Praise for Leonard B. Scott's bestseller

CHARLIE MIKE

"May be the greatest war story to come out of Vietnam
. . . There's violence and compassion, gore and tender-
ness, arrogance and humility, friend and foe."

Columbus Ledger Enquirer

"An exceptionally fine addition to the literature on the
Vietnam War . . . a first-class reading experience."

Military Review

"A hymn on the theme of valor—that of the American
soldier and that of the North Vietnamese enemy as well."

The New York Times Magazine

"Military men and women have praised it for its honest,
accurate, and realistic portrayal of the Vietnam War and
the people who fought it."

The Atlanta Journal Constitution

"A moving and important portrait of a group of heroic
young men who fought hard, and of survivors who came
home to get on with the business of living."

Publishers Weekly

Also by Leonard B. Scott
Published by Ballantine Books

CHARLIE MIKE

THE LAST RUN

LEONARD B. SCOTT

BALLANTINE BOOKS · NEW YORK

Library of Congress Catalog Card Number: 86-91570

ISBN: 0-345-33646-1

Text design by Holly Johnson
Cover design by James R. Harris
Illustration by Glenn Madison

Manufactured in the United States of America

First Edition: June 1987
10 9 8 7 6 5 4 3 2 1

THE LAST
RUN

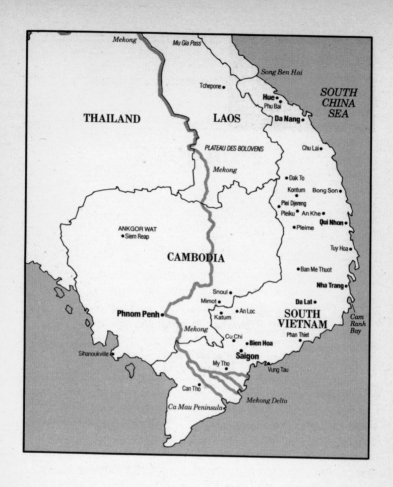

PROLOGUE

1 September 1970

Private Nguyen Tran Nuu lay trembling in the darkness as the earthen tunnel began to shake around him. It was time. They had come as his senior sergeant had said they would. He crawled toward the entrance, got to his feet, and crouched in the square fighting position. Then he slowly raised the camouflaged trapdoor above him a few centimeters. From the outside, the rise in a clump of grass would have been hardly noticeable.

The first lumbering American armored personnel carrier clanked into view, bellowing like a wounded water buffalo and knocking down small trees. Until then, Nuu had seen the rectangular mechanical boxes only from a great distance, and the size of the monster and the noise it made shocked him as it rumbled by only thirty meters in front of his position.

Riding on top of the carrier were six Yankees, all of whom wore watches like rich men. Four were white-skinned, two were black, and each had a rifle in his hands and a bandolier strapped across his chest.

Nuu, still trembling like the ground around him, asked for strength from his ancestors as the APC disappeared from view and a second burst out of the tall grass. He shut his eyes, remembering his sergeant's words, and felt better knowing everything the man had said had come to pass: The Americans had come along the predicted route in a single column and were obviously not expecting an ambush. In fact, they thought they were about to attack General Headquarters.

Nuu began to prepare for what he had been training to do for two months. His company had been ordered to the old tunnel complex for the purpose of setting up this ambush. The complex ran the entire length of the ridge, and digging and camouflaging the fighting holes had taken many weeks. Rehearsals took up the rest of the time. Now he felt his confidence coming back. He knew what to do. He was to wait until the seventh armored carrier passed, then destroy the eighth. His attack would halt and confuse the column. The rest of his comrades were spread out in similar positions to the north and would shoot the other vehicles and any Yankee soldiers who were within the killing space. After he destroyed the carrier, he was to crawl to the tunnel corridor that led to the far side of the ridge. There he would follow the path to the reorganization point. One platoon would remain in the complex and fight from bunkers until told to withdraw.

Nuu squatted down and lovingly picked up his RPG-2 antitank grenade launcher. He ran his hand over the smooth, hard wood of the casing that would protect him from the heat of the metal tube, and he blew dust from the handgrip's trigger. Night and day he had practiced the procedures of loading, aiming, and firing the weapon until they had become second nature. Now his fears completely dissolved. The power of his old friend would destroy the huge monster.

Nuu pulled a HEAT antitank grenade from his back pouch and inspected it quickly as the fifth carrier rumbled past. The type-50 Chinese high explosive antitank grenade had three basic components: a warhead containing a conical-shaped charge, a motor, and a flexible fin assembly that wrapped around the motor. He carefully inserted the missile into the muzzle, making sure the metal ring slid up and released the spring-loaded fins that partially extended within the tube. With a slight twist he locked the projectile into place and patted the large, 82 mm warhead that would easily penetrate the APC's armor plate. The missile would assure him an award of Valiant Fighter Third Class and make him honored among his family.

The seventh APC rolled from view, and Nuu pushed back the hidden door. He stepped up onto the firing step, quickly pulled a prepositioned grass mat over his body, so as to blend with the vegetation, and placed the launcher on his shoulder. The eighth APC clanked down the path made by the others. Nuu aligned the sights and aimed at the front portion of the hull a meter down from the driver's hatch. He took a deep breath and slowly squeezed the trigger. The launcher jolted in a cloud of smoke and sound as the grenade swooshed out of the tube. The fins sprang out and, fully extended, stabilized the missile as it streaked toward its target.

The massive APC shuddered with the warhead's impact. The blast charge detonated and instantly turned the cone into a concentrated, directed jet force that blew a hole through the armor like a hot knife through jello. The driver was killed instantly by the shock wave; milliseconds later, the molten steel that blew into the compartment decapitated him and slammed his body against the engine wall. The right pivot steering level was shoved forward and the accelerator was depressed by the weight of the headless corpse as it crumpled down and became pinned between the steering device and seat. The carrier's right track churned forward as the left remained motionless, causing the vehicle to pivot in a constant right turn.

The few men on top of the APC who weren't blown off by the explosion jumped off to take cover. One of the soldiers lay on the ground, too stunned to move, as the runaway monster turned abruptly and ground him beneath its track. Another man rolled away and crawled frantically to get out of its path, but too late. The fourteen-ton APC rolled over his feet, crushing them into bloody pulp. The engine's roar drowned out his hysterical screams as more APCs were caught in the devastating grenade attack.

Nuu backed down and closed the trapdoor above him. There was no need to shoot again. He paused for a moment, listening to the chaos outside, and smiled. He had done his duty and made his ancestors proud. He knelt down and began crawling into the tunnel's darkness.

Three hundred meters from Private Nuu's fighting position one of the North Vietnamese Army's youngest and brightest lieutenant colonels peered through the command bunker's firing portal. Lieutenant Colonel Dinh Luong Sy smiled at the sight of three APCs burning and two more smoking. His general's plan was a masterpiece!

The slightly built colonel turned and glanced quickly at the map beside him. He knew the old headquarters tunnel complex in which he stood would soon be under siege. Thirty minutes before, the Yankees had helicoptered a battalion-size force into the valley behind him as part of an operation to find the general's headquarters. Now they would surely come to the aid of the mechanized unit that had been ambushed.

The general had planned the ruse months ago and sent him to the old tunnels to carry it out. The Americans relied on their electronic surveillance devices too heavily, and easily fell prey to their own intelligence. They constantly sought the location of the general's headquarters, so he had simply provided it. The general ordered the establishment of a radio station that sent out bogus traffic consisting of old information. The transmissions were designed to ensure detection. He'd even used old radios whose peculiar signature identified them as his to broadcast to ghost units.

The general had also planned the ambush knowing the Americans would base their attack strategy on the terrain. The Yankees would find the old tunnels, as planned, and waste days searching through them. Old documents would be left to confuse them even more.

Colonel Sy shook his head in admiration. They had come to find his general but had instead fallen victim to him. The general was now forty kilometers to the west in a command tunnel forty feet below ground. The Tall One had outfoxed the American aggressors again.

As Sy stepped down into the tunnel to join the two escaping platoons, he looked over his shoulder at the lieutenant who had to stay and fight on to give the others time to escape. The young officer smiled confidently as only the young could. Sy forced a smile in return, knowing the soldier would die. He and his few men would be the Americans' only victory. His death had been planned, with everything else, by the general. The general had spoken with great sadness as he explained the reason for the sacrifice to the victim: The Americans had to have a small victory so that they could claim the operation a success; otherwise more would come.

Sy had seen the agony in the general's eyes and had understood. His leader was buying precious time to build and strengthen his southern liberation forces. The price for ultimate victory had to be paid for, once again, by the young, who would die, sadly, as the liberation's truest heroes.

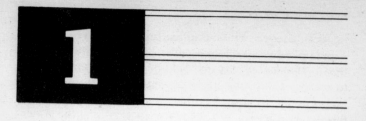

1

2 September

Bo Dau Mountains
Thirty-six kilometers southwest of Phan Thiet

The rain forest awoke in a gray shroud of smoking mist. The vapor swirled as six dark figures with painted green and black faces arose slowly from the jungle floor and stood motionless. They wore heavy rucksacks and camouflaged fatigues and had jungle flop hats pulled low over their foreheads.

The leader stood four feet in front of the others. His narrowed brown eyes methodically searched the area as he concentrated on the sounds of the awakening forest. Sergeant Matt Wade, team leader of Ranger team 3-1, was following a procedure he'd learned from experience. He was fine-tuning his senses for survival. Chirping insects, birds squawking in flight, wind rustling the branches in the canopy—all were absorbed and stored for reference. Every sound, smell, and sight, all constantly changing with time of day and weather conditions, was important.

Experience had taught him many lessons. Once, the absence of crickets chirping on one side of a trail had warned him of an NVA ambush. Another time, two shriveled ferns among a stand of lush, vibrant companions gave away a sniper's camouflaged position. The jungle had to be understood. Otherwise it became an undefeatable enemy.

The twenty-one-year-old sergeant tilted his head in another direction to listen. His lean, rugged face exposed taut muscles above his square jaw. He was rangy at five-feet-ten, and his heavy rucksack hung from his broad shoulders as if it was part of him. Seven months of stalking the enemy in the jungle had trimmed his body to nothing but bone, muscle, and sinew.

Wade's team had been inserted at dusk the day before by helicopter and had laagered for the night. They were thirty kilometers inside enemy-controlled territory and were to move to a trail seven klicks away. It was a kill-mission; they would ambush whoever came down the trail and collect papers and documents for intelligence purposes.

The sergeant shifted his Colt submachine gun to his left hand and pulled a pouch of Beechnut chewing tobacco from his leg pocket. He turned and looked into the faces of his team as he filled his cheek.

The first team member his eyes fell upon was a short, wiry, nineteen-year-old black man, Specialist Fourth Class Jeremiah Flowers—"The Rose." Rose, the team point man, held up his thumb and flashed a big grin. Wade couldn't help but smile back. Rose was ready, as always. Despite his toothy grin, Rose was a merciless killer. He had shot his first man at the age of sixteen during the Detroit race riots in 1967. Four months before he'd been on Team 1-3 during the Cambodian mission. He was the only team member to survive, and now he lived for revenge.

Wade shifted his gaze to his good friend and assistant team leader, Spec-4 Kenneth Meeks—"Thumper." The six-foot-tall soldier had massive shoulders and narrow hips. He was built for speed and agile strength, like a thoroughbred racehorse. He had been starting fullback for Penn State, but dropped out his sophomore year when his brother had been killed at Hue during the Tet offensive of 1968. He had joined the Army and volunteered for Vietnam with one obsession—to justify his brother's death. Thumper had been in Vietnam for only five months, but he was already one of the most highly decorated men in the Ranger company. Like Rose, he had come from another team.

When all of his old teammates had been wounded or rotated home, he'd joined Wade's team. Thumper was the rock of the unit; he was unshakable under pressure and totally dependable.

Wade's eyes turned cold and narrowed as he glanced at the next two men. They were cherries, new men assigned to the team despite his protest. Robbins and . . . damn, he couldn't remember the other one's name. Robbins was easy to remember because of his red hair and freckles. The other one was . . . uh . . . Stevens! That was it. Stevens had long hair and acted as if he didn't give a shit. Rose had called them Red Rob and Shitbird Stevens.

Wade's gaze softened as it shifted to the last team member. Spec-4 Carl Rostov was standing guard watching their rear. The twenty-nine-year-old soldier was the oldest and most experienced man on the team. In 1961, his family had tried to escape from Czechoslovakia, but Carl had been the only one to make it. His mother had been killed, and his father and brother imprisoned. Carl served with Belgian mercenaries in Africa for three years and later emigrated to the United States. He was known as "Russian" and was built like a thick tree stump. He had brutish features and the gait of a bull. Russian was driven by a passionate hate of Communists.

Wade put his hand on his friend's back and whispered, "Watch the cherries for me, Carl."

The burly soldier nodded silently without taking his eyes from the jungle. Wade kept his hand on the soldier's back, a sign of the special friendship he felt for the man. Unlike the others, Carl had been on Wade's team since he'd taken over seven months before. Russian had been his mentor and had taught him many secrets for survival in the jungle. They had been through many rough missions together and had lost five men over the months. It had been Carl who had stood by Wade, who had talked him out of depressions over losses, and who had helped him grow into a confident leader. Wade owed the man his life, but Russian never asked for anything but his friendship.

Wade quietly waved at Rose to begin the trek. Rose

grinned cruelly as he brought his M-16 up to his chest and started walking toward the west. Thumper waited until the soldier had taken ten steps, then followed behind in the slackman position. He carried an M-79 grenade launcher and would stay ten to fifteen paces behind the point man, protecting his flanks and back.

Wade was about to step off and follow Thumper when he heard the distinctive "click" of an M-16's selector switch. He spun around, grabbed Robbins's fatigue shirt, and jerked him to within inches of his face. The sergeant's stare made the cherry cringe.

"*Don't ever* do that again!" Wade whispered harshly. "You never push a selector with your thumb. That click you just made could be be heard fifty feet away. Hold the damn thing and turn it slowly and it won't make noise." Wade stepped back and pointed his finger at the offender's face. "And *don't ever* take your weapon off safe until you have a target. The point man is the *only* man who has his weapon on 'auto.' You'll shoot somebody if you trip or get spooked." Wade's eyes softened as he realized the young soldier was shaking. "Look, I know this is new to you and it's not all your fault. But you gotta watch and learn quick. Don't move, don't fart, don't do anything unless I do. You stay as close to me as stink on shit and you'll get through this mission. You got it?"

Robbins lowered his eyes in submission and nodded. Wade felt sorry for the kid and put his hand on his shoulder. "No sweat, you'll get the hang of it. Now turn around and tell Stevens what I told you. And whisper."

As Wade was about to turn, he noticed Russian looking at him with a slight grin. Wade smiled. The Czech had given him the same lesson seven months before.

Private First Class Bill Robbins wasn't in awe anymore. At first he'd been spellbound by the huge teaks and mahoganies that soared to over a hundred feet and blocked out almost all sunlight. The thick vines, clinging and twisting in every direction, and the giant ferns were like those he'd seen in pictures in *National Geographic,* but the pic-

tures hadn't prepared him for the misery. Five minutes in
the jungle was enough to make it all look the same. Vibrant
shades of green became monotonous blurs as his eyes fixed
on the back of Sergeant Wade walking five feet in front of
him.

The team had been moving for two hours, but to Robbins
it felt as if they'd humped for two days. Without a doubt,
the past fourteen hours had been the most miserable in his
life.

Yesterday's helicopter insertion and the short move to
the night laager position had been scary but strangely ex-
citing. Then came the night, and the excitement had
quickly given way to terror. The others had slept while
he'd lain awake shivering and praying on the damp ground.
It had grown so dark that he couldn't see his hand in front
of his face. Shutting or opening his eyes made no difference. And then came the sounds; horrifying cries and
screeches of unknown animals and insects. Close to midnight, what sounded like a platoon of NVA crept toward
the laager. He awoke Rose. The angry soldier had listened
for only a minute, then slugged him. "Ya dumb shit, that's
the wind blowing the branches in the trees," the young
black man had said.

It wasn't the wind—Robbins knew it. It had been NVA.
For the rest of the night he'd balled up, waiting to die, only
to feel unseen creatures crawling over his feet and legs and
buzzing insects biting his face and hands.

The shivering horror of the night before seemed like a
bad dream now as he grew certain he would pass out from
the heat.

The team broke from the rain forest into an expanse of
head-high elephant grass. Rose found an animal path and
they followed it. The thick grass stalks blocked all moving
air. The sun's heat beat down unmercifully and made the
small path a sweltering torture chamber.

Robbins wiped the sweat from his eyes with the soaked
olive drab towel around his neck and leaned forward to
again try and catch up to Wade. The twenty-five-pound
radio he carried in his rucksack along with the rest of his

fighting gear was gaining weight. Yesterday he judged his pack to weigh seventy-five pounds; today it felt like 175 as it dug into his shoulders and cut off the circulation to his arms and hands. My God, I can't even feel the M-16 I'm carrying, he thought in desperation.

Sergeant Wade looked behind him and sighed. Robbins had fallen too far behind again. The young soldier's face was flushed and he looked about ready to drop—as did Stevens. Wade kept moving for a few minutes until the team had crossed the open area and again entered the rain forest. He then motioned for Thumper to signal Rose to halt for a break.

Robbins, exhausted, fell back on his pack and shut his eyes to stop the dizziness. Stevens dropped wearily down beside him, wanting to puke or die. At that moment it didn't matter which. Either one would be relief.

Wade shook his head and whispered to Thumper, "We're gonna have to slow down or they ain't gonna make it."

Thumper reached for his canteen. "I wish Lieutenant Dickey could see them. Maybe he'd listen to you next time. These guys just got off the plane from the States a couple of weeks ago. They don't know their butts from holes in the ground, and they aren't even climatized yet."

Wade took a drink from his friend's canteen and gave it back. "We'll give 'em ten minutes to rest and then move out. Go back and make sure they drink plenty of water. I'm going up with Rose and pull security."

Stevens finally opened his eyes and looked at Robbins. "Man, this is bullshit."

The redhead's eyelids struggled upward slowly. "Yeah. I'm thinkin' this Ranger business isn't for me."

Stevens snickered as he lay his head back. "You just now figured that out? Shit, I knew this was bullshit all last night when I didn't get a bit of sleep. I'm gettin' out of this unit as soon as we get back. I wanna hump with a regular line company. At least you got lots of people to keep you company at night. Six dudes in Charlieland don't cut it, man.''

Robbins smiled through his misery. He was glad to know he wasn't the only one who'd been miserable during the night. He was about to shut his eyes again when he saw Russian looming over him with a strange look in his eyes.

"No move," the barrel-chested soldier hissed, and raised his rifle up as if to beat the cherry with the butt.

Robbins threw his hands up to protect himself as Russian slammed the M-16 down, just missing his head. Stevens and Robbins sprang to their feet to run from the crazy man, but Russian still held the rifle butt to the ground. They then saw a thin, iridescent green body writhe and curl around the weapon stock. A bamboo viper's head was pinned beneath the rifle butt.

"Cut his head off," Russian demanded.

Both men looked at each other in disbelief. Neither was about to get close to the well known two-stepper—so called because its victims, once bitten, took only two steps before dying.

Thumper brushed past the two startled men and pulled his knife. He cut the deadly snake's head off in one swipe. Russian walked over to the cherries, and with a look of disgust took hold of Robbins's fatigue shirt-sleeve and pulled him over next to Stevens. He motioned them both to sit, and then knelt in front of them, whispering, "You do not listen to what my sergeant say. He tell you do nothing he does not do. My sergeant did not lay down. No one lay down in the jungle until you check the ground first. The snake a good lesson for you. No matter how tired you become, you must be alert."

Thumper leaned over Russian's shoulder. "You were lucky. Both of you drink a full quart of water and then we'll move out."

Two hours later, the team found the trail they were to ambush and hid themselves in a thicket of bamboo only fifteen meters away. Sergeant Wade had positioned himself and the cherry, Robbins, together. Ten meters to his right were Thumper and Rose; to his left, at the same distance, were Russian and Stevens. Hidden near the trail were deadly Claymore mines.

Wade was almost out of patience as he set down the radio handset. Because of the new men, the ambush had taken too long to set up, a situation which could have killed the whole team. The cherries didn't know or understand the procedure and had to be talked through it step by step. Stevens had really screwed up and walked out onto the trail. It'd taken Russian five precious minutes to erase his footprints and rearrange the plants he'd disturbed and crushed. Any dink could spot footprints and see a trampled path leading to a hide position.

It was that damn Dickey's fault. Lieutenant Marvin Dickey, his new platoon leader, had ordered Wade to take the new men on the mission. The platoon was short of people, and the L-tee had taken new replacements without sending them to the Mini-Ranger school at An Khe. The course was two weeks long and taught basics for survival. It also weeded out those who weren't physically or mentally tough enough for the dangerous work. Dickey had made the decision not to send the cherries to the school over the protests of Sergeant First Class Gino, the Third Platoon sergeant, and over all the other team leaders as well.

Dickey was a dumb-ass for not listening to his experienced sergeants. Damn, Wade thought, if Major Shane, his company commander, knew about the situation, he'd have the shavetail Dickey's ass!

But wishing wouldn't make the situation any better. Major Shane and the rest of the company were in Da Lat, one hundred miles away, while the Third Platoon was based in Phan Thiet, working independently for the Corps G-2 with dumb-ass Dickey in charge.

Since Dickey had taken over a month before, the platoon had gone to hell in a handbasket. The bastard was getting good men killed with his stupid orders and lack of experience.

Wade let out a deep breath. He had to relax and put his

anger aside. Anger dulled the senses. He lay watching the trail for thirty minutes when, to his far right, a small, thin NVA soldier appeared. The man wore khaki pants and a gray shirt, with an ammo-pouch vest strapped to his chest. He wore no hat, his black hair was neatly combed, and he seemed to be grinnning. He carried an AK-47 in the crook of his arm. Another soldier appeared behind him, and then three more, all similarly dressed and armed, but wearing soft, floppy, boonie-hats.

Wade pressed himself closer to the ground as the enemy moved farther into the kill-zone. He tried to keep his hand from trembling, and he began to press the Claymore mines' detonator.

The world seemed to explode into a dark, brown-black cloud only a few feet away. The thunderous, earsplitting *"boom!"* was followed quickly by two more loud thunderclaps of sound as the other team's mines exploded.

Wade rose to his knees and fired into the billowing cloud. He saw one soldier kneeling to his right. He brought the figure into his sights and squeezed the trigger. The man pitched sideways, then tried to get up. Wade was about to fire again when he heard the distinctive *"ping-pop"* of a grenade's level falling free and the striker detonating the primer cap. He spun around in time to see Robbins throw himself to the ground after tossing the grenade. The green sphere sailed only ten feet, hit the bamboo, and bounced back to the side of the prone soldier.

Wade screamed *"Nooo!"* as he threw himself backward and tried to flatten himself on the ground.

A vehement, explosive *"crack!"* shook the earth and slammed his head down, then up, as his body was flung on its side. He lay stunned, hearing nothing but a dull ringing noise that careened through his brain. His body felt as if it was wrapped in a tight cocoon of small pins that stuck and prodded his every nerve. A blur appeared, a blur that became a man screaming at him and grabbing him, but Wade couldn't hear the words or feel the hands.

Thumper shook his team sergeant again. "Matt!"

Russian busted through the bamboo and fell to his knees

beside Thumper. He pushed the big soldier back gently and began to inspect the sergeant's wounds. Stevens followed behind Russian, holding a bloody bandage to his arm. He'd been shot through the biceps. Stevens took one look at Robbins's ripped corpse and fell to his knees, gagging.

Thumper knew Russian had plenty of experience with wounds and picked up his M-79. One look at the five bodies sprawled on the trail told him the ambush had been set up perfectly. He yelled toward Rose, "Secure the south end of the trail. I've got the north."

Russian pulled back Wade's shirt and sighed in relief. He patted Thumper's leg. "The sergeant is stunned, his wounds are not bad. He will lead us again."

Thumper relaxed his taut body and smiled. He clapped Russian's shoulder and stood up. His smile dissolved upon seeing the torn, blood-splattered body of Robbins. He walked over and put his hand on Stevens's shoulder. "Come on, kid, we gotta search the bodies."

Stevens looked up with tear-filled eyes. "But we have to . . . can't we . . . ?"

Thumper shook his head sadly. "There's nothing we can do for him now. Come on, we gotta hustle."

Wade regained consciousness and opened his eyes slowly. Robbins lay beside him, his eyes open, blank, seeing nothing. The dead man's face was gray-white; his freckles seemed transparent.

Wade turned his head away. He felt sick. He tried to sit up but his head seemed too heavy. He shut his eyes to stop the throbbing, gathered his strength, and tried again. He swung up to a sitting position and focused his eyes on Thumper, who was wrapping a clean bandage around Stevens's arm.

Thumper, seeing the sergeant sit up, patted Stevens's back reassuringly and moved closer to Wade. "You feelin' better, huh?"

Wade looked around quickly; they were next to a large, open area.

"How'd ya get me here?"

"Russian carried you. How's your shoulder?"

Wade looked at Thumper strangely, then glanced quickly down at his right, then left shoulder. His fatigue shirt, on the left side, was stained deep crimson. Until that instant, he hadn't felt a thing. Suddenly, as if his eyes had to see and confirm the injury, he felt a dull ache. He prodded himself and realized he wasn't hit bad; there were just a few sensitive areas, which meant a few embedded fragments. Thumper was whispering to him.

"The bird is on its way. We collected all the shit from the dinks but had to destroy the weapons and leave 'em. Stevens took an AK round through the upper arm. The kid played 'John Wayne' and stood up after the Claymores blew."

Thumper glanced over his shoulder at Robbins's body. He'd had to wrap a poncho around the soldier's middle to hold in the intestines. The grenade blast had almost severed the body at the hip.

"I didn't see the dink who threw the grenade. Did you?"

Wade shook his head. "It wasn't a dink; Robbins threw it. The kid got excited. It hit the bamboo and bounced back."

Thumper slapped his weapon's stock. "Damn that Dickey! The cherries should never have come!"

Wade's head was still ringing, but he could hear the familiar popping of helicopter blades as a bird made its approach.

Phan Thiet
Third Platoon Ranger Base Camp

A helicoper landed in a cloud of dust and four men hopped out. Wade had refused to get off at the Evac hospital and had stayed on the bird as it continued its flight to the Ranger camp. He and the three other team members walked directly toward the sandbagged Tactical Operations Center.

Sergeant First Class Gino, the Third Platoon sergeant, stood waiting for them outside the TOC entrance. He was stocky, about thirty-five-years old, and had the tough look of a mafia hit man. His beady brown eyes fixed on the approaching team sergeant. Wade threw down an NVA pack partially filled with papers and documents at Gino's feet.

"Where the hell is the lieutenant?"

Gino looked into the sergeant's angry eyes, then at his blood-stained shirt.

"He's on the telephone to the Ol' Man explaining what happened and why he used untrained cherries."

Wade glared at Gino for a few seconds, then softened his stare.

"You called and told 'em, didn't you?"

Gino smiled faintly. "Yeah, as soon as I heard what happened. I called Da Lat and told Childs what Dickey had done. Major Shane called a few minutes ago and sounded pissed!"

Wade reached for his chewing tobacco pouch but stopped. It was in his left leg pocket, but his arm hurt too bad to move. Gino noticed his discomfort and inspected the wound.

"You gotta get that cleaned up."

Wade withdrew the tobacco with his other hand.

"Not before I talk to that dumb shit lieutenant! This platoon and this operation are fucked up . . . and it's because of *him*! I'm not goin' out again with cherries. It's gonna get us all killed!"

A tall, dark-haired first lieutenant walked out of the TOC door and, seeing the team, broke into a smile.

"Good job, men. You got the documents and five confirmed kills!"

Wade's face flushed, and he tossed the tobacco pouch to the ground.

"Yeah, and we got one man killed and one wounded because of your stupid order!"

The lieutenant's smile vanished. "You watch your mouth, Sergeant!"

Gino quickly stepped between the two men and put his hand on Wade's chest, pushing him back. "Wade, you report to the medics and get your shoulder checked. Rus-

sian, you take him! Thumper, you stay and debrief us.
Move!''

Wade pushed Gino's hand away. "Lieutenant, I hope
you're satisfied! Your stupidity killed that cherry!''

Russian grabbed Wade's waist roughly and pulled him
away. "The sergeant is delirious! He is upset and doesn't
know what he says." Rose grabbed Wade's shirt and began
tugging.

Wade fought their grip.

"Lieutenant, you killed Robbins, you son of a bitch.
You murdered him and . . .''

Lieutenant Dickey pointed his finger at Gino as the men
pulled Wade away.

"You heard that! He cussed me! He . . . he . . .!''

"He's shot up with morphine, Lieutenant," said Gino
blandly, picking up the NVA pack.

Dickey stammered, "Yes, but that's insubordination!
That's verbal assault! I want charges written up on him!''

Gino eyed the lieutenant pathetically. "It'll never hold
up. Major Shane will never sign off on it, so forget it. Come
on, Lieutenant, we've got to debrief Thumper and get the
report to G-2.''

Dickey put his hands to his hips. "You called Da Lat,
didn't you? You told Sergeant Childs about my orders, and
he had Major Shane call me . . . didn't you?''

Gino motioned Thumper inside the TOC. As soon as the
big man disappeared, Gino shoved the NVA pack into the
lieutenant's arms.

"Yes, sir, I did! You screwed up, sir! You didn't listen
to me or the team sergeants. Wade was right. You did kill
Robbins and yesterday Welch and Gymon. They all died
because of your stupid, fucking order to take untrained
cherries to the field. You better accept that fact and start
listenin' or you ain't gonna have a platoon! You better start
lookin' around and throw out the bums you accepted in
this unit. We got potheads, dopers, and shitheads! You
coddle them and won't let me throw 'em out!''

Dickey smiled cruelly. "That's it! Sergeant Gino, you're
relieved! I've been waiting for you to say something like

this. You never liked me! You've always fought every order I've given. Well, you've finally done it. You're through."

Gino shook his head tiredly. "Lieutenant, you can't relieve me. Major Shane will have to do that! Now, like I said, we got to get this information to G-2. Are you gonna debrief, or me?"

Dickey spun around on his heels. "We'll see, Sergeant! I'm calling the major now and we'll see!" He brushed past Gino and hurriedly entered the TOC door.

Da Lat
Temporary Headquarters
Sierra Company, Seventy-fifth Rangers

Major Ed Shane slammed the telephone handset down angrily and stood up. "That's it! I want the Third Platoon back here now!"

Sergeant First Class Jerry Childs slowly raised his eyes from the report he was reading. "Sir, you're gonna have to clear that with Corps. The Third Platoon is their baby."

Shane paced back and forth like a caged panther. He was six feet tall and thin, but had powerful shoulders, developed from years of competitive swimming.

"Screw Corps! I've had it. I'll go to Corps tomorrow morning and talk to the G-3. The Third Platoon has lost three men in two days and doesn't have enough experience to do the job. Damn it! It's Corps's own damn fault for giving me nothing but new replacements instead of experienced men from line units like we need. Dickey can't control the platoon. He's new and doesn't have enough experience."

Childs threw his legs up onto the desk. "Gino says the L-tee is a shithead."

Shane began pacing again. "What do you expect? He doesn't know anything. I'll get him squared away. Corps won't give me any other officers. Damn! They say we're pulling out of Nam and can't fill us up to strength, and yet they keep asking us to do more."

22

Childs lit a Camel and blew out a cloud of smoke.

"Sir, when you're at Corps, you better be calm. General Wayland doesn't like Ranger-types, and now that his deputy, General Burton, is gone, we don't have many friends up there."

Shane stopped pacing. "Yeah, I know; but the situation is getting too bad to continue like it is. We can't do the mission Corps wants unless we have support. I think once I explain the problems to Wayland's operations officer, he'll understand."

Childs shook his head. "Sir, the G-3 is new and don't wipe his ass unless the Corps commander approves it. You gotta have help in convincing General Wayland we need support. Talk to Colonel Ellis, the intelligence officer for Corps. I hear he's got his shit together. He's got a couple of tours as a grunt. He'll understand our problems. Hell, we really work for him anyway. He's the one that uses all the intell we gather. I'd say he's got to help us to help himself."

Shane stared into the weathered face of his small operations sergeant and couldn't help but smile. Jerry Childs looked like a range rider from an old Western: hard, lean, and craggy-faced from being outdoors for most of his life. Three tours in Vietnam had etched three lifetimes of experience into the leathery wrinkles at the corners of his dark, deepset eyes. His flattop haircut, constant scowl, and drill sergeant's bark marked him as a "lifer" to the younger Rangers, but a respected lifer, a total professional.

Shane put his hand on the sergeant's shoulder. "You know, Jerry, Major Colven told me before he left that I'd best take good care of you. He said you were a contrary ol' bastard, but as good as they come. I don't know why you extended your tour another six months, but I'm damn glad you did. I don't know what I'd do without you."

Childs, never one for showing emotion, averted his eyes. "Well, sir, I been in the Army a few days and know how Corps operates—fucked up!" He stood and began walking toward the door. "I'll call Aviation and get you a bird for tomorrow. You best sit and write down all our problems so you won't get emotional when you talk to them paper-shufflers.''

Shane began to offer a heartfelt ''thanks'' for the advice, but the grizzled sergeant walked out of the office.

Childs strode into the communications room, thinking how much Shane and his ex-commander were alike: high-strung and fiercely concerned for the welfare of their men. Major Colven had rotated home three months before, but it seemed like yesterday that Colven shook his hand for the last time and told him, ''Take care of Shane. Keep him outta trouble. And Jerry, take care of my Rangers.''

Childs stopped by the field phone and starred blankly at the wall. The discussion about Corps and his thoughts of Colven had brought back painful memories.

Just four months before the company had been a proud, unbeatable unit, staffed with the best men he'd ever worked with. But then came the Cambodian mission. The damn Corps paper-shufflers, who'd never humped a ruck, had ordered the Rangers into Cambodia to find NVA base camps for the larger American units to destroy. The teams found the base camps, all right, but Corps took away their helicopter support in the middle of the operation, leaving them helpless and outnumbered. The result was the death of twenty Rangers and as many wounded, all experienced and all irreplaceable.

Childs's face reddened with anger. The faces of those men still haunted him at night. They screamed out to him, asking ''why?'' And he didn't have the answer.

Corps had said it was a mistake. A fucking mistake! A misrouted message in a misrouted system. A bureaucratic error where no one was to blame. A mistake. Yeah, a mistake that had killed his men and had sent others home broken.

The sergeant glanced down at a piece of paper beside the phone. It was the note he'd made when Sergeant Gino had called from Phan Thiet. Sergeant Wade had been wounded and a cherry killed. The note was yet another reminder that the bastards at Corps weren't finished with the company yet.

After the Cambodian disaster, Corps, in its infinite wisdom, cut off replacements. Within a short time, most of the experienced men left in the company rotated home. Without experienced leaders to train newer men, the casualty rate climbed. Major Shane had fought for and gotten replacements, but Corps would only give him men who'd just arrived in-country. The company was now at only sixty percent strength, and was mostly filled with cherries. And, as if to throw salt on the wounds, Corps had recently split the company. Third platoon was in Phan Thiet, while the other two platoons were here in Da Lat.

The company was dying, and Childs was helpless. Tomorrow, Major Shane's trips could mean life or death for Sierra Company, Seventy-fifth Infantry, Airborne Rangers. His major was the last hope, but no matter what the outcome of the major's trip, he'd stay and fight with the company to the end. He loved the company; the men were his personal responsibility and they needed him. They were the reason he'd extended his tour and stayed on. He'd take care of his men and help Shane as Colven, his old commander, had asked.

Childs began to crank the field phone's handle but a wave of guilt swept through his body as an image of his wife filled his head. She was sitting in the porch swing in front of their small house, waiting. Her sad expression tore a gash in his heart. She needed him, too.

The sergeant shut his eyes and clenched his teeth. Linda would understand. She was a professional soldier's wife. She knew he had to stay. He couldn't leave his men when they needed him.

Tightening his body, he threw his shoulders back and took in a deep breath. "I'm sorry, honey," he muttered, then grabbed the phone handle with determination and began cranking.

Phan Thiet
District Office, Military Intelligence

The corps's assistant intelligence officer finished reading and tossed the report onto his desk. "This confirms it."

A captain seated by the desk stood. "Yes, sir. The documents brought in by the Rangers this afternoon confirm that the Thirty-third NVA Regiment is definitely moving. The pieces are falling into place. We haven't had any attacks because they are moving into the mountains and consolidating. The Forty-second and Thirty-third regiments are now confirmed."

The intelligence officer stood and walked over to a wall map. "Let's say you're correct. They are consolidating. Even so, it certainly isn't for an attack. They're moving to the farthest point from our remaining ground forces."

"Sir, they're doing exactly what they did prior to Tet '68. They will reequip, train, and then break up and strike."

The major pulled at his chin in thought, then picked up the report from his desk. "What's this last line mean?"

"I'm not sure, sir. That was found in a diary on a radioman or a signal repairman. His last entry stated he was happy to be returning to work for the Tall One and ultimate victory. The 'Tall One' caught my attention. The analysts are translating the rest of the diary, but I know of only one time before that I have seen that phrase."

"Well?"

"General Binh Ty Duc was called the 'Tall One' by Ho Chi Minh in 1967 after the battle at Dak To."

The major's eyes opened wide. "My god! Do you realize what this could mean?"

The captain smiled. "Yes, sir."

The major quickly gathered the rest of the report together and strode toward the door. "I'm sending this out right now to Corps Headquarters. Colonel Ellis will shit when he sees it."

Phan Thiet
Twenty-third Evac Hospital

Sergeant Matt Wade leaned back against the emergency room wall and stared out a window into the darkness. Two hours before, an orderly had cleaned his wounds and explained that the small hospital was understaffed and had only one doctor. A patient had hemorrhaged earlier and the doctor would see him as soon as he could.

The emergency room door opened only a bit. Wade forgot the pain in his shoulder and broke into a smile when he saw a familiar face peer around the door.

"Come on in, Thump. There ain't nobody here but me."

Thumper took one more glance around and strode in. "Damn, Matt, these medical types are really assholes. They won't let anyone in until you're on the ward. I've been here for hours trying to see you."

Wade grinned. "I know. I heard you and Carl arguing with the orderly from in here. . . . Hell, the whole hospital could hear ya!"

Thumper shrugged his shoulders and sat down beside his friend. "Yeah, well, Russian didn't understand why we couldn't see you and got pretty upset. I don't know if that orderly understood Czech cuss words, but he looked awfully scared. A staff sergeant came out and ordered Russian outta the hospital and called Gino."

Wade eyed the big soldier suspiciously. "And what about you? I thought I heard somebody say 'no visitors until tomorrow.'"

Thumper lowered his head. "Aw, hell, Matt, I had to check you out or Russian would have bugged me all night long. You know how he is."

Wade nodded. Carl was his mother hen, but he knew Thumper was concerned, too, and wouldn't have slept either. In fact, he, Wade, would have done the same thing.

"Haven't they given you anything for the pain yet?" asked Thumper as he stood and looked over the open wounds.

"Naw, but they will as soon as the doc comes. How's the team?"

"They're fine. We'll sleep in tomorrow and rest up. Then we'll see what Dickey is going to screw up next." Thumper's eyes shifted from Wade's wounds to his eyes. "Matt, you ought to take it easy when you get out of the hospital, go on R&R and relax awhile. I hear Bangkok is nice."

Wade narrowed his eyes. "What are you trying to say? Is Dickey gunning for me?"

"No, nothing like that. It's just Russian and me think you deserve a break. You were lucky today. You've been running patrols for seven months straight and your luck has about run out. Today was a good lesson for us all. It's time you took it easy."

Wade leaned up. "Come on, Thump. I know you too well for you to bullshit me. Spit it out."

Thumper lowered his gaze. He was silent for several seconds as he tried to find the right words. "Matt, you scared me today . . . I mean *really* scared me. When I ran over and saw you layin' there, I thought . . . I thought we'd lost you. Matt, you've been pushin' hard for seven months. You've been going all out. And lately you've been actin' like this war is something personal. You've been going on missions when you didn't have to, and taking chances you normally wouldn't. You can't keep this up. You gotta slow down or one day you won't make it. Please. Take it easy and relax awhile. For me, huh?"

Wade suddenly felt weak inside, but forced a smile. "Sure, Thump, I hear what you're sayin'. Now get out of here and get some sleep."

Thumper patted his sergeant's leg, but avoided looking into his eyes. He could tell by Matt's voice that his advice hadn't been taken well. Thumper strode to the door without looking back. He didn't want to see a friend die. And Matt Wade was going to die . . . unless he changed.

Sergeant Wade closed his eyes to stop the tears as Thumper walked out the door. His friend's words had hit like shrapnel. Thumper had told him the truth that he hadn't wanted to admit to himself. He had blamed bad luck and Lieutenant Dickey for too long, but now the blame had to be placed where it really belonged—on himself, Sergeant Matt Wade.

Thumper was right—the war had become too personal. Within the chaos and pain of Vietnam, Wade had found the success, respect, and admiration he'd always strived for.

Up to the time he'd been drafted, his life had been a series of failures that seemed to leave him no future but the farm. All his hard work in school, all his trying to make something of himself, seemed never enough, but the Army was different. Within its rigid system, grade point averages and college test scores meant nothing. His physical strength, natural leadership ability, and overwhelming desire were exactly the attributes the Army rewarded. He excelled in basic training and was selected for accelerated schooling to become a noncommissioned officer. Later, when he volunteered for the Airborne and Ranger Schools at Fort Benning, he discovered a different kind of Army. At these schools, designed to push students to their physical and emotional limits, and then a step beyond, he'd found another man inside himself, a man who loved the stress and physical rigors that others seemed to hate. Students weakened and failed around him while he grew stronger and asked for more.

He had arrived in Vietnam, confident and ready to lead, only to find he wasn't prepared. Ranger school had given him the basics, but there was no substitute for the real thing, where people really died. With time and Carl Rostov's help, he gained the experience he needed and soon became a combat leader, a success again.

Team leaders Zubeck, Selando, Griffin, and himself were the last of the veteran team sergeants, but he was the standout, the best, and that meant continually proving it. That was exactly what he'd been doing for the past months. He'd been pushing himself to be a somebody. He'd been using the men he loved to gain his own self-respect. Now, Thumper's visit had made him realize the truth: He *was* a success, but only because of his men, and he suddenly felt a need to be with them. He didn't need a break or rest, as Thumper had suggested. He just needed to lead and to keep his men from harm. Success from now on would mean getting them all home safely.

The doctor pushed open the emergency room door. An orderly followed him. The doctor's face showed the strain of long hours without sleep as he tiredly examined Wade's wounds. Without speaking, as if saving energy, he pointed to a nearby stainless steel cabinet and held out his hand. In a few seconds, the orderly handed him a prepared needle and syringe.

Wade shut his eyes as the needle pierced his skin, and he felt the tingling surge of the injected fluid. The doctor withdrew the needle and spoke wearily. "Okay, Sarge, that will put you out for awhile. One of the fragments is deep, and I'll need to go in. The other is sitting just under the skin and won't require much work."

Wade glanced at the punctures. The lump under the blue, discolored skin looked like a round, jagged splinter.

"You lie back, and when you wake up it'll all be over. I'll be back when you're out."

Wade lay back on the padded table and shut his eyes as the doctor and orderly walked out of the room. He remembered how his granddad had pulled a large splinter from his leg years ago. The vision of the old man tugged at his insides and stirred emotions he hadn't felt in some time. He missed his grandfather.

Joshua Wade was a farmer, like his father before him. Both had tilled the same soil and cursed the same unpredictable Oklahoma weather. Wheat and cotton were their crops, and 360 acres of rich bottomland was their life. The Wade home was built by Amos Wade in 1917 on a bluff overlooking the South Canadian River and, upon his death, had been given to his son, Joshua. Josh and his wife, Elma Wade, reared a son and a daughter. The son married young and later went to Korea and was killed, leaving a pregnant wife.

Josh and Elma brought their son's wife to their house to live, but loneliness overcame her. She ran off with an oil-crew roughneck, leaving a baby boy.

The Wades raised the boy as their own, and he grew strong working the fields, but he had problems in school.

He was kept back a grade, and then another, before it was discovered that he was dyslexic—he read words backward. Elma read the texts to the boy night after night, and through their combined hard work, he passed junior high school.

Elma died in 1963, and they buried her on Black Jack Hill alongside two generations of Wades. The old man and the boy passed the hill every day on their way to the fields, knowing Elma was watching over them.

The boy grew into a strapping man who learned to love the land, but hated its demands when he also learned to love football. His grandfather didn't approve of the game. He said there wasn't time for sports when the land needed working.

Matt made the time; he'd come home tired from practice but always did his chores so the old man wouldn't give him that look. His grandfather didn't say much—didn't have to; that look said everything.

Matt was older than his classmates because of his difficulties in school, but he was good on the ball field. He knew his grandfather didn't understand the way it felt when Matt read about himself in the papers, or when the townspeople made a fuss over him; it didn't matter. He didn't even mind when the old man never went to a game. But the "look," that look, always tore him up inside.

When Matt graduated high school he received a partial football scholarship to Southwestern State College. He studied hard, but with working nights to pay the rest of his way through school he fell behind in his grades. Nothing had ever been easy for him; he'd had to fight and struggle his whole life. Again he'd done his best only to fail, to earn a grade point average that told him he had no future.

He went back to the farm and to his granddad, who never did understand why he wanted to be more than just a farmer anyway. Matt tried to explain why he had to make it on his own, to earn self-respect before he could accept the Wade heritage.

The draft notice came six months later. The old man said nothing. He just got on his tractor and plowed all day. In fact, he never mentioned the notice until the day he drove his grandson to the bus station.

The door to the Greyhound opened and the old man

cried. Matt hadn't seen him cry since Elma died. His grandfather hugged him and wouldn't let him go. The bus driver had to honk the horn twice before the old man finally dropped his arms in acceptance and defeat. Those tears and his grandfather's parting words tore through Matt's heart: "I'll miss you, son."

Matt wrote home often but never received any mail until finally, just before he shipped out to Vietnam, a short letter arrived. The scribbled lines from his grandfather's arthritic hands were hard to read, but they spoke of love and pride—love of his precious land, and pride in his grandson. He wrote, too, of Matt's father, who'd been killed in Korea, and how his dad was, like Matt, "hardheaded, but good." He ended with, "Come back to me, Matt. Come back to me and Elma. We love you."

The doctor walked back into the emergency room, followed by the orderly. "Is he out?"

The orderly opened Wade's eyelid with his thumb. "Yes, sir. But it looks like he's been crying."

The doctor merely glanced at the tears on the young sergeant's face as he pulled on his surgical gloves. "Get me a probe ready."

3

3 September

An Lou Mountains
Fifteen kilometers north of LZ English

The hidden NVA machine gun chattered and spit out a deadly tongue of blue flame as it made another sweeping burst.

Lieutenant John Dalton Gibson lay waiting to die on a jungle trail fifteen feet from the gun. He pressed himself closer to the ground, trying to will his body to dissolve into the protective earth. His rigid frame jerked involuntarily at the sound of each burst, anticipating the impact of the bullets. He knew it was just a matter of time before the gunner raked him to make sure he was dead.

A small rivulet of blood trickled down the incline of the trail and backed up against his cheek. The riddled body of Harris, the point man, lay sprawled on the path only four feet in front of him. The blood was his.

Gibson opened his eyes when he felt the warm stickiness on his face and shuddered in revulsion. He wanted to scream and vomit, but he did neither. His survival instinct prevailed. He remained motionless.

His platoon had been ordered earlier that morning to secure a jungle covered hilltop. They'd walked along a small trail up a ridge toward their objective. Gibson had halted his men only two minutes before and had motioned Harris to check out the crest of a hill twenty-five meters ahead. Harris, a lanky Texan, had taken only ten steps, then froze. Gibson had crept forward cautiously to see what the problem was when the hidden machine gun opened up. Harris was hit in the chest and was knocked backward violently. He died before hitting the hard clay of the trail. Gibson had seen the blue-orange flame in the split second he'd thrown himself to the ground. The gun was in a bunker just off the trail ahead of Harris.

Gibson couldn't stand the smell of the blood any longer and chanced shifting his head. He lifted up only slightly and immediately felt a surge of hope. He saw that he was in a slight depression, a dead space the gunner couldn't see. Gibson looked behind him to spot his men just as the gunner fired another burst. The bullets cracked only inches over his head and made impact with splintering thuds into the felled tree behind which his first squad lay huddled. The rest of his men were hidden behind trees and rocks farther back along the trail. They were all pinned down.

Gibson's feeling of hope again turned to one of helplessness as he realized he couldn't crawl back to his men without being exposed. It was at least ten feet to the log, with no cover in between. He waited until the machine gun quit firing and barked to his platoon sergeant: "Sampson!"

"L-tee?" came back in a surprised voice from behind the log. "You okay?"

"Yeah. Can the third squad move around to the right and try and flank em?"

"They already tried, sir, and Botkins was hit. We can't move."

Gibson felt defeated. They were out of range for artillery support, and the left side of the ridge was too steep for maneuvering. There were no options left except . . . Damn, he'd been trained to do it but . . . shit! "Sampson, I'm gonna rush the bunker. Throw something to your left to draw the dink's attention. I'm gonna toss a grenade and try and get behind them. When you hear me yell, come running quick!"

"Are you sure, sir?"

"Hell no, I'm not sure, but it's all we got. Throw something in thirty seconds."

Shaking horribly, Gibson took off his rucksack and pulled a grenade from his web belt. He had to concentrate on one thing at a time. He pushed the selector on his M-16 from *safe* to *semi* and drew his leg up, readying himself to rise and throw the grenade. Damn! The grenade! He hadn't pulled the pin yet.

Sergeant Sampson was going to toss his helmet for distraction but realized it wouldn't be enough. He decided instead to give the NVA gunner a live target. He picked out a large tree ten feet to his right and hopped to his feet in a dead run.

The gunner swung his barrel and fired at the fleeing target. The bullets followed the sergeant like mad hornets. Sampson hit the ground and rolled behind the protective tree as hot lead stitched the air where he had been.

Gibson tossed the grenade, fell to the ground, and grabbed for his weapon. The grenade hit three feet in front of the bunker's firing portal and lay for several seconds before disintegrating in a vehement blast.

Gibson jumped to his feet and ran up the hill toward the billowing cloud of debris, praying the gunner couldn't see him. He ran as fast as he could but felt as if his body was in slow motion. He hurdled two fallen logs and sprinted the last ten meters of open ground before diving into the grass to the right of the bunker, out of view of the gunner. He lay on his stomach, his chest heaving and his muscles loose as rubber. He should have been elated, but he only felt sick. There was no small tunnel entrance at the back of the bunker, as he'd expected. Instead, he found himself laying on the edge of an extensive trench system.

Gibson fought back the sour bile pushing up his throat. The trench meant he faced a helluva lot more than a couple of dinks and a machine gun. Shit, what have I gotten myself into? he thought, as he slowly raised his head and peered into the six-foot-deep trench that zigzagged around the contour of the hill. To his right, the bunker was dug into the side of the trench and covered with a mound of dirt expertly camouflaged with growing plants and grass. Suddenly, the machine gun opened up. Its sound was muffled within the bunker but still it startled him.

"Oh God," Gibson whispered to himself, trying to control his shaking. The smell of gunsmoke and freshly dug soil filled his nostrils as he lowered himself into the trench and edged along the near wall toward the bunker's entrance. He stopped just short of the small opening and took the last grenade from his belt. Without hesitation he pulled the pin and let the spoon fly. He held the primed grenade for two seconds, then tossed it in and fell back against the wall. The explosion threw him forward as red dirt tumbled down all around him, but he kept his feet and ran firing into the dust-filled bunker. Two dark shapes lay silhouetted in a heap in front of a small firing portal. He held his breath and fired at the bodies; the sound was deafening within the small confines. Then dust overcame him, and he began choking. He threw himself toward the entrance for precious air. He sucked in a deep breath and raised his head to yell for his platoon. His mouth had just formed the words when six feet away two NVA ran around the corner of the trench. Gibson raised his weapon in a single motion and fired from the hip. The first surprised soldier took another step, seemingly unhurt, then suddenly doubled up as if hit in the solar plexus. The bullet had passed through his stomach and blown out his back to strike the second soldier in the side. Gibson fired twice more, this time aiming. Both men suffered for only milliseconds before their heads jerked back in instant peace.

Gibson tryed to yell out with confidence, but his voice failed him and he squealed like a desperate child: "Help meeee!"

A hand appeared from around the corner of the trench. Gibson jerked his M-16 up but the hand was gone. An object fell directly at his feet. A Chicom grenade! Gibson fell back into the bunker entrance and rolled just as the bamboo-handled device exploded. He jumped to his feet, knowing that whoever threw the grenade would be coming. He ran out into the trench just as a small North Vietnamese rushed around the corner, firing his AK-47. Bullets cracked by Gibson's ear as he pulled the trigger. The soldier fell like a rag doll as the top right part of his head blew back and splattered the dirt wall. A bloodcurdling scream killed the silence, and a second NVA charged around the trench corner. Gibson pulled the trigger, but nothing happened. He was out of ammunition.

The soldier fired wildly and pitched forward, tripped by his dead comrades. Gibson lunged and rammed his rifle barrel into the man's back. The soldier grunted and spun around, grabbing for Gibson's throat. The lieutenant jerked the weapon up and viciously slammed the butt into the soldier's face. The sickening, bone-crunching thud wasn't heard by Gibson as he screamed crazily and struck the smashed face again and again.

A hand reached out and grabbed the lieutenant's shoulder. Gibson spun around with the bloody weapon, ready to kill his attacker, but met the stare of Sergeant Sampson. The sergeant looked into the dirt- and blood-streaked face of the young officer and spoke gently. "He's dead, L-tee."

Phan Thiet
Third Platoon Base Camp

Russian was sitting on his cot, patting a small, yellow dog, when Rose walked into the large tent and tossed his shaving bag over to his bunk.

"Russian, my man, the shower is most def-initely what's happenin'. You and Bitch looks like you could use a cleanin', too."

The Czech looked up from Bitch and sniffed the air. "You smell like a woman, Rose."

Rose laughed with his usual deep chortle and put his wrist to his nose. "This is Essence of Horny. The Phan Thiet ladies most def-initely can't resist it. The Rose is gonna profile and get him some prime toooonight!"

Russian grunted and lay back on his cot, still patting his dog.

"Come on, old man. You come with us tonight. The

Rose will find ya an old blind chick that don't mind makin'
it with hairy, foreign dudes like you."

Thumper strode into the tent with an olive drab towel
draped around his thick neck.

Rose motioned toward Russian as the big, bare-chested
soldier walked by him. "Thump, the ol' dude needs to get
laid, man. I've been rappin', tryin' to explain to him there's
sweet thangs out there just dyin' for our love and a-feck-
shun!"

Thumper brushed past Rose with a smile. "Yeah, and
they want our mon-nay!" He sat on his cot and picked up
his fatigue shirt.

"Russian, I talked to Sergeant Gino at morning chow.
He's still pissed that you threatened an orderly last night.
You'd better come with Rose and me this afternoon when
we go downtown so that Gino don't put you on detail."

Russian raised up to a sitting position. "The orderly, he
is imbecile. He the one who make the trouble. He should
let me see my sergeant when I ask."

Rose grinned knowingly at the Czech. "Yeah, and I bet
you asked reeeeal nice, too."

Russian glared back, looking as if to kill.

Thumper walked over quickly and stood between the
two men, trying not to laugh. "Russian, Lieutenant Dickey
wants to see me at the TOC. When I get back, we'll go by
and see Matt, then hit the town and get us some real food.
Whaddaya say?"

Russian's harsh glare dissolved. "Yes, I go, but keep
the crazy one away from me."

Rose looked around from behind Thumper. "Looky
who callin' *me* crazy. You da one the medics wanted to
lock up, man!

Russian began to spring up, but Thumper put his hand
on the Czech's shoulder and spoke softly. "It's all right,
Carl. Rose is just pulling your chain."

Russian pointed his finger at the black soldier's smiling
face. "One day I going to pull his head."

Rose began strutting back to his cot. "Well allll right,

we going to town and find us some sweet thangs tonight. We gonna rock 'n' roll and make 'em scream with delight.''

Thumper exchanged glances with Russian and both men shook their heads.

Nha Trang
Corps Headquarters

When Lieutenant Colonel Robert Ellis, Corps G-2, intelligence officer, walked into the large office, a young major wearing camouflage fatigues immediately rose to his feet.

Colonel Jeffries, Corps G-3, operations officer, remained seated behind a desk and motioned toward the tall major: "Colonel Ellis, meet Ed Shane, commander of Sierra Rangers. He's just flown in from Da Lat."

Ellis shook Shane's hand warmly. "Good to meet you, Ed. Your men have done a great job getting me information."

The G-3 gestured to a nearby chair as he began to speak. "Bob, the major has requested you be present to hear about some problems he's having. He hopes that between the two of us, we can help him. Go ahead now and brief us, Major."

Shane explained the personnel situation and the problems with the split company. When he finished, Colonel Ellis exchanged glances with the G-3 and sighed.

"Well, I'd say the Rangers's problems are our problems," Ellis said. "The personnel situation is going to be sticky because we have to work through the G-1, Colonel Rite. Rite is a pompous ass, but based on what Shane has told me I think we can arrange things. The company being split is easy to fix. I suggest that Major Shane move his entire company to An Khe, his permanent camp, and begin a comprehensive training program just as he requests."

The G-3 nodded in agreement and turned to Shane.

"How long would this program of yours take if you received replacements in . . . let's say two days?"

Shane could hardly contain his joy as he answered. "Three weeks, sir, maybe four, depending on the quality of veteran replacements."

The G-3 stood and walked around the desk. "Ed, you start your company moving back to An Khe as soon as possible. Go down and see my air transport officer and tell him what you need in air support. You come back day after tomorrow and we'll brief the general on what's happening."

Shane shook hands with the two officers, thanking them, and left the office.

The G-3 shook his head. "Okay," he said to Ellis, "how are we going to get around Rite and the general?"

Ellis smiled confidently. "Don't worry about Rite. I'll scare him a little. The general is a different story. Getting Wayland to eat cake requires icing . . . and I think I know what icing he likes." His smile vanished. "But I'm going to need your help. The information I received from Phan Thiet yesterday matches with what my people have pieced together, but it's going to take the Rangers to confirm it. Shane was right—the Rangers have got to be in top condition to do the job."

The G-3's eyebrows lifted. "And what job is that?"

Ellis stared at a wall map across the room. "They're going to find the NVA's Second Division that is consolidating northwest of Phan Thiet." He broke his eyes from the map and fixed them on the colonel. "And that division is co-located with the commander of all Commmunist forces in South Vietnam, General Binh Ty Duc."

Lieutenant Colonel Sy stood at a trail intersection and raised his canteen to his parched lips. Behind him, resting along the twisting jungle trail, were the men of the Second Company of the Thirty-third Regiment, the men who had ambushed the Yankee armor column two days before.

Sy swallowed two gulps of tepid water and lowered the tin water bottle. Standing in front of him, staring with hate-filled eyes, was the Second Company's commander, Captain Trung. Sy knew the captain considered him a higher headquarters meddler and that he had caused the death of the stay-behind platoon. He avoided the angry eyes and sat down facing away from him. In a few minutes he wouldn't have to endure the looks any longer. The captain and his company would be taking the eastern trail and marching to a natural mountain fortress to rejoin the Thirty-third Regiment. The captain would go never knowing that the general himself had planned the operation as a ploy to divert attention, and had sent him, Sy, the general's special staff officer, to oversee the operation. The general knew a company commander would not understand the greater purpose of the sacrifice and would not have left men to die.

When Sy saw the senior sergeant approaching with a young private, he knew his wait was over.

Captain Trung stepped in front of the young colonel and glared at him with disdain. "Here is your escort," he said sarcastically. "You requested a squad, but the squad you would have had you left in the bunkers days ago. Private Nuu is all I can spare."

Colonel Sy stood up, disregarding the captain's lack of respect, and smiled faintly as he looked into the questioning and hurt eyes of Private Nuu. They were still red from crying. He obviously didn't want to leave his unit.

Sy hefted his pack to his shoulder. He felt sorry for the boy, but it was a long journey back to headquarters, and Sy needed him. Sy picked up his AK-47. There was no need to say anymore to the captain. The man would never understand. Sy simply pointed to the western trail and motioned Nuu to lead the way.

Captain Trung and the senior sergeant watched the two men until they disappeared from view. The sergeant shook his head with disgust. "Liberation Headquarters is a greater enemy than the Americans."

Captain Trung stared down the empty trail and spoke almost in a whisper. "Perhaps, but I know this: One day there will be a day of reckoning for those who killed their own."

The sergeant nodded in silence. He hoped he would be there on that day. He hoped he would be the one who pulled the trigger.

Phan Thiet
Third Platoon Base Camp

Lieutenant Marvin Dickey dropped his salute and motioned for Thumper to sit by his desk.

"Specialist Meeks, I'm very impressed by your performance. I've been reading your file, and I see you have been awarded two Silver Stars. The citations make you out as quite a hero."

Thumper had caught the hint of sarcasm in the officer's last words and knew he was trying to manipulate him. The lieutenant's lack of genuineness solidified Thumper's first opinion of the man: He was an asshole.

Dickey leaned forward in his chair, looking for a reaction, as he spoke again. "Yes, Meeks, you have quite a record, much too good to be just an assistant team leader. So today I'm making you leader of your own team. This means a promotion, of course, and starts you off on a new career."

Dickey let the good news sink in for effect and casually picked up a pad of paper. "There is one little thing to clear up, and then we can get down to the business of assigning you some people. I need a small statement about what Sergeant Wade said to me yesterday. Just a few paragraphs would be fine." Dickey extended the pad toward the stone-faced soldier.

Thumper kept his eyes on the forehead of the officer and spoke dryly. "I will not accept the position of team leader, sir."

Dickey dropped the pad as if it were hot. "What do you mean, *you* won't accept?"

Thumper didn't change expression. "I mean, sir, I don't want to be a team leader. I'm happy with what I'm doing now."

Dickey's hand shot up and he pointed his finger at Meeks's face. "You'll do what I say or I'll move you to another team anyway."

Thumper controlled his anger and kept his stoic expression. "Sir, I respectfully request to call Major Shane."

"I'm the platoon leader, soldier! You'll follow *my* orders!"

"Beggin' your pardon, sir, but you're new and don't know that Major Shane personally assigned me and Specialist Flowers to Sergeant Wade's team. It is *his* policy to have at least one experienced team per platoon."

Dickey sat back in his chair to think. He didn't know his commander that well, having only seen him a few days before being assigned to Phan Thiet. But in that brief contact, it was obvious that the major was much too close to his men and relied too heavily on his NCOs. Meeks was probably right about the major personally assigning him, but all was not lost.

Dickey forced a smile. "All right Meeks, I won't make you take a promotion if you really don't want it. But you should really think it over, and if you change your mind, the job is open to you. You're dismissed. . . . Oh, before you go, I need the statement. You can sit here, and perhaps I can help you."

Thumper decided to drag it out. He was having fun. "What statement was that, sir?"

"The statement concerning the events yesterday . . . when Sergeant Wade was insubordinate, of course."

"I'm sorry, sir, but I didn't hear the conversation yesterday . . . at least I didn't hear any insubordinate remarks."

Dickey's face flushed in seething anger. "You're playing games, Meeks! Don't mess with me. Write the damn statement!"

"Is that an order, sir? I mean, write that I didn't hear anything?"

"Get out! Get out and send Rostov and Flowers to me immediately!"

Thumper shot to his feet and executed his best hand salute. Dickey ignored the salute and screamed. "Out!"

Thumper held his salute, knowing the officer had to render one in return, according to regulation. He found great pleasure in seeing the system really work, sometimes— especially in this case.

Dickey threw a quick salute in defeat, then quickly turned his back to Thumper.

Thumper marched smiling from the room. He could hardly wait to warn Russian and Rose. The lieutenant was definitely in for a bad day with team 3-1.

Phan Thiet
Twenty-third Evac Hospital

Sergeant Matt Wade sat on the side of his bed, laughing as Thumper recounted his story about Lieutenant Dickey. "Rose told him he was hard of hearing and didn't hear a thing. Then Russian walks in and tells him he doesn't understand English very well, even had Dickey explain what insubordination was, then says he didn't hear anything either. I guess we'll all be on shit details for a month!"

Wade fell back against his pillow, laughing harder. He could see Dickey trying to talk Carl into writing up charges. The lieutenant was lucky the Czech hadn't broken his neck.

Rose strutted over to the bed and began eating Wade's food from the hospital tray.

Wade shook his head. "Damn, Rose. Now I know why you came to visit."

Rose looked up with his mouth full. "We goin' out tonight. I need strength for the ladies."

Russian closely inspected his sergeant's bandage. "You be back soon, yes?"

"Sure. The doc says it's fine—a couple of stitches is all. He's sending me to Bien Hoa Air Base tomorrow to get some X rays."

"Why X rays?" asked Russian worriedly.

Wade leaned back on the elevated bed. "He wants to see if there are any small fragments left in there. He won't dig 'em out, but he says he wants it in my records. The damned X ray machine here is broken, so I gotta go to the Air Force hospital. Stevens flew out an hour ago."

Thumper sat down beside Wade. "How was Stevens?"

"He won't be back. He's going home. Lucky kid just got here, and he gets a million-dollar wound."

Thumper looked carefully at Wade's shoulder. "Very painful?"

The sergeant shook his head reassuredly. "Nothing a few beers wouldn't take away. How's about you guys sneaking some in?"

Thumper exchanged grins with Rose and lifted a Claymore bag from the floor. "We always take care of our team sergeant, now don't we?"

Wade laughed as Rose looked around the open ward. "Hey, Sarge. You got any nurses in here, man? I wanna see a round eye and a round ass."

Wade pointed to the door. "Thump, get lover-boy outta here and get him the clap, will ya?"

Rose shook his head as if hurt. "That was cruel, man, real cruel. The Rose done seen them movies. I got me some A-numba-one, reinforced rubbers from stateside." He broke into a wide grin. "This Ranger is ready for action!"

Thumper patted Wade's leg. "I'll see you when you get back. Take care and don't mess around with any of them Air Force nurses."

Wade frowned. "Don't worry, I've seen the VD movies, too."

Rose strutted for the door, followed by Thumper, but Russian remained before his sergeant and good friend, holding out his hand. "Take care, my Sergeant."

Wade shook hands and patted Russian's arm. "You watch them tonight, Carl. Don't let 'em drink too much and make sure they get back before curfew, all right?"

Russian brightened visibly at having this responsibility placed on him. "Yes, my Sergeant."

Wade smiled to himself as the bullish man had gone. Russian never called him by his given name. It was as if his upbringing or his regimented military training wouldn't allow any simple word of familiarity. Wade had once tried to make him assistant team leader, but Russian led by slaps and harsh verbal attacks, which young Americans couldn't understand. Russian was well aware of his dictatorial ways and gave up the position voluntarily, but he remained devoted to Wade and would follow him to hell, if ordered.

The thought of Russian taking care of the others, as asked, caused Wade to smile again. The Czech would take the request as an order and follow it to the letter, constantly hounding them to drink less, for to Russian no matter the consequences, an order was always accomplished.

Wade felt no less affection for Thumper and Rose. To him, they were all like brothers, and he knew they all felt the same. Oh, they argued, complained, and fought each other at times, but only to a point. It was as if they all understood that what they had was special. Carl and Rose fought like cats but woe unto the man who said anything bad about one of them in the presence of the other. Thumper and Rose had come from other teams that had been just as close. Rose's friends had all been killed; Thumper's had been wounded or rotated home, yet they never mentioned their old friends. Wade knew they thought of them, but the unspoken rule was never to mention the past. The past didn't matter.

Wade felt incredibly strong. He had been given strength by three men—*his* men. Their lives were in his hands and the responsibility weighed heavily on him, but he wouldn't have wanted it any other way, because they really were his brothers.

Da Lat
Temporary Ranger Headquarters

Sergeant First Class Jerry Childs viciously snubbed out the remaining one inch of his cigarette to get even with its foul taste. He'd smoked a pack waiting for his major. He cussed himself for starting again after quitting for almost a year. The cigarettes were winning. He was losing the battle for self-control.

Major Shane had called him that afternoon from Nha Trang after the meeting with Colonel Ellis and the G-3. The news was what he had hoped for. He waited up to hear the details. Childs looked at his watch—9:10. He was about to stand when he heard a jeep pull up outside. Seconds later, Shane walked in, followed by Pete, his driver.

"'Bout damn time, sir. I been losin' my beauty sleep. Pete, get me and the old man a couple of beers."

Shane tossed his map case to the desk and sat down tiredly. "We're movin' back to An Khe starting tomorrow. We got lucky 'cause there were C-130s in Vung Tau. Two birds will be in Phan Thiet tomorrow at 1300 to pick up the Third Platoon, and at 1400 we've got three birds to pick us all up. You'd better call First Sergeant Demand and tell him the good news."

Childs took the beers from Pete and handed one to Shane. "Sir, I already called An Khe and told Top. He'll have everything ready for us like he always does. Damn, he was so excited I thought I could hear him pissin' his pants."

Shane took a long drink and lowered his can. "Jerry, you were right about Colonel Ellis—he's going look out for us. He's going to get replacements for us from the 173rd, so it looks like we've finally got everyting we've asked for. Now all we gotta do is figure out a training program."

Childs took a quick sip of his beer and sat down the can. "Sir, I've been sittin' up 'cause I wanted to talk to you about that. As you know, we've done this before; just before the Cambodian operation, we got the whole company together and had a small training program. But this is gonna be a helluva lot different. We don't have the experienced men we had before. It's gonna take a lot of planning and hardass training to get the new men and line troops from the 173rd made into a Ranger unit that's worth a shit. We're gonna have to get the lieutenants to the airfield and fly every day to get them experienced in the back of a bird dog. Right now, they're okay but not good enough. Our radio operators are terrible and so are the majority of our teams, and we got a bunch of shitbirds we need to get rid of."

Shane looked into his sergeant's eyes and began to smile. "You waited up to tell me something I already know?"

Childs was surprised Shane had seen through him so quickly.

Shane picked up his beer, knowing what Childs really wanted, and decided not to make him wait any longer.

"Jerry, I know we're not even close to where we should be. I could handle the training, myself. I've been to all the schools and know what's to be done . . . but I'm not. You are."

Childs's head lifted immediately. His lips wouldn't smile but his eyes did. The major was giving him what he wanted, what he knew he could do like nobody else could—train Rangers.

"Sir, I hoped you'd say that, but you know, I gotta do it my way. Once you give me the mission that's it. I make Rangers . . . or I break them."

Shane held the gaze of his sergeant and raised his beer as if in a toast. "Make me some damn good ones."

4

4 September

0900 Hours
LZ English

The morning air kicked up into a red dust cloud as the helicopter landed. A single passenger, Lieutenant J. D. Gibson, hopped to the ground and slung his sixty-pound rucksack up to his shoulder. He walked down a row of parked HUEYs toward a road he knew led to the main base, also known as LZ English, home of the 173rd Airborne Brigade. He reached the road and stopped.

Six months ago, he'd walked down the same dusty road and gotten on a bird that took him to his platoon and the war. He'd weighed 175 pounds then, and wore new olive drab jungle fatigues. He now weighed 155 and his uniform was bleached almost white from the sun and relentless monsoons. Six months ago his ruck had seemed to weigh a hundred pounds as it tore unmercifully into his back and shoulders. Now it was a part of him, like his helmet and M-16; they were constant companions, old friends.

Six months—an eternity—ago, he had wanted to see action, but when he'd gotten it, it sure wasn't what he'd expected. He'd been trained well at Fort Benning, but they hadn't prepared him for real war. Instead of the forty-man platoon with which he'd been trained, he'd had twenty-six. There had been no gruff platoon sergeant like in the movies, no John Wayne or Aldo Ray to take him under his

49

wing and show him the ropes. He'd had instead a twenty-year-old staff sergeant who had only been in the Army three years. War wasn't leading charges and killing. War was responsibility—the overwhelming, day-in, day-out responsibility to ensure that the young men in his platoon lived to see another day. War was misery, heartache, and sore, tired muscles; covering the dead with ponchos, medevacing the wounded, and praying he wouldn't have to do it all again. War was making decisions that could send men to their deaths. It was constant moving, trying to find an elusive, dedicated enemy before he found you. Killing was easy; he had nine notches on his weapon's stock, but there was no high, no glory, no gratification in killing. Killing was easy, but humping was hard, losing his men even harder, and telling his platoon "good-bye" an hour before the hardest of all.

Gibson let out a sigh and began walking up the steep road. He put all thoughts out of his mind, except making it up the hill to the main base. Thoughts of the past and future were meaningless; thoughts were only dreams, and dreams didn't count in war. "It don't mean nuthin'," he mumbled to himself as he brought his rifle to the crook of his arm and leaned into the hill.

Between two plywood barracks, a group of sweaty men, stripped to the waist, stood cheering in the middle of a dirt basketball court. They hollered again as a tall, lanky black man threw out his fist and knocked a small blond soldier to the ground.

"You stay down, muthafucker! Don't be foulin' me again!"

The blond shook his head and spit out a glob of blood. He stood up shakily and held up his fists. The lanky soldier grinned cruelly and moved in to finish him off. Suddenly, something hit the ground in front of him and someone screamed, "*Grenade!*" The players ran like scattered quail and hit the ground rolling.

The blond hadn't moved. He had noticed that the grenade's pin hadn't been pulled. He looked up and saw a helmeted soldier on a rise by the road. One glance at the faded fatigues without rank and the scuffed white boots told him it was a *grunt* just out of the field. The soldier was lean and of medium height; his rolled-up sleeves exposed the burned, brown skin and ropy muscles of his forearms.

The seething black man got to his feet and strode menacingly toward the helmeted soldier on the rise. "You better pray, muthaf . . ."

The soldier's hand came up in one motion, holding the M-16. The bolt slammed forward, chambering a round with a metallic "clank."

The tall man froze as he stared into the impassive pale blue eyes of the soldier—eyes that somehow he knew wouldn't blink when the trigger was pulled and his brains were blown out. The black man backed up a step. "You crazy, man?"

The soldier spoke dryly. "Back up and move out. The fight is over."

One of the other players snickered. "He ain't gonna shoot, Jack, he's bluffin'." Jack's eyes shifted from the icy blue pools to the name tag above the shirt pocket. Immediately, his eyes widened in recognition and he spun around.

Another of the players pleaded, "Jack, he's bluffin', man!"

Jack snarled, "Shut up, fool! He ain't bluffin! That's Gibson!"

Every player's head turned to the soldier in disbelief. Just an hour before, they'd had to stand in an awards ceremony rehearsal. The battalion commander himself had announced the ceremony would be for a Lieutenant Gibson who'd be coming in from the field. He'd explained that Gibson would be receiving a Silver Star for singlehandedly crawling into a NVA bunker and killing two soldiers inside. Four more NVA had attacked him while he was in their trench system; he shot three and killed the other with the butt of his weapon.

The players all turned to leave—all except the blond,

who picked up the grenade and tossed it to the lieutenant.
"Thanks, sir. He probably would've whipped my ass."
   Gibson turned and began to walk back to the road.
   "Uh, sir? Were you? Were you bluffin'?"
   The lieutenant's only answer was silence. His steps
kicked up miniature clouds of dust.

Phan Thiet
Third Platoon Base Camp

Thumper wiped his grenade launcher with an oily rag and
looked up at the approaching soldier.
   "Rose, you better stay out of sight. If Russian sees you,
you're gonna be mincemeat!"
   "Man, that dude is a walkin' bummer. Last night, he
wouldn't let us do shit! I had to do somethin' so I could
be with Chee. Shit, man, that chick wanted me, *bad*!"
   "Yeah, but sendin' that broad over and sneakin' out
pissed him off. We spent two hours lookin' for you, and
it took everything I had to hold him off you when you
showed up."
   Rose smiled slyly. "That chick I sent over was hot,
wasn't she?"
   Thumper tossed down the rag. "That was the ugliest
woman I ever saw!"
   "Shit, man, Russian ain't no Hollywood star his own-
self! The chick was hot to trot!"
   "Yeah, well, she had her hands in my pants more than
I have in a month. She grabbed Russian's dong and nearly
ruined him when he jumped up from the table."
   Rose fell to his knees with laughter. "Man, I was only
trying to help the old bastard. He'll understand, man. No
sweat!" He looked around the camp, still chortling.
"Where is he anyway?"
   Thumper motioned toward the TOC. "The platoon got
orders to move to An Khe today. Gino has got him loading
some radio equipment on air pallets. He'll be back soon
enough, and he'll be lookin' for you."
   "Man, Russian will forget everything by the time Gino
gets finished with him," said Rose none too convincingly

as he glanced over his shoulder toward the operations center.

"Yeah, well don't be so sure. You'd better start packin' your gear. We're going out on the first C-130 that comes in."

Sergeant Gino, carrying a folding chair, stomped out of the TOC so mad he couldn't speak. He'd stayed up most of the night because of the late call from Childs telling him about the move to An Khe. Childs had told him that two C-130s would be arriving at 1300 hours to move them out. He, Gino, had stayed up and written a complete, detailed loading plan to include time schedules for packing, moving equipment, and loading. The plan was a masterpiece of organization and textbook scheduling. He'd called in his sergeants and team leaders at 0800 and briefed them about the entire loading sequence and gave them a copy of the schedule so they could coordinate and systematically move men and equipment without confusion. The load-out was going to move like clockwork.

Then, 1000 hours, just five minutes ago, the Air Force Operations at Vung Tau had called and blown up his entire plan and all his late-night hard work. The two C-130s that were *supposed* to come in at 1300 weren't coming—mechanical problems. But good news, said the airmen. They had two other birds for support. They'd be in even *earlier*. One would be in at 1100 hours and the other at 1200 hours.

Gino set his chair down and sat ten paces in front of the operations center so he could see the base camp and airfield. Murphy's Law must have had the Air Force in mind, he thought.

There was no time to rewrite the plan now. He had to do what all good NCOs did at times like this: holler, kick ass, and get the impossible done.

A Ranger strolled out of his tent one hundred meters away. Gino stood up and bellowed. *"You! Come here!"*

The soldier changed his direction and began walking over. Gino put his hands on his hips. *"Move your ass!"*

Gino recognized the soldier, who had one of those 'what

have I done now' looks on his face, to be one of the newer men.

Gino pointed to the tents behind the soldier. "Hawkins, I want you run into every tent in this base camp. You will tell every team leader, assistant team leader, and every man over the rank of Spec-4 to report to me in *five fucking minutes!* Do you understand?"

"Yes, Sergeant."

"Move it!"

LZ English
Headquarters, 173rd Airborne Brigade

Lieutenant J. D. Gibson entered the deputy brigade commander's office wearing new jungle fatigues and a Silver Star medal pinned to his left pocket flap. He came to a halt and saluted smartly. "Sir, Lieutenant Gibson reports as ordered."

A gray-haired colonel wearing glasses low on his nose stood and reached across the desk. "It's a pleasure to meet you, Gibson. I'm sorry I didn't attend the awards ceremony, but I can hardly get away from this desk any more."

Gibson quickly dropped his salute and shook the colonel's surprisingly strong hand.

"Sit down, son. First, I want to say you did a helluva job as a platoon leader with Bravo Company. Your platoon alone had more kills than six of our rifle companies last month. Most important of all, you did it with very few casualties. That's a sign you're a helluva trainer as well as leader. Congratulations on your Silver Star."

Gibson only nodded. The office seemed uncomfortably stuffy to him after having lived outside for six months.

"One more thing." The colonel smiled. "Lieutenant Gibson, because of your outstanding performance, I'm sending you to Nha Trang, where you will be replacing my liaison officer to Corps Headquarters. This will both enhance your career and benefit this brigade."

Gibson knew he should say something but he didn't know what the hell a liaison officer was. He stammered for a moment and finally offered, "Thank you, sir." Then he allowed his stone-faced stare to fix on the colonel's forehead.

The deputy commander got up and held out his hand again.

"Lieutenant, I expect good things from you down there. You talk to my S-1 across the street and he'll explain your duties. I understand you'll be leaving this afternoon, so good luck to you."

Gibson shook the colonel's hand again and was about to turn away when the colonel asked, "Did your hair turn in the field or is it natural?"

"The field, sir." Gibson replied, impatiently. He wanted out of the stuffy office.

"Well, Lieutenant, don't worry about it. I've had gray hair for twenty years myself."

Gibson forced a smile and exited the office quickly. The battalion commander had mentioned his prematurely gray hair, too, and so had everybody else who knew him before he went to the field. He looked thirty rather than twenty-three years old.

He walked out of headquarters building and pulled off the medal. He felt naked without his ruck or weapon, and the new fatigues felt uncomfortable. "Don't mean nothin'," he said to himself as he crossed the street to find out what the hell a liaison officer was.

Nha Trang
Corps Headquarters

Colonel Bob Ellis nodded as he walked past the G-1's Vietnamese secretary, then turned into Colonel Rite's office. The rotund Corps personnel officer looked up from his desk in surprise and rose to his feet. "What are the intelligence spooks doing in my part of the world? Is one of my secretaries suspected of spying?"

Ellis forced a thin smile and sat down without being asked.

Rite bristled beneath his hospitable exterior. Ellis was a junior colonel and knew better. He'd been assigned to Corps only three weeks before, but he was already one of the general's fair-haired boys, and he was flaunting the relationship.

Ellis drummed the arm of the padded chair with his fingers as he got down to business. "Charles, we have a problem. It's been brought to our attention that our replacement policy for the Corps Ranger Company isn't working well. In fact, it's in shambles. As far as I can tell from written past policy, the company is supposed to draw a *few* new men from in-country arrivals, but the majority are to come from veterans in the 173rd Airborne Brigade.

"Major Shane, the company commander of Sierra Rangers, tells me they haven't received veterans from the 173rd in over four months. The situation could be construed as almost criminal, especially based on the recent casualty rates of the company."

Rite's face flushed in anger. This son of a bitch Ellis was telling him he wasn't doing his job! The damn West Point junior colonel had said *our* policy when he damn well meant *his*, the G-1's, policy!

Ellis stopped his drumming and casually looked past the G-1 toward the window. "Charles, I know this was probably just an oversight on our part, but we need to get the Rangers back to full strength immediately."

Ellis's eyes shifted from the window to Rite and locked on. "We need to call the 173rd today and ask for one hundred men. They should be volunteers with at least four months experience. They'll report to An Khe in two days."

Rite smiled smugly and shook his head. "That's impossible. I could get a few men in a couple of weeks, maybe, but not a hundred. It's out of the question. I know this Ranger Company works for you, but there are a lot of other priorities. As personnel officer for this Corps, I have to allocate resources to *everyone* as best I can."

Ellis sighed wearily and pulled a folded piece of paper from his fatigue shirt pocket. He unfolded it slowly for effect and momentarily glanced over the contents before looking up at Rite. "Charles, I called the 173rd G-1 an hour ago and explained our situation. He's an old friend, by the way. He was one of my company commanders in '67. He tells me he can put a message out to his units and have a hundred volunteers with no problem. As you know, the 173rd is in a pacification role, so all he needs is a call from you and a backup message later. He says he can have the men in An Khe in two days with no problem.

"And about priorities . . . . I have here a memo signed by the general that says the highest priority of this Corps is intelligence gathering." Ellis stared at Rite. "That means my Rangers. I think you'd better make the call to the 173rd. They're waiting to hear from you."

Rite felt like throwing the heavy ashtray on his desk into Ellis's smug face, but he took in several quick breaths to restrain his anger and not show his emotions. His authority had been usurped, but he knew Ellis had him by the balls. He, Rite, had consciously ignored the replacement policy of the Rangers, and if Ellis brought the situation to the general's attention, there would be one personnel officer out on his ass—especially after the general had made that statement about high priorities. Shit, there was nothing to do but play ball and hope to regain strength in another inning.

Rite softened his expression and raised his brow in conciliation. "Sure Bob, I'll call them today and send the message first thing tomorrow. The general will want to sign it himself, won't he?"

Ellis stood up. "Of course. Just have it on my desk by 0700, and I'll see to it. Thank you, Charles. I knew you'd appreciate the situation and take positive action. I'm sure the general will appreciate it, too."

"I'm here to help," said Rite, burning holes into Ellis's back as he walked out the door.

Colonel Ellis glanced down at the blank piece of paper in his hand and smiled as he passed by the secretary.

Phan Thiet
Third Platoon Base Camp

The base camp was in turmoil. Sergeant Gino had people running around and packing gear everywhere, trying to meet the earlier flights. Team 3-1 was still scheduled to fly out on the first bird, so they had to get their gear to the airfield as soon as possible.

Thumper had called the hospital to tell Wade about the move, but he'd already been flown out by med-evac to Bien Hoa Air Base. The orderly had promised to pass on the information as soon as Wade returned the following day.

Thumper finished packing Wade's gear, hefted the bags to his shoulder, and began the 300-meter walk to the airfield. He didn't feel the weight of the heavy bags. His mind was on the all too familiar base at An Khe. The thought of returning there brought back many painful memories.

He'd said good-bye too many times in An Khe. Grady, his first team sergeant and close friend, had rotated home from there. Mary Ann, a Red Cross worker who had lived in a compound close by, had said good-bye there, too.

Mary Ann, especially, had taken a piece of his heart when she transferred to Saigon. She was a woman he could have held onto for a lifetime. Since then she had written many letters, but somehow he couldn't put feelings on paper to reciprocate. He sat for hours thinking of her, but he couldn't bring himself to write a single line. Finally, about a month ago, her letters stopped coming. He shut his eyes to stop the emotions that made his knees feel weak. He missed the tall, raven-haired woman who had made him feel so good, and he missed the old team he loved. Of Team 2-2, three had been wounded in Cambodia, and two had rotated home. That left him, the last original member.

He opened his eyes and took a deep breath for strength. When he'd been moved to Matt's team three months ago, he had found a new home, and Russian, Rose, and Matt had taken the place of the others, but his old friends would always have a special place in his heart.

Thumper tossed Wade's bags onto a pallet and returned to the tent. He quickly stuffed his belongings into two duffel bags and began to walk back to the airfield. Sergeant Gino saw him and yelled for him to come to the TOC.

Thumper cussed under his breath and walked toward

the sergeant, who still sat on his folding chair directing the
load-out.

Rose lay back on his rucksack behind a tent, hiding from
the watchful eye of Gino. He had just dozed off when a
powerful, hairy arm clamped around his neck and jerked
him up. Russian pushed him away, causing him to fall over
his rucksack. Rose rolled to the ground and sprang to his
feet to meet his attacker.

"You do not follow my orders," Russian growled. "You
make me a fool."

Rose immediately lowered his fists and began backing
away from the approaching huge soldier.

"No man, I was just . . . No, Russian, shit, man, back
off. I . . . I . . ." He spun around and ran screaming,
"Thum-*per*!" . . . Thum-*per*!"

Thumper stood up at the sound of the bloodcurdling
scream and smiled as Rose ran straight for him. Russian,
followed by his dog, chased Rose at a slow lope.

Rose skidded to a halt behind Thumper and Gino, and
pointed excitedly toward the advancing bull.

"He . . . he's gonna kill me!"

Thumper sat back down and shook his head. "I told you
he was pissed."

Russian halted a few paces in front of Thumper and
glared at the Rose.

"I teach the crazy one a lesson."

Thumper sighed. "Carl, I understand how you feel, but
we'd just be another man short. Besides, Sergeant Gino
here needs a detail man to load out equipment."

Rose whined, "Aw, shit, Thump."

Thumper ignored the remark. "Why don't you and Bitch
go on down to the airfield," he said to Russian. "We'll be
in An Khe in a little while, and we'll get to chose our bunks
while lover-boy is still working. He won't be in until this
evening.

Russian grunted and lowered his eyes to Thumper. "He
will not work. He just talk."

Gino stood up, offended. "The hell he will! I'll make him sweat!"

Satisfied, Russian threw one last cutting stare at Rose, then went to the tent to collect his equipment.

Rose fell to his knees with a pained expression. "Damn, Thump, you can't do this to me, man."

"You're staying, or I'll let Russian have you."

"Shit, man, you messin' with me and . . . and I got a slight problem."

Thumper's eyebrows raised slowly. "Yeah?"

"Well, I tried to piss awhile ago and . . ."

Thumper shook his head with a sigh. "You'd better get to the medics before they pack up their penicillin. What happened to the stateside rubber?"

"Aw, man, she wanted me *now*, you know what I mean?"

Thumper, trying to contain his laughter, gave an exaggerated nod and pointed to the medics' tent. "Move out and get your shot. You got work to do!"

Rose got up, mumbling. "I swear, man, you try to help a buddy, and he done gets hos-tile. You try to be nice to a lady, and she gives you the clap. This world is fucked up, man."

Bien Hoa Air Force Base
433rd Wing Hospital

Sergeant Matt Wade had arrived that afternoon at Bien Hoa, wearing a sling. He had his X rays taken, but there were no flights scheduled back to Phan Thiet until the following morning, so he was ordered to a convalescent ward to wait.

As soon as he saw the ward he knew he wasn't going to like it. A short Staff sergeant in hospital whites grinned when he noticed the lanky buck sergeant wearing camouflage fatigues and black beret.

"You're just the man I've been looking for," said the ward master as if he was eyeing a new slave. "You're not leaving until tomorrow, so today you're mine. You'll be in charge of getting this ward, and the next one over, cleaned up. You'll have nine men. All are able to walk or push a broom. You'll find mops and brooms at the end of the hall.''

Wade glared at the staff sergeant with disgust. ''And what will you be doing?''

The ward master smiled smugly as he stood up from his chair. ''I'm going to a USO show at the air base—you just gave me the ticket.'' His smile dissolved into a serious frown. ''Don't make any trouble, Sarge, or you'll be doing this for a week. I can have you scheduled for a reexamination based on my observations. That should take at least another day or two, and I can keep doing it until I'm tired of you. Now, you just do the job and you'll be gone tomorrow.''

Matt had seen his type before. They were in control of their little world and could deal misery and woe to their captives. The bastard held all the aces. Matt made a mental note to one day make a special trip back and finish the conversation. He held back his anger and resigned himself to be cool. ''Where's the detail?''

The ward master smirked as he walked for the door. ''Next door. And Sarge, make these floors *shine*.''

Nha Trang
Corps Headquarters

Colonel Ellis stood to the side of General Wayland's desk, pointing to a wall map. ''We have confirmed that the Thirty-third and Forty-second NVA regiments are assembling in this mountainous area here. Reports indicate the Thirty-ninth regiment will link up in the next three weeks to form the Second Division.''

The gray-haired Corps commander seemed preoccupied and merely glanced at the map. ''Colonel, you're wasting my time. You know my orders are pacification. That area you so casually pointed to is over one hundred square kilometers. It would take three divisions to find them. And if we did find them, Washington would never accept our casualities.''

Colonel Ellis pressed. ''We don't need three divisions,

General. The Rangers will find them for us, like they found
the base camps in Cambodia. The Rangers can pinpoint
their main base, and we can send in a B-52 strike to destroy
it."

The general's eyes told Ellis he was interested, but not
convinced. Now for the icing, thought the colonel.

"Sir, Region Headquarters is aware of this buildup, as
is the South Vietnamese government. I think you'll agree
they will look very favorably upon this Corps should we
reduce this potential threat . . . especially since recent reports indicate that the commander of all Communist forces
in South Vietnam, General Binh Ty Duc, is co-located with
the Second Division."

Wayland leaned forward in his chair and studied the map
more closely.

"When would the Rangers go in?"

"Four weeks, sir. We would want the NVA with their
base camp fully operational and feeling relatively safe.
Plus, we need to bring the Rangers up to full strength. We
haven't been taking very good care of them recently."

The general leaned back in his chair, thinking aloud.
"You know, we haven't had any positive press since the
Cambodia invasion. An operation like this . . ." His eyes
locked on the G-2. "I approve the plan. You brief me in
one week on the details and prepare a briefing for Region
Headquarters."

"Yes, sir," Ellis said with satisfaction. He decided to
try one more hand. "General, I've already informed Colonel Rite to begin filling the Rangers back up to strength,
and I'm moving the Rangers to An Khe where they can
begin a rebuilding program. I hope you approve?"

"Yes, of course. Do whatever is necessary."

"Thank you, sir. . . . Oh, I'm sorry, sir, but when you
mentioned 'press' I was reminded—I wasn't sure if you
knew the Associated Press would be at the awards ceremony this evening?"

The general's eyes lifted immediately. "What
ceremony?"

"The Aviation Battalion is awarding several pilots Distinguished Flying Crosses. I thought you were . . ."

Wayland suddenly reached over and snatched up his phone. "Get me Rite up here, now!" He slammed down the receiver and looked back at Ellis.

"How'd you hear about this?"

"Sir, the Aviation commander and I are classmates and had dinner last night. I thought you knew about the ceremony or I wouldn't have . . ."

Wayland raised his hand, interrupting the G-2. "It's a good thing you did mention it. At least I have one staff officer who understands the power of the press. Thank you and keep up the good work."

Ellis came to attention, then briskly strode to the door. He'd pulled it off perfectly. He felt like skipping, but kept his measured gait until passing through the aide's office to the hallway.

The portly G-1 personnel officer ran up the stairs and called out to him. "What's the general want? Do you know?"

Ellis fought to keep a straight face. "Not really, I just mentioned to him the awards ceremony this evening and. . ."

"Jesus! What ceremony?"

Ellis calmly restated what was said and grinned as the colonel bolted into a nearby office. Ellis chuckled as he strolled down the hallway.

Colonel Rite quickly picked up a telephone and called downstairs to his public affairs officer.

"What's this about an awards ceremony at the Aviation Battalion?"

"Yes, sir, they're awarding two DFCs."

"Was the general invited?"

"Yes, sir, but I checked his calendar and he has a meeting with the Fourth Division commander for dinner so . . ."

"Shit! You should have told me! My god, the press is

going to be there! He'd cancel the Fourth's general to . . .
shit, never mind, just get in my office, now!''

Rite slammed down the receiver and hurried to the general's office.

The aide looked up from his desk. ''He's waiting on you,
sir.''

Rite opened the door and cringed as the general looked
up from his desk. ''Goddamn it, Charles! How come I
wasn't . . .''

Rite walked out of the general's office five minutes later,
red-faced. Goddamn that Ellis. He did this to me, that
smart-ass son of a bitch. He came into *my* office and as
much as ordered me to fill the Rangers with experienced
men. And now this. *This!* I'll get you, Ellis. I'll get you
and that prima donna Ranger outfit you think so much of.

Southern Liberation Military Headquarters

Private Nguyen Tran Nuu forgot his weariness and hunger
as he stood just inside the entrance of the command tunnel.
He and Colonel Sy had completed their long march to headquarters and were waiting for one of the general's staff
officers to clear them for entry.

Nuu could not believe the size of the tunnel. Unlike
those he had seen before, the corridor was large enough
to accommodate three men walking shoulder to shoulder,
and electric lights were strung along the six-foot-high earth
ceiling for as far as he could see.

Colonel Sy noticed the private's eyes widening. ''This
is your new home. I think you will like your position in
the Security Battalion. I will talk to the commander and
see if you can be assigned a new RPG-7 to take the place
of the RPG-2 you left behind.''

Nuu lowered his head. ''Thank you, comrade Colonel,
but I should return to my platoon. They need me.''

Colonel Sy put his hand on the boy's shoulder. ''That
is impossible, my friend. You now know the location of
our headquarters. The tunnel is a secret and no one is allowed into the valley without permission. Very few even

know of its existence. For the sake of security, you must now become one of the Guard Battalion that secures the complex. But it is a great honor to serve here. Your family will be very proud."

Nuu recalled who had halted them a kilometer from the entrance and searched their packs. He and the colonel had been escorted down a trail that passed through four heavily fortified checkpoints. The soldiers all wore clean uniforms of the same style and color, and even wore their red collar rank insignias. Their weapons were new, as was their equipment, but the most striking thing about the soldiers was how well-fed they all looked. One thing he had learned since coming to the south was that the liberation army lived day to day on scant rations. There had been days—sometimes weeks—when he had been given only a handful of sticky rice for a day's ration. Perhaps serving with the Guard Battalion would not be such bad duty after all.

Nuu looked at the young colonel sheepishly. "Comrade Colonel, do you think they have a uniform that will fit my frail bones?"

Sy laughed and patted the boy's shoulder. "Yes, my friend. I will see to it."

"Sy, you have returned!"

Sy turned around at hearing the familiar voice call his name. "Yes, Senior Colonel Chinh, I have come back to haunt you after sending me away so long."

Nuu backed up against the earthen wall and stood at attention. He had never seen a senior colonel before but recognized the four silver stars on the officer's shoulder insignia.

The old colonel warmly shook hands with the young officer and motioned to Nuu. "Is this a hero from the Thirty-third Regiment that ambushed the column?"

Sy smiled. "Yes, comrade Colonel, and he was my escort on my difficult journey back. He desires only a new uniform before being assigned to the Battalion."

Colonel Chinh looked at the small frame of the private and winked. "I think he desires a good meal first." Chinh turned to the sergeant posted at the entrance. "Call the

senior sergeant and have him pick up this hero of the
Thirty-third. Tell the sergeant to feed him well and assign
him immediately.''

The colonel took Sy's arm and began leading him down
the corridor. ''Now tell me about the ambush. We received
a report, but we have been waiting on your firsthand ac-
count. The general is very interested.

Sy looked over his shoulder at Nuu. ''I will check on
you tomorrow and see to the RPG-7. Thank you, my
friend.''

Nuu nodded only slightly as he stood at attention, still
shaking from his shock that a senior colonel would address
him as a hero.

The two officers turned right at the second corridor and
walked down wooden steps to the second of four levels.
The first was the security level, which housed the troop
billets and Logistics Directorates rooms. The second level
was the largest and held the staff billets and Political Directorates rooms. The third level, their destination, was
the Military affairs section and held the large briefing and
planning rooms. On the fourth level were generators and
communications equipment. The complex was like a buried ship, complete with kitchens, sewage facilities, and
electric ventilation. Surrounding the main headquarters
tunnel were many smaller tunnels designed to confuse an
attacking force. If an attack did come the entire headquarters could escape without detection by utilizing four
main communications tunnels that exited kilometers away.

Colonel Chinh walked into the briefing room and sat
down at a large table. ''It is unfortunate a platoon was left
behind, but . . .''

''I understand, comrade,'' said Sy.

The colonel's eyebrows raised. ''Yes, and that is why
the general sent you. He knew you would understand and
appreciates your loyalty. Not many can see the future as
we do.'' Chinh motioned to a nearby chair. ''The Tall One
is about to leave the headquarters to visit General Sang's
consolidating division. He plans a political meeting in con-

junction with the visit for which you will need to make arrangements."

Sy grinned ironically. "He plans to tame Sang, the Tiger?"

The colonel laughed. He was glad to have Sy back. Sang, the Second Division commander, was making himself a thorn in the general's side by his verbal attacks on current strategy. Sang was too impatient; he needed to be put in his place.

"Yes, he will give advice to the Second Division commander, and probably a lot more than advice." The colonel leaned closer to Sy and lowered his voice. "The general needs to get out of the tunnels. He has been very depressed and needs to breathe fresh air among his beloved soldiers. You will accompany him and prepare him for the political matters, and I will have to remain here and send you messages to keep the Tall One informed. I wish I could let you rest after your long journey, but there is much work to do. We cannot have any political directorates surprise us at the meeting. You know what must be done?"

Sy met the old man's eyes and nodded in silence. He would have to contact his spies within the directorates and determine if there were shifts in the political mood or outside pressures being exerted from party members with different views from those of Premier Van Dong. There is currently a power struggle being waged in Hanoi that could have an impact on the strategy of the war. It had been a constant battle between the military and political leadership since the death of Premier Ho Chi Minh last year. Many party members were leaning heavily in favor of China's views and were attacking the pro-Soviet members.

Colonel Chinh rose to his feet. "You do not have much time. The general leaves in three weeks. You and I must keep our general out of the political fight or the victory we seek will elude us for a long, long time."

Sy smiled reassuringly. "General Binh Ty Duc will have no surprises, comrade. I can promise you."

An Khe
Sierra Company, Headquarters Base Camp

Thumper sat down against the outside wall of the barracks and stared at the brilliant scarlet sunset. The first group of the Third Platoon had arrived at An Khe after being delayed in Phan Thiet for over two hours. After all the hollering and cussing by Sergeant Gino to ready his men for the early flight, the plane had broken down after landing. The platoon finally arrived at 1600 hours and had been trucked across the sprawling base to the permanent Ranger camp.

First Sergeant Demand, the senior NCO of the company and custodian of the Ranger camp, met them with his usual speeches—"Rules of the Ranger Camp" and "Virtues of Cleanliness." "Top" Demand was an institution within the Rangers. He loved to talk and preach, and sometimes you couldn't distinguish between the two, but whatever he said, everybody listened.

Top had marched them to the mess hall after they stowed their gear and gave his other speech, "Rules in the Mess Hall." After chow they were told to stay in the area and help the other platoons coming in that evening from Da Lat.

Thumper relaxed for the first time all day and pulled out his billfold. The plastic-coated picture of Mary Ann was the first thing he saw when he opened the rubberized jungle wallet. She held the same smile he'd seen countless times yet never tired of, and wore a baggy Red Cross uniform that couldn't hide her perfect proportions. He'd taken the picture of her only fifty paces from where he sat. It was the last time he'd been with her, except in his dreams.

Thumper flipped the plastic partition over to the next picture and smiled. It was the man he longed to be with more than anyone else in the world—his brother. They'd been raised along the Susquehanna River and had been together constantly. When the officer came to the house and told the family Rob had died at Hue, Thumper couldn't believe it. His brother couldn't have died without his knowing it. They were too close. He'd known when Rob was happy and sad, and when he fell in love with Peg. They felt each other's pain. He knew everything about his brother. But he hadn't known this. And what made it worse, he hadn't know why.

Thumper went back to college among students who hid behind draft deferments and decried the war as a waste. Still, he knew his brother couldn't have died for nothing. Finally, he gave up his education and starting position as fullback on the football team to find the reason.

He'd found his answer one day several months ago as he stood in a formation honoring those who had fallen in his company. The major had said, ''You know the devotion you feel for your fellow soldiers and the closeness and respect it engenders. You do all this, and people ask, 'Why? Why did he have to die?' They died, Rangers, for you and me. They died protecting their friends to their left or those behind them. They did their best so more like them wouldn't fall.

''No, Rangers, soldiers don't die for great causes or even for countries. They march forward and give their lives for their friends and fellow soldiers, who they know would do the same for them. . . .''

Thumper lowered his head, absorbing the silence. He was at peace with his brother's death. He could almost hear Robby's laughter on evenings like this. His laughter and the memory of Mary Ann's smile were all he had when he was alone, but those two things were enough, for he knew he would have them forever.

5

5 September

Bien Hoa
433rd Flight Hospital

Matt Wade had been awakened at 0630 and told to report to the hospital helicopter landing pad to catch a flight to Phan Thiet. He had hurried to the pad only to find that the chopper wouldn't arrive for another twenty minutes. A passing orderly told him he could wait in the hospital mess hall.

Wade poured himself a cup of coffee and strolled into the dining area. He took several steps and froze. Directly in front of him, seated in the empty dining room, was a beautiful, auburn-haired woman clothed in a black jump-suit that was covered with unit patches. Across from her was a rotund, middle-aged man wearing a loud Hawaiian-flowered shirt. The young woman glanced up at the sergeant with large, questioning, brown eyes. Wade couldn't help but stare. She was the first round-eyed woman he'd seen in three months.

The plump man grinned and motioned to a chair beside him.

"Sit down, my friend, and join us."

Wade hesitated, but the civilian stood and pulled back a chair and extended his hand.

The sergeant shook hands as the portly man loudly introduced himself. "I'm Walter Goldstein and this lovely lady you saw yesterday at the USO show."

Wade's bewildered look revealed he hadn't seen the show. The woman raised her head in amusement while her companion recovered from his error. "Well, uh, there were so many there that . . . Well, let me introduce Sophia Salin, the best little singer in Southeast Asia!

The small woman nodded silently in Wade's direction, disappointing him. He'd wanted to touch her hand.

Walter sat down, motioning to the sergeant's sling. "What happened to you, my boy?"

Matt slid the chair back to put more distance between himself and the loud voice. "I took some shrapnel in the shoulder, sir."

"Don't call me 'sir.' Hell, I'm just a dishonest agent trying to make a fast buck!" Walter laughed in an obnoxious hee-haw. He looked over at the woman, who rolled her eyes. "See, she agrees!" he guffawed even louder.

Wade forced a chuckle, wishing he hadn't sat down. No round-eye was worth losing his hearing for. He listened to the loud, resonating voice for five minutes and tried to look interested as Walter babbled on about unfamiliar people whom he claimed he had coached and made into star performers. From what he could gather from the one-sided conversation, Wade deduced that Walter was taking the woman on a tour of camps to make her name a household word.

Wade's eyes kept betraying him and stole glances of the obviously bored woman who looked like a miniature version of Sophia Loren but younger. He couldn't help but wonder if her name was a stage gimmick to cash in on the resemblance.

She wore no makeup or lipstick. Her eyes were huge and expressive, as were her full, perfectly proportioned lips, which turned up slightly at the corners. Her thick brown hair cascaded to her shoulders and partially covered her left eye as she sipped her coffee. She brushed her hair back with delicate fingers, as if she was aware of his stare, and shifted her head.

There! thought Wade, taking a mental picture. The exact pose he wanted for his mental scrapbook. Perfect. It would be a picture he could look at again and again when he wanted to recall true, natural beauty.

She looked into his eyes, but he quickly shifted his gaze to Walter. There was no point in meeting her gaze, in inviting her in. He knew he would not see her again after today, and in any case, she was beginning to bring back to him painful memories of Kathy. He'd loved Kathy so much it hurt. She had the same natural beauty as this woman, but her hair was blond. She'd left him when he flunked out of school. He tried to hold on, but the harder he tried the further he pushed her away. Every day for a week after returning to the farm, he drove the sixty miles back to the college, and although tired after plowing all day, he would wait for hours until she returned to the women's dorm. Each time she came back later. She began to seem distant, as if she was disappearing into a fog. The last night he'd waited till midnight before she finally returned—this time with a date. She didn't speak or even acknowledge his existence as she and her date passed by him on the same bench where he always waited. On that very bench, a month before, he'd told her he loved her.

Her silence that night broke his heart. It was the most painful loss he'd ever experienced.

Suddenly Wade was again aware of the agent rambling on, but he did not notice the woman's curious stare.

An orderly yelled into the mess hall. "The bird is inbound!"

Wade immediately got to his feet to make his apologies and be off, but to his surprise the obese agent and his lovely client both stood and began collecting their bags.

The agent grinned broadly as he picked up a briefcase. "Looks like we'll be traveling companions; isn't that great?"

Damn! Wade thought as he turned his back on the agent and frowned. "Yeah, great," he mumbled.

The woman, stepping in front of the sergeant, saw his dour expression. She smiled knowingly, but Wade didn't notice as he let the agent pass in the hope that the obnoxious man would select a seat as far from him as possible.

Nha Trang
Corps Headquarters
173rd Airborne Liaison Office

At 0700 Lieutenant J. D. Gibson walked into a small stucco
building adjacent to the huge Corps headquarters chateau.
Two staff sergeants arose, smiling, from behind battered
desks. The thinner one motioned to a door. "Your new
office, sir."

Gibson stepped into the small cubicle and surveyed his
new home. He hated it already; there were no windows.

"Sir, how'd you like your BOQ room?"

The lieutenant had been picked up at the airfield the
night before and taken directly to the bachelor officers
quarters.

Gibson sat on the sergeant's desktop. "The room's all
right. It's just gonna take some gettin' used to. I haven't
had clean sheets and a refrigerator stocked with beer in
quite awhile."

The sergeant smiled broadly; it had been his suggestion
to have beer for the new liaison officer.

Gibson gestured toward his office. "Will you move my
desk out here by the door? I need to see sunlight and have
a breeze."

The thin sergeant's smile dissolved as he exchanged a
quick glance with the other sergeant across from him.

"Sure, sir, but I thought you'd like . . ."

Gibson stood, shaking his head apologetically. "I'm
sorry, but I can't stand to be closed in. Why don't you all
just introduce me to the G-3, and I'll help you move it
later?"

The sergeant looked bewildered and nodded to his partner, a young black, for help.

The black sergeant stepped around his desk.

"Sir, I think you'd better sit down and let me explain
what you're really going to be doing around here. I know
the brigade S-1 told you one thing, but he doesn't know
how it really is."

Gibson sat down and listened, confounded, as the sergeant explained that he seldom, if ever, went into Corps

Headquarters, let alone see the Corps G-3 operations officer. His job was to ensure that visiting high-ranking 173rd officers and their guests were billeted in VIP quarters and escorted to restaurants, shopping spots, and tourist beaches. He was to drive the VIPs wherever they desired and see that they enjoyed their visit. The sergeant's primary duties were to collect Corps messages to the 173rd headquarters and send them out on the earliest aircraft possible. The black sergeant took a message from his desk and used it as an example.

"You see, sir, I picked this up from G-1 this morning. The message directs that the 173rd is to provide volunteers for the Corps Ranger Company. The only requirement is that the volunteers have at least four months in country. Volunteers are to be sent to Sierra Company Rangers in An Khe. Sir, all I do is put this in a pouch and send it out this afternoon."

Gibson listened for another couple of minutes with the realization that despite what the brigade S-1 had said, he wouldn't be making any decisions, attending any meetings, or consulting about 173rd activities or operations. He was nothing more than a flunky, a "gofer" for the brass.

The final blow came when the sergeants walked him outside and showed him his personal jeep.

It was new, hand-painted with five coats of shiny, dark-green paint, and waxed to a sparkling sheen. The seats were white naugahide with a large, colored, and embroidered 173rd patch on the back of each. The tires were painted with tire black; the floor mats were light blue. The sergeants had thought he'd be pleased. The lieutenant almost vomited.

He prided himself on being a field soldier. The men in the bush thought of rear echelon types as "gettin' over" and "skaters." To be called a REMF, a rear echelon mother fucker, was the worst possible insult to an infantryman. Gibson stared at the jeep in disbelief. To drive such a vehicle was like tattooing "REMF" on his forehead.

He spun around and walked directly for his office. He

had to call brigade right now and tell them he'd made a mistake. This job was definitely not for him!

2,000 feet elevation
Twenty miles southeast of Bien Hoa Air Base

The medevac helicopter climbed to gain cruising altitude. Wade had managed to convince the right door gunner to let him sit with him in the side crew compartment, while the agent and woman sat in the passenger bay behind the pilot and copilot.

Wade, wearing headphones, sat back in the nylon seat and listened to the pilot talk to the copilot about the entertainer.

"You get a load of that black jumpsuit she's wearing?"

"Yeah, she looks like she was poured into it."

"She's gotta be a 36-Charlie at least."

"Man, you're blind! She's a 38-Delta not e-ven countin' the nipples."

The door gunner, listening to the same conversation, poked Wade in the ribs and grinned. Wade smiled back to be friendly, but he thought it unfair that the woman didn't know she was being talked about. The wind and engine noise made it impossible to hear the crew without the headphones.

The Huey reached cruising altitude and leveled. Wade leaned over to look at the land three thousand feet below and could see a gray ribbon snaking its way through a green tapestry of jungle-covered mountains. It was Highway 1 leading them to Phan Thiet.

Suddenly his earphones popped with static and a voice came over the radio ordering the pilot to pick up a wounded soldier somewhere below. The pilot argued that he had civilians on board, but the voice was emphatic: the medevac was the only help available, and this was an emergency. The pilot agreed reluctantly and took the radio frequency of the ground unit needing help.

The bird banked left and began losing altitude. The door gunner, who was a medic, reached under his seat and unstrapped a medical bag. Wade leaned back on the padded fire wall as the copilot dialed the ground unit's frequency and called over the radio.

An excited voice responded immediately and gave the unit's location. Wade could see they were passing over the highway and heading north into mountains. The chopper leveled at two thousand feet for only a minute and then suddenly banked hard right and dropped like a rock, leaving Wade's stomach in his throat. Thank God I'm only on for the ride, he thought, as the bird passed over a steep, tree-covered ridge only five hundred feet below.

The medevac streaked down a small valley and headed for a spiraling yellow smoke cloud a kilometer away. The pilot held ninety knots for five hundred meters, then lowered the bird's tail into a flare, breaking the forward airspeed in half. The bird fell into the dissipating yellow smoke and settled to the ground. They had landed in a small open area by a stream. On all sides was dense jungle; sweat-soaked GIs stood in the tree line with weapons ready. Two men broke from the trees carrying a black soldier on a poncho litter. His chest was bare and wrapped with a blood-stained bandage. The medic beside Wade hopped out and helped the men hoist the unconscious soldier into the passenger cabin, where the crew chief dragged him in between the pilot's seats and the passengers. The medic bent over the soldier as the bird lifted off. Suddenly the men in the tree line raised their weapons and began shooting into the jungle. Wade could only hear faint "pops" above the engine roar, but he tensed instinctively and tried to make himself smaller.

The chopper shot forward, barely clearing the treetops as the crew chief yelled "Taking fire!" into the radio transmitter.

Wade heard "pings" and prayed the small vibrations he'd felt weren't what he thought.

"We're hit!" screamed the pilot, trying to gain more altitude. The copilot spoke as if intoxicated, "I'm hit, I . . . I'mmm hit bad . . . I'm . . ."

The chopper began shaking in a faint vibration that steadily grew into a teeth-chattering lurch. The engine began to scream louder as if in pain. Wade knew he was about to die.

The shuddering chopper just cleared a steep ridge when the pilot lowered the nose and sped down into the valley to pick up airspeed for control. The bird fell rapidly, quieting the engine's tormenting whine and horrible shaking. Wade felt a twinge of hope until he opened his eyes. They were headed down a narrow, tree-covered valley with rugged mountains on both sides. Directly ahead loomed a larger mountain.

The pilot knew it was hopeless and only prayed he could raise the chopper's nose into a flare before hitting the jungle canopy. Their hope for survival was to settle in. He fought the shaking controls and spoke into the transmitter almost apologetically: "We're going in."

Wade saw the treetops rushing past at eye level and pressed himself against the fire wall. He heard the sickening slap of the skids hitting the branches and braced himself.

The pilot tried to pull up, but suddenly the bird nosed over as if tripped by a snare. The huge rotating blades struck the canopy, exploding in a succession of thunderous "cracks." The fuselage was thrown upward and flipped on its left side as the tail rotor tore into the top tree branches like a buzz saw and disintegrated in an explosion of shrapnel. The tail boom snapped off and the dying bird screamed its last with an earsplitting grinding of gears. The medevac helicopter crashed down into the waiting jungle canopy.

Wade, who had been pinned against the fire wall by centrifugal force, was thrown upward as the wreck plummeted. The seat belt seemed to be tearing him in half and was squeezing the air out of him. His eyes bulged outward, forcing his eyelids open. The sounds of screams from the passenger compartment were drowned out by the deafening cracks and pops of broken limbs and the horrid screeching of branches scraping down the metal fuselage like amplified fingernails on a blackboard.

The Huey pitched violently side to side as it fell fifty

feet before jolting to an abrupt halt, impaling itself on a dead mahogany. A jagged limb had torn through the passenger cabin and protruded through the open door. The dead bird lay on its side twenty feet off the ground, looking as if it had been stabbed by an up-ended pitchfork.

The jungle was deathly silent. Leaf and twig fragments filtered down, shrouding the wreckage in a woody dust. The sun's rays poured through the path of destruction in the canopy above and basked the fuselage in an eerie diffusion of light.

Matt Wade lay motionless against the fire wall. After a moment, his eyes fluttered and then opened. His head was spinning, and he thought he was in a dream. It had to be a dream. He was in a deep, dusty tunnel looking up at the sun. Then he shook his head and concentrated. It wasn't a dream.

Wade felt as if he was broken in half. There was no sound, no motion, only pain and the warmth of the sun on his face. *I'm alive!* he thought in astonishment, but he quickly shut his eyes and forced himself to check his body movements. Please God, oh God, please, he prayed, as he tried to sit up. He couldn't move. God, no! He fought the feeling of desperation and tried again. His head and shoulders moved but his midsection wouldn't respond. Wade fell back, tears rolling down his cheeks, and then suddenly grabbed at his waist. *The seat belt!* he thought. The damn seat belt is holding me! He wanted to scream out in relief as he began to unbuckle the strap when a ghastly sound seemed to tear right down into his soul. It was a gurgling, inhuman sounding rasp. He freed the belt and crawled groggily to the passenger bay. "Oh, shit!" The agent had been partially lifted out of his seat belt by a branch that had smashed through the cabin. The jagged branch had torn through his skull and ripped him upward. His body was stretched out, with his lower thighs still restrained by the seat belt. The woman's blood-covered body was held by her belt and sat supported by Walter's exposed stomach. Twenty feet below, lying crumpled on the jungle floor, were the two bodies of the medic and wounded soldier.

The gurgling sound snapped Wade's head toward the pilot's seat. He pulled off his sling with a jerk, grabbed the protruding limb, and swung over to the pilot's door. The pilot's front plexiglas window had smashed in from the top and scraped down the pilot's helmet and visor. The jagged edges had finally penetrated his throat, pinning him to the seat. He was suffocating on his own blood. Matt smashed the side window with his boot and grasped the window. He strained with all his might but could move the plastic only an inch. It was not enough to clear the pilot's chin. Frothy blood gushed over his hands, making the plastic slick. He lost his grip. The window snapped back like a steep spring. "Oh, Jesus." He tried again but it was useless. Seconds later the pathetic gurgling ceased.

Wade sat back on the door, feeling sick and defeated.

His mind had taken many unwanted pictures. Pictures that would haunt him for the rest of his life. He fought their grisly images and concentrated on the one in the mess hall. She had been so beautiful, so . . . Shit! He cleared his head of all thoughts except how to get down and away from the crash, knowing the dinks would be there long before a rescue party.

Wade crawled to the edge of the passenger bay and looked for a way to climb down. The limb that had pierced the cabin forked only a few feet past the fuselage. He scanned the interior for something to use as a rope. "The seatbelts!" He could snap them all together. That would give him at least twelve feet—enough for him to climb down and drop the rest of the way.

Wade collected his own belt and the medic's, then reached down to unfasten the woman's. He'd have to let her body fall. He had reached under her and just grasped the release when she moaned. He jumped back, almost losing his grip. "My God, she couldn't possibly be . . ."

Wade quickly lowered himself into the cabin and, bracing his feet against the fire wall, released her belt. With his hand still under her small waist, he began lifting. He used the agent's body to slide her up far enough to finally swing her clear to the pilot's door.

Wade pushed back her blood-matted hair. Her eyelids rolled back slowly as he patted her face. "Come on, come on, open your eyes, little lady." He quickly checked her head for cuts or gashes. He found a lump just above her nape, but no wounds. The blood had to be Walter's, he thought, as he felt over her body for obvious wounds and fractures. Her twitching hands lay at her side with fingers curled inward like an invalid's. Wade had seen it many times before. She was in shock. He completed his check, then unzipped her jumpsuit, revealing skin as white as clean sheets. She wore a black lace bra and matching panties. Again, he looked for wounds or discolored skin and felt for broken bones. Thank God, she had none.

He turned her toward the incline of the slightly tilted bird to get the blood flowing to her head and began massaging her arms and shoulders while constantly talking to her.

"Talk to me. Who are you? Talk to me." He patted her face again, but this time harder. "Talk to me! Say something, damn you!" Her eyes locked onto him and tried to focus.

"Come on, talk to me. *Talk to me, lady!*" Her lips quivered, then puckered, "Wa . . .Walter?"

"No, I'm not Walter, but keep talking, lady. Come on, keep talking."

Her eyes had a bewildered look but didn't leave him.

"Where . . . where is Walter?"

Wade lifted her very slowly to a sitting position and began rubbing her shoulders and neck. Her head rolled forward, then slowly lifted.

"Where's Walter?" she said again almost pleading for an answer.

Wade raised her chin and looked into her cloudy eyes. They were large and sad, like a beaten puppy's, and they broke his heart. He hugged her tightly.

"He's dead. . . . He's dead, but you're alive." He moved back from her but held her shoulders firmly. "You're alive, lady. There's nothing we can do for Walter. We gotta get the hell outta here, or we're gonna die, too."

Her tearful eyes turned away.

"Look at me, damn it! You gotta snap out of it. You're a survivor. You made it. Now, keep survivin', and be strong. Fight to live. Fight, lady, 'cause it's all we got.''

Her eyes narrowed and she sniffed back her tears. "Are the rest dead?"

"Yeah, but there's you and me and we're gettin' the hell outta here." He released her to see if she could sit up alone. She fell back but threw out a hand to brace herself.

Wade stood, satisfied she was out of shock. "I gotta find a way down. Zip yourself up and don't move from here. Don't look in the chopper. I'll be talking to you so I'll know you're all right. You talk back. You got it?"

She nodded.

"No, I said talk!"

The woman looked up, glaring. "Yes, I've got it!"

Matt grabbed the jabbed limb and lowered himself into the cabin.

"Where you from?"

"New York," she said softly as she zipped up her jump suit.

"What?"

"New York!"

Wade grabbed the agent's head. "Where in New York? Tell me about it."

The woman began talking as Wade pulled Walter's head free and let him fall.

"What was that?" she asked worriedly, interrupting her own prattle.

"Just clearing out equipment. Keep talking."

Wade could now see the disfigured crew chief who was dangling down held only by his seat belt. It could have been me if the bird had fallen on the other side, Matt thought as he unstrapped a litter from the fire wall and placed it sideways in the door. He could now stand in the compartment and hold onto the limb. He was about to release the crew chief's belt when he saw the black cord attached to the man's helmet. The cord ran to the top interior of the aircraft, where it was stored in a coil. That's it! There had to be at least ten feet. With this cord and the other from the medic's side, he knew he had his way down.

"And from Queens I moved up to Brooklyn and began singing in Greenwich Village, then . . ."

Wade climbed out of the cabin five minutes later holding a seat belt with the black cord tied to its back.

The woman had her back to him. She was looking up toward the treetops and talking about a club in New York in which she'd sang.

Wade tossed the belt down beside her and massaged his left arm.

She started and turned to him. "Are we going down now?"

"Yeah, I think this will work. I'm gonna lower you down first and . . ."

"Think?" she cried out. "I'm not going just on a *think*!"

Wade shook his head tiredly. "Okay, I *know* it's gonna work. Just come here and put your hands up."

She got up reluctantly and raised her arms.

Wade placed the belt under her arms and tightened it snugly.

"It's simple. We're going to climb down into the cabin and then I'm going to lower you. All ya gotta do is put your feet on the tree and walk down. Hold your hands on the cord, but whatever you do, don't raise your arms above your head or you'll slide out. Now, watch how I climb down into the cabin and follow me."

"Is Walter in there?" she asked, glancing toward the cabin.

"No, he's on the ground with some others. Don't look at the ground or Walter. Just watch me."

Wade sat on the edge of the compartment and lowered himself to the stretcher. The woman followed behind him and sat down as he had instructed. She had begun to look down when he snapped, "What's your real name?"

She tossed her head up, staring at him as if he'd just read her personal diary.

"Well? What is it?"

Her face hardened. "Virginia. Virginia Wolinski."

"Well, Ginny, you keep your eyes on me or I'll kick your skinny butt out right now."

She glared at him, looking as if she wanted to claw the tinny hillbilly drawl out of his throat.

Wade had tied the cord end to a D-ring on the chopper floor and cut pieces of canvas from the seats to protect his hands. He placed the cord around his back in a belay position, as he was taught at the Fort Benning Ranger School.

"Okay, Miss, whatever you name is. Go."

She hesitated only an instant then pushed herself out. Wade took her weight across his shoulders and lowered her slowly.

The small woman went down easily, landing on the crew chief's back. She shuddered and quickly stepped off the corpse, sobbing in horror.

Wade spoke to her calmly. "Look up at me and release your belt. . . . Good. Now back up and keep your eyes on me."

Wade tested his weight and then began sliding down the cord. His left arm and shoulder screamed out in pain as he tried to slow his descent, but the pain was too much. He released his grip, falling the last eight feet. He hit heavily and rolled to his stomach.

Virginia ran to him and tried to turn him over.

Wade brushed away her hands. "I'm okay." He got to his knees and let out a deep breath. He felt relieved but totally fatigued. His adrenalin had run out. He wanted only to fall over and rest to regain his strength.

Virginia leaned over apprehensively. "What are we going to do?"

Wade took in another deep breath, then stood. "We're going to collect whatever we can from the others, then move."

She looked over her shoulder at the bodies and began sobbing again. "I . . . I can't touch them."

Matt didn't say anything as he walked toward the first body.

6

Nha Trang
Corps Headquarters

Major Shane and Sergeant Childs had flown in to Nha Trang that morning. They now sat in Colonel Ellis's office as he explained that they wouldn't be briefing the general as planned. Ellis had already resolved their replacement problem. But he took the opportunity to advise them they would be involved in a secret operation in four weeks and to be prepared.

Childs didn't like secrets and protested. "Sir, we appreciate your helping us, but we need to know what you have planned. It could influence our training program, if it's something special."

"No, the operation will be nothing you don't normally do, but for security reasons I can't tell you any more yet. I'll come to An Khe in two weeks and brief you."

Shane leaned forward, worried. "Sir, we'll have a chance to provide input to your plan, won't we?"

The G-2 understood the major's fears. He had been a commander himself in '68 and knew how top brass could muddle an operation by not asking for a commander's advice and input.

"Yes, Ed, you and I will go over the whole operation before we firm it up."

Satisfied with the answer, Shane exchanged glances with Childs to see if he had any more questions.

Childs shook his head.

When the colonel saw they were both contented, he leaned back in his chair. "What else can I help you with?"

Shane had one more request. "Sir, we're short of experienced officers. Could you see if any are available?"

The colonel immediately reached for the telephone and dialed.

"Colonel Rite please. . . .Hello Charles, this is Bob. . . . fine, thank you. I have Major Shane of the Ranger company in my office and he needs some experienced officers. As you know, the general has a personal interest in the company and would appreciate your assistance. . . . Yes, I know they're hard to get, but I'm sure you'll be able to help us. . . . Yes, I understand. Thank you."

Ellis put down the receiver. "He's such an ass!" I don't know if I helped you or not, Ed. I've been pulling his chain pretty hard to get your replacements. He's diggin' in his heels on this one."

Shane nodded in understanding. "Thank you for trying. We can get by."

Ellis stood. "When do you start your training program?"

Shane smiled at Childs. "You'll have to ask my expert, sir."

Childs collected his map case and got to his feet. "Sir, we're starting tomorrow when the replacements get in. We'll probably be siftin' through a bunch of them and kickin' out some of our own."

"I thought I recognized you, Sergeant Childs," Ellis said with a sidelong glance. "You were a Ranger instructor at Fort Benning, weren't you?"

"Yes, sir, I was in charge of Camp Darby."

"How well I remember," said Ellis with a chuckle. "You don't remember me, but you tried your damnedest to get rid of me."

Childs eyed the colonel's gold and black Ranger tab on his left shoulder.

"You got the tab, sir, so you musta been okay in my book."

Ellis laughed aloud. "Come on, I want to take you both to lunch and hear how you're going to train them. It'll bring back lots of memories, I'm sure."

The three men walked for the door. Ellis slapped Childs's back. "You still call 'em 'ragbags'?"

"Hell, sir, they *are* 'ragbags.'"

Lieutenant J. D. Gibson was fed up. He was tired of clean sheets, running water, and cold beer. He wanted out *now*.

The lieutenant paced back and forth in his office deciding to do something about it. He'd go over right now and talk to the G-1 and ask to be transferred to a field assignment.

His earlier call to the 173rd the day before had been a disaster. The brigade S-1 had told him the general himself had selected him and he'd have to stay as the liaison. The only way he could be released was to have Corps assign him a new job, but he certainly couldn't return to the 173rd.

Gibson pushed open the screen door and walked toward the Corps Headquarters. Even if he couldn't go back to his Airborne unit, he'd at least try for another field assignment.

Gibson felt self-conscious in his uniform. When he'd arrived the night before, he was told he had to have all new fatigues on which all skill badges and insignia had to be embroidered. The sergeant was going to order the fatigues for him. In the meantime, he had borrowed a set from a lieutenant named Fielding, an Air Defense Artillery officer who was the Fourth Division's liaison. The fatigues were much too big for Gibson, but at least they were new. To hell with the way I look, Gibson said to himself. He had to try. He marched into the large downstairs office, where two pretty Vietnamese secretaries and a captain sat.

Captain Holden glanced up at the lieutenant's approach. One look told the captain much that he wanted to know: here was a first lieutenant in the Air Defense Artillery, obviously new in-country, and fitted with jungle fatigues which were too large. He'd learned long ago to read the

man's rank and branch of service before looking at his face.
It saved time. He waited until the officer stopped in front
of his desk before speaking.

"What can I do for you, Lieutenant?"

"Sir, I want to talk to Colonel Rite about transferring
to a field unit."

The captain put down the pictures of the awards ceremony of the day before and stared at the lieutenant standing before him.

The lieutenant was five-eight or five-nine, tanned, and
had unusual gray hair. He wasn't wearing parachute wings
or any other patches except the Corps patch on his
shoulder.

"Why do you want a transfer?"

"Sir, I want to be in a line unit. I feel I could contribute
more in a field assignment and . . ."

The captain held up his hand, interrupting him. "Don't
say anymore." He turned for his officer assignment book.
He was not one to stop an officer who wanted to go to the
field. The lieutenant would be easy to place, and finding
a replacement liaison would be no problem. No sense bothering the colonel with something he could do himself. He
found the book and turned to the air defense vacancies.
"No sweat, Lieutenant. Consider it done. We aim to please
around here."

The door to the colonel's office opened, and Colonel
Rite walked out holding his coffee cup. "Mey, get me some
coffee, will you?"

The closest Vietnamese girl rose with a smile. Her white
tunic clung tightly to her delicately proportioned body.
With a slight bow, she took the cup from the overweight
colonel and shuffled to a table nearby.

The colonel walked to the captain's desk and quickly
scanned the pictures lying there, then glanced up at the
lieutenant's odd gray hair.

The captain gestured toward the young officer. "Sir, he
wants a field assignment, so I knew you wouldn't mind my
taking care of it."

The colonel nodded, took the cup of coffee from the

petite secretary, and walked back into his office. He sat
down and took a sip of the hot coffee, then suddenly lifted
his head with a grin. "Ellis, you son of a bitch, you wanted
an officer . . . well . . ." He yelled toward the door:
"Steve!"

The captain opened the door in seconds. "Yes, sir?"

"Send that lieutenant to Sierra Rangers."

The captain stepped the rest of the way into the office,
thinking he had't heard the colonel correctly. "Sir?"

"Send that lieutenant to Sierra Rangers," the colonel
repeated.

"But, sir, he's air defense. He's not qualified to . . ."

"Steve, I *want* him in Sierra Company."

"Yes, sir, but . . ."

"*Now*, Steve."

"Okay, sir." The captain walked out, shutting the door.

The colonel smiled broadly. Ellis, this'll teach you not
to screw around with me. I can screw back. He reached
for the coffee cup with a chuckle.

The captain shook his head, perplexed, and sat down.

"Sorry, Lieutenant," he said, "looks like you're going
to a Ranger company."

Gibson yelped with joy. "Really, sir?"

The surprised captain stared at the grinning lieutenant.
It wasn't the reaction he'd expected. The phone rang on
one of the secretaries' desks. She answered and spoke
softly to the captain.

"It is for you, sir."

"Tell 'em to hold just a sec." He leaned forward for a
pencil. He looked up at the lieutenant's name tape above
his right pocket.

"Take this note, Fielding . . ." he looked down, writing
rapidly on a notepad. "To Sergeant Alcord down the hall.
He'll cut your orders." He tore the paper off the pad and
handed it to the young officer and picked up the telephone.

"No, sir, I'm not Fielding. It's 'Gibson', sir. John Dalton Gibson. The fatigues are . . ."

"But your name tag says . . . aw, never mind. Sergeant

Alcord is down the hall. Give him the information." He
put the phone to his ear. "Captain Holden, G-1 office. . . .
Oh, hello, sir, sorry I had you on hold. Yes, I've got the
report right here. . ."

Lieutenant Gibson ran down the stone steps of Corps
Headquarters to the liaison office. It had taken Sergeant
Alcord only a few minutes to fill out the necessary paperwork, although he had explained that the actual orders
would take five days to process. Still, if the lieutenant
wanted to report today, he could do so and the orders
would follow.

Gibson hurried to his desk, opened the middle drawer,
and took out a photograph of the platoon he'd left only a
few days before. They were his "Banshees," the death
angels he cared so much for. Well, guys, I'm going to the
Rangers. Hot damn!

Gibson quickly collected his other belongings and
pushed open the screen door. He would drive to the BOQ,
pack his gear, and come back for the final time before
leaving. "Damn! The Rangers!"

Cam Tiem Mountains

Matt Wade stood holding a compass trying to determine
which direction was south. He remembered they'd crossed
Highway 1 and had headed north into the mountains. He
figured they couldn't be more than fifteen kilometers away
and could make the road by tomorrow.

Wade wore the crew chief's mesh survival vest and .38
caliber pistol. The sleeveless vest was standard issue for
all pilots and crew, with a pocketed front holding a first
aid kit, hand flare, deflated plastic bag for water, matches,
knife, compass, and pen gun with flares.

Virginia wore the medic's vest, which held identical
items. She stood staring at the agent's neck chain, which
Matt had given to her minutes before.

Wade folded the compass and whispered firmly, "Let's
go."

Virginia stood fast, still staring at the thick gold chain

and Star of David medallion. Wade took the chain from her hand and put it around her neck.

"We gotta move. Stay five feet behind me and stop when I do. Don't talk and don't step or grab anything that might make noise. We're going to leave a fake trail, then double back and head south."

She looked at him tiredly and began to nod, but stopped as another thought occurred to her. "What's your name?"

Wade shook his head, put his finger to his lips to quiet her, and began to move.

"Look, I'm sorry. I just forgot, okay?"

The sergeant kept walking.

Virginia sighed and looked at Walter's corpse one last time. "Shalom," she whispered, fighting back her tears, and began to follow the sergeant.

Nha Trang
Corps Headquarters

Colonel Ellis, Major Shane, and Sergeant Childs had just returned from lunch and began walking up the Corps Headquarters steps when a shiny jeep honked its horn and squealed to a halt beside them. A wide-eyed lieutenant yelled as he hopped from the Jeep. "Sir! Sir!"

J. D. Gibson couldn't believe his luck; he'd seen the camouflaged fatigues and black berets of the two Rangers as soon as he pulled in. The tall Ranger was a major and had to be the commander of the company.

He ran up the steps to Major Shane. "Sir, I'm sorry for honking, but I wanted to introduce myself to you. I've just been assigned to your company."

Childs shook his head in amusement and glanced at Shane, whose mouth had fallen open. Shane recovered quickly and stared at the gray-headed Air Defense Artillery officer in the incredibly ill-fitting uniform.

"L-tee, you couldn't possibly be assigned to me. I can't use an ADA officer."

Gibson looked down at his uniform. "Oh no, sir, this uniform is . . ."

Ellis put his hand on Shane's shoulder and tossed his

head toward the Headquarters entrance. "Rite did this. Come on, let's go talk to him."

Shane glared at the mumbling lieutenant. "You stand by that . . . that *pimp mobile* until I get this straightened out."

Gibson looked in the direction the major was pointing and almost cried when it was obvious he was pointing to his jeep. Shane and Ellis jogged up the steps as the lieutenant tore at his shirt and threw it toward the vehicle.

Childs watched as the gray-haired officer yanked a dirty duffel bag from the back seat and pulled out a faded fatigue shirt. "Goddamn it, I'm not an ADA officer!" He put on the shirt and glared at Childs.

Childs stared in disbelief at the faded shirt with sewed-on parachute badge, combat infantryman badge, and Ranger tab over the 173rd Airborne insignia.

The seething lieutenant approached Childs menacingly. "You still an asshole, Childs?"

The sergeant's jaw tightened and met the officer's glare, but suddenly softened, recognizing him.

"Yeah, and I see you're still up to your old tricks, huh?"

Gibson's frown turned into a grin. "Good to see you, Sarge. Been a long time."

Childs held back a smile and extended his hand. "You were company commander of Ranger Class Nine as I remember. I gave you a twenty-five bad spot report for jumping into Ledo Drop Zone with a fuckin' turtle."

Gibson shook hands warmly. "Pretty good memory for an old cuss like you. That was two years ago."

"I could never forget a Ragbag that killed the class mascot."

"How was I supposed to know I'd fall on the damn thing? As I recall, you made us give it a full military burial!"

Childs couldn't help but crack a grin, remembering the entire Ranger class trying to keep from giggling as Gibson read the eulogy of a fallen comrade who'd died heroically during a parachute drop, smashed flat in the act of cushioning the drop of a fellow paratrooper.

When Colonel Ellis and Major Shane walked down the steps, they were obviously upset. Shane halted abruptly, seeing the lieutenant's faded shirt, and looked at Childs for an explanation.

Childs quickly introduced the officer and explained the error in their first impression. As he talked, Shane and Ellis's smiles became bigger and bigger until they burst out laughing. Colonel Rite had insisted that the lieutenant could contribute in some way to the unit; besides, there were no other officers available.

Ellis patted Shane's back. "You'd better get him outta here before Rite finds out he outsmarted himself. I'll get his orders cut immediately so he won't get pulled."

Shane grabbed the lieutenant's arm. "Come on. You're taking us to the airfield."

"Where are we flying to, sir?"

"An Khe, L-tee. An Khe and your new home."

Cam Tiem Mountains

The sergeant cussed and prodded her for almost two hours before finally stopping. Virginia Wolinski, exhausted, fell back on a rock stream bank. She had never felt so miserable in all her life. She looked up at the first blue sky she'd seen since leaving the crash. They had found a stream an hour before and followed it up to a rocky ravine where the sun finally revealed itself and gave her hope. At last she felt free of the dark, wet world she'd just traveled through, a world from another time where an endless maze of enormous, unbranching tree trunks soared upward into a green canopy so thick it turned midday sunlight into twilight. The jungle was an incubator of oppressive humidity and stifling heat, a brown, silent hell where fungi and bacteria lived on the dead and parasites fed on the living, where she was just an inconsequential speck waiting to be devoured by its vastness.

She shut her eyes, dreaming of another place that some people called a jungle, too—but New York City wasn't a jungle to her. It was her home, her family. She understood it, and it had made a survivor of her. She loved the constant motion of its sights, sounds, and smells. It had taught her painful lessons, but in its way had also given her its protection, and she desperately wished she were back there now.

The sound of splashing water broke her trance, and she opened her eyes. She heard it again and raised up on her elbows. The sergeant was on the opposite bank of the stream, throwing water up on his bare chest to clean his shoulder wounds. His body was hard and lean. The contours of his upper torso rippled with muscle. He wasn't particularly handsome, but there was a ruggedness about him that had caught her attention from the first moment she saw him. He exuded confidence; it showed in his walk and in the way he held his head. His eyes seemed to penetrate beneath the surface of things. She'd known his kind in the city. They were easy to pick out of a crowd by the way they led rather than followed. He was a survivor, too, a man who felt at home in his jungle. In that he was like her. But now she was at his mercy; he was her only hope, and she didn't even know his name.

The sergeant stood and looked at her, but his eyes told her nothing. He picked up his shirt and vest, then crossed the stream. He looked tired as he sat down beside her and opened the first aid kit from the vest.

"This is a good spot to rest, isn't it?" she whispered, sitting up.

He rubbed some ointment on his wounds and glanced around.

"Naw, it's too open. We'll rest when we get to the top of the ridge ahead of us."

She stared at him, unbelieving. "I'll never make it. I don't even think I can stand up."

He put on his shirt. "You can still talk, so you can walk. Let's go." He stood and threw on the vest.

She shook her head in determination. "I'm not going another step unless you at least tell me your name."

He began walking, then stopped and looked over his shoulder. "It's Wade. Now get up and move your ass!"

Her eyes narrowed defiantly as she got to her feet.
"You're an asshole, Wade. You know that?"

The tired soldier turned and began walking. "Yep."

An Khe
Ranger Base Camp

Rose tiredly dragged the last heavy ammunition box to the
edge of the two-and-a-half-ton truck and sunk to his knees.
"That's the last one, man."

Thumper and Russian wordlessly picked up the ends of
the eighty-pound box and walked toward the steel conex
container a few yards away.

Rose slid off the back of the truck and picked up his
jungle fatigue shirt. "Thump, man, if you gonna piss off
the L-tee again, leave me outta it."

Thumper shut the steel door of the storage container
and wiped sweat from his eyes. "Why you blaming me?
You could have wrote the statement Dickey wanted."

Rose rolled his eyes at Thumper and motioned toward
Russian. "No I couldn't and you know it. This foreigner
woulda killed me."

Russian nodded with a confirming grunt. Thumper
grinned. "Rose, you needed the exercise anyway. Dickey
is just giving us a little payback. Six hours of unloading
trucks is probably just the beginning."

Rose snickered. "This is white man's work . . . Hey,
let's skate back to the barracks before that dumb shit gets
back and finds somethin' else for us."

Thumper glanced around for the officer and quickly put
on his shirt. "Take the point, Rose, and get us outta here."

Minutes later the three team members walked into the
barracks and had to step over a pile of beer and C ration
cans. Four men from Team 3-2 sat in the corner listening
to a Jimi Hendrix cassette while passing a joint.

Thumper kicked a beer can in their direction. "You
going to smoke that shit, get out of the barracks!"

A thin soldier wearing a colored headband and sunglasses smiled at him smugly. "Who says?"

Thumper squared his large body to them. "Me."

Russian stepped up beside him. "Us."

The soldier kept his smile. "Hey man, mellow out, it's cool. We leavin'."

Thumper kicked another can toward them. "Pick up your trash first!"

"Sure, man, it's cool." The three men giggled and began picking up the cans to the beat of the music.

Thumper shook his head in disgust and walked down the aisle to a small room, followed by Russian and Rose. He sat down on his bunk and looked up at the others. "Somethin's up. I haven't seen an officer or senior NCO lift a hand to stop the shit that's goin' on."

"Is the whole company here?" asked Russian.

Thumper leaned back against the wall. "Almost. There's still one more flight due in from Da Lat, and the major and Childs are at Corps, but that still doesn't explain why the other leaders haven't taken charge and started kickin' ass."

Rose stepped back and looked in the barracks bay, then leaned back into the room, whispering.

"Looky here, I heard from Pete that this is all planned, man. The major told the big boys to leave us alone and wait."

"Wait for what?" asked Thumper, sitting up.

"Pete says they're bringing in a bunch of line doggies from the herd, and they're gonna fill us back up to strength. He said somethin' about they was waitin' until they got here, and the major was gonna turn Childs loose on us to start smokin' our asses."

"Ooh, shit!" said Thumper.

Russian eyed Rose, not trusting him.

"Peteroski tell you this for sure?"

"Man, Pete is the company clerk, ain't he? We're tight, man. He wouldn't give the Rose no flaky skinny."

Thumper stood up. "Pete is good people. He wouldn't exaggerate about something like this, plus it all fits. . . . Look, tomorrow it's probably gonna hit the fan. We better get our area squared away and look strac to keep Childs off our backs. I got a feeling if Pete's right, Childs will be inspecting all our equipment and dealin' out big-time trouble.''

Russian nodded in agreement, but Rose shook his head.

''Man, that's lots of shit to be cleanin'. I want to hit the vill tonight and . . .''

Russian's glare halted his protest.

''Okay man, no big thing. I can't find my rubbers anyway.''

Private First Class Peteroski, the company clerk typist and the major's driver, parked his jeep by the Third Platoon barracks and got out to lift the hood. A small yellow dog ran from the side of the building and leaped at the back of his legs.

Peteroski smiled and bent over to hug the playful ball of fur. ''Bitch, I missed you, girl. Old Russian been takin' care of you?''

Peteroski ruffled her fur in reflection. Bitch had belonged to his close friend, Joseph Dove, who'd been killed during the Cambodian mission. Russian had adopted her and was her constant companion when he wasn't in the bush. Bitch liked everybody and loved to be played with, but she especially liked to be fed. When Russian was on a mission, she stayed in the TOC and, strangely, always stayed close to Childs.

Peteroski gave her a last pat and stood up, shaking his finger. ''Now let me get to work.''

''You skatin' a-gin, Pete?''

Peteroski smiled, recognizing the familiar voice of Lieutenant Bradley Lee Avant. The officer was short, powerfully built, and could have been considered handsome, but he always kept his head shaved. He'd come to the company just prior to their leaving for Da Lat and had been assigned First Platoon leader. According to his files, he was a graduate of North Georgia Military College and had gone to law school for a year-and-a-half, but he certainly didn't show it. In Da Lat, he had always kept everybody laughing with his corny Southern drawl and quick wit.

"Sir, I'm not skating. I'm about to change the major's jeep oil filter."

"I see. And ya was gittin' instructions from the dawg, right?"

Pete laughed as the officer leaned over and patted Bitch's head. "Dawg, is you a coon hunter, a possum hunter, or is you really a mechanic?" Avant stood up and motioned toward the barracks. "Pete, I hope the ol' man knows what he's doin' not lettin' us do something about the troops. I ain't smelled so much pot since visitin' Atlanta during the hippie antiwar marches."

Pete merely nodded. He knew these things were going to change pretty fast. He'd overheard the major and Childs talk about their plan just before leaving for Nha Trang.

Avant sighed and threw Pete a wave as he opened the barracks door and went in. Pete gathered his tools from the front seat and opened the hood.

Lieutenant Dickey stomped out of the Headquarters building and glanced quickly around the Ranger camp. Seeing the major's jeep, he knew he had found his culprit and marched straight for the vehicle.

Pete was leaning over the engine when Dickey stopped in front of the jeep and pointed his finger at the clerk. "You, soldier, what's your name?"

Pete looked up at the obviously irritated officer. "Peteroski, sir."

"You're the one! You were seen taking a fan from my room."

"Yes, sir?"

"You don't just walk into an officer's billet and take his property."

"I had permission from Lieutenant Avant, sir. I was to pick up all Company fans and distribute them in the troop barracks."

"Not without my permission you don't. Who is this Avant? Who does he think he is?

Avant, having heard the conversation, pushed open the screen door and walked out. "Ol' cousin Avant is the Company supply officer. And him is me. And he *thinks* he's is a good-un'.''

Avant walked up to Dickey and held out his hand with a smile. I'm Brad. Don't think we've met yet.''

Dickey ignored the gesture and stared coldly. "You can't order an enlisted man into my billet and have him take my fan.''

Avant dropped his hand but still held the smile and glanced over at Pete. "Why cousin, Pete ain't never *en*-listed, he was drafted. Weren't ya, Pete?

Dickey fumed. "You know what I mean.''

Avant slowly turned his head back toward the taller officer and his face hardened to stone. "You mean, did I, the duly appointed supply officer of this company, assign Private First Class Peteroski the responsibility of collecting *company property,* as per the instructions of the company commander, Major Edward Shane, for the explicit purpose of cooling troop billets? You bet your sweet ass I did!''

Dicky was completely taken back by the sudden change from Avant's country boy drawl to articulate verbal assault. He knew that if Shane ordered the fans taken, he was powerless to pursue the matter any further.

Dickey backed up a step. "Very well, you can keep the fan, but I will take this up with Major Shane as soon as he returns.'' Dickey turned on his heels and marched straight for the officers' barracks.

Avant broke into his smile again. "Nice ta meetcha, cousin.''

Pete shook his head in awe. "Sir, where did you learn to . . .''

Avant winked. "In law school. They always said beat them with their own words and they'd know they done been whipped.''

"Why didn't you finish law school, sir?''

"Pete, I was a student and workin' for my po Daddy's law firm till he found out I was bangin' his secretary. How was I supposed to know she was his sweet young sugar baby.''

"Really, sir?''

Avant's smile dipped slightly. "Yeah, most of it." His expression changed as he motioned toward Dickey, walking away in the distance. "Pete, remind me now and then not to like that guy, will ya?"

Cam Tiem Mountains

Matt Wade reached the crest of the ridge and sat down heavily against a large mahogany. Several seconds passed before the small woman appeared and fell down beside him. Wade leaned forward, grabbed her arm, and pulled her toward him. She groaned and sat up. "Can't you leave me alone?" she pleaded.

"Yeah, but the ants won't if you lie down like that. Sit against the tree."

She crawled to the trunk and sat back. "Are we going to make it?"

"Yep."

"How much farther is the road, for God's sake?"

"It's down this ridge in the valley. I just don't know how far. It's gonna be dark in awhile, so go to sleep. We'll make it tomorrow."

The woman scooted closer to him and shut her eyes.

Two hours later she awoke feeling something digging into her scalp. She opened her eyes, but it was so pitch black it was as if she was buried. She felt in her hair and touched a hard-shelled creature that immediately attached to her finger. She shrieked and flung her hand up, striking the sergeant, who shot up.

"What's the matter?" he whispered harshly, as she frantically brushed at her tangled hair.

"Oh God," she mumbled as she ran her hand through her hair, praying the creature was gone. "Something . . . something was in my hair and . . ."

Wade reached out in the darkness, touching her, and put his arm around her shoulder. "Come here, damn it. Sit between my legs and lie back on me. Whatever is out there will get me first, okay?"

The woman unhesitatingly scooted over his leg and lay

back, still shaking. His arms folded over her protectively and he gave her a gentle hug. "Try to get some sleep."

She lay rigid for awhile but finally relaxed in his warmth. She drew up her legs. She'd almost forgotten what it was like to be held by a man who didn't paw at her. All the painful memories of the past seemed as if they had happened only yesterday. She'd slept with many men at first. It was part of the business. A woman trying to get a start had to pay the price. Mostly one-nighters like her singing engagements. The "interviews" and "auditions" usually meant a night in bed with the club owner or manager. Those were the days just after she'd left her home to make it on her own. She couldn't go back and she couldn't go forward. The booze and grass made some of them tolerable, but there was always the revulsion the next morning. Walter had ended the bad times. He'd heard her sing and had taken her under his wing. He had thrown away her cheap makeup and had given her a new name and, more important, hope. Walter was obnoxious at times, but he kept her away from the seedy club owners and managed her career. He was a has-been, and he knew it, but he believed in her, honestly believed she had what it took to make it. She had needed his confidence. They had needed each other. They had both gotten over bad times and were looking for better.

She cried silently, touching his necklace, praying he'd died quickly and still believing.

An Khe
Ranger Camp

The jeep's lights shined briefly on a long, white, one-story structure before extinguishing and leaving the passengers in the darkness. Major Shane, Childs, and J. D. Gibson had been picked up at the An Khe airfield and taken to the Ranger Camp's officer/senior NCO quarters.

Shane walked to the motel-like building and stopped at the first door on the end. "L-tee, you'll be bunking in Hootch Four with Lieutenant Dickey. This is my room. If you need anything, come on down. We've got an officers' call at 0800 in the headquarters just down the slope. See you then.''

"Yes, sir,'' said Gibson, picking up his duffel bag. Childs walked ahead and pounded on the door midway down the building. "Gino, open the damn door. I need a beer!''

Gibson knocked on the fourth door. There was no response. He knocked louder and tried the door; it was locked. The lieutenant looked up and down the dark building. The major and Childs had disappeared into their rooms. Gibson knocked on the door and waited for several seconds, then threw down his bag. Screw it! In minutes he had his poncho and poncho liner spread out by the door. He'd slept outside with his platoon for six months; one more night under the stars was nothing new.

Lieutenant Dickey turned over in his bunk. Some idiot knocking on my door at 10 p.m. The nerve!

He reached up and touched the TEAC tape deck play button and lay back down.

10 p.m.! Who could be so dumb, he thought, as he shut his eyes and concentrated on the soft music.

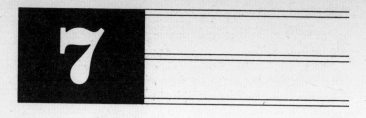

7

6 SEPTEMBER

Cam Tiem Mountains

Matt Wade awoke to the woman's gentle breathing. She had snuggled close to him and was sleeping peacefully. He shut his eyes to block out the morning's dim light, trying to absorb her softness and warmth a little more. She smelled of damp clothes, but it was wonderful to have her so close. He'd made love to many women but had never slept a whole night with one.

He savored her body a minute longer, then shook her gently. She only moaned and snuggled closer.

"Come on, we gotta move." He leaned forward and tried to stand.

"All right, already. I'm up, I'm up." She sat up and patted her hair cautiously. Wade walked behind a tree and relieved himself as she slowly stood and tried to stretch her sore muscles.

"I've never ached so bad in all my life," she whispered, as she went behind a boulder and unzipped her jumpsuit.

Wade heard a muffled shriek and pulled his pistol. He ran to the boulder and cocked the hammer back. Taking a deep breath, he jumped clear, ready to fire.

Virginia stood with her jumpsuit around her ankles, biting her hand and trying not to scream. She saw him and pleaded in terror, "Get it off . . . get it off me, please!"

Perplexed, Wade lowered the pistol. "What's wrong?"

She shut her eyes and bowed her shaking legs like a chapped cowboy.

Wade sighed and holstered the pistol. A leech was attached to her inner thigh, close to the edge of her lace panties. "I gotta get some matches."

She immediately opened her eyes. "No! Don't go."

Wade returned seconds later and knelt down in front of her smooth, quivering stomach. He struck a match and let it burn a few seconds, then blew it out and tried to touch the hot end to the corpulent parasite, but the woman was shaking so badly he couldn't touch it long enough to work. "Hurry!" she shrieked.

"Quit shaking, damn it."

He held her waist and placed his head on her navel to try and stop her shaking. She grabbed his head, digging in her fingernails in desperation. Wade lit another match, trying to control his own quivering hand. The feeling of her velvety skin on his forehead and the profusion of dark pubic hair spilling out from the bikini panties was unnerving. He blew out the match and held her tighter as he touched the hot match head to the bloated leech. The parasite shuddered and fell off.

"There, it's gone."

She immediately shoved him back and grabbed for her jumpsuit. Wade sighed and took out another match. "Better hold up, you gotta 'nother one under your arm."

She shrieked, dropping the material as if it was on fire, and threw her arms up, shuddering uncontrollably. "Get it off me! Oh, God, please get it off. Pleeease!"

Wade stood and circled her, inspecting for more, unable to keep from noticing that her ample breasts were as rigid as rocks. He again held her waist and pulled her to him to stop her shaking. It took two tries but the leech finally succumbed.

He backed away. "You can pull up your drawers now."

She glared at him as if wanting to kill and pulled up her suit.

"You took long enough!"

Wade met her glare with a disgusted sigh and spun

around. He unbuttoned his shirt as he walked to his vest and found two of the gray bloodsuckers on his right side. He lit matches but their position was awkward to reach with his sore arm.

The woman stomped over to him and grabbed the matches away. "Bend over," she commanded.

Wade looked into her angry eyes and reluctantly began to stoop over. She dispatched both quickly and slapped his buttocks. "Now the pants, Mister."

He stood abruptly and grabbed the matches. "Not on your life."

"Fair is fair, Wade," she snapped.

"You wear underwear, lady, I don't. I'll check myself out."

Her face showed no surprise, just anger. "Wade, you, you . . ." She couldn't find the words for her humiliation. "You bastard!"

Wade picked up his vest. "South is that way. I'm leaving in one minute. You can follow me or you can go on your own. I don't give a damn either way."

She saw in his eyes he meant exactly what he said, making her even more angry. No man had ever looked at her with such disdain before. She controlled her desire to slap him and turned to pick up her vest, knowing she had to follow.

Wade removed the partially filled survival water bag from his vest, took a long drink, then offered her one.

She pointedly reached for her own water bag. It was empty.

Wade still held his out with a condescending grin. She snatched it from his hands. "What about food? Surely you could find some roots or something?"

Wade shook his head, mumbling, and began walking.

"I'm starved, Wade!"

He kept walking and disappeared over the crest.

"Damn you," she whispered, and hurried to catch up.

An Khe
Ranger Base Camp

Major Ed Shane pushed open his hootch door and stepped out into the cool morning air. He'd gotten up early to inspect the troop barracks and company area while his men still slept. He gazed down the gently descending hill to the barracks and began to take a step, then stopped abruptly.

From the corner of his eye he saw a strange shape, and turned. A figure was rolled up in a poncho beside one of the rooms. "What the . . . ?" He marched over and tapped the sleeping figure with his foot.

Lieutenant Gibson threw back the poncho and grabbed for a nonexistent rifle.

"Whoa, L-tee, it's just me."

Gibson sprang to his feet, wearing only boots and fatigue pants. He'd used his shirt for a pillow. "Damn, sir, you scared the hell outta me. I guess I was really out of it."

"Why are you sleeping out here, for Christ's sake?"

"The door was locked, sir. I tried knocking, but . . . "

Shane's eyes narrowed, and he pounded on the door, waited a few seconds, and pounded again.

Lieutenant Dickey opened the door, yawning, wearing light blue pajama bottoms. Seeing the major, he stiffened immediately. "Sir?"

"You didn't hear knocking last night?"

Dickey's eyes shifted to the bare-chested soldier, then back to Shane. "No sir. Did someone knock?"

Shane eyed the tall officer suspiciously. "Dickey, if you sleep *that* soundly, you'd better find yourself another profession . . . and get rid of those damned PJs! You'd look like an ass running to a bunker if we got mortared."

Dickey shrugged his shoulders. "Sir, my stereo must have covered the noise. I'll keep it turned down from now on."

Shane stared at the lieutenant, thinking to himself: He should never have given me an excuse. I hate excuses. That's strike one.

The major motioned to Gibson. "Get our new L-tee squared away, Dickey. Show him the shower point and then the camp. And remember my meeting at 0800."

Dickey began to say "Yes, sir" but Shane had turned around and headed for the troop barracks.

Dickey rolled his eyes and stepped out the door. "Toss

your stuff in the corner, cherry. I'll divvy up the room later."

Gibson stepped closer to the taller officer as he put on his shirt. "What did you call me?"

"Cherry. All newbies are called . . . "

Gibson raised his hand abruptly. "First, I'm not a cherry. Second, I heard you turn on your music *after* I knocked. I was going to pound your damn door in but had already laid out my gear and decided to give you the benefit of the doubt . . . until now. I don't know what your problem is, but don't screw with me."

Dickey raised his head arrogantly. "I don't have a problem. I told you and the major what happened."

Gibson shook his head in silence. He'd seen Dickey's type before and knew argument was useless.

Dickey opened the door wide. "I'll be dressed in a few minutes and show you the camp."

As he began picking up his poncho liner, Gibson wondered it he'd made another mistake in coming to the Rangers. The door next to Dickey's opened and out stepped a short, stocky soldier who looked like "Mr. Clean." Gibson couldn't help but stare at the shaven-headed officer as he approached with an extended hand and a huge grin.

"Howdy, cousin, I'm Brad Avant, First Platoon leader. I couldn't help but hear y'all. I'd be tickled ta show ya 'round Rangerland."

Gibson wasn't sure how to take the silly grin and cracker drawl, but he shook hands. "J. D. Gibson. Thanks for the offer, but Major Shane told Dickey to take . . . "

Avant shook his head dramatically, stopping Gibson in mid-sentence. "No, no, no. I, the resident Welcome Wagon host, *must* have the honors." Avant lowered his voice. "Plus, Dickey is an asshole, and it wouldn't do for the men to see you with him."

Gibson eyed Avant. He still wasn't able to figure him out, although Gibson prided himself in making snap judgments based on appearance and brief conversation. Avant went from exaggerated drawl to perfect pronunciation all in the same sentence. And his humor and last direct statement didn't jibe. It was as if there were two different men talking out of the same mouth.

Avant winked. "I know what you're thinkin', cousin, but don't worry none. I ain't crazy. I'm your new best friend. Believe me."

Gibson looked into the eyes of the officer and suddenly felt a strange warmth for him. He couldn't put his finger on it, but he felt Avant was right.

Avant broke into an even wider smile, as if reading his mind, and backed away, pointing at Gibson's patches. "Mercy sakes, but we have a gen-u-wine veteran from the 173rd. Man, do we need your experience. Where'd ya go to school?"

"Texas A&M. How 'bout you?"

"North Georgia Military, then on to law at Emory in Atlanta."

"How come you're in the . . . "

"Infantry?" helped Avant. "I didn't finish law school. Ya see, cousin, I done seen the light one night. The light spoke ta me and said, 'Boy, you've been a killer since three and a bullshitter since two. Go and be infantry. Go forth and rape, pillage, and plunder fo yo country.' But hell, that's another story. Come on! Get your shaving gear. I'll show ya where we shave, then we'll tour Rangerland."

Ten minutes later, Gibson and Avant had finished shaving and stood on a rise outside the shower building.

"J.D., as you can see, An Khe is one big mama of a base. It takes an hour just to drive around the perimeter. Ya see the big boulder mountain off to our right? That's Hong Kong mountain and the big landmark of An Khe. The actual town is just outside the main gate, but it ain't much to see. Mostly cheap tailors and sleazy bars. Hell, J.D., ya even pay for the clap in them joints."

Avant pointed out the road far below them. "That road leads to the center of the base where the Fourth Infantry Division and a slew of support units are. And, my friend, just below us here is Rangerland."

Gibson followed Avant's hand as he pointed down the

grassy slope to the small camp. A dirt road split the camp, with eight small plywood barracks on one side and the single-story headquarters building and sandbagged operations center on the other. Gibson couldn't get over how open the area was. It looked like grazing land on a ranch in Texas rather than a fortress. The terrain was completely void of trees except for a small valley just below the barracks. The only sign that it was in fact a fortified base was across the valley and up a barren hill, where large, wooden observation towers stood.

Avant noticed him looking at the towers. "There is a tower about every five hundred meters, and in front of them is enough concertina wire to go around the world. There's a swath plowed a klick wide all the way around the perimeter and at night it's all lit up like a ball park. Ya see down there? The mess hall is just below the barracks in the valley, and across from it is the Mini-Ranger school. It has a rappeling tower and a couple of shacks used for classrooms."

Avant turned around and pointed at the long, white structure. "*That* is what we call the motel—and it's where we just came from. It's the officers' and senior NCOs' hootch. Why don't you get your gear and throw it in my room? No use you bunkin' with Dickey."

Gibson frowned, thinking of the earlier encounter with the arrogant officer. "Brad, what's Dickey's problem?"

"Cousin, he's a Yankee. Whaddaya expect? I believe the boy thinks he got commissioned field marshall instead of loo-tenant. He's supposed to be real smart, but looks to me it's book smart, not people smart. He got a real knack for pissin' people off every time he opens his mouth."

Gibson nodded in agreement. "Well, what about the other officers. What're they like?"

"Major Shane is super, I'm super, you're super, Dickey is an asshole, and Foley is okay. Dave Foley is a West Pointer and is the operations officer and acting executive officer. He came in just before I did and seems to have his shit together when it comes to planning and flying missions. He ain't a field soldier, though. He's strictly a staff type.

Foley makes no bones about not liking the infantry. He shoulda been an engineer, but the Academy boys was kinda short on grunts. Foley is smart and knows he ain't no John Wayne like us.''

Gibson looked at Avant, shaking his head in bewilderment. "What makes you think I'm a John Wayne type? You don't even know me.''

Avant threw his arm around Gibson's shoulder and began walking him toward the motel. " 'Cause, cousin, ya just left the bush and you're still alive. That's pretty damn good credentials. Plus, ol' Brad is a fair judge of character. I got straight As in jury selection. I read people like a book. When I heard you talkin' to Dickey this morning I knew you thought he was an ass. That means you're a pretty good judge of character, too. Face it, cousin, we're alike. All I gotta do is loosen you up a bit. You ain't smiled since I metcha. The troops gonna think you're a badass that knows it all.''

Gibson stopped in his tracks and backed away from the officer. "Avant, you're unbelievable. You don't know me from Adam and yet you decide I'm John Wayne, got character, and have to smile all the time, for christ's sake!'' Gibson's hard stare broke and he cracked a slight grin. "But you got one thing right. I'm a good judge of character, and Brad, you're the craziest son of a bitch I've ever met.''

Avant laughed loudly and tossed his arm over Gibson's shoulder again. "Cousin, we gonna make a helluva team, with me bein' crazy and you keepin' us straight. Damn, this company better watch out!''

Major Shane sat at his desk, waiting. Lieutenants Gibson, Avant, and Foley sat in folding chairs around his desk, with First Sergeant Demand, Childs, and several senior NCOs leaning against the far wall.

Shane glanced at his Rolex GMT Master—0803 hours. The door opened and in strode Lieutenant Dickey. Shane stared at the late officer as he took a seat beside Avant.

Strike two, he said to himself, as he looked back at his scribbled notes.

"Today, at 1300 hours, we receive two planeloads of replacements from the 173rd. When they arrive, we begin a comprehensive training program. Because of officer and experience shortages, we are going to consolidate our training. I will oversee the program, along with First Sergeant Demand, but Sergeant Childs will be in charge of all initial screening and training. Platoon sergeants, along with selected, mature Ranger veterans, will act as trainers and cadre. We are considering all other men students. They will take all training, and they will be thrown out if they can't hack it. Officers will be trained separately by me. First Sergeant is your point of contact for all training equipment, chow, billeting, and vehicle support. What are your questions?"

No one spoke. Shane stood. "Good. We'll have a daily meeting during morning chow to discuss problems and how things are going. Those of you who don't know each other, introduce yourselves. I'm going to the airfield and lay on some bird dogs for officer training. I'll see everyone at lunch." The group snapped to attention as the major walked for the door.

When the major had gone, Gibson introduced himself to Lieutenant Foley, who, Gibson thought, looked out of place with his thick, black-rimmed glasses and bookish appearance.

Foley talked in a squeaky voice, but had a suspiciously strong grip. He also wore a Ranger tab, which told Gibson the man had more character strength than his weak-looking exterior suggested.

Gibson felt a tap and turned around to stare at a bantam black first sergeant who held out his hand. The senior NCO could have been picked out of a crowd as a first sergeant. His frame was small, but his shoulders were broad and powerful. He looked like a boxer, but was dressed in starched-stiff fatigues and shiny black jump boots. His smiling face exposed gleaming white teeth and twinkling eyes. "L-tee, it's good to have a fellow sky-soldier join my Rangers."

Gibson shook hands with First Sergeant Demand, and trying not to show his discomfort in the man's vicelike grip, returned the pressure. Demand's eyes showed the pleasure he took in the contest and finally released his hold. "Good, L-Tee, you'll do fine. First Sergeant likes shaking hands with real paratroopers. If you need anything, you see ol' Top."

"It's a pleasure, Top. I'm glad to be here."

Lieutenant Avant took Gibson's arm and walked him to the door, whispering, "Sorry, cousin, forgot to warn you about Top's handshake. He nearly broke my hand the first time I met him." Gibson opened and closed his stiff hand. "What else haven't you told me about him?"

"You'll see when you eat chow this evening."

Cam Tiem Mountains

Matt Wade stepped out of the jungle and cussed. Before him was a wide, meandering river blocking their route.

The woman came up behind him and sat down tiredly. "Don't even ask. I can't swim that."

They had reached the valley floor an hour before and made good time through the sparse jungle. Wade thought the road wouldn't be more than a few kilometers away.

He scanned the far side, then looked up the near banks for a place to cross. To the west looked best. "Come on, Ginny, we'll walk up aways and find a place to cross."

The woman looked up, genuinely surprised at his tone of voice. He had spoken without growling.

She put her hand out, and he pulled her up. "We're finally becoming a civil person, aren't we?" she said sarcastically.

Wade just sighed and began walking along the bank.

Four hundred meters down, where the river widened further and had a sand bar in its center, they stopped and Wade took off his boots. He tied the laces together, put the boots around his neck, and began wading out into the muddy water. It only came up to his knees. "Okay, take off your shoes and come on."

He held her hand and they crossed to the sand bar. The

water had only come to their waist. Wade released her hand and tested along the other side. The water was much deeper, coming to his chest in only a few steps. Shit!

He waded back and sat down, studying the bank only twenty meters away.

Virginia stood over him. "Forget it, Wade. It's too deep. I can't make it."

Wade's jaw muscles rippled as he clenched his teeth. He'd had all he could stand. "Look, I'm sick and tired of your saying 'I can't'! We've made it this far, and we're gonna keep on makin' it."

"How?" she asked smugly.

Wade stared at her for a moment, then looked at the far bank. "I'll think of something."

The woman shook her head and pulled out the two empty water bags. "While you're thinking, Einstein, you can fill these." She tossed the bags to the sand in front of him.

Wade only glanced at the quart containers, then shifted his gaze back to the river. He stared for several seconds before suddenly looking back at the bags. "Take off your clothes!"

"What?"

"You heard me, get 'em off."

Wade grabbed one of the bags, blew into it like he would a balloon, closed it, and then picked up the other.

Virginia was beginning to think he'd finally gone crazy. Wade looked up after filling the second bag. "*Now,* or I'll take them off!"

Realizing he meant what he said she began to unzip her suit. "You'd better have a good reas . . . "

The sergeant swiftly unbuckled his pistol belt and took off his pants, stopping her in mid-sentence. He hadn't lied; he didn't wear underwear!

She quickly continued unzipping her suit and stepped out of it.

"Tie a knot at the end of each leg." he commanded.

"Why are we doing this? I don't . . . "

Wade grabbed the suit away from her and quickly tied

the knots, then put the air-filled bags inside the suit and pushed them up the legs to the knots. He then tied the other end into a large knot, waded out into the water, and lay down. The inflated legs supported him like water wings.

He waded back and threw her the wet jumpsuit, then picked up the pistol belt and trousers, placing them around his neck.

"Let's go."

"What about my vest?"

"Leave it." Wade grabbed her hand and waded into the river. They made it a quarter of the way before the water rose to his chin. Virginia was already floating. He pulled her in front of him, directing her head toward the bank. "Kick like hell." He shoved her toward shore.

She screamed "No!" but began kicking with all her strength.

Wade tried to sidestroke but the weight of the vest and pistol belt dragged him down. He took a deep breath and sank.

Virginia made the bank easily and climbed up the slope. "You bastard! You son of a . . ." She turned, looking for him, but he wasn't there. *"Wade!"*

He broke from the water midway across and gasped in a deep breath before disappearing again.

"Oh my God. Wade!"

She waded out to her waist, crying out for him, when he suddenly popped up in front of her gasping for air.

"Wade!"

She grabbed for him, but he got to his feet and stood up in front of her, taking in deep breaths. She sniffed back tears of relief and put out her hand to help him.

He waved her back. "Turn around till I get my pants on."

She looked at him in disbelief. What was left that he was afraid she might see? She could hardly keep from laughing as she shook her head at the absurdity and turned around. *"Now,* we're even, Wade," she said, glancing back over her shoulder.

An Khe
Ranger Base Camp

The last truck pulled away in a cloud of red dust, leaving ninety-five replacements from the 173rd. They wore green jungle fatigues and baseball-style hats. They assembled quickly in a ragged formation at the command of Sergeant Gino. Next to the replacements stood a formation of ninety-eight Rangers wearing their camouflage fatigues and flop hats. Childs had directed that they were no longer authorized to wear the black beret until they completed training. Behind the two formations were the platoon sergeants and twelve selected cadre who wore black berets and olive drab T-shirts. Thumper, Rose, and Russian stood in their ranks, having been selected as instructors.

Sergeant Gino centered himself on the formed company and commanded, "Com-pan-ee, A-tench-hut!"

Childs strode from the headquarters building and mounted a small platform of wooden ammo boxes.

Gino saluted smartly. "Company prepared for training."

Childs returned the salute and barked, "Pa-rade *rest!*"

He put his hands on his hips and surveyed the two formations. "*People*, my name is Childs. I'm the senior Ranger instructor. My job is to make you look, think, and act like Rangers. In two weeks, those who complete the training will be called Rangers and will be awarded the black beret. No man, regardless of rank or experience, is guaranteed to make it. You must *earn* the right to be called Ranger. You are now *maggots, ragbags,* and *shitbirds.* You 173rd replacements are *maggots.* You cherries who *were* in the company are *ragbags*, and *all* of you are *shitbirds*! My platoon sergeants and instructors are proven Rangers and will be addressed as *Ranger.*

"This company is an elite organization, and we only want the best. Our job is tough, demanding, and dangerous. Those who can't hack the training will be thrown out in a heartbeat. You can quit at any time. All quitters and washouts will be sent to a leg unit immediately. You must obey all our rules and regulations to the letter, or you're *out*!

You must pass all training or you're *out*! You must show enthusiasm and motivation or you're *out*! There are no excuses or appeals. If I say you're out, you're *out*!''

Childs paused for effect and lifted his head slightly higher. "All shitbirds wearing headbands, beads, peace medals, and sunglasses and have their hair parted in the middle, fall out to my right. *Now*!''

Twenty-two men ran from the formation and quickly formed into two ranks beside the sergeant, who stared at them with disgust.

"You shitbirds smoke pot and do dope. I can smell it from here. You got ten seconds to get in the proper uniform or you're *out*. One, two, three . . . ''

The ground quickly became littered with colored bandanas, glasses, and necklaces. Several made no move to take off their "indicators."

"Nine . . . ten! You, you, you, and you, get out of my sight. Report to Headquarters. You're out! The rest of you are hereby warned. If you smoke grass or use dope or *ever* put any of that shit on again, you'll find yourself on a plane to the stockade. Get back in ranks. *Now*!''

Childs waited until they fell back in before putting his hands back on his hips.

"Now shitbirds, the first rules: For the next two weeks, *nobody* smokes, drinks booze or beer; *nobody* eats candy or any pogeybait; and *nobody* leaves the Ranger camp unless it's official. You will eat only what the mess hall serves or the C rations we give you. You are restricted to the company area. Lights out at 2100. First formation every morning is 0500. Physical training will be twice a day, 0600 and 1630.''

Childs pointed to the 173rd replacements. "Maggots, you will draw equipment and weapons immediately following this briefing. You and your equipment will be inspected in two hours.''

He then pointed to the other formation. "Ragbags, you will be inspected in one hour. Before I dismiss the company, does anybody want to quit?'' Three hands shot up— two from the "ragbags" and one from the 173rd "maggots." Childs snickered, then bellowed, "*Move out, quitters!* Anybody else?" No one moved.

"We'll see about that. Pla-toon sergeants, take charge of your shitbirds."

Major Shane stepped back from the window, smiling. "It's begun, Top."

First Sergeant Demand chuckled. "Yes, sir. Ol' Childs is in Ranger heaven pushin' them kids. I just hope we don't lose too many."

"Top, I don't care if we only end up with two platoons. At least we'll have dependable men who know what they're doing." Shane walked for the door. "The first three barracks are full of 173rd replacements, right?"

The first sergeant shook his finger at his commander. "Sir, they're 'maggots' now, but yes, sir, they're in the first three and the 'ragbags' are in the next three.

Shane laughed. "Okay, Top. The maggots and ragbags. Damn, I sure hope the brass don't visit; it'd sure be tough explaining nicknames like those. Let's go down and see how they're set up."

Thumper, helping with the assignment of weapons to the 173rd replacements, stood in front of a group of twenty-five men. "Anybody here that has had experience with the M-60 machine gun, step up to the table."

Five men stepped out of ranks. The first was a lanky, six-foot-tall redhead, whose fair skin was sunburned to the color of a beet. His forearms were tattooed with a panther on the right and a dragon on the left. His face was smooth and covered with freckles, but his lips were thin and held a natural, mean scowl.

Thumper motioned him back. "You look a little skinny to be humpin' a 60."

The redhead snickered as he snatched up one of the twenty-five-pound guns from the table and expertly disassembled the weapon in thirty seconds, then reassembled it in the same time. He ran a function check then tossed the weapon to Thumper.

"It's got a worn cam roller and the drive spring needs replacing. The hog will jam in the first burst."

Thumper smiled at his error in judgment. "What's your name?"

"Private First Class Woody Stecker. I was a 60 gunner in the Aviation Battalion."

Thumper tossed the weapon back. "Fix it, Woodpecker. It's your gun now."

The soldier held the gun affectionately, but glared at the big man. "The name is *Stecker*."

Thumper shook his head. "You're redheaded and look as hard as woodpecker lips. You're 'Woodpecker' now. Next man, grab a 60."

Childs began his equipment inspection precisely on time and became a human tornado. Few men were unaffected by his wrath as he strew clothes and equipment all over the dirt road. Childs approached the final soldier and stared into the trembling man's eyes. "Are you shakin'?"

The soldier seemed terrified, but he shook his head "no." Childs backed up a step, eyeing the man from head to foot. He was a short Indian with a huge nose that looked as if it had been broken several times. His face was horribly scarred from acne or chicken pox. A silver cross hung exposed from dogtags outside his shirt. Childs didn't recognize him and knew he had to be one of the cherries assigned to the Third Platoon while at Phan Thiet.

Childs pointed to the cross. "Get rid of that, ragbag."

The Indian's eyes widened further as he spoke in a whisper, "I can't."

"What?"

"I . . . I cannot. I am a believer and it is a symbol of truth."

"Bible-thumper, I said, take it *off*!"

The soldier, looking skyward, whispered a prayer and shook his head again.

Childs reached up to grab the chain. But the young Indian's hand shot up, grasping the sergeant's wrist in a death grip. "The Lord called me to the Rangers. Please do not take the cross."

Childs stared into the brown, pleading eyes and released the chain, stepping within inches of the soldier's face.

"You keep the cross, Preacher, 'cause you got guts. But, if you *ever* grab me again I'll knock your ass to kingdom come. Your gear better be squared away or you're gonna need a congregation to pick up all your shit." Childs tore through the soldier's equipment, inspecting everything twice. He finally tossed down a two-quart canteen and grabbed the startled man's arm and dragged him to the front of the formation.

"You ragbags see this ugly Indian? Whatever he's preachin', you'd better listen, 'cause he's the only one that's got his gear squared away. I'll be back in one hour to reinspect, and if you ain't straight, I'll make *believers* outta *you*!"

Childs turned to the small Indian. "Preacher, you're now the chief of this tribe of ragbags. Square 'em away."

Highway 1
Cam Tiem Mountains

Virginia Wolinski fell to her knees on the hard-paved road and touched the hot surface as if it was gold. "We made it! We really made it!"

They'd only traveled an hour after leaving the river before finally stumbling onto Highway 1.

Wade stood on the shoulder of the road with his hand up to block the sinking sun's glare as he scanned both directions.

"We might be too late to get picked up by a convoy."

"What?"

"The convoys don't move after three, so they don't get caught on the road after dark. This is VC country."

"But surely we can . . . "

His head turned suddenly and he stared up the road again. "What is it?" she said.

"A ride."

A minute later Wade flagged down a small, three-wheeled, Lambretta pick-up. The driver, an old Vietnamese man with brown, wrinkled skin and wisps of long gray hair hanging from his chin, stared at the couple as if they were aliens. Wade quickly inspected the vehicle. In the pick-up bed were dozens of one-foot eels and other assorted rotting fish.

Using what little Vietnamese he knew, Wade talked to the old man, who knew a few English words. Lots of hand signs filled in the story. The old man had taken a full load of fish and eels to market in Xuan Loc, ten miles distant, and was returning with the unsold. He had thought Wade was a robber, but now, as he realized that all the couple wanted was a ride, he grinned broadly.

Wade took Virginia's arm and motioned her toward the pick-up bed. "Get in, and let's get outta here."

Virginia took one look at the eels and yanked her arm free from his grasp. "No way, Wade. I'm not getting in there with those things!"

The sergeant rolled his eyes and sighed. "Look, Lady, take a look inside that cab. There's no room for both of us. Hell, there's barely room for me. These Lambrettas are nothing but motor scooter's with a chassis."

"Wade, I'm not getting in the back. *I'll* ride up front with the gentleman and *you* ride in the back."

The sergeant lowered his voice and turned his back to the driver. "Lady, for all I know, that ol' man could be VC and takin' us to his friends. I gotta ride up front and cover him so he don't try no funny business, you understand?"

Virginia looked nervously at the old Vietnamese, then back at the eels. "But . . . Oh, God, I hate you for this, Wade."

She climbed reluctantly onto the back bumper and held her nose as she stepped gingerly into the slimy bed. "Wade . . . I . . . I'm going to be sick."

The sergeant hopped quickly into the cab before she changed her mind and motioned for the old man to go.

"Wade? *Wade!*"

The driver jerked the vehicle forward, knocking Virginia back screaming.

Ten minutes down the road Wade looked back at the woman, glad he was in the front and away from the horrible odor of the fish. The vehicle's man-made wind was keeping the stench in the back. The old man was chattering away in a high singsong pitch as if the American understood every word he said. The woman looked at him pleadingly, but Wade kept smiling and nodding to keep the old man happy.

Twenty minutes later the vehicle slowed. Wade could see a cluster of clapboard huts along the road just ahead. He'd seen many such "rest stations" while on convoys. They were nothing more than thrown-together shacks that gave a few farmers a chance to sell black market Cokes and cigarettes to GI truck drivers during piss breaks. Some "stations" were more elaborate than others, offering everything from candy to prostitutes for an exorbitant sum.

The old man pulled off the road to the jubilant welcome of three barking dogs and a small, smiling boy.

The vehicle had barely stopped when Virginia scrambled over the tailgate and ran to a small table holding stacked cans of Cokes and beer. Wade yelled, "Hold it," but it was too late; she grabbed a Coke can and was immediately struck by a long branch of bamboo. An old woman stepped out of the hut, scolding her in high-pitched Vietnamese, and raised the stick for another blow.

The driver barked out to the old woman, but she struck the auburn-haired American anyway.

Virginia ran to Wade, still holding the Coke. "Stop her, Wade!"

The sergeant grabbed the stick but also snatched the can from Virginia and handed it back to the woman, who smiled, exposing a dark, red mouth full of betel nut.

The small boy tugged at Wade's trousers. "You numba one GI, you souvenir me cigarette?"

Matt smiled, knowing the boy was the mouthpiece for

the old couple. Kids picked up the GI language quickly and did most of the dealing.

"Don't smoke, kid, and don't have MPC. We cheap Charlie."

The boy's smile vanished. "You fucking numba *ten*, Joe!"

The driver spoke to the boy, obviously wanting to know what was said and listened to the boy as he pointed disgustedly at the two passengers.

The old man stiffened visibly and spoke quickly to the boy.

Virginia whispered to Wade. "What's happening?"

"It seems we're not wanted since we don't have money."

"But I've got money."

The boy pointed an accusing finger at Matt.

"You numba fucking ten. You ride with Papa-san and pay no mon-nay. Papa-san say you no tell him you no have mon-nay!"

Wade put his hand out to Virginia. "Give me the MPC."

"Huh?"

"The money, lady."

Virginia unzipped her vest pocket and withdrew a small, soggy wad of the military payment currency script. Matt's eyes widened in disbelief, as did the boy's. She had three twenties and a ten in the small, colored notes.

"Ginny, we could buy the whole place with this. Why're you carrying so much?"

"Mad money. Can I have a Coke now . . . and some food?"

Wade took a twenty and handed it to the wide-eyed boy.

"You give papa-san for ride and tell him take us to Phan Thiet now."

The boy held up the money excitedly and talked quickly with the old man, who showed no emotion except shaking his head and then spoke in a higher pitch.

The boy shook his head at Wade. "Papa-san say he no can go Phan Thiet now. It too late. ARVN shoot him, think maybe he VC. You stay. Girl come morrow, she give you short time. You stay, drink beer, chow down big time.''

Wade sighed, disappointed, but nodded toward the boy. ''We drink and eat, leave tomorrow. You have C rations?''

''Bucoo, Joe, cost you this money, okay.''

''Okay.''

Minutes later the couple sat in the floor of the hut with a stack of C rations. Virginia had just opened a can of beans and franks and wolfed down a large bite when Wade snatched the can from her.

''Slow down! You wanna get sick? Eat slowly and chew your food a long time before swallowing. Your stomach hasn't had food in awhile and needs to adjust. You shouldn't have drank those two Cokes so fast, either.''

Virginia rolled her eyes and began chewing in slow motion.

The boy walked in, tossed down the several ponchos and poncho liners that Wade had requested, then sat beside Wade and touched the hair on his arm. ''You kill bucoo VC?''

Wade took a bite of chopped ham 'n' eggs and shook his head.

The boy stroked the hair in fascination and looked at the woman.

''You have same same?''

Virginia pushed back her sleeves, exposing her fair skin.

The boy leaned over, inspecting her fine hair, and smiled. ''You same same me.'' He then looked at her chest. ''Bucoo boobs. You have baby-san?''

Wade hid his grin and raised his brow, waiting for the response.

Virginia pushed down her sleeves self-consciously and folded her arms across her breasts.

''No, I don't have a child, I'm just . . . well, I'm . . . ''

''American,'' said Wade, nonchalantly taking another bite.

''Yes, American. American girls have . . . we . . . well, we . . . ''

Wade smiled at her discomfort and pulled the boy over to him.

"American girls are bigger than Vietnamese. They get bucoo fat drinking bucoo Cokes." The boy eyed the woman and then the two empty cans laying beside her. He nodded in understanding.

Virginia glared at Wade and took a large mouthful of beans. The boy looked up at Wade. "GI lady boom boom same same Vietnamese?"

Wade coughed to keep from laughing and nudged the boy. "Get some more Cokes, kid."

An Khe
Ranger Base Camp

At exactly 1630, Childs stepped up on the ammo boxes and faced the formation of bare-chested men who were ready for physical training. He shook his head and sighed. "Shitbirds, I've been around the world, two state fairs, a carnival, and seen ducks screw, but I've never seen anything like you. The inspection was a joke. You shitbirds have violated one of the major rules of the Rangers—attention to detail. You must pay attention to detail in order to survive. Well, I got somethin' for you. This little run we're goin' on is designed to clean out the cigarettes, booze, candy, and *dumb-ass*! Anybody wanna quit before we begin? Too bad. *Left face! Forward, harch! Doubletime, harch!*"

The formation of men was led by Thumper, who was to ensure they kept a steady, eight-minute-per-mile pace. Childs ran along the side of the formation with the platoon sergeants. Thumper led them down the hill to the perimeter road for one mile, then turned them around and started back. The men ran silently, not singing the traditional Airborne cadences. When a soldier tried to sing out, Childs would yell *"Shut up!"*

Five hundred meters from the Ranger camp, Childs began hollering, *"Only five hundred meters, girls, then it's over!"* He yelled again as they got closer, "We're almost there, it's almost over!"

He allowed the formation to climb halfway up the hill only one-hundred meters from the barracks before stopping them. "Shitbirds, I got a little surprise for you! *About face!* We're gonna do it again! *Doubletime, harch!*"

The formation had lost no one on the first run, but by the time they reached a half mile, twelve men had fallen to the side.

Childs stopped the formation and faced them toward him as he stood on a rise, stalking back and forth with hands on hips.

"You just learned a lesson, shitbirds! Don't ever let your mind think it's over! If you were on a mission and had to run to a helicopter pickup zone and found you couldn't use it, you'd have to run to another PZ—and another until you finally got picked up. A Ranger must never think something's over. *It ain't never over till the fat lady sings at your funeral!* You see them wimps that fell out? They let their *minds* beat them! They're the ones you'd have to carry on a mission 'cause they *thought* they couldn't make it! Shitbirds, remember this lesson. *It's all in your heads!* You have to drive on and push through pain. You must toughen your mind as well as your body."

Childs pointed to the camp a half mile away. "You shitbirds walk on back and cool down before chow. And remember, *it ain't over till the fat lady sings!* Move out!"

The formation of men began walking back to the camp, except for a lone soldier in camouflage fatigue pants who began jogging. Childs recognized him immediately; it was the small Indian he'd inspected earlier. One of the men yelled out, "Show 'em, Preacher! Us ragbags is bad!"

The Indian passed by a group of maggot replacements that jeered at him. "That's one ugly Indian, man!"

"Ragbags ain't shit!"

A ragbag yelled back, "You 173rd maggots are *wimps*!"

One of the 173rd replacements broke into a run and easily caught up to the Indian and passed him.

"Go, maggot!" hollered the 173rd replacements, encouraging their group's competitor.

The Indian increased his pace and took back the lead,

to the cheers of the ragbags. The replacement maggots began hollering and screaming for their man to catch up. Thumper watched in disbelief, for the replacement that had run to catch the Indian was the tall redhead, Woodpecker.

Childs stood on the rise, watching not the runners but the screaming men who seemed to find identity in the names 'maggot' and 'ragbag.' "I'll be damned," he thought as they hollered and ran to see who would win.

"Move it, maggot!"

"Go, ragbag, beat his ass!"

The two runners ran neck and neck up the hill. The redhead pushed ahead and sprinted for the first barracks, but the Indian caught up to him with a surprising burst of speed and slapped the wall of the building first. Both men fell to their knees, out of breath and gasping for air. The redhead finally got to his feet and stood over the small soldier. "I'll beat your ass next time."

The Indian raised his head, looking skyward, then looked at the glaring soldier. "Only if the Lord gives you strength."

The first of the soldiers arrived. "Who won?"

The redhead motioned disgustedly toward the Indian. The ragbags yelped with joy and raised the victor to their shoulders as the 173rd maggots gathered around their defeated runner. "No sweat, man, you almost beat that ugly shit."

The two groups faced each other, yelling and trading insults, when Childs stepped between them. "*At ease! Shitbirds!* Get cleaned up and get to chow!"

The groups of men mumbled and walked away, leaving Childs with something very unnatural on his tough face— a grin.

The mess hall rocked as a booming voice filled the room.

"Moooove out, Troop-ar! Eat my good Army chow and mooove out!" First Sergeant Demand stood by the food line bellowing, "One piece of cake, Troop-ar! You holdin' up my line!" The mess hall was full when the bantam soldier turned toward the dining area.

"Some of you troop-ars not appreciatin' the first sergeant's latrine! You been writin' little notes on my walls and smokin' nasty cigarettes. You troop-ars keep that up, you gonn be sleepin' in the bunkers! I heard some cussin' in my chow line. Don't be cussin' around yo' first sergeant. I like clean things!" The senior sergeant turned back to the food line. "Mooove out, Troop-ar!"

Major Shane sat at a table with his officers and senior NCOs and noted Lieutenant Gibson's stare at the black sergeant. "L-tee, you'll have to get used to Top when you eat. He always does this. This is his mess hall and he takes great pride in a shipshape camp. Don't use profanity around him and never, never throw any trash on the ground."

Gibson broke his trance from the bellowing man and nodded to his commander, grateful for the warning. Lieutenant Avant nudged him. "I told you Top was different."

Shane leaned back. "Sergeant Childs, how is your program coming?"

Childs motioned to the dining area where men sat eating. "You see anything unusual over there, sir?"

Shane glanced at the men. "No, should I?"

"Sir, take a look at their uniforms."

Shane looked again, but shook his head. "They look alright."

"Sir, you'll notice the camouflage-fatigued ragbags over there, and the green-fatigued maggots on the other side. I think we got us two separate armies."

"We have cammies for the replacements; issue them."

"No sir, not yet. I got a feelin' this is exactly what we need."

Shane looked at Childs strangely, then broke into a grin. He winked knowingly and leaned forward for his glass of tea, but noticed Gibson looking at him as if he wanted to speak.

"Gibson, what do ya wanna say?"

The lieutenant stiffened. "Nothing, sir, except . . . "

"Well?"

"Sir, I feel I should be with the replacements. They're

from the 173rd and so am I. I think I should take the same training they are so that I'll have credibility. I'll take off my rank if I need to."

Shane eyed the lieutenant, then looked at Childs, who winked approvingly.

Shane's eyes shifted back to the L-tee. "It's not fair to the ragbags if the replacements have an officer."

Gibson elbowed the shaven-headed officer beside him. "Sir, I'm sure Lieutenant Avant will accept the position of ragbag leader. He *is* a North Georgia graduate and all."

Avant swallowed a piece of cake. "Sir, it would be a profound honor indeed to show this Aggie what a real leader is."

Shane hid his pleasure with a frown and leaned back in his chair. There was the officer training program to consider. He knew he could train them after Childs's two-week program, but . . .

Childs spoke up. "Sir, I think it's a good idea to have some internal leadership to keep the armies under control. It could get out of hand."

Shane pointed his finger at Gibson. "You are now a maggot."

"Thank you, sir."

Shane then pointed at Avant. "And you're a ragbag."

"An honor, sir," said Avant. "I shall uphold the name with dignity and pursue the . . . "

"Get outta here!" interrupted Shane, unable to contain his smile any longer.

First Sergeant Demand rocked back on his heels as the men kept filing into the mess hall. He suddenly came to attention and marched directly toward three blacks who had just walked in.

First Sergeant's eyes had narrowed to slits as he approached the first, who was tall and wore his shirt partially unbuttoned, exposing a long, black shoestring necklace with a black plastic closed fist on its end.

Demand stopped four paces from the tall soldier, who stared at him defiantly.

"Boy, what yo think this is—a black panther headquarters?"

"I ain't no boy," said the tall soldier, glancing at his two smiling friends.

"You sure ain't a man, and you ain't dressed like a soldier. I guess you're right—you ain't a boy. You a *wimp*! A weak, incompetent, malingering pus-say. Now, wimp, you got ten seconds to get that unmilitary paraphernalia off your funky body, or the first sergeant's gonna introduce you to his black power fist upside your wimp head, *clear*?"

The tall soldier squared himself to the glaring sergeant and smirked.

The first sergeant took a step closer, speaking softly. "You got your hands full fighting dinks. I don't think you wanna complicate your life and try out the first sergeant." The broad-shouldered sergeant's stare was cold and cutting. He whispered almost inaudibly, "Five seconds, wimp."

The soldier's eyes nervously shifted back and forth. He turned slightly, glancing at his friends, who wouldn't return his look. The men around them backed up quickly. He looked back at the small, muscular man before him, who, no doubt, meant exactly what he said. His hands shot up for the necklace.

"Now, button up your shirt, boy. They gonna think yo queer."

The first sergeant's eyes shifted slowly to the other two black men, both of whom quickly took off their necklaces and began buttoning their shirts.

"Moooove out, troop-ars! You holdin' up my line!"

Rose sat across from Russian staring at his food and feeling sick. Russian looked up after eating his meat loaf. "What is wrong, Rose?"

Rose shut his eyes wearily. "Man, I ain't run in months and my stomach is saying 'fuck you.' "

The Czech took Rose's food tray and smashed the meat loaf into mush with his fork, then mixed the meat with the mashed potatoes. He pushed the tray back. "You must eat small bites and drink water or you will become weak."

Rose shook his head and leaned back in his chair. "I can't, man. Don't feel like eatin' nothin'."

Russian stood and walked around the table and sat down beside the black soldier. He picked up a spoon and held it toward Rose. "You will eat or you not leave. You must have strength for tomorrow. Eat!"

Rose sighed and took the spoon. "Man, you're worse than my mama."

Seated behind Russian in the corner of the mess hall were the Ranger cadre team sergeants who were the experienced junior leaders of the company. Thumper had been asked to join them to represent Wade.

Sergeant Zubeck, an athletically built six-footer who was team leader of 2-1, sat at the head of the table and leaned back in his chair. "Childs is in complete charge of the training program and wanted me to tell you he has total confidence in our ability to train the men. He's giving us the authority to kick out any man who shows he's weak or gives us any back talk. He said if we say a man goes, he goes."

Sergeant Selando, a half-Mexican and team leader of 1-3, snickered. "Then you can kiss a third of them goodbye. We had a bunch that barely made the run today. Wait till tomorrow when they're sore and tired."

Thumper leaned forward. "What about the guys from the 173rd? How much should we expect them to know since they've come from regular line units?"

Sergeant Zubeck rolled his toothpick to the other side of his mouth. "Thump, we gotta assume they don't know much. They've come from just about every unit in the 'Herd' and all have different levels of experience. Most of the young line dogs only do as they're told. They're not used to thinking on their own. Most can't read maps or talk on the radio with the right procedures to call for helicopter or artillery support. What they do have, though, is time in the bush. They know how to move, shoot, eat, sleep, and live in the field. That alone makes them better than cherries who are scared to death the first couple of times out.

"We'll teach them the Ranger basics and build on expertise later. The ones you're looking for are those that can think on their feet and catch on quick. Don't waste your time on weakies and dummies. There isn't time to train 'em. If you see one with a weakness, correct him immediately. If he improves, watch him a little longer. If he doesn't improve, toss his ass out right and concentrate on the others."

As Thumper thought about Robbins's torn body, he knew he would give no mercy to any student, and the doubts he had about his abilities as a trainer dissolved. He had the experience to do the job and he would do it. He vowed to himself that no student of his would die like Robbins.

Sergeant Zubeck rose from his chair. "I don't know about the rest of you, but I'm hittin' the sack. Tomorrow is gonna be kick-ass, and I wanna be the one who's kickin'."

Thumper left the mess hall and walked down the road toward his barracks, but suddenly changed direction. He had to satisfy his curiosity. As he opened the door to the replacement maggot barracks, he was met by blaring music from a cassette player.

"Give me a ticket for an airr planer. . . "

Sitting on the closest bunk beside the cassette player was the reason Thumper came. The man's eyes were closed, and he was singing along with the music.

Thumper had been watching Woodpecker all afternoon, convinced that the surly redhead would have quit before the run. He had constantly complained and given smirking, indignant looks to all the Ranger cadre. It was obvious to Thumper that Woodpecker had an attitude problem and wouldn't make it . . . at least it had been obvious until Woodpecker had raced the Indian.

When Stecker opened his eyes, he showed no surprise at seeing the big, bereted soldier staring at him, and he kept singing.

Thumper bent over and pressed the "stop" button. "How come you raced the ragbag?"

Stecker picked up the cassette player and pushed the rewind button. " 'Cause nobody beats Woody Stecker, especially no cherry."

"He beat you," said Thumper with a half-smile.

Stecker looked up with a scowl. "This time he did. Next time he won't."

Thumper saw his opening and attacked. "You mean you're gonna stick around for a next time?"

Stecker tossed the cassette to his pillow. "Yeah. I'm gonna whip his ass, and then I'll . . . uh . . . "

"Quit?" said Thumper, already seeing the answer in the soldier's eyes. "I thought you probably would. I just wanted to check to see if my hunch was right."

Thumper turned to leave, feeling a twinge of sadness. "No sense you hangin' around to run. The first time you give another Ranger instructor one of your 'give a shit' looks, you'll be out on your ass . . . if not knocked on it." Thumper began to walk for the door and motioned to the soldier's equipment. "Might as well pack your bags. You'll be gone by noon tomorrow."

"Fuck you," growled Stecker.

Thumper spun around. "Pack 'em now! You're out!"

Stecker jumped to his feet in rage. "Fine! You assholes in your berets make me sick anyway! You all walkin' around like you're somethin' special, and you ain't shit! I got more experience than most of ya, and you treat me like a fuckin' cherry!

Thumper glared. "So that's it? You thought you'd just come here and get handed a beret? You expected to volunteer for the Rangers and that'd automatically make you one? Well, I got news. It's a helluva lot more than that."

"Says you! I got plenty of experience in the bush. I'm the best 60 gunner around and could go out on a patrol right now. But no. You assholes wanna play stupid-ass games and go on runs that don't mean nothin'."

Thumper turned his back and walked for the door. He wasn't going to waste his time any longer. He began to push the door open but stopped himself. He remembered when he'd first arrived at Penn State to play football. He'd been the most sought after high school fullback in the state and had thought the team would accept him with open arms. They hadn't. In fact, it seemed the coaches and older players wanted to get rid of him by the way they rode him. He'd thought he was good and would easily make the team, but he was almost cut the second day out. The head coach had told him, "Meeks, you have an attitude problem. You think you're good. You were, in high school, but this isn't high school. You're either going to play our way and change your attitude or you're gone."

Thumper knew Stecker had something strong inside of him that made him compete against the Indian. It was that something that separated some men from others—something that was worth saving.

Thumper turned around to try. "Do you know how to use 'resection' when you're trying to find your location on a map? How about the bursting radius of a Mark-82? Okay, an easy one. What is a salute report message?"

Stecker mumbled a "Screw you" and sat down on his bunk.

Thumper stepped closer, pointing his finger at the redhead's face. "No, *Mister Experience*, I'm not letting you off so easy. Answer the questions. Do you know *any* of them?"

Stecker shook his head with disgust. "Games, man. You're playin' games and it don't mean nothin'."

"It isn't games! You can't answer simple questions that any Ranger could. You can't navigate in the jungle without reading a map, and resection is used to pinpoint your exact location by using a compass. You can't call in air support if you don't know where you are, and you sure as hell can't drop bombs, Mark-82s, unless you know their bursting radius, or they'll splatter you or the team. You spot some dinks but you can't tell higher headquarters over the radio because you don't know how to use the salute report format. S-a-l-u-t-e—size, activity, location, unit, time, and equipment.

"Woodpecker, you may be good in the field, but you aren't a Ranger. You gotta know everything I just told you and a helluva lot more. Tracking, advanced first aid, artillery, and gunship fire adjustment, enemy weapons and uniforms, radio codes, ambush techniques . . . shit, I could go on, but I think you get the idea."

Stecker's intense gaze met Thumper's. "And runnin'? What the hell does that teach?"

"It tells us who really wants to be here and who doesn't. It tells us who's weak and who'd flake out of a mission. You saw the ones that fell out today. Would you want them on your team?"

Stecker lowered his head. "No. But why you-all gotta be such assholes? There's other ways to get your point across."

"Charlie is an even bigger asshole, and he gets his point across with an AK-47. We don't have time to be nice guys and convince you this training is necessary. You either accept it or you don't."

Stecker sat silent for a moment, pondering Thumper's words. At last he said, "You reckon you could at least call me Stecker instead of Woodpecker? My buddies in my old unit called me 'Woody.'"

"Sure, maggot, I could, but I won't. Woodpecker is to remind you you're in *this* unit . . . . Now, what's it gonna be? You wanna be 'Woody' in a leg unit or 'Woodpecker' with us?"

Stecker stood up and sighed. "I guess Woodpecker ain't that bad." He held out his hand. "Thanks."

Thumper ignored the gesture and walked for the door. "Don't thank me. You haven't made it yet . . . maggot."

Woodpecker snickered. "I will . . . and I'm beatin' that ragbag, too."

Unseen by the redhead was Thumper's smile as he said to himself, "Thanks, coach," and headed for his hootch.

Highway 1

Matt Wade sat outside, leaning against the bamboo frame of the hootch and holding the .38 on his lap. The old couple and the boy were sleeping behind the rest station store in their thatch-covered hut.

Wade took in a deep breath of the cool night air and quietly got to his feet. He walked into the hut, knelt by the sleeping woman, and nudged her gently. She didn't stir. Wade poked her harder and put his hand over her mouth, whispering, "Be quiet and get up."

Her eyes opened wide and she sprang up.

"Shhh! Get your stuff and follow me."

"Why?" she whispered.

"We're moving to another place to sleep in case the dinks come sneakin' around."

She quickly balled up her poncho liner and followed him. Wade walked for several hundred meters to a slight rise and spread out his poncho.

"We'll sleep here and go back when it gets light."

Wade laid down and put the .38 by his head. The woman laid down beside him and spread the poncho over them both. Wade looked up at the stars for a moment, then shut his eyes.

"Wade?"

"Yeah?"

"Eh . . . I . . . well, I just wanted to thank you for taking care of me. I know I seemed bitchy at times, but I just didn't know what to do. . . . I know you acted mean to make me angry so I'd forget what happened but . . . but, well, you got me through it and I appreciate it. If I can do something . . . Wade? . . . Wade? . . . *Wade?*"

"Huh . . . what?"

"Did you hear anything I just said?"

"Huh?"

"Go back to sleep. I just said 'thank you.'"

The sergeant turned his back to her and sighed tiredly. "No sweat."

For several minutes she lay in silence, listening to his breathing and trying to understand why he bothered her so. It had to be the way he looked at her. His eyes never seemed to see her as a woman, only as a burden. The first time she looked into those eyes in the mess hall, they seemed to be absorbing rather than seeing her. It was like he was reading her life's history in a book. Later, when he sat down, she'd caught him staring again, but then his look was strange and distant. From that moment on, he'd never looked at her in any other way.

Virginia snuggled closer to him, putting her arm over his waist. "No sweat" was all he'd given her in return for her gratitude, but she needed more—even if she couldn't understand why. Well, tomorrow was another day.

8

7 SEPTEMBER

Thanh Van Vuong stirred the embers of the small fire and pushed the blackened pot closer to the coals.

Pham Do Kinh rose from his hammock and squatted down by the fire. "Do we have enough to buy the ducks?"

Vuong glanced at the two large stacks of cinnamon next to his hammock. "One more tree should give us a full load and more than enough money."

Kinh smiled and leaned over to check the simmering rice. "Your grandfather was right. There are many cinnamon trees in the valley. We will have to give him some duck eggs for his wisdom—once we buy the ducks."

Before Vuong could reply, he heard a noise and looked up. He dropped his chopsticks and froze as three North Vietnamese soldiers approached with their weapons pointed at him and Kinh.

Sergeant Van looked about the camp and stepped in front of Vuong. "Why are you here?"

The squatting men exchanged nervous glances. Vuong looked at the rifle barrel pointing at his head, then up to the sergeant, and stammered. "We . . . we are collecting cinnamon. The valley has many trees and we are collecting some to sell and buy ducks for our farms."

The sergeant raised his brow, unconvinced. "What village did you come from?" he snapped. "How long have you been in the valley?"

Vuong gulped several times to control his shaking. "We came from Hien Thien, twelve kilometers to the east. My grandfather told us of this valley and the cinnamon trees he had seen here many years ago when he was a boy. We walked here. . . . Have we done something wrong? We are . . . "

"Who sent you here?" barked the sergeant, shoving the barrel of his AK-47 into Vuong's Adam's apple.

Vuong eye's widened, and he felt his bowels loosen. He tried to speak but words wouldn't come. Swallowing the last of his saliva, he tried to talk again. "Naaa . . . no one sent us. We are just farmers trying to make money for . . . "

Sergeant Van began shaking his head side to side and lowered the rifle barrel. "You lie. You are spies sent by the puppets."

"We are farmers! We only . . . "

Sergeant Van fired a single shot into the intruder's head. Vuong fell back into the fire and flopped on the coals as blood spurted from the hole in the side of his head and smoked around the puncture. Van casually lowered the barrel to the squirming body and fired another bullet into the farmer's skull. Vuong's head jerked with the impact and his body ceased to move.

The sergeant raised the rifle and pointed it at the other man, who was crying and holding his open hands out to him. "No, no, we are just farmers. In the name of Buddha, believe me!"

Van raised his weapon and motioned to the newly assigned private. "Nuu, come here."

Nguyen Nuu was standing open-mouthed, still in shock at what he'd just seen. He felt sick and weak inside as he stared at the body smoldering in the fire.

"Private Nuu, come here!"

As Nuu boke from his trance and stepped forward, the smell of burning human flesh overwhelmed him.

Vann took the RPG-7 from Nuu's hands and gave him his AK. "Kill him. They came too far into the valley and have seen the small rice and sweet potato fields. He will talk of what he has seen.''

Kinh fell at Nuu's feet and grabbed his legs. "Please don't kill me . . . please believe me. I have done nothing.''

Nuu looked desperately at his sergeant. "He is just a farmer.''

Vann's eyes were cold. "He is a threat. Kill him.''

Kinh sobbed and looked up at Nuu pleadingly. "Be . . . believe me!''

Nuu looked at the man, who couldn't have been a few years older than himself, He shut his eyes, praying for forgiveness, and pulled the trigger to end the man's pleading. Kinh screamed from the impact of the bullet that tore through his spleen. He rolled on the ground shrieking like a crazed animal, trying to reach the burning wound.

Nuu gagged and quickly lowered the recoiled weapon to put him out of his misery. He stepped closer, putting the barrel on the man's head, and fired. Blood and brain tissue splattered his new uniform as the bullet blew out the back of the farmer's skull and covered the ground with gore.

Van took his rifle and patted Nuu's back. "You did your duty." He looked at the other private and motioned toward the bodies. "Bury them.''

Senior Colonel Chinh stood in front of a large wall map and pointed at a group of blue pins positioned west of An Khe. "Reports indicate the puppets have not set up programs in these villages. They protect only the road to the east. Do we have teams available to bring these hamlets into the liberated zone?''

One of the colonels sitting at the large table nodded as he looked at a map he held in his hand. "Yes, comrade, I have a team in Binh Dinh province. They could be contacted immediately and ordered to the hamlets to begin the project. It is the Thach San team and they are always successful.''

Colonel Chinh tapped the map with his bamboo pointer. "Send the order. We must have another twenty villages within our liberated zone by the time the general meets with the committee. We must show substantial progress or the representative for Political Indoctrination and Expansion will cry for more support. His contacts within the party are powerful and pressure will be brought to bear to increase military support. I do not need to tell you the consequences of such actions. Our force is bled dry as it is. We cannot detail fighting men to civilians who are inept. We must keep control and not let the politicians influence our strategy. I want you all to look at your districts and give me suggestions on which hamlets we could claim or regain using our own assets."

Chinh walked to his chair and gave a quick wink to Major Sy, who had provided him the information about the expansion member who was voicing discontent toward the general's slow and deliberate village expansion program.

Sy left the briefing room. He had three more committee members yet to check and he wanted to see if Private Nuu had received his new RPG-7.

An Khe
Ranger Base Camp

Lieutenant J. D. Gibson didn't feel like eating after the morning's grueling three-mile run, but he didn't dare show he had a queasy stomach. He took a bite of runny scrambled eggs. At the other end of the long table, Brad Avant took a bite of toast, chewing slowly to keep from throwing up.

The run had taken its toll. Ten men fell out from Avant's ragbags, but only six had quit from the replacement 173rd maggots. The formation of maggots hooted and hollered when both lieutenants had to report their losses to Sergeant Childs after the run. As they had the day before, the maggots and the ragbags remained separated in the mess hall. Even the Ranger cadre was split. Childs had divided the instructors and trainers, assigning them to each of the groups. They, too, had come under the spell of the competition.

First Sergeant Demand stood in his usual position by

the chow line, bellowing like a drill instructor. "Moove out, troop-ars. We got eggs, bacon, grits, toast, oatmeal, Post Toasties, and cold milk. *Eat First Sergeant's* good Army chow and move out!"

Lieutenant Avant gagged at the word "oatmeal" and picked up his tray. Gibson quickly followed the officer through the mess hall door.

Outside, Avant took a deep breath and spun around. "Damn you, J.D.! What the hell ya git me into? I'm supposed to be the crazy one, remember? And you up and volunteer us to be shitbirds. Cousin, I almost died runnin' up and down my formation this mornin' tryin' ta keep my boys from fallin' out."

Gibson shrugged his shoulders. "Hell, Brad, ya wanna be John Wayne you gotta lead by example. Your ragbags are wimps. I can't help that."

Avant broke into his silly grin. "You're trying to piss me off, ain't cha, cousin? You really think your boys gonna show mine somethin'? Well, I got news. Your boys are pissin' in the wind. Tell you what. I bet my Indian is gonna whip your redhead in the run this afternoon."

Gibson shook his head, "Childs wouldn't let 'em race this morning, so what makes you think he'll let 'em this afternoon?"

Avant threw his arm over Gibson's shoulder. "I got my sources, cousin. Just put up or shut up."

Gibson thought for a few seconds. "Your Indian won last time, so he's already proven himself. Let's see . . . that makes the odds two to one. I got ten bucks to your twenty says you're full of shit and my man wins."

Avant patted Gibson's shoulder. "Cousin, you got yo'-self a deal."

Lieutenant Dickey sat outside Major Shane's office, waiting for him to return from breakfast. Dickey felt confident that the paperwork he held in his hands would impress the major. The statements and fact sheets clearly demonstrated insubordination on the part of Sergeant First Class Gino and Sergeant Wade while in Phan Thiet. Their gross misconduct had set a dangerous precedent within the platoon and had undermined his authority as commander.

He had also written a paper pointing out the lack of discipline of two officers in Shane's command, namely Avant and Gibson, whose continued disregard for the "Code of the Officer" was appalling. Well, someone had to stand firm on the principles and customs of the Army. Dickey knew he was doing the right thing by bringing these matters to the commander's attention. Shane would see he was right and help him in the quest to reverse the undisciplinary trend.

When Shane walked through the front door, he took off his beret and immediately strode toward his office.

Dickey stood at attention as he passed. "Sir, I request to see you."

Shane kept walking. "Sure, come in."

Dickey marched in and executed a salute as Shane sat down behind his desk. Shane casually tossed a salute back and motioned to a nearby chair. "What cha' got?"

Dickey handed the papers to Shane and sat down. "Sir, I wanted to make you aware of some problems I've encountered."

Shane set the papers down and began reading. A few minutes later he looked up abruptly toward the door.

Dickey felt a wave of euphoria, knowing Shane was about to call for the first sergeant to bring Gino and the others.

"Hey Pete, bring me a cup of coffee, will ya?"

Dickey turned ashen white as Shane put his feet up on the desk and motioned toward the papers. "What is this bullshit?"

Dickey stammered, "Sir, I . . . I thought you . . . "

"Dickey, what the hell is your problem? You act like a damn prima donna. You give orders like a general instead of a lieutenant. Son, you gotta lead your men, not order them. This bullshit you gave me is a good example. You're stomping on piss ants and can't hear the elephants about to run over you. I know what you're saying the problem is, but you're wrong. *You* are the problem. You gotta get involved with your men and learn their strengths and weaknesses. This is a Ranger unit, where our men work independently as teams. They're a different breed and need a different kind of leadership. You understand all that?''

Dickey nodded. By now he wanted only to be done with the session and to get out of the office. It was clear the major was not only a part of the dicipline problem here, he was a major cause of it.

Shane swung his legs down from the desk and gathered the papers into a stack. ''Young man, you're smart and could be a helluva fine officer if you'd watch and learn from officers like Avant and Gibson. Learn from them quick and show me something, or I'm afraid you won't make it in my unit. I don't need toy soldiers. I need combat leaders.''

Shane held the papers out to Dickey, who immediately stood, saluted, took the paperwork, and marched from the office without speaking.

Shane shook his head and yelled, ''Pete, where's my coff . . . ''

''Right here, sir,'' said Peteroski, walking in the door.

Highway 1
Twenty-one miles west of Phan Thiet

Wade and Virginia sat in the back of a partially-filled deuce-and-a-half truck heading for Phan Thiet. They'd been picked up by a convoy ten minutes before. Wade sat looking out at the scenery as Virginia stared at him. The sergeant finally couldn't take it any longer. ''Okay, what is it? Why you lookin' at me that way?''

''Can't take it, huh?''

Wade shifted his shoulders so as not to see her. ''Never mind.''

''Turn around, Wade, I want to talk to you.''

''Forget it.''

''Alright, I'm sorry for staring . . . and I'm sorry for being bitchy. Turn around. Please?''

Wade sighed and shifted back, but avoided looking at her.

"What is your Christian name?" she asked evenly.

"Matthew, but I go by Matt."

"Where are you from?"

"Oklahoma."

"Why did you stare at me in the mess hall when we first met?"

Wade looked into her searching eyes to see if she was mocking him. Her look was serious. "You . . . well, you reminded me of somebody. I'm sorry if I made you feel uncomfortable."

"Did you love her?"

"Jesus, lady!" Wade shifted around again. "What business is it of yours? Just leave me alone. Damn, I said I was sorry."

"You did love her, I can tell. Look Matt, I've slept with you two nights and saw you buck-naked. You saved my life, and we don't even know each other. Don't you think we could at least talk?"

Wade sighed. He didn't want to admit it, but the small woman had gotten to him. She'd bitched and complained but always did what he said and tried her best. She was strong and filled with such fiery determination that he couldn't help but like her. Of course, her natural beauty couldn't be hidden by the sweat and grime, but it was her eyes that were too much for him and what he tried to avoid. Those large brown eyes made him feel so powerless that he knew he'd weaken and say something he'd regret. They were traps that had probably broken countless hearts already. He didn't want his to be the next one. He knew he'd been hard on her and gruff when he didn't need to be, but if he'd been otherwise, he would have fallen victim to her, and he'd been burned by one woman already.

Wade turned around slowly but still avoided looking at her. "Whaddaya wanna talk about?"

Virginia smiled and leaned back against the sideboards, looking at him. She had won the first battle. "I'm going to be honest with you. I've never met a man like you before." She grinned. "Of course, I've never been saved before, either."

Wade shook his head, unsure if this was a compliment or the start of a drawn out "thank you." "Lady, I'm an Okie. People say all Okies are different, so don't think nothin' of it."

Virginia ignored the remark and asked what was really on her mind. "Matt, did you ever have any girl friends? I mean friends, not lovers."

Matt looked skyward. "Yeah, I had a coon dog named Sally. She was as good a friend a man could . . . "

Virginia laughed and playfully hit his arm. "You know what I mean."

Wade smiled and shrugged his broad shoulders. "I guess not. I didn't have sisters, or any girls that lived nearby. When I got big enough to notice the difference I was put back a few grades in school, and everyone thought I was a dummy. I had a girl friend in high school, but she wasn't a *friend*-friend. To tell you the truth, I just wanted in her pants to find out if the big boys' stories about sex were true."

"Were they?" asked Virginia coyly.

Wade smiled, embarrassed. "Nope. The first time I was scared, she was scared, and it was a disaster."

Virginia laughed and scooted closer to him. She liked his smile. At least it seemed genuine.

"In college I met a girl who looked a bit like you. She was a good friend but not a *friend*-friend either. She was special. But things changed."

Virginia noticed the light fading from his eyes. "It didn't work out, huh?"

"Naw, she could do a lot better than me. I don't blame her. I just wish it could have been different, that's all. You know what I mean?"

Wade broke his self-imposed rule and looked into her eyes for the answer. She didn't have to speak. Her eyes spoke for her. He tried to break their hold by forcing a smile, but they only grew larger, increasing their power over him.

Virginia wished she could meet the woman that had hurt him so badly, and wring her neck. He was looking at her,

Virginia, as she knew he'd once looked at the other woman. He was looking for understanding. Virginia reached out and took his hand. "I wish some things in my past could have been different, too."

She lowered her eyes, and then told him about a young girl's struggle for success—the good and the bad, and how, eventually, she'd met Walter and they'd shared a dream of making it to the top. Wade found himself with his arm around her as she recalled the bad times and wished somehow he could take the painful memories away. But he also laughed with her, feeling her joy as well as her pain. Sharing together somehow felt comforting to them. They had unashamedly opened their souls to each other about their feelings, and they had found understanding.

Virginia laughed and raised her hands as if holding a camera. "Click! There. Now I have one of your little mental pictures, like you just told me you took of me."

Wade lifted his chin and turned his head slightly. "I shoulda never told you about that. You were out of focus. Anyway, this is my best side."

Virginia grinned. "Huh-uh. I saw your best side at the river, remember?"

Wade lowered his head in embarrassment. "Hell, Ginny, I don't even remember takin' my drawers off."

"You were so mad at me you probably don't even remember you almost drowned."

"I did not! I bounced off the bottom like they taught us in water survival class."

"So that was it. You bounced."

"Yeah, I was bouncing just like you did when those leeches took a liking to you."

"And I suppose you got some of those little mental pictures of me then, too?"

"You bet I did!"

"Damn you, Wade."

The sergeant quickly raised his hands. "Click! There. I got the real you. Bitchy!"

"Wade!"

He grabbed her and kissed her forehead, but just then

the truck began slowing. Wade pointed ahead. "We're here, Ginny. We made it."

Virginia stood up beside him and hugged him tightly. "God, it's ugly . . . but oh, so . . . so beautiful!"

An Khe
Ranger Base Camp

The hot afternoon sun gave no mercy. The men of the Ranger company fired their weapons through the liquid heat. The company had marched to the firing range four hours before and had broken into small groups that rotated among training stations.

Thumper studied a paper target and shook his head. "Preacher, it's easy to see why the cowboys always beat you Indians. You only hit the target once!"

The small, brown-skinned soldier shrugged his shoulders. "David only used a sling shot."

"Yeah, well, you got a sling shot? You're gonna need something to hit the target before Childs sees this. Come on, let's try it again, but how about this time, you open your eyes, huh?"

Rose watched as two of his students set up their Claymore mines in front of a line drawn in the dirt, which represented a trail. He waited until they were finished, then faced the group of twenty men at his station.

"What you dudes just seen is exactly how *not* to set up a kill zone. They directed the blast of their Claymores to blow straight across the trail—*wrong!* The only dinks they gonna kill is the dude who stands in front of them mines.

"Looky here." Rose repositioned the crescent-shaped explosives. "If you put 'em at an angle so they blow *down* the trail you can kill more dinks. Plus, when you add the other team's mines, you got yourself a cross-blowing effect, and that, dudes, *definitely* fucks up Luke the Gook's day!"

Sergeant Gino, holding an M-16 rifle, paced back and forth in front of his group of students.

"Once you blow your Claymores, you raise up and kill anybody still standin'. The thing you gotta remember is—don't shoot on automatic." He suddenly turned and fired the weapon on auto. *Burrrrrrup!*

"Now look what I gotta do." He pushed the magazine release, letting the empty magazine fall to the ground, and then quickly inserted another. "You see what happens if everybody shoots on automatic? You all have to change magazines at the same time! This, people, gives the dinks time to recover from the shock and start blastin' back! Remember—once you have the initiative, *keep it*! Only two team members shoot auto. The rest shoot in the semiautomatic mode; this ensures a steady rate of fire into the kill zone. Next thing you gotta know is . . . "

Childs had stood awhile observing behind Gino's class, then walked down the road to another class thirty meters away. The round-robin training was working better than he'd expected. The men were asking good questions and seemed attentive. It was a good day to be a soldier, he thought, as he stopped and listened to Russian explain methods of throwing hand grenades.

"Never *throw* grenade if brances are close overhead. The grenade not kill Communists . . . it kill *you*. Toss grenade like your game—softball, I think you say. Underhand. It don't hit branches this way. You must yell 'grenade' so comrades know to get down."

At 1400 hours Childs blew his whistle and gathered the company around him.

"Shitbirds, I heard some of you complaining 'cause you didn't eat noon chow. Rangers can never expect *anything*. Don't expect food, water, mail, or gettin' home in one piece. Don't *expect* nothin', and then you won't be disappointed. It's part of the mind game. You got to Charlie Mike—*continue the mission,* regardless of the odds, weather, terrain, or the enemy. You gotta Charlie Mike and drive on! Remember, shitbirds, never till the fat lady sings do you get what you *expect*!"

Phan Thiet

Sergeant Matt Wade stood by the Phan Thiet air terminal fence watching the plane that would take him to An Khe land. Behind him, with her back turned to him, was Virginia, seething. Since getting off the truck two hours before, they had been constantly busy. First they'd gone to flight operations to report the crash. There they were interviewed by a major to whom Wade showed, on a map, where he thought the wreck was and by which route they'd made it to the road. Later, two more officers repeated the whole debriefing process and had Matt and Ginny fill out reports about the deaths of the others. The officers had said the work was necessary so that notification of next-of-kin could begin. The major had made his jeep available and ordered them to the hospital for a screening. When they'd arrived, Wade found out he wasn't on the list of missing. The hospital administration had thought he was still in Bien Hoa and was holding a message that he was to report to An Khe immediately to join his Rangers. Virginia had torn into the orderly who delivered that message like a buzz saw. She demanded that Wade be given time to rest and recuperate. Wade dragged her out of the hospital to tell her that he had to go, that there was nothing that could be done. They'd arrived at the airfield only minutes before, and learned that a plane was about to land.

Wade pushed off the fence and put his arm over the angry woman's shoulder. "Will you please stop acting this way? I'd like to remember you with a smile."

Virginia spun around. "You know damn well you don't have to go. You deserve a rest!" Her angry eyes misted, and she hugged him tightly. "I . . . I wanted to be with you for awhile."

Wade walked her over to a nearby bench. "Ginny, you gotta understand something. We wouldn't be with each other anyway. I'm enlisted. I'd be placed in an observation ward till they thought I could leave. You rank as an officer and would be housed across the base in the BOQ with an armed guard at your door. I'd love to stay here if I could be with you, but the system doesn't work that way. Me

leaving makes it easier, believe me. . . . Now get your
head up and smile and let me see the Ginny I know."

Virginia raised her head, forcing a smile, and hugged
him again. "I'm going to miss you."

Wade returned an affectionate squeeze and looked into
her eyes. "You sure you wanna go on with the tour?
You're going to be all right?"

She nodded confidently. "Yes, I've got to. It was Walter's dream, and he worked hard to get me here. I'll make
it okay."

Wade smiled at her determination. "You can do anything you set your mind to. I know. I've seen ya. You take
care of yourself. I . . . I kinda got used to ya. I'm going
to miss you, and I'll damn sure never forget you."

Virginia looked sadly into his eyes. "I won't forget you
either, Matt."

Wade began to turn away, but then mumbled "Ah,
hell," and grabbed her. He kissed her passionately, then
spun around and walked to the aircraft.

Virginia wiped her tears quickly. "Wade!"

He turned. She brought her hands up. "Click!"

He smiled, shook his head, and continued walking.

Virginia watched him disappear into the tail of the plane.
"I'll always remember you, Matt. Always."

An Khe
Ranger Base Camp

Childs marched the company back at 1600 hours and let
them put up their gear before beginning their run. He ran
them only two miles before stopping the company one-half
mile away from the Ranger camp. "Shitbirds, I'm gonna
let the two men who raced yesterday do it again."

The formation of men broke out into a thunderous yell
of approval. Childs waited until their roar died down, then
put his hands on his hips.

"*But*, I don't think it's fair that *only* two men have the
opportunity for such good exercise. So, every ten seconds
one maggot and one ragbag will race to the barracks. The
group with the most wins eats first in the mess hall, *and*

only runs two miles tomorrow morning. The losers run four!''

The rumbling of moans that came from the ranks only increased Childs's pleasure.

"Major Shane and First Sergeant have already run ahead and will log the winners. L-tees, organize your people and have 'em ready. We begin in one minute!''

Gibson and Avant ran down their respective formations and pulled out those most likely to win the first runs to accumulate points.

The small Indian and thin redhead walked up to a starting line that Childs had scratched out with his foot.

"On your marks . . . get set . . . do it!''

The redhead sprinted ahead while the Indian held back, keeping a steady pace. The other men hollered and screamed as the first two runners bolted up the road, their sweat-streaked bodies glistening in the sunlight. The redhead reached the bottom of the hill twenty meters ahead of the Indian and leaned into the hill, churning up a cloud of dust. The Indian began picking up his pace and then broke into a sprint. Fifty meters from the barracks he sped past the redhead and took a commanding lead.

Major Shane couldn't help but yell encouragement to the two men as they neared the barracks, straining with all their might. The Indian slapped the wall five steps in front of the thin soldier and broke out into a loud war hoop. First Sergeant Demand calmly raised his clipboard and placed a mark under ragbags.

Fifteen minutes later the last two runners ran up the hill. They were Lieutenants Gibson and Avant. The maggots and ragbags lined the road hollering as Gibson began his sprint. The shaven-headed officer waited a few more paces to begin his. Avant caught Gibson just short of the barracks, but Gibson threw himself into a belly slide and banged into the barracks first.

The 173rd maggots went crazy in jubilation and quickly got their dazed leader to his feet, pounding his back, yelling and laughing.

A minute later, Childs mounted his platform holding the

results of the races and scanned the anxious faces. "Shitbirds, the score is ragbags—81, 173rd maggots—84. Maggots win!"

The formation of maggots turned into pandemonium as
the losers looked on in dejected silence.

Childs waited for the men to settle down, then raised
his hand. The maggots quieted immediately.

"Shitbirds, you all ran hard. I didn't see a single maggot
or ragbag give up. You put out one hundred percent and
. . . and, well, *ya done good*! Tomorrow the losers only
have to run three miles!"

Major Shane turned his back on the happy, yelling company. Their all-out effort and proud faces had gotten to
him. He had to get away or he'd do something dumb, like
show his emotions. His men had run their hearts out. They
were truly becoming a Ranger company.

As he strode for the mess hall, he thought of the young,
gray-haired lieutenant, J. D. Gibson, who had wanted to
achieve credibility with his men. He'd gotten it the moment
they saw their leader straining to run up the hill, and he'd
gotten much more. He and every other man who ran had
earned each other's respect.

Shane pulled open the mess hall door and looked back
at his company one more time. They still had a long way
to go, but today he had a company of men he felt privileged
to lead. They were winners.

After Lieutenant Avant handed J. D. Gibson his hand-
kerchief, he kept his palm out. "You owe me five dollars,
cousin."

"Bullshit. We're even. I beat you."

"That wasn't the bet. The Indian won, so pay up."

"Brad, I'm bleedin' to death and all you care about is
money!"

"I want my money before you die, maggot. Jesus, that
was dumb, slidin' in like that. It's a wonder you didn't
break your neck."

"I won, didn't I?"

"This time, cousin—this time."

The two officers entered the mess and sat down at the officer/senior NCO table. Shane and the other officers were already half finished eating. Shane was telling Lieutenant Foley about the run. "And the Indian boy touched first. . . he yelled out a war hoop that woulda made Crazy Horse blush with envy. Lieutenant Dickey, what's that Indian's name, anyway?"

Dickey looked up, surprised to be brought into the conversation. "Sir?"

"The Indian lad that won. What's his name?"

Dickey's face turned white. "Uh, well, sir . . . he was only in Phan Thiet for two weeks and I . . . "

"You don't know his name?" growled Shane coldly.

"Sir, I didn't have time to . . . "

"Don't give me excuses!" Shane stood up quickly and pointed to two soldiers wearing cammies who, he knew, were in the Third Platoon. "What are those soldiers' names?"

Dickey looked at the two men, then back at the major as if snake-bitten. "Sir, I don't know, but I . . . "

Shane cut him off by throwing down his napkin. "That's it. *First Sergeant!*"

Sergeant Demand marched quickly to the table. "Yes, sir."

Shane pointed to Dickey. "Have this officer out of my company by nightfall!"

"Yes, sir."

Dickey's face flushed, and he stood up, glaring at the major. "Sir, I protest this humiliating treatment in front of subordinates. To be relieved of my duties because of not recalling names is ridiculous and beyond comprehension. It is most certainly based on improper grounds."

Shane's eyebrows shot up. "Lieutenant, you're relieved exactly because *it is* beyond your comprehension. You may appeal in writing to the next higher headquarters, as I'm sure you will, but do it when you're out of my area. Now if you would be so kind, *get out of my sight!*"

Dickey gave Shane a look of disdain and then strode to the mess hall door, with First Sergeant Demand at his heels. Shane took a deep breath to control his anger and looked at Avant. "Now, what is that Indian kid's name?"

"Black Eagle, sir. He's a Sioux from North Dakota and says he was an all-state miler from Wilson Indian School."

Shane picked up his fork and broke into a smile. "That kid sure can run, can't he?"

Thumper, Rose, and Russian sat in the mess hall eating when a familiar voice growled, "Move over Three-one."

All of them immediately rose with a smile as their sergeant approached with a tray.

"Matt! About time!"

Wade hadn't realized how badly he missed his men until he felt their backslaps and handshakes. Rose looked him over as he sat down. "Man, you look like shit! Didn't them REMFs feed you?"

Wade told them the whole story and leaned back. "So, you're lucky I'm here at all. I ain't never gittin' on another medevac, that's for sure!"

Rose pounded the table. "Man, a roundeyed singer, no less! Damn, I wish it'd been me!"

Thumper had noted Wade's distant gaze as he talked about the woman. He obviously wasn't telling the entire story. Russian patted his sergeant's back. "The past is forgotten, my Sergeant. You were lucky and we are thankful."

Rose poked Russian. "Man, he didn't bang her! What you talkin' about, thankful? If I'd been there, she wouldn . . . "

Russian grabbed Rose's neck, partially lifting him from the chair. "You talk too much, crazy one."

Wade laughed. Russian and Rose would never change. Just then, First Sergeant Demand walked in and took up his usual position. "Thump," Wade said, "did Top give his usual speeches?"

Thumper raised his finger in the air, imitating Demand. "Troop-ars, cleanliness is next to Godliness and yo first sergeant is next to God. Troop-ars, wash your nasty bodies twice a day and stay away from the painted ladies of An Khe.''

Wade laughed and leaned back in his chair. ''He's given the same pitch to us twenty times. He's gotta get some new material.''

Wade noticed Rose eyeing the young girls working behind the serving line, as was his custom. ''Rose, you'd better quit leering at those dink KPs like you do. If Top sees ya lookin' at his girls, he'll bust your head for thinkin' dirty thoughts.''

Rose leaned farther back in his chair to get a better look at the girls who were giggling at him. ''Man, the tall one digs me. I can tell she wants the Rose, baaaaad!''

Thumper patted Rose's back. ''Remember the last time we were here and you messed with one of the KPs?''

''Aw, Thump, why'd ya bring that up? Shit, man, that chick didn't know what she was doin', man.''

Wade grinned, ''Rose, as I remember it, she knew *exactly* what she was doin'. How much she steal from you anyway?''

Rose dropped his head. ''Man, the chick just wanted a little souvenir of a good time, that's all.''

Russian pointed an accusing finger. ''She take your money, watch, ring, and camera.''

Rose shrugged his shoulders. ''Hey dudes, lighten up, will ya? It was a lousy camera anyway.''

Sergeant Wade lay back on his bunk, staring at the ceiling, when Thumper walked into the room and pulled up a chair.

''You okay, Matt?''

''Sure, no sweat.''

''You look beat. I thought you'd be asleep.''

''Naw, I'm still on an adrenalin high. The last couple of days have finally caught up with me. Just trying to sort things out.''

''Take it easy for awhile, Matt. You don't start your block of training for two days. Rest up and get your strength back.''

"I'll be okay tomorrow. It just kinda got to me all at once."

"What was she like?" asked Thumper. He suspected it was more than the chopper crash keeping his friend awake.

The sergeant kept his gaze on the ceiling. "Ginny was alright. She was tough, but pretty as a picture. And she had these eyes you could swim in and . . . " He caught himself and looked at Thumper, who stared at him as if he already knew. "Look, Thump, I liked her. Nothing happened, she just kinda got to me toward the end. It wasn't a big thing."

"Hey Matt, I understand, believe me. It's just that it's obvious it *was* a big thing. At least, she's kept you awake when you oughtta be sackin' it. Are you gonna try and keep in contact with her?"

"Naw, she wouldn't even know who the hell I was if I wrote."

"Come on, Sarge. You don't believe that."

Wade looked back at the ceiling. "It doesn't make any difference anyway. She's on tour and I wouldn't know how to get in touch. It just makes me feel better knowing there's girls out there like her, you know?"

Thumper lowered his head, thinking of the Red Cross girl he'd loved.

"Yeah, I know."

They both sat in silence for a moment, then Thumper stood and walked for the door. "Matt, we're gonna meet some others like them when this is over. We know how it can be, and we'll make it happen again."

Wade looked up at his close friend and smiled faintly. "Yeah, one day, Thumper. Thanks."

Wade lay his head back, feeling very tired, and closed his eyes. He hoped it really would happen. For now, he only had a picture. A picture that slowly faded as sleep finally overcame him.

Virginia Wolinski rolled over in bed, unable to sleep. Her thoughts were on the man who had held her for two nights, protected and secure against the jungle. The heat of his kiss still burned her lips and made her think about how he'd looked at her when he stepped away and stared into her eyes. From that look she had realized at once that he didn't want to leave her, and that had made her feel content.

Very soon, now, she would be seeing him again. She hadn't dreamed it possible when he'd left, but she'd just walked out the terminal door when an Aviation commander drove up. He wanted to see her about filling out some "special" paperwork. The paperwork gave her an idea that turned into her ticket to see Matt Wade once more. She closed her eyes and a brief smile played across her lips as she thought of his kiss once more.

9

11 SEPTEMBER

An Khe

Beads of sweat trickled down Thumper's camouflaged face as he stopped in mid-step and slowly turned to his sergeant. He pointed ahead, balled his hand into a loose fist, and grinned. Wade returned a single nod and ran a finger across his throat.

Thumper winked in acknowledgment and raised his weapon to the ready position. Slowly turning, he crouched and began to creep forward again.

Wade followed carefully a few paces behind. He still had not seen the enemy, but he knew his friend's skills were unquestionable.

The big Ranger stopped again and rose up slowly. "*Bang*! Shitbirds—you're dead! Everybody freeze in your positions. Don't touch your weapons and don't move a muscle until we inspect you."

Six surprised and upset students lay hidden in ambush position just off a trail. Thumper and Wade had sneaked up on them from behind and caught them all facing the trail with no rear security.

Thumper shook his head and walked toward the trail to check their Claymore dispositions as Wade inspected their equipment and individual positions.

Wade had been back three days and was fully rested. He'd become deeply involved in the training program in an effort to forget about the woman. With his busy schedule, he'd been successful.

Wade inspected the first two men, then picked up the third soldier's M-16 and sighed as he pointed the barrel at the man's face. "Tell me what your weapon selector switch is on."

The wide-eyed student stammered, "I . . . I don't know, Ranger Sergeant."

Wade pressed the barrel into the cringing man's forehead. "In that case this weapon has a mind of its own. And right now it wants to blow your brains out for being stupid. A weapon kills dinks and it can kill you or your friends unless *you* control it." Wade tossed the weapon down at the soldier's side. "Did you just learn something?"

"Yes, Ranger Sergeant, keep my weapon on safe until I've got a target."

Minutes later, the six students sat on the trail as Thumper critiqued their ambush. "You did a good job of setting up the Claymores and hiding yourselves but you failed to designate a rear security team. Based on terrain, sometimes you don't need to, but in this case you had a trail forty meters behind you. I smelled you first. Which one of you uses "Old Spice" after-shave?"

One of the students frowned and raised his hand. Thumper motioned his hand down. "Rule! You never wear after-shave or freshly washed fatigues, and you never smoke, take a shit, or eat C rations in ambush position. Dinks have been in the bush a long time, and the slightest trace of a different smell tells 'em you're there."

Wade sat behind the students, listening. There was no one better than Thumper for teaching them. He was a natural-born Ranger. He had a gift, a sixth sense for feeling when something or someone was there.

Wade knew he was lucky. He had that sense, too, and so did Russian and Rose. It was one of the reasons that together they made the best team and were all still alive.

When Thumper finished his critique, he looked over at Wade. "You want to add anything, Matt?"

Wade got to his feet, "Yeah. You-all didn't do too bad.

You were found by the best tracker in the company, Specialist Meeks, here. Don't feel bad about it; learn by it. If you got questions, ask. Tonight you've got some training that is super-important. Don't let your brain vapor-lock just because you can't see in the dark. Remember what we've been teaching you.''

Lieutenants Gibson and Avant were leaning up against a tree at the mouth of the thickly vegetated valley by the Mini Ranger School. They were waiting their turn to walk "Death Valley." The Ranger cadre, hidden in the valley, was waiting to ambush them as they walked down a designated trail. The training was designed to teach point-man skills and to tune their senses. If they saw the cadre first, they wouldn't be killed. Twenty men had entered so far and by the sound of the blank ammunition popping, none had fared too well.

Gibson picked a stalk of grass and put it in his mouth. "You know, Brad, I thought I was pretty good in the field, but this training has really been good for me. I thought since I'd been to Ranger School this would have been a snap, but it isn't. This morning we set up a perfect ambush and I'll be damn if Specialist Meeks didn't make us. Said he heard one of us moving around."

Avant stretched his legs out. "Don't feel bad, cousin. Ol' Brad got his ambush all set up and one of my guys farted so loud the whole base camp knew where we was at.''

Gibson spit out the grass stalk in laughter. "Really?"

Avant raised up and stared at his companion. "Well, I'll be damned. You can laugh. After all this time you finally did it. This training must be gettin' to ya, boy."

Gibson smiled. "No, the training hasn't, but you have."

Avant leaned back against the tree. "J.D., I know you told me you wanted to be a career officer and all, but why you doin' all this? The liaison job would have been good for your career."

"I like a challenge, Brad. That job wouldn't have been."

"Yeah, and it wouldn't have got you killed, either. This

Ranger shit will put your ass in a body bag back to Texas.
What really drives your train?''

Gibson was silent for a moment, trying to put feelings
into words. "I guess it's trying to be the best. I gotta know
I'm one of the good ones. We've seen the shitty officers
that issue orders by a book instead of experience. I want
to be a leader men can have confidence in."

"So there was never any doubt that you wanted to be
an officer?''

"No. I knew when I was just a kid and saw my Dad
marching his company down a road singing cadences, all
in perfect step. It sent chills up my back. I remember I
wanted so bad to be with them. There was never a doubt
after that. I knew what I wanted. . . . How 'bout you,
Brad? Did you always wanna be one?''

Avant lowered his head. "Cousin, you're lookin' at who
I thought was gonna be the next Clarence Darrow. I went
to North Georgia because my daddy thought I needed the
discipline. I got a reserve commission when I graduated
because it'd look good in my profession. I was gonna be
a big lawyer like my daddy and one day run for office.''

Gibson sat up. "What happened?''

Avant smiled reflectively. "I fell in love with a wonderful girl who happened to be my daddy's secretary. I
went to her place one night to surprise her. I surprised her
alright, her and my old man. It was a pretty ugly scene.
Come to find out ol' daddy was payin' for the apartment,
car, and her. I couldn't look at mom anymore, knowing
what it'd do to her if she found out, so I did the decent
thing and left. The Army seemed a nice place to work
things out for awhile. I'll go back to law school someplace
else after I get out. Like Childs says, it ain't over till the
fat lady sings.''

"You went to Ranger School and Airborne school—you
didn't have to do that just to work things out in your head.''

Avant resumed his silly grin. "Cousin, I gotta be the
best, too. Damn, boy, I couldn't let some nasty Texas career officer be the only leader in the Army. Ol' Brad has

gotta be *numero uno*. And he gonna prove it in Death Valley."

Gibson put out his hand with a sly grin. "Five bucks says I make it through and you don't. I think you lawyers say 'put up or shut up.'"

Avant took his hand. "Boy, John Wayne will be proud of me today."

An hour later Gibson sat at the other end of the valley in sweat-soaked fatigues. He'd completed the walk, having been "killed" twice. He saw Avant emerge from the vegetation wearing a grin, and knew he'd lost.

The officer walked up and put out his hand. "Pay up, cousin."

Gibson was about to reach into his pocket but suddenly looked up. "Wait a minute. How'd ya know I was killed?

"Sergeant Zubeck told me."

"Zubeck wouldn't have talked to you unless he killed you."

"He zapped my ass good. So did Selando. But you still owe me, cousin."

"No way! The bet was . . . "

"The bet was, *you'd* make it through, and I wouldn't. Well, cousin, I didn't make it through, but that's irrelevant. The bet was if *you* made it through, and *you* didn't. Case closed. Pay the lawyer."

Gibson got up slowly, looking as if he was going for his pocket, but instead he jumped out, grabbed Avant's head, and wrestled him to the ground. The two tired and sweat-soaked men fought for only seconds before both started laughing.

At dusk, Sergeant First Class Childs gathered the company around him and had the men sit down. "Shitbirds, you just completed your classes on smells. You now know the enemy ain't superman or any better than you. He eats different than we do, so he smells different. His shit smells different and the food he cooks smells different. When he's in the bush, he don't know you're there so he acts slack. You can usually smell him first or see his tracks or signs.

So far, you've been using sight and smell to find him. Tonight you're going to learn to hear him."

Childs paced back and forth with his hands on his hips, looking into the young faces staring back at him. He pointed toward the valley. "Tonight's class is called the 'the night of horror.' In a little while, you'll see why. I'm going to break you down in small groups, and you'll spread out. You'll have one cadre Ranger with each group, and he'll explain what you're hearing. You'll be out all night, then road-march fifteen miles tomorrow. Everybody *must* make the march or you're out. You haven't eaten today and tonight you won't sleep. Tomorrow we find out who is a Ranger and who isn't. Does anybody want to quit now and go to the mess hall and eat? I understand they're having steak and French fries."

One soldier stood up. Childs ignored him and kept talking. "And for dessert they got ice cream on top of strawberry shortcake."

Another man stood, then another. Childs glanced around for more and threw his shoulders back. "Everybody shut your eyes and don't open 'em. Shitbirds, this is your last chance. Nobody will see ya. Just get up and move out of the ranks to the back. If there's a doubt in your mind that you might not have it and can't live and stay in the jungle with only six men, this is your chance. Remember, shitbirds, today is the easy day. Tomorrow will be agony, and it ain't gonna get any better."

Seven men got up and joined the others in the back. Childs smiled to himself. He'd bet Major Shane at least eight would be affected by lack of food, even for a day. A man's stomach would always overrule the brain if he let it.

"Open your eyes, shitbirds! It's show time!"

At midnight, Thumper whispered to his group of ten to gather close around him. "Okay, what were the last sounds we heard, Black Eagle?"

"One man walking down the trail going east to west."

"Good. How do you know he was on trail, Woodpecker?"

"There was no noise of branches or vegetation being disturbed."

"Good. Johnson, was he lookin' for us?"

"Don't think so. He was movin' too quick to be huntin'."

"Right. Shepard, was he wearing boots or Ho Chi sandals? Shepard? Shepard? Somebody wake that son of a bitch and tell him he's out!"

12 SEPTEMBER

Childs looked at his watch and raised his whistle to his mouth. *Sweeeeeeeeeeeeee!* It was 0700 hours and time for the road march. The company walked out of the valley like zombies. He'd made sure they hadn't slept by throwing artillery simulators all through the night.

"Move it, shitbirds! You're on my time! Cadre, make sure they're all carrying at least sixty pounds in their rucks. If not, use rocks. Hey, shitbirds, anyone wanna quit?"

Childs halted the company at the twelfth mile of the march. *"Five minute break."*

Toward the rear of the strung-out company formation the small Indian, Black Eagle, fell back on his rucksack, exhausted. He shut his eyes, knowing he wouldn't be able to get up and complete the last three miles. He was finished. The past six days of constant running and marching with a heavy pack and little food or sleep had broken him. He was too tired and sore even to get out of his pack or check his feet. It was over. He had let down his savior and himself. When Childs blew the whistle, he would be out.

"You gonna make it, Preacher?"

Black Eagle opened his eyes slowly. The sweat-soaked man standing over him was leering at him with a cruel grin. It was the tall redhead. Black Eagle lowered his eyes in silence.

"I never thought you'd make it this far. You ain't got it."

Tears trickled down the Indian's face, and he said nothing. Childs blew his whistle and bellowed. "Saddle up and *move out!*"

Woodpecker chuckled coldly. "This is it, Indian. The white men done whipped your ass again, huh?"

Black Eagle forced his head up. "Go with God, my friend."

"I ain't your friend! Get up or you're out. This is the last march!"

The Indian dropped his head to his chest in silence.

Woodpecker snickered as he began walking. "I knew you wouldn't make it."

Black Eagle shut his eyes to pray for guidance in his defeat, but suddenly was lifted to his feet.

"Damn you, Preacher. You gotta make it so I can beat your ass on the run."

"It's over for me. I haven't the strength to . . . "

Woodpecker grabbed his arm roughly and pulled him along. "Not till the fat lady sings, Preacher. Where's that God you talk about? He sure as hell picked a loser in you, didn't he?"

"I cannot. . . "

"Move, damn you! One foot in front of another. Yeah, just like that, one foot in front of the other. Ain't there somethin' in the Bible that says the Lord gives strength to the weary?"

Black Eagle slowed and stared at the redhead. "You know Isaiah?"

Woodpecker pulled him forward again. "Nah, I don't know that shit, but my old lady used to read to me from the book when I was sickly. We didn't have much money. The book medicine was free. What'd Isaiah say?"

Black Eagle lifted his head. "'He gives strength to the weary, and to him who lacks might. He increases power.

"'Though youths grow weary and tired, and vigorous young men stumble badly.

"'Yet those who wait for the Lord will gain strength; they will mount up with wings like eagles, they will run and not get tired, they will work and not become weary.'"

Woodpecker released the smaller man's arm and walked ahead. He looked over his shoulder. "You're an Eagle, ain't ya?"

Black Eagle bent forward and increased his pace to catch up. "Yes, I am an Eagle, and you are a helper, the Lord sayest. 'And I will ask the Father, and he will give you another helper, that he may be with you forever.'"

Woodpecker set his eyes to the front. "I ain't no helper, Indian. I'm the guy that's gonna whip your ass. Come on, we got some catchin' up to do."

Childs mounted the platform and looked over the gaunt faces of the company. There were only 112 left. Days of eating only two meals and training for fifteen hours had taken its toll. He knew they'd been pushed enough.

"Shitbirds, that was the big cut. We lost twenty-one on the march. There will be no PT tonight or tomorrow. You get a day of rest tomorrow. Get your feet checked and gear cleaned. Do it!"

The unbelieving men didn't move. They knew it had to be a trick of some kind. Childs wouldn't give them a break. It was impossible for him to give any compassion. Childs stepped off the platform and barked over his shoulder, *"Move, Shitbirds!* Before I change my mind!"

Lieutenant Gibson lifted his head tiredly. "You heard him. Let's move it, maggots."

Avant felt too weak to speak. He merely motioned his men to the barracks. The company dissolved slowly, leaving a single soldier who had fallen to his knees. Black Eagle lifted his arms and looked skyward. He had raised his wings to soar above the pain in his body, to fly with his happy heart above the misery and ache. He chanted the warrior ancestors' song of victory. Before, he had always sang silently. Smaller than most of his red brothers, he was considered weak and his words were not heard. His academic successes and track awards meant nothing to his proud people, who lived in the glory of the past. He had dropped out of Trinity Bible College to become a warrior like his ancestors, for only to the words of a warrior would his people listen.

Today he had fallen in the struggle but was lifted by a warrior of another color, whose spirit had given him renewed strength to win his battle of faith.

Black Eagle knew there would be more battles to fight, but now there was another eagle to soar with him.

Matt Wade sat with his team on the floor of the barracks. As he stretched out his sore legs and leaned back against the wall, Russian's dog, Bitch, pranced over for an approving pat. Wade stroked the small animal's head affectionately. "That was it," he said. "That was the last of Childs's torture chamber. It'll all be downhill from here on out. Childs will ease up on PT so the men can get their strength back and concentrate more on training."

Rose lay back against his bunk. "Good thing, man. I'm as beat as they are, and I didn't even carry a ruck. Man, I looked at a *Playboy* the other night and pinned up the food advertisements. It ain't right when ya think more about food and sleep than you do poontang."

The dog left Wade and sat on Rose's lap. "Russian, Bitch is fatter than ever. Ain't she in training, too?"

The Russian grunted and snapped his fingers. Bitch came to him immediately. "Little one is a Ranger, like us."

"Yeah, but we ain't got but two meals a day. How does she rate?"

"The KPs feed her."

Thumper sat up worriedly. "Russian, you'd better watch the dinks around that dog. Rose and I were in Phan Thiet one time and saw this dog get hit by a truck. The Vietnamese had that squashed mongrel hung up and skinned in two seconds. This guy brought out a blowtorch and started cookin' it on the spot. The dinks were crowdin' around all laughing and jumping around like it was Christmastime." Thumper looked at Wade and winked. "Come to think of it, guess who was jumping around with the dinks, waitin' to chow down."

Rose started pushing away from Russian and looking

for a fast exit. "Hey Thump, man, I just had a little bite . . . "

Russian hugged the dog protectively and snarled at Rose. "You do this?"

"Well, hell, Russian, I just wanted to . . . It was just a little bite and . . . "

Russian grabbed Rose's leg and pulled Rose to him. "You no touch little one again!"

Private First Class Peteroski ran down the hill and pulled open the barracks door. On the floor in front of him, Russian held Rose down so Bitch could lick his face. Sergeant Wade and Thumper were laughing uproariously as Russian scolded, "Do not lick him! Bite him! He eat your brother!"

Pete shook his head in bewilderment and spoke excitedly. "Come on, Matt, the old man is looking for you. We got a call and you're flying out tonight!"

Russian released his hold and let Rose up as Wade got to his feet.

"Settle down, Pete. What's this all about?"

"We got a call from Corps about you savin' some singer. The old man told 'em he didn't know anything about it and they musta had the wrong unit. Well, some colonel got on the line and really let the ol' man have it. Major Shane wants you right now!"

"Aw, shit!" said Wade, shaking his head.

Thumper stood and put his arm over his sergeant's shoulder. "You didn't tell them what happened?"

"It was no big thing. I didn't think it was . . . "

"Come on, Sarge!" said Pete, holding the door open.

Major Shane leaned forward in his chair. "So you're telling me crashing in a chopper and saving a young woman's life was no big thing?"

Wade shrugged his shoulders apologetically. "Sir, we were only fifteen clicks from the road and . . . "

"Never mind, Wade, It doesn't matter. I understand." Shane walked around the desk and put his arm around the worried sergeant. "But next time do us a favor and tell us when you crash in a chopper, okay? Top, you'd better get him to the airfield.''

Shane extended his hand. "Sergeant Wade, I'm just sorry I can't be there for the ceremony.''

Wade shook hands, relieved that his commander wasn't angry with him, but before he even released his grip, First Sergeant grabbed his arm roughly. "Come on, He-ro. You got a plane to catch.''

Two hours later the Huey settled down on the concrete runway at Nha Trang airfield, where a captain was waiting with a jeep for Wade. The cool evening air was blowing off the ocean and felt good to Wade as they drove to a hotel next to the headquarters.

The Captain, who was the public affairs officer for Corps, explained that the award ceremony would be at 10 a.m. the following morning. The Corps commander himself would award the Soldier's Medal. Wade fought to stay awake as he listened to the itinerary, which would begin when the captain picked him up at 0900.

Wade left the Captain and walked into the plush room alone. He headed directly for the bed, but immediately noticed a wine bottle in a bucket of ice on the nightstand. A card rested against the silver bucket. Wade sat down on the bed and picked up the card. "Thanks again!'' it said and was signed, "Virginia, Sophia Wolinski, the best little singer in Southeast Asia.''

Wade smiled and lay back on the bed. No tellin' how she called from whatever fire base she was at to do this, but knowing her, if anyone could find a way, she could.

Wade shut his eyes, too tired to think any more about her, and dozed off in exhausted sleep.

The still, sultry night air was alive with the sound of crickets as Sergeant Gino walked up the road toward the white motel. He glanced at the luminous hands of his watch. The sergeant was upset with himself. It was after eleven, and he should have been in bed a good hour ago. He'd made the rounds of the barracks and stopped off at

Selando's room for a quick beer. He'd ended up drinking four and shot the shit for over an hour. Damn, he thought to himself, I need sleep to keep up with these young kids, not beer.

As he approached the hootch door, all thoughts stopped. The familiar sound of the crickets had been momentarily replaced by a distant, but distinctive, metallic *thunk*.

Gino froze, hoping he'd imagined it, but he heard the noise again: *thunk.*

"Oh, shiiiit! The sergeant spun around and yelled at the top of his lungs, *"Incoming! Incoming!"*

His warning was still echoing off the barracks walls as he heard the faraway sound again. "Thunk. . . . Thunk." Gino ran for a nearby bunker. At least, he thought, he wasn't the only one who wouldn't be getting any sleep for awhile.

Black Eagle stirred in his sleep when someone ran by his bed screaming, "Mortar attack! Hit the floor!"

Black Eagle turned over, mumbling to himself that it was all just part of a bad dream, but something in him couldn't completely deny the reality of the warning.

Within the darkness of the small barracks, panic-stricken men began yelling and running in every direction for protection. Black Eagle's stomach tightened with fear and his chest refused to bring in enough air to breathe, but still he didn't come awake. He dreamed he was falling from a plane at night without a parachute. Death was coming but he couldn't see the ground to know when.

Forty yards behind the barracks, an ear-shattering explosion finally shook him into reality. He flung himself to the floor as dirt and gravel debris pelted the tin roof like a metal hailstorm. Dust, knocked free from the ceiling and walls, filled the barracks with a choking cloud. He coughed and gasped and tried to dig himself directly into the cement floor. The thunderous second explosion seemed farther away but the plywood walls and tin roof creaked and moaned in agony.

Private First Class Woody Stecker knew he was hit. He lay stunned beside a metal conex container, feeling his blood run down his face and back. He didn't know where he was hit or how bad but by the blood loss he figured he wouldn't ever see the sun again. His body was covered by a light coating of dirt and he felt strangely peaceful. He couldn't hear anything but a loud ringing and wondered if his eardrums were punctured. It didn't matter—he was dying anyway. He shut his eyes and thought about what he'd done wrong to get himself killed this way. He'd jumped up, hearing the warning yell, and had run out the back door. The steel conex looked like a good place to hide but he couldn't dig his way under the damn thing. The round had hit only twenty yards away while he was digging. It had tossed him up, then slammed him down. Now he couldn't feel a thing but sticky fluid running down the back of his head. Shit, he thought, it's blood. Not only that, but my legs don't work, my arms won't move, and God, I must look horrible. They'll probably puke when they find me. Funniest damn thing, though, I'm dying and suddenly all I want is some French fries or chicken fried steak or fried okra or. . .

Childs stood on the road looking down the hill toward the camp. The first two mortar rounds had made impact in crunching blasts of white, orange light just behind the Third and Second Platoon's barracks. Childs had heard the warning yell from Gino and had run out his hootch door, counting seconds to himself. He'd gotten to nineteen when the shells hit. The second volley would tell him if his Rangers were in trouble. The unseen gunners could adjust the range slightly and wreak havoc and destruction upon the camp. An explosion to his far right caused him to relax. They weren't adjusting on the camp. The round had hit in the open field between the Ranger camp and the Red Cross compound. It was random shooting, intended for harassment more than anything else. A second explosion followed close behind the first, almost in the identical spot. Two guns, thought Childs. They'd probably fire one more volley and hightail-it out.

Major Shane ran from the bunker to check the camp,

but noticed Childs and slowed to a walk. He stopped beside the sergeant and looked at the distant guard towers. They were bathed in dull yellow light from flares popping high overhead. Two more explosions erupted close to the Red Cross compound. The tower machine guns rattled and their red tracers streaked into the blackness.

Childs motioned toward the distant machine guns. "Those idiots on the perimeter are wastin' good ammo. The way they're shooting, they must think two dink divisions are attackin'. Them dinks skated after lobbing those last rounds. They'll be halfway to North Vietnam in an hour. Them little bastards are smart. They know to drop only two or three volleys. Scrambled choppers would spot their signature."

Shane smiled for a second, thankful to have the old veteran, then became serious. "Jerry, what were you doing standing out here like that? Hell, you didn't know where that second volley was going to land."

Childs shrugged his shoulders. "It ain't my time yet." Childs began walking down the hill so as not to have to discuss the matter any further. He didn't know how to explain it any better, but somehow he honestly knew he was in no danger. The sergeant took several steps and spoke over his shoulder. "Tell you one thing, though. The dinks did us a favor."

"How's that?" asked Shane.

Childs snickered as he continued walking. "They reminded our shitbirds we still got us a war goin' on."

A flashlight shone directly into Woody Stecker's face and blinded him. "Damn, man, you hurt? You're a fucking mess."

The redhead heard nothing, but he was happy someone had finally found him. At least he would die knowing they'd found his body.

Childs walked up beside Rose, who was holding the flashlight. "Is he hurt?"

Rose bent over the soldier and shook his head. "Naw, he's just stunned. But the mess sergeant sure gonna be pissed. Shrapnel tore through the conex and ripped open his big cans of cooking oil. It's all over the dude."

Childs bent over the redhead. "What the hell you doin' out here? The bunker is beside the barracks, dummy. You was lucky this time. The shrapnel missed your head by only a foot."

Stecker looked up at Childs as if he was speaking Chinese.

Rose shook his head. "I don't think he can hear ya, Sarge."

Childs stood up and put his hands on his hips. "Get the dumb shit to the medics and have 'em check him out. . . . Then get him cleaned up. Christ, he smells like an oily sardine."

Nha Trang

Matt Wade rolled over and immediately opened his eyes. There was someone in bed with him. The lights were out, and he remembered he hadn't turned them off.

He thought at first it was just his imagination, but as he came fully awake, he definitely felt an arm over his waist and a warm body next to him. It had to be a prostitute sent up by the captain, but the light fragrance she wore was certainly not Vietnamese. Wade turned his head slowly to get a look at her when the girl snuggled closer and giggled.

Wade hopped up immediately and pounced on her. "You crazy lady! What the hell you doin' here?"

Virginia fought his grip, laughing and kicking her feet. She freed her hands. "Click! I got you."

Wade got up and turned on the light. "Damn you, Ginny, you scared the hell out of me."

She was wearing a camouflage jumpsuit and jungle boots like his. She raised up to her elbows. "I see you still sleep in your clothes. Your language hasn't improved any either. You miss me?"

Wade looked at his watch; it was a quarter to twelve. "It's midnight, for God's sake! What are you doing here?"

"Answer *my* question and I'll answer *yours*."

Wade sighed. "Yeah, I missed ya . . . kinda."

Virginia smiled. "Same here. That's why I came. I can't let my hero get a medal without my being there, can I?"

173

"Yeah, but you put me in for the medal. That was a dumb thing to do."

She snapped tartly, "It was not. You deserved it."

Wade smiled when he saw the anger in her eyes. "Alright, Ginny, thank you. How'd ya get in here, anyway?"

Virginia's eyes narrowed. He looked into them. She shook her head and got up.

"You know, I've done nothing but think about you. When I came up and saw your door open, I almost cried from happiness. You were lying here so peaceful I . . . I, Matt, tell me you really missed me, too."

Wade put his arms over her small shoulders.

"I missed you a lot, Ginny. I didn't think I'd ever see you again. I'm glad you came."

Virginia stared at him for a moment, then hugged him tightly. "God, you feel good. I think I became addicted to sleeping with you in the jungle."

Wade returned her hug, wanting desperately to kiss her, but not sure whether he should. She pushed away from him and walked toward the door. Wade sighed inwardly with relief. "I'll see you in the morning for breakfast and . . ."

She reached the door, but turned off the light instead. "No you won't. You're going to hold me all night like before. I need you to hold me, Matt."

"Ginny, I . . ."

The sound of her jumpsuit being unzipping sent chills up his back. "Are you sure, Ginny? I can't promise you . . ."

"Yes I'm sure . . . but how the hell do I get out of these boots?"

Wade laughed and reached out in the darkness. "Come here."

13 SEPTEMBER

At 1000 hours, the Corps adjutant came to attention. "Attention to orders. By direction of the secretary of the

Army, Sergeant Matthew R. Wade, 427-48-5001, is hereby awarded the Soldier's Medal for . . . "

Virginia stood smiling among a group of officers and photographers assembled on the lawn adjacent to the headquarters. General Wayland stood in front of the bereted sergeant who, except for a sparkle in his eyes as he looked at Ginny, showed no emotion.

". . . displayed exceptional courage and reflects great credit upon himself, his unit, and the United States Army. Signed, John B. Minzer, secretary of the Army."

Wayland stepped forward, pinned the medal on Wade's shirt-pocket flap, and shook hands. "Congratulations, Sergeant. You can be very proud of this. Now smile and face the cameras for the people back home."

Wade forced a smile. He could hardly wait for the ceremony to end. It was taking so long, and he hardly had any time left with Ginny as it was.

The photographers had the general pin the medal on two more times before they were finally satisfied. Then the officers came by and shook hands, but Wade didn't see their faces. Ginny had disappeared, and he was looking for her. When the crowd finally dispersed, leaving him on the platform with only the PAO captain, he located her under a banyan tree, where she was being interviewed by a group of correspondents.

Wade came up behind the group and motioned for her to come to him.

She smiled brightly and excused herself as she waded through the men to the sergeant.

"Hold it, Sophia, that's perfect—and could you both turn a little more?" A photographer took several pictures. Wade stood with her for one more picture, then began gently pulling her away.

"Just one more?"

Wade shook his head and kept walking.

She hit him playfully. "I'm working on my career and you want to play Tarzan and Jane."

"Well, Tarzan has gotta catch a chopper. He doesn't have much time."

She put her arms around his waist. "Matt, I've already talked to some people about that, and they can use you here at the headquarters. We'd be able to see each other and . . . "

Wade stopped and put his hands on her shoulders. "Ginny, I'm not the paper-shufflin' kind. I could never take a rear area job as long as my guys are in the company. They need me . . . and I need them."

Virginia's eyes narrowed as she backed away from him. "You're caught up in it, aren't you? Do you think you're going to win the war all by yourself? Matt Wade, this war had been going on for years and will keep on going, with or without you. Get out now before it's too late. I . . . I need you."

Wade kept his distance, and his expression grew stone-hard. "Look, you're askin' for something I can't give. I'm not a REMF-ass paper-shuffler! And I'm sure as hell not leaving my men. You either accept that or you don't. It's up to you."

Virginia shook with anger. "You hard-headed hick!" But even as she spoke she knew she couldn't change him. She could see that in his cold, determined stare. "At least write to me and call if you ever get some time off . . . won't you?"

Wade's grim expression dissolved, and he came to her and lifted her chin. "You bet. Ginny, I'm gonna miss you. Don't you know that?" Ginny forced a smile through her tears. "You'd better miss me," she said, and then dug into her purse. "Here, I've got something for you so you'll remember me." She pulled out a gold chain and placed the long, thick necklace over his head. "You come back to me, Matt."

Wade lifted the medallion on the chain's end. It was gold and had engraved miniature parachute wings and a Ranger tab. On the back was inscribed:

"CLICK"
Love You
Ginny

Wade held her tightly and kissed her.

"Hey, Sarge, we gotta go!" yelled the captain.

Wade sighed and kissed her forehead. "Where're you located, so I can write?"

"Saigon USO Headquarters. They forward my mail to me. Take care, Matt."

The sergeant turned to go and looked over his shoulder. "You too, Ginny."

Virginia watched him with tears running down her cheeks. As he got into the jeep she yelled, "Hey!"

Wade knew before he turned around and quickly raised his hands.

They both said "click" at the same time.

Sergeant Wade arrived back at the Ranger camp to find the company rappeling off the forty-foot tower. Major Shane and First Sergeant Demand, who were observing the training, called him over.

"You a gen-u-ine *hero* now, Ranger?" asked Demand, grinning.

Wade saluted his major and retorted, "Yep, Top, I'm almost first sergeant material."

Shane shook his hand. "Did everything go alright?"

Wade couldn't help but smile. "Yes sir, even better than I expected. How's the training going?"

"Outstanding. This confidence-building stuff is good for us. Next week we'll be breaking up the men into teams. I thought about breaking up your team to spread out the experience, but I've decided against it. I'm going to be using you on the more difficult missions. You'll get first choice of the students, so start thinking about who you want."

"Thank you, sir, for not breaking us up. We'll do you a good job."

Shane patted the sergeant's back. "I know you will."

Thumper set down his food tray beside Wade and was joined by Rose and Russian. "Well, how was it? The REMFs hassle you?"

"Naw, they were all right. They feed good."

Rose leaned over. "Getcha any women?"

Wade rolled his eyes up. "You must be rested and eatin' good. You're back to your ol' ways."

"Man, a dude gotta unload or his eyeballs turn white."

Russian pushed Rose back with his arm. "You talk terrible things. I try to eat and you say such words."

"Man, I'm just tellin' it the way it is. Why, if I'd been there, I'd . . . "

Russian turned with a scowl. Rose picked up his fork and stabbed the spaghetti savagely. "Russian, you a bummer, man. Why they take foreigners in our Army beats the shit outta me."

Wade waved his fork for attention. "You guys keep your eyes out for two good replacements for the team. The ol' man is giving us first choice. We need a 60 gunner and a radio man."

"I got just the man we need for the 60," said Thumper quickly. "It's that redheaded 173rd replacement called Woodpecker. He's the best I've seen on the range. He's skinny, but he's a humper."

"The guy that ran against the Indian?" asked Wade.

"That's him. He'd be my first choice."

"Okay, I'll watch him this week. Anybody see a good RTO?"

Rose spoke with his mouth full. "Man, whoever it is, just make sure he ain't foreign, will ya?"

16 SEPTEMBER

The days passed quickly for Wade. He taught map reading and land navigation to men who had just rotated from Thumper's station on artillery and gunship supporting fire adjustment. They seemed attentive and interested, but Wade could tell that a problem was beginning to develop. Now that the men were getting plenty of food and sleep, they were becoming difficult to control. Two nights before, the ragbags had raided the 173rd maggots' barracks and sprayed shaving cream in all the beds. The maggots reciprocated the following night by sneaking in at midnight and dousing the sleeping ragbags with canteen water. A fight had broken out that caused four men to lose teeth and several others to require stitches. The two groups of men had become so competitive that Childs had to keep them constantly separated or they'd yell and jeer at each other, disrupting the classes. Childs had admitted to the cadre that he was worried he'd carried the competition too far.

Wade marched his last class of the day back to the barracks and gave them five minutes to get ready for the evening run. When he walked to the PT formation a few minutes later, he couldn't believe his ears. Childs was addressing the company. "Shitbirds, I'm cancelling the last half-mile race that was scheduled for tonight. I . . . "

The company of ragbags and maggots booed and yelled out in protest. Childs, fuming, held up his hand for silence, then called Lieutenant Gibson and Lieutenant Avant to the platform. "We're causin' dissension instead of team building," he whispered to them. "We should cancel the son of a bitch."

Gibson shook his head. "It's important to them. They've been waiting for this last race and they're ready. You gotta let 'em do it."

Avant agreed. "Sergeant Childs, you have to let the race stand. My men are higher than kites. They need the race to blow off steam. Hell, if you don't let 'em run, were gonna have more trouble."

Childs understood. He stood up to face the company. "Shitbirds, I've reconsidered. The race will go on, but only one representative from the ragbags and maggots will run. And this will be the *last* run!"

The company hooted and hollered their approval as Childs stepped off the platform shaking his head. He hoped he hadn't made a mistake.

The maggots chose Woodpecker, for he had been training secretly every night. The ragbags chose their proven winner, Black Eagle.

Thumper walked the two men down the road to the starting point, gave them a few minutes to stretch and warm up, then stood at the starting line. "I'm going to be shooting my .45 so the others will know it's started. Good luck to you both. *On your marks . . . get set . . .* " *Boom!*

Black Eagle used the same strategy as before: He began at a moderate pace to feel out his opponent, but to his surprise, the redhead fell in behind him.

At the halfway point, Black Eagle picked up the pace and pulled farther ahead, but Woodpecker kept up his steady churning until he reached the bottom of the hill before beginning his practiced sprint.

Childs, standing at the finish line, watched Woodpecker pass the Indian halfway up the hill, two hundred yards before the end of the race. As if he was playing to the shouts and screams of the company that lined the road, the skinny redhead pumped his long legs like pistons and took a commanding lead. Childs thought it was over when the redhead's face suddenly contorted in pain and he pitched forward. He rolled on the ground in agony—with a cramped calf muscle, judging by the way he grabbed his leg. The screaming ragbags yelled louder as the Indian jumped over the fallen runner without losing stride and raced for the finish line. Childs stepped back to let the winner pass but the Indian slowed to a jog and looked over his shoulder at his writhing competitor. The ragbags were screaming for their man to continue, but he turned around abruptly and jogged back to the maggot.

Childs felt a tingling sensation run up his spine as the Indian pulled the taller soldier to his feet and supported him with an arm around his waist. The Indian strained with the weight, but began jogging to the line again. The crowd of shitbirds became silent as they watched the two men struggle for their goal. The redhead moaned in pain but continued to hobble along, his face contorted, but his eyes, like those of the Indian's, set in determination.

Childs backed up as the two men labored together in a final exhausting effort and fell across the line at the same time. The comany of silent men broke into a roar of jubilation as Childs looked down at the two men and fought back the urge to lift them up and hug them both. In seconds, the runners were pounced on by hollering, laughing ragbags and maggots, all of whom wanted to shake their hands and slap their backs. Childs squared his shoulders back and walked through the gathering crowd as the two runners were lifted onto the shoulders of yelling shitbirds.

Major Shane walked up behind Childs and tapped his shoulder. "What were you saying about two *separate* armies?"

Childs frowned and started toward his platform, but halted after a step. There wasn't a thing he could say to the company. The actions of those two men had said it all. He grunted to himself and looked over his shoulder at the major. "Looks like we got us some Rangers after all, sir."

The following morning First Sergeant Demand announced in the mess hall that a chaplain was visiting and he wanted every man to attend a service to be held outside after chow.

Wade finished eating breakfast with the team and got to his feet. "Come on, guys, let's hear the sermon and get ready for the helicopter class."

Thumper and Russian stood, but Rose remained seated. Wade motioned them on and sat down. "What's the matter, Rose, ya not feelin' good?"

Rose didn't look at his sergeant as he snapped, "I ain't gonna hear no holy shit! There ain't no law says I gotta go and I ain't goin', man."

Wade had never seen Rose so adamant and tried to ease the tension. "No sweat, Rose. You don't wanna go that's fine, but what's the problem? You know I'll have to explain to Top why you're not there."

Rose stared at his sergeant for a second as if about to speak, but suddenly looked away. "No, man, it ain't for talkin' about. Man, I ain't goin', that's all. If Top wanna hassle me, let him."

Wade got up and put his hand on his friend's shoulder. "He won't hassle you. I'll make sure of it. You'd better take the back door and wait in the barracks. We'll be up later."

Rose looked up at his sergeant. "Thanks, Matt, for not

pushin', man. It's . . . it's a personal thing.'' Wade nodded in silence and headed for the door. Rose closed his eyes for a moment and saw the smiling face of the Reverend Jeremiah Washington Flowers, his father. Rose's fists clenched in anger just thinking of the man who promised him and the family everything and left them in squalor and, much worse, shame. His father was the Lower East Side's pastor and preached in an old Safeway store every Sunday. He preached hope to those who were beyond it and dreams to the dreamers. As a fourteen-year-old boy he'd been one of those who believed his father, until a young pregnant girl said his dad was her baby's father. He'd even believed his dad when he said it wasn't true, but his mama cried a long time and never smiled again. A month later the reverend left on a Saturday and never came back. They said the reverend left with the congregation's donations for the new church, but the boy didn't know for sure, because he never went back. A teenage black boy without a dad wasn't uncommon in Detroit's Lower East Side, but being ''The Reverend Flowers's boy'' was. The welfare his mama took to feed her family he could endure, the snickers and whispers he couldn't.

Years later the whispers ended with the riots, and his work for the people gave him respect. Then trouble ended and the people wanted to believe in dreams again. He joined the Army to pay the bills and get away from the dreamers. He played the Army's game and found that the jungle was no different than the streets. Dreamers died believing they wouldn't and he survived because he believed he could.

He found respect among those who believed in one another and hope in a system that rewarded survivors. He wasn't Jeremiah Flowers's boy anymore. He was ''the Rose,'' a man who believed only in his friends and himself.

11

20 SEPTEMBER

With two days left in Childs's training program, Wade still hadn't decided on an RTO. The radiomen had to be smart and able to memorize countless call signs and frequencies, plus speak the peculiar radio language fluently. Wade talked to Sergeant Selando, who'd been teaching the radio procedures class.

"Ya seen anybody who seems to have the knack?"

"Yeah, there's a couple, but you want the real star, he's sittin' right behind you." Wade turned around. There were five men sitting eating C rations.

"That kid has got a memory like an elephant. I guess it's from his school-teaching."

One of the men looked up, a big Texan Wade remembered from the training classes. That must be him, Wade thought. "Thanks, Selando, he looks big enough to hump."

Selando saw who Wade was looking at and shook his head. "Not him." He pointed to the small man leaning against a tree. "Him."

Wade looked at Selando in disbelief. "You gotta be kiddin'!"

Selando laughed. "Look, I wouldn't shit you. He sure doesn't look like much, but the Indian memorizes the stuff like it was scripture. You asked who the best was and that's him. If you don't take him, I'm going to."

Wade shook his head, mumbling. "Well, he ain't foreign, that's for sure."

That evening at chow, Wade broke the news to the team. "So I decided on Woodpecker for the 60 gunner and. . . Preacher for the RTO."

Rose tossed down his fork. "Preacher! That ugly little dude! No, Matt, he's a Jesus freak, man!"

Russian nodded in approval. "Yes, he will be good. He listen good in my class."

"Whatcha talkin' about, man? He's as weird as you are. The Indian is a Bible-thumper. Aw, Matt, no, man! He ain't cool!"

Thumper reached over to Rose's plate and took his cake. "Matt, I think you picked us some good people. Woodpecker is experienced and I hear Preacher is smart. The Lord knowth how we needth a goodth influence."

Rose snatched the cake away just as Thumper raised it to his mouth.

"You's a smart alec big dude! The Preacher is gonna drive us crazy with his holy shit. He ain't never gonna pull the trigger, man."

Wade scooted back his chair. "Rose, lightning is gonna strike any second now."

Thumper and Russian slid their chairs back, too. Rose stared at their grinning faces, and shook his head disgustedly. "You're all dreamers!"

22 SEPTEMBER

Sergeant First Class Jerry Childs stepped up on the platform and placed his hands on his hips. Before him stood a company of 110 men all dressed in newly-issued camouflage fatigues and jungle hats. He paced back and forth, then halted. "Shitbirds, you are the survivors of two weeks of hell. You have proven to yourselves, the instructors, and me that you have earned the right to wear the black beret. Today the initial training is over. Tomorrow we begin team training.

"Some of you are going to the Commo platoon, and the rest are assigned to teams. You are all going to become an elite unit known and respected by our friends and our enemies. Today you become Rangers! Remember what you've been taught. Your life and the lives of others will depend on it. You're no longer maggots . . . or ragbags . . . or shitbirds. You are men who will continue the mission, Charlie Mike, till that fat lady sings. I pronounce you all *United States Army Rangers!*"

The formation erupted in a thunderous roar and tossed their hats skyward.

Childs came to attention. "Award the berets!"

The cadre filed down the rows of men, placing a black beret on each man's head.

Lieutenants Avant and Gibson were given their berets by Major Shane. The major shook both their hands and winked. "You think Childs was bad, wait till tomorrow when I teach you both to fly backseat in a bird dog."

Avant feigned fainting and fell on Gibson's shoulder. "Aw, sir, we were going to drink a little beer tonight and celebrate."

Shane laughed and began walking to his headquarters. "Top has a little party planned with a movie. You two be there . . . sober!"

Both officers saluted smartly. "Yes, sir!"

Black Eagle and Woodpecker moved their gear into the Third Platoon barracks and began unpacking their equipment under the watchful eye of Rose.

"Where you from in the world, Woodpecker?"

"Monroe, Louisiana."

"Where'd ya get them cool tattoos, man?"

Woodpecker smiled proudly, pointing to the colored dragon on his right forearm. "I got this 'un in New Orleans and the panther in Columbus after Jump School. Look mean, huh?"

"Really, they're bad, man. I'm gonna git me a rose put on my arm when I get back to the world. Maybe some boss jump wings too."

Preacher glanced over at the black soldier as he spread his poncho liner on the bed. "You'd be wasting money, Jeremiah, your skin is too dark."

Rose spun around, stabbing the air with his finger. "Don't *ev-er* call me by that name, Indian! I wasn' talkin' to your skinny red ass!"

Nonplussed, Preacher smoothed out the nylon material and looked up. "Sorry, Rose, I thought you . . . "

"Man, don't talk to me! I ain't said shit to you!"

"I was only trying to . . . "

"Shut up, holy man!"

Woodpecker poked Rose's back roughly. "Back off."

Rose spun around, looking up at the tall redhead's face. "Don't you take up for this mutha's slack. He's a holy man and ain't gonna pull no trigger to save yo white ass!"

"Just leave it be, Rose."

"You leave it, man! He ain't got the guts to kill. He'll let you down, man. His holy shit ain't gonna save you. The mutha' shouldn't be here!"

Black Eagle shook his head at Woodpecker pleadingly.

The Louisianan gave Rose a last warning glare and began folding his clothes. The black soldier brushed past Woodpecker and pulled open the barracks door. The man who called him Jeremiah was like his father. He would let him and his team down just like his father had let down the family. Preacher lived on faith, on dreams—but dreams went away on a Saturday and never came back.

Rose stepped out of the barracks and looked over his shoulder. "He ain't gonna pull the trigger, man! He ain't gonna pull the trigger!"

Woodpecker tossed his barracks bag to the floor. "That dude got a chip on his shoulder. I don't know what his problem is but he ain't got no right hasslin' you."

Preacher looked out the screen door toward the road. "I've talked to some of the cadre. Did you know that in Cambodia Rose saw his whole team killed? He was hidden and lay there unable to help. He waited until the NVA patrol began picking over the bodies, then attacked. He killed eight men, Woody. He killed them and instead of escaping back to the Vietnam border he went west, deeper into Cambodia to hunt for more.

"An American unit found him three days later carrying NVA equipment from the men he'd killed. They said all he wanted was more ammunition so he could continue the mission. The unit had to disarm him and bring him back by force."

The thin redhead threw his hands up. "That explains it! The dude is nuts."

Preacher turned around and shook his head. "No, my friend. He is a great warrior. No matter what harsh words he speaks, Rose is a warrior and must be respected."

Woodpecker arched an eyebrow. "Preacher, you respect him all you want, but I'm watchin' his black ass and ain't lettin' him hassle ya."

Preacher lowered his head. "It's my problem."

Woodpecker tossed himself on his bunk and looked up at the ceiling. "No it ain't. We're in this together. Preacher, there's just you and me. We stick together, and *nobody* hassles us. The other team members seem friendly enough, but you know and I know, we ain't one of them . . . not yet."

First Sergeant Demand announced at evening chow that he had a movie for the company as soon as it got dark. At 1830, the assembled men sat on the slope of the hill behind the mess hall, where several white-painted plywood sheets rested against the chow hall wall. The bantam soldier stepped up onto a wooden ammo-box stage in front of the screen and faced the audience.

"Rangers, some of you ain't been to the first sergeant's movies, so I gotta explain the rules. No pissin' on the first sergeant's flowers. If you gotta get rid of the Cokes and beer we providin', you visit *my* latrines!"

The new men were surprised to hear the old veterans "boo" loudly. The first sergeant raised his hand and the noise ceased immediately.

"The other rule is *no* abusin' my projectionist, Private

Peteroski, with cussin' or throwin' rocks if the film breaks.''

Again, the old vets laughed and booed. This time, the new men caught on to the game and booed, too. Demand let the noise build, then raised his hand. ''This is a graduation party tonight, so beer and Cokes is free.''

The men yelled, ''Yeah!''

''Mess sergeant provided free popcorn, but salt is one dollar!''

''Boo!''

''Tonight's movie is one of the first sergeant's favorites, *Care and Maintenance of the M-16A-1 Rifle!*''

Thunderous boos!

''Okay, Rangers, you don't wanna see my movie, we'll see the mess sergeant's favorite. *Bambi!*''

Again loud boos!

Demand shook his head as if in disgust. ''Alright, Rangers, ya don't want his, then we'll show that Hollywood smut they call art. You gonna have to see ol' Gregory Peck in a movie called *The Chairman*. Roll 'em, Pete!''

The audience hooted and clapped in approval as the old projector began clanking and threw a bright tunnel of light onto the painted wall.

Thumper leaned forward and tapped the two men in front of him. ''You guys keep your empty Coke cans. This is going to get interesting.''

Woodpecker and Preacher exchanged confused looks and turned to the big soldier. ''Why?''

''You'll see. Just keep 'em handy.''

Sergeant Wade leaned closer to Thumper as he sat back on the slope. ''Where's Rose?''

Thumper rolled his eyes to his right. ''He's sulking over by the projector. He already had a run-in with Preacher and Woodpecker.''

Music began blaring from the speakers that popped with static.

Wade shook his head. ''You gonna talk to him, or me?''

''I already did, but he's really got a thing about Preacher.''

"You better talk to Russian, and we'll keep Rose off his back till he gets used to him."

Thumper nodded and leaned back on the slope. Three-one had six good men but they still weren't a team. As long as there was dissension among them they were only partly effective and very vulnerable.

Thumper looked over at the sullen black soldier. Rose would have to get over his mistrust of the Indian because if he didn't, one of them, or maybe the whole team, would pay a horrible price.

"Lieutenant Foley and I will be teaching you both how to fly in the back seat of the L-19 bird dog." He motioned toward Avant. "Brad, you've already flown and know most of the procedures, but the training won't hurt you."

Lieutenant Foley had been working the past two weeks as operations officer and had been busy planning and co-ordinating the teams' ambush missions. He took off his thick glasses and rubbed the bridge of his nose. "Sir, Colonel Ellis from Corps called this evening and said he'd be flying up this week to brief you on an operation."

Shane nodded and stood up. "Let's go get a beer and see Top's movie. Gibson, stay close to the other L-tees and learn the rules."

"Beggin' your pardon, sir?" said the gray-haired Lieutenant, not sure he'd heard right.

Shane winked at Avant and smiled. "Just stay close and duck when your fellow officers do."

Gibson, totally bewildered by his commander's warning, began to speak up, but Avant grabbed his arm. "Come on, cousin. Me and Foley will protect you."

Gibson, Avant, and Foley sat a little to the left of the humming projector. They'd had a few beers, as had most of the other assembled men lying on the sloping hill. Gregory Peck had had a miniature receiver implanted on his body and was on his way to China. A low growl could be heard above the soundtrack of the movie as Bitch yanked, chewed, and pulled on one of Russian's bootlaces. Nobody said anything about the dog's noisiness. She was a member of the company and was allowed her shortcomings.

Gregory Peck had just walked through a gateway and a Chinese Communist soldier was questioning him.

It was then that Gibson and the other new men were introduced to the traditional Ranger reception to the first sergeant's movies. As soon as the Communist held up his AK-47 to stop the famous actor, twenty beer cans sailed toward the unknowing guard. They struck the wooden screen with a clatter, followed by yells and screams from the Ranger audience. The camera then shifted to another guard and again beer cans sailed; but this time, many more came from the new men, including a partially-filled can of Gibson's.

It's great! he thought. You get to take out your frustrations on the screen. A few seconds later, the camera zoomed in for a close-up of a banner of Mao. Cans and rocks almost blocked out the picture. The Rangers screamed, hollered, and hooted. Gibson turned to Avant, who was lobbing cans like mortar rounds. He was lying back and laughing so hard that J.D. thought he might bust a gut-muscle. Gibson readied two cans of his own for the next opportune shot.

Major Shane and Sergeant First Class Childs left the movie as the final reel began. They went to Shane's office to discuss the upcoming operation and Colonel Ellis's visit.

Shane spread out a map sheet on his desk. "Jerry, you'll be running the operation on fire base Mustang while I get the officers trained. I figure you'll be out there about eight days, time enough for each team to run two or three patrols. According to the Fourth Division S-3, they've had plenty of activity by local units, so you'll probably have teams in contact. If you think it's gettin' too heavy, give me a call and I'll come out with support from the Fourth Divison."

Childs studied the map a few seconds and looked up. "Sir, the only problem I see is this area west of fire base.

There's a village out there. Our guys aren't used to workin' around people.''

Shane nodded in understanding. "Yeah, I know. I suggest you put Sergeant Wade's team in that area. They have a lot of experience and know the difference between VC and local friendlies. I'd be afraid to put in an inexperienced team. They'd be too trigger-happy, shoot first and ask questions later."

Childs took a grease pencil and marked beside the village 'Team 3-1.' "It's done, sir. We'll have the teams move out to the fire base tomorrow and they'll be in the bush the following day. I just hope we get some kills to make 'em thirsty."

Shane picked up an intelligence report and handed it to Childs. "Based on this, I think our teams will get the kills."

Childs read the report and snickered. "Looks like we're gonna have us some veterans pretty quick. The dinks better quit being so open or my boys gonna fuck up their day, big time."

Gregory Peck was being chased by the Chinese Reds. He was trying to get to the Russian border, where Russian troops had just appeared to help him escape. The music was up as loud as it would go to compensate for the Rangers' screaming and yelling. One soldier jumped up to throw a rock and was hit from behind by several cans. As he turned, he was hit by more. The Russians fired mortars and killed several Chinese, again to the hoots and hollers of the audience. Gregory Peck looked as if he might escape when suddenly a large red hole appeared on his forehead . . .

One of the Rangers had filled a plastic bag full of red Kool-Aid and thrown it. When it hit and "killed" Gregory Peck, an even louder yell went up.

In minutes, the movie was over. The laughing men cleaned up the mess and began walking up the hill. J. D. Gibson was still smiling as he strolled with Foley and Avant back to their hootch. Avant threw his arm over J.D.'s shoulder. "Whatcha think, cousin?"

Gibson set his face in a frown. "Shocking behavior. Hardly becoming to gentlemen and officers. I have only one question. When we gonna do it again? That was great!"

Wade lay on his bunk rereading the letter from Ginny he'd received that afternoon. Her neatly penned lines were somehow what he'd expected: chatty at first, then direct and simple. She was describing her feelings for him as if she was beside him, talking.

Thumper walked in and sat beside him. "She wrote you already, huh?"

Wade folded the letter and began to put it back in the envelope.

"Yep, she's really something."

"Are you going to write her back?"

"Tomorrow, I'll scribble somethin'."

Thumper lowered his head. "Matt, don't wait till tomorrow. Do it right now. I was gonna write tomorrow, too, but it never came. Do it now when you're thinkin' about her. She went to a lot of trouble to see you in Nha Trang, and she deserves your thanks."

Wade sat up, surprised at Thumper being so serious. "I probably shouldn't have told you about it, Thump."

The big soldier smiled. "What are friends for if you can't share a little happiness?" His smile dissolved quickly. "Friends also share their mistakes, and I made one in not writing back to Mary Ann. Don't make the same mistake, Matt. Take it from a friend. Write her and tell her what you feel."

Wade swung his legs off the bed and stood up. "I'm *going* to write a letter, my friend, and so are *you*. Deal?"

Thumper shook his head sadly. "No. It's too late for me."

"Bullshit!" blurted Wade. "It ain't over till the fat lady sings, remember? We're both gonna knock out a couple a pages right now *and that's an order*. Hell, you're the one who convinced me!"

Thumper raised his head and stared into Matt's eyes for a moment, then winked. "Deal!"

Woodpecker swung his legs up to the bed and leaned back. He'd been talking to Black Eagle for several minutes and shook his head in bewilderment. "Damn, Preach, that's a helluva reason to join the Army. Gettin' to be a warrior so's your people will respect you. Sounds all turned around to me."

Preacher smiled and began taking off his boots. "My people are different in ways you can't understand. Why did you join the Army?"

"I didn't. My draft board joined me up. Didn't matter none. I didn't have no good job or nothin'. I needed the bread and three squares a day. I went to jump school cause it kept me outta Nam a little longer, plus the extra fifty-five dollars a month. Man, I'm gonna buy me a Harley when I get out and see the country. Ya see that flick, *Easy Rider*? That's me, man."

"Motorcycles are dangerous. You know how to ride one?"

"Are you kiddin'? You know how much a hog costs? Shit, I'll learn how. And when I do I'm gone from Monroe."

"You would leave your family like that, just leave?"

Woodpecker smiled. "We're a different people, and you wouldn't understand."

"What would you look for when you left your family?"

Woodpecker lay back on his bed with a distant stare. "Me, man. I'd be looking for me."

Russian walked into the barracks and glanced at Rose's empty bunk. "Where is the crazy one?"

Preacher tossed his boot to the floor. "He's in the third barracks listening to some tapes."

Russian frowned and turned around. "I will get him. It is time for sleep."

Woodpecker raised up to his elbows when the Czech left. "Russian is a big mama looking after his kids, ain't he?"

Preacher raised his head up. "He is a great . . . "

"Warrior, I know," blurted Woodpecker, finishing the

sentence. Woodpecker threw his pillow at Preacher. "I hope you hurry up and get to be one them warriors you think so much of so you'll quit talkin' crazy."

Preacher casually picked up the pillow and suddenly let out a war hoop and jumped on Woodpecker's bed. "A red-haired scalp is what I need!"

The two men wrestled and laughed for several seconds before realizing they were being watched. Wade stood at the end of the bunk with Thumper.

Wade shook his head. "Thump, I think I selected us some real weirdos."

Thumper nodded his head solemnly in agreement, but broke into a smile as he replied. "Glad *you* picked 'em and not me."

Political Officer Le Xuan Can stepped out of the darkness into the light of the kerosene lamp. Before him squatted the hamlet elders of An Chon. The thirty-two-year old soldier took off his wide-brimmed French slouch hat and squatted down, meeting their gaze. "I come with joyous news, my friends. The Provisional Revolutionary Government has declared your hamlet part of the new liberated zone."

An old man wearing a cloth tied around his head spat and looked at the others, snickering. "Another government's words."

Le Can smiled. "Yes, I know you have seen many governments, and all have brought promises; but this time, I bring more than words. I bring truth. Is it not true the puppets claim this a strategic hamlet? Where are the puppets? Do they help you? They cower in their base, miles from here. I am here and will bring medical support and a teacher. These are truths.

"The New Provisional Revolutionary Government is already victorious. The Yankees have ceased their search-and-destroy operations and now stay in defensive positions. The North is no longer being bombed, and the PRG sits in Paris at a conference as the genuine representative of the people.

"I come to consolidate the government's power. We must show the world we are powerful and hold most of the country in the liberated zone."

The old man shook his head. "Politics mean nothing to me. All I have are my water buffalo and my grandchildren. You come to take our rice and sweet potatoes to support your government."

Le Can sighed and lowered his head. "It is not *my* government, old one. It is *your* government, and we ask for nothing but that your hamlet proclaim its liberation. I am here—what more truth do you ask? I am now assigned to this province from the District Committee. Your hamlet will hold elections and elect a Peasant Liberation Committee and establish your own priorities so that we may help you with them. What do the puppets offer?"

The old man said nothing, but Nguyen Thi Thanch rose to her feet beside him. She was frail and her hair was closely cropped. "Old Bao has lost his sons to the struggle, as all of us have. We are tired of this war and only want to plant our rice in peace. Bao has lost hope; but what you say is true. The puppets do not help. Promise you will not take our children, and we will join with you again."

Le Can stood and bowed to the woman with respect. "We need your youth to stay here and help you. I promise they will not be asked to volunteer. Your decision to help us will be received with great joy. I will return to your hamlet in two days with a teacher and medical team to demonstrate our help. Tell the people this and receive us with open arms and hearts, for it is the new beginning for An Chon."

Le Can stood in the darkness with the hamlet chief as the old ones returned to their huts. "You did well, Comrade Huu. Your mother spoke with authority."

The chief stared at the closest hut. "Yes, she understands the needs of our home; but your promise not to take the youth must not be broken. They are all we have left."

Le Can turned to his two men, who were escorting him. "Tell Comrade Huu what they call me."

The closest soldier stepped closer. "Le Can is known as 'Thach Sanh'—the peasant knight. He speaks the truth and keeps his word."

Le Can put on his French Legionnaire's hat and placed his arm around Huu's shoulder. "You will be rewarded for our efforts. When I return in two days, introduce me as Thach Sanh. Have the whole hamlet waiting for us. Young and old must take away a lasting impression. It will help the cause and give them hope to have a hero address them."

Huu knew Le Can was indeed a hero of the Liberation Army. He had been awarded the Valiant Fighter Award, Third Class. The French hat was a symbol of his past exploits.

"A hero does not impress those who are tired of war," Huu said. "The medical team and teacher are what they need and should be introduced with great words."

Le Can squeezed the chief's shoulder tightly. "You are wise, Huu. I hear what you say. So it will be. I will bring a red banner for you and ensure you are elected to the hamlet committee. Good night, my friend. In two days, you will be a hero yourself."

23 SEPTEMBER

Fire base Mustang was shrouded in the red dust cloud kicked up by the departing deuce-and-a-half trucks. Childs stepped out of the tactical operations center and hollered out to the assembling Ranger teams, "Team sergeants report to me! Assistant team leaders move your people to the tents across the road!"

Childs and the communications platoon had come out earlier to the ARVN camp and set up the TOC.

Childs walked into the large underground bunker, followed by the team sergeants. He had a map hanging from the thick-timbered wall. "You received your team area of operations before coming out, right?"

The sergeants all nodded and took out their maps.

"You've got the rest of the day to plan your routes and coordinate them with me. You'll be going out at dusk at staggered times so we don't have anybody running into each other. This is different than you've been trained, because you're not being infilled by chopper, and you'll be moving at night. When you drove up you saw that this fire base looks like a big tit. To the west is rice paddies and in the other directions are open rolling hills leading to the mountains. You'll cross the open areas and reach the mountains tonight so you won't be seen. Tomorrow afternoon, after resting up, you'll establish ambushes. The whole idea is training. You'll get used to each other and

197

have time to work out the glitches. *But remember*, there
are dinks out there! Follow the rules we taught you. Don't
be half steppin' or Charlie is gonna light your ass. The
ARVNs haven't been too active, so Charlie thinks he can
walk around with no problem. You're here to convince
him he done fucked up thinking it was over. Stay alert,
and *kill me some dinks*! Sergeant Wade, you stay a minute.
The rest of you start planning your routes."

Wade moved closer to the map as the men filed out.
Childs waited till they departed and motioned to a chair.

"Sit down, Wade. You have a village in your AO, so
take it easy and don't blow away any civilians."

Wade didn't like the mission and let out a sigh. "Sarge,
I've never worked in such an open area before, and I sure
as hell haven't been around any villages."

"I know that," retorted Childs, "but you got more experience than the others. That's why I picked your team.
Just skirt around the village tonight and set up your bush
in the foothills past the rice paddies. Anything that moves
at night is bad guys, so grease 'em."

Wade shook his head. "It's a long hump tonight, at least
eight klicks. Hell, we don't move at night in the
mountains!"

Childs studied the young sergeant's face for a moment.
"It ain't like you to complain. Whatsa matter?"

Wade lowered his head a few seconds before looking
up. "I'm good in mountains. I know what's got to be done
up there, but this open stuff is new to me. Here I am,
supposed to be training new men and now I'm just as
cherry as they are. Not a very good example, huh?"

Childs, realizing his sergeant wasn't feeling his usual
confidence, leaned back in his chair. "Wade, you'll do
fine, believe me. I was with the Cav my first tour and this
is all we did. I wish I'd had your experience when I first
got here. Look, it's no different. Instead of jungle you got
the night to protect you. Once you get past the vill, it's
like a regular mission."

Wade felt a little better from telling his sergeant how he
felt. He looked at the map more closely and smiled. "Well,

Sarge, the village of An Chon better not have any sleep-walkers 'cause they gonna pay big-time if they do."

Wade spat a brown stream of tobacco juice into a Coke can as his team studied the map he'd spread out on a foot-locker. "I marked the route. Does anyone have any suggestions?"

Rose looked up. "Yeah, forget it. It's all rice paddy, man. I ain't got duck feet."

Woodpecker ran his finger along the line Wade had drawn and tapped the village location. "It's gonna depend on wind direction if we're gonna get that close to the village before we go around."

Wade was surprised how the redhead had spoken so knowledgeably and leaned over the map. "Why?"

"I was with the Second Battalion, 503rd for awhile before going to the Aviation Battalion, and worked an area with lots of vills. The dinks have dogs and water buffs that'll smell us a klick away."

"Water buffs?" asked Thumper, smiling.

"Yeah, their buffalo can smell a GI bucoo far away and then goes *dinky dau*. The dinks put their buff pens on the outskirts of a vill and when the buffs start snortin' and stompin' around, the dinks know they got GIs coming. The dogs are inside the hootches and when they get wind of us, they'll start howling, lettin' everybody know, too."

Wade patted the redhead's thin back. "I knew you were good for somethin'."

Rose leaned back, mumbling. "The dude is full of shit, man. We gonna have to hump farther to get around the vill now."

The sun had just disappeared below the horizon when the first six teams passed through the perimeter gate. Wade's team 3-1 was the first out and headed due west toward the rice paddies.

Woodpecker had experience negotiating the narrow dikes and moved easily while the others slipped and fell in the rice paddy's two feet of muck. Initially they moved slowly, but by the time the darkness came, the rest of the team had gotten the hang of it. The paddies were interspersed with islands of high ground thickly vegetated with soaring bamboo thickets and other growth. The half-full moon reflected off the water, silhouetting the team and making them perfect targets.

After moving for an hour, Wade halted the team alongside one of the islands to regain his composure. He'd been in some hairy situations, but he'd never felt as nervous as he did right now. The team, walking along the dikes in the moonlight, would be powerless if they were ambushed, with no place to go and no cover. A Ranger team lived on stealth and depended on its senses, especially those of sight and sound. The night stole the team's sight, and the crickets, frogs, and damnable creaking and moaning of the bamboo took away their hearing. They walked along the dikes with only one hope—good luck, and luck was a nonfactor to a professional.

Wade knew they were getting close to the village. He took several deep breaths to control his shaking and upset stomach, then licked his finger and held it up. The wind was out of the east. At least they were downwind and wouldn't have to walk so far to skirt around. He took another deep breath, praying their luck would hold for another hour, and began walking again.

Le Xuan Can sat by the firelight and, with a smile, set down his diary. The peasants of the local villages here had done exactly what those in Binh Dinh Province had done; they complained of the hardships of the struggle and begged that the youth not be taken. He always promised the peasants not to take their young, but he knew what would really happen. The old teacher would fill the young hearts with the fiery words of Ho Chi Minh. Soon they would overcome their parents' fears, and they would beg to serve in the struggle. They would become a youth regiment in the People's Army; the peasants would then work harder to feed their children and their comrades. He had seen the phenomenon too often not to know the eventual outcome. Only time was needed, time and patience. The puppets and Yankees had left the peasants alone to hold their roads and cities, while the liberators of the true government held the people's hearts. Tomorrow, he, the Thach Sanh-peasant knight, would begin his slow march to victory, and the children of An Chon would soon . . . very soon, be marching along with him.

Matt Wade put down the radio handset and bought his CAR-15 to his lap. They had reached the foothills an hour before and found enough dense vegetation to laager in the standard wheel formation—sitting back on their packs shoulder-to-shoulder and facing out in a circle. One at a time, each man would watch for an hour and hold the radio to make periodic commo checks. The radioman at Mustang had just called him, and he'd replied by pushing the side bar twice. Two squelch breaks was the code for "all is well, no change in situation."

Wade was about to wake Thumper, but hesitated and looked up at the stars. The air had a twinge of dampness that only the night could bring, and the chirping crickets reminded him of the evenings on which he had sat with his granddad on Buggy Creek Bridge.

They often turned the dogs loose in the creek bed and let them run coons to the draw just below the bridge. His granddad would sit on the tailgate of the old Chevy pickup and chew tobacco, hardly ever speaking, and Wade would sit with him, always wondering what his granddad was thinking in his silence. One night, when he was sixteen, Wade finally had the courage to ask: "Granddad, what do ya think about when sitting out here?"

His granddad had stood and walked to the edge of the old wooden bridge and spat into the darkness.

"Me and Elma used to sit here for hours listenin' to the dogs and crickets. I come out here to be with her again."

He had walked back and sat down beside his grandson and looked up at the stars. "The night is special time, Matt. It's got a life of its own . . . and it holds a lot of good memories."

Wade cleared his thoughts and lifted the heavy medallion from his chest, thinking of the auburn-haired woman. "Memories," he said to himself, and tapped Thumper.

24 SEPTEMBER

Le Xuan Can reached out and turned up the wick of the kerosene lamp, basking the earthen walls in a golden hue. The wooden slats creaked as he sat up and placed his feet on the slanted, clay-packed floor and looked around. The room had changed little in the seventeen years since he'd been there last. That time he had been wounded in the legs by a French mine. The old underground complex had been a hospital; now it was used as a headquarters and supply base for the People's Liberation Armed Forces. The tunnel complex, known as *The House,* was dug into the side of the hill. It had three large rooms connected by tunnels. A bamboo thicket hid the main entrance, and the escape tunnel was on the far slope near a boulder. Three cell members used *The House* as a permanent base and received the coded radio messages over the AM transistor radio from Hanoi. From here the struggle had been coordinated and planned for the district in the past years. *The House* was only three kilometers from An Chon, yet few knew of its existence.

He slept in the first room nearest the entrance, where the others still slept in hammocks supported by huge teak support timbers. His was the only wood-slat bed, a place of honor.

Le Can rose to the sound of a faint whistling. Above him were the bamboo ventilation tubes that passed through the earth ceiling to the outside. He walked through the small, narrow tunnel to the second room that served as the headquarters and radio room. A young soldier of sixteen sat at a desk monitoring Hanoi Liberation radio.

"Any news, comrade?"

The boy turned with a smile to Thach Sanh and held up a notepad. "The fighters have taken a puppet base in Binh

Dinh province, and the Province Commissar asks for an update from all districts in two weeks.''

Le Can nodded. When he went to Kim Suu to transmit his report, the leaders would be pleased.

Returning to the sleeping room, he pushed open the clay- and root-matted door and climbed the cut-out earthen steps. Gray, early morning light greeted him as he stepped out of the entrance and closed the door. He stood in a small open area which, except for a narrow exit leading to a leveled spot alongside the hill, was completely enclosed by thick bamboo. He stepped out of the thicket to where three of his men lay on ground sheets and a fourth stirred the embers of a small fire. The old man stirring the embers gave him a casual glance. ''We will eat soon if you bring wood.''

Le Can, putting on his French hat, smiled at the old man's lack of respect. It was the teacher, Doan Ty, a contrary old man, but a master both of words and of cooking. Le Can picked up several sticks and set them down by his friend, who wore tattered khaki shorts and a black peasant shirt.

''We eat, then I go with the others to An Duc and talk to the hamlet chief. I will return this afternoon and we go to An Chon, where you will begin teaching.''

Doan Ty placed a blackened tin pot partially filled with water on the coals and cocked an eyebrow.

''You call it teaching. I say it is preaching. It is no matter. The result is the same. Is the medical team going with us?''

''Yes, but they go with me to An Duc first. The hamlet is in need of them. It will not take us long. The puppets and Yankees have given this area up. They only hold on to their precious road.''

''How long before you strike their outposts?''

''Not for another four months, when we have enough support. In another month we will begin mining the road to show the people we are fighting.''

''How many children does An Chon have?''

''Nine that will be old enough. An Dat has twelve, but

is close to the road. I will talk to the chief today and have the children go to An Chon." Le Can smiled and patted Doan Ty's back. "It will save your old legs many steps, yes?"

Rose halted the team and motioned Wade forward. They had gotten up at first light and climbed the first small hills to get deep into the forest. They planned to move a kilometer into the foothills, then head west toward a trail that led to the mountains and set up their ambush.

Rose whispered faintly, "Somebody's got a fire."

Wade sniffed the air and caught the faint but distinct odor of burning bamboo. It was coming from the south. "Let's check it out, but stay on the high ground and parallel this slope we're on."

Rose patted his M-16 affectionately. "We gonna get some, I can feel it."

Wade motioned the others up and told them about the change in plans, then nodded at Rose to move out. They stalked along the face of the hill, weaving their way through scrub trees and thick thorn bushes for fifty meters until the land suddenly sloped away into a small valley. They could see a small, dissipating cloud of smoke drifting up from the trees below.

Cautiously, Rose began to move down the hill, keeping close to a large banana tree grove. He came to a slight outcrop and froze. The team immediately knelt down. Rose lay down slowly and peered over the outcrop. Thirty yards below, five Vietnamese squatted by a fire.

Rose raised his hand and motioned his team sergeant up. Wade crawled forward and peered over the outcrop just as four of the VC stood. One of the Vietnamese, wearing a strange, wide-brimmed hat, walked into a thicket of bamboo and disappeared. Wade crawled back a foot and waved the rest of the team toward him. He was about to assign positions and targets when Rose poked him and pointed down the hill. The VC wearing the strange hat reappeared from the thicket holding a khaki satchel. He spoke to the other men as he picked up his rifle and began

walking down the slope. Three other soldiers slung their
weapons and followed. They were all carrying AK-47s, and
one of them, who also carried a large medical shoulder
bag, turned and waved to the remaining soldier, an older
man who wore shorts.

Wade cussed under his breath. There was no time to
assign targets. He'd have to let them go. Damn! Had the
dinks waited only thirty seconds more, his men would have
been in position and . . . Shit!

Wade tapped Rose and pointed to his own eyes. Then
he pointed to the remaining soldier. It was a signal for Rose
to watch the old man. The sergeant backed up and motioned Thumper to him as he pulled out his map.

"Thump," he whispered, "We gotta wait here and see
what the dink does. We can't get any closer or he'll hear
us and we can't shoot or the guys that are left will hear.
We'll wait awhile. If he looks like he might leave, grease
him."

Wade tapped Preacher and held out his hand for the
radio handset.

Sergeant First Class Childs was shaving, using a small
signaling mirror, when the RTO yelled from the TOC. "We
got a sighting from Three-one!"

Childs tossed down the razor and ran for the bunker
with half his face still covered with white shaving cream.

The radio operator handed the handset to the sergeant.

"This is Hotel Three. Go."

"This is Three-One, spotted five VC, from John, one
right, two point one up. Four carrying AK-47s heading
southeast. One VC remains by fire, am observing, will in-
itiate later. Out."

Childs stood and looked at the map where scattered
black dots had men's names beside them. He found
"John" and plotted over one grid square to the right, then
up 2.1 grid squares. The location was almost three kilometers due west of An Chon in the foothills. Come on
Wade, kill the bastards.

Doan Ty finished cleaning the rice pot and squatted by the fire. He couldn't help wonder how many such fires he'd been warmed by in the past years. The orange and red embers were old friends and had provided his ancient bones much comfort. It should be a simple mathematical problem, he thought. I have been with the struggle for ten years, multiplied by 365 fires a year is 3,650.

The thought of so many days made him lower his head in reflection. It was ten long years ago that he had left his school classroom and joined the struggle. Uncle Ho had told him, "Words are more important than guns. The people's struggle must have teachers to educate the young for the future . . . for the future holds our ultimate victory."

Ty smiled to himself, thinking of the many young faces he'd made followers. Uncle Ho would have been pleased to know his recruit of ten years before had become a master teacher.

Ty shoved dirt on the dying embers and stood. He decided to listen to the radio and talk to the remaining three men in the underground complex to pass the time. He stretched his arms upward and headed for the thicket.

Wade waited five minutes for the old soldier to come out of the bamboo before finally deciding to check it out. He whispered to Thumper, "I'm going down there and see what's in that thicket. Somethin' ain't right."

Thumper nodded and signaled to the others that the sergeant was going down and for them to cover him. Wade took off his pack and checked his CAR-15 one last time before going over the outcrop.

He low-crawled for ten meters and stopped. In front of him, sticking out of the ground by a thorn bush, was a two-foot-high, four-inch-round bamboo post. Several inches down from the top were cut-out square holes. It looked almost like a periscope.

Damn, it's a breathing tube or chimney, he thought. His stomach knotted into a ball and his throat craved moisture. He knew what the tube meant. Taking a deep breath to calm himself, he continued crawling down the hill.

Thumper couldn't see his sergeant through the vegetation. He waited for what seemed like hours until he noticed a movement by the bamboo thicket. Wade had crawled to the side of the bamboo and was trying to see through the thick stalks. The sergeant stood, took a step to the side, and peered through the small opening. Cautiously, he stepped forward into the thicket and disappeared. Thumper raised the M-79 launcher and clenched his teeth, waiting for the sound of the CAR-15. Seconds passed, but nothing happened. Suddenly he saw Wade's back as he stepped backward out of the thicket. Wade looked up toward him and motioned them down quickly.

Childs sat holding a cigarette. He wanted desperately to light it, but he wouldn't. He'd gone two weeks without one, and he'd promised himself he wouldn't start again. The radio speaker crackled and a whispering voice filled the bunker.

"Hotel Three, this is Three-one, over."

Childs brought the handset up. "Hotel three, Go."

"We found an underground bunker with at least one dink inside. He doesn't know we're here, we're checking it out. Out."

Childs turned to the radio operator. "Get on that other radio and call Fourth Division S-3, *now!*"

Wade positioned Russian up the hill to watch for anyone approaching, and whispered to the others. "We got an underground bunker of some kind. The entrance is in that bamboo. I'm gonna toss in a grenade and follow it, then . . ."

Woodpecker stepped closer, interrupting in a whisper, "There's got to be an escape hatch somewhere. If any more are in there, they'll flank us."

Wade's eyes widened. "Damn, you're right. Preacher, you stay here and cover the entrance. If that door opens, shoot the son of a bitch and toss in a grenade. The rest of us will scatter out and try and find the escape door."

The Indian nodded apprehensively and took a grenade from his ammo pouch.

Woodpecker pointed up the hill. "It's gotta be on the side of the hill where they could sneak out without being seen. It's on the far left or right."

Wade pointed to Thumper. "You and Woodpecker take the left. Me and Rose will take the right. If you find it, signal Russian and he'll signal us. I'll tell Russian what's happenin'."

The two teams broke up and began the search. After fifteen minutes, Wade was beginning to think it was hopeless. Rose leaned against a tree and was about to reach for his canteen when ne noticed something. Black wire was attached to the tree. When he backed up, he could see a small antenna hidden in the branches. He followed the wire down to where it was buried in the soil. Rose snapped his fingers at Wade and began pulling the wire up. The American-made communications wire yielded easily to the pressure as it had only been buried an inch. A long furrow quickly kicked up and snaked down the hill toward a large boulder. Wade and Rose followed the wire to the rock and saw the faint square outline on the ground. Both men looked at each other at the same time—the escape door!

Wade gathered his team at Russian's position on the hillside. "Thumper, you and Woodpecker watch the front entrance. Russian stays here and watches. Me, Rose, and Preacher will go in from the escape tunnel. Thump, if you hear us firing, back up and wait till they run out. Don't throw any frags in the cave, it might get us. And watch out for them throwing grenades before they come out. If we can't get in or it looks like there's a bunch of 'em, we'll throw in a gas grenade and wait for 'em. If I blow my whistle, everybody comes back here to Russian. Any questions or suggestions?"

The men all shook their heads.

"Okay, let's find us some dinks."

Using his knife, Rose began slowly prying open the wood- and soil-beveled door, which was constructed like a plant bedding box to hold the grass and foliage of the surrounding area. Had they not found the wire, they would never have located the entrance. Preacher held his weapon ready as Rose inched the door back gently, exposing a small black hole. Wade knew immediately he couldn't go down. The entrance was too small for his shoulders. Rose dropped his pack and pulled out his .45. "I'll go alone."

Preacher shook his head and dropped his pack. "I'll go with you."

Wade tapped Preacher, whispering, "Let him go, it's too tight for two."

The sergeant handed Rose his penlight and buck knife. Rose tossed down his flop-hat and put the penlight in his mouth. He slid the knife under his belt and took one last deep breath of fresh air before lowering himself into the darkness.

Doan Ty got to his feet. He could tell the young boy was tired of the conversation and would rather listen to the radio. Ty nodded to the second soldier, who glanced up only momentarily from writing in his notebook. Ty entered the short tunnel to return to the sleeping area. A soldier he'd talked to previously lay in his hammock sleeping. Ty turned around, retraced his steps back into the radio room and entered the tunnel to the third room, where the rice was stored.

Deciding to kill some of the ever-present rats, he lit the kerosene lamp.

Rose reached the tunnel floor and moved forward only three steps before making out a wall directly to his front. There was just enough light from the open door above to see that the tunnel made a ninety-degree right turn. Throwing a grenade into the entrance would have been useless. He flicked off the penlight and held his breath as he edged around the corner. Damn! He peered down a twenty-foot corridor, five-feet high and two and a half feet across, that slanted down at a thirty-degree angle. At the end of the corridor was a faint light. Son-of-a-bitch, why do I do this shit, man? Beads of sweat stung his eyes as he moved slowly down the inclined floor, praying there were no hidden traps or snakes. The hard clay walls smelled of musty smoke and damp cloths as he got closer to the end. He could now make out that the tunnel made a turn to the left and that the light was coming from around the bend.

Rose wiped the sweat from his forehead and shut his eyes for a moment to regain his confidence. Grasping the pistol tighter, he began to peer around the corner when a sound made his body turn to stone in rigid fear. It was a faint scampering noise coming in his direction. Suddenly, several large rats scurried around the corner and crashed into the terrified human obstacle. The foot-long furry creatures squealed and fought past his legs, leaving Rose shaking so badly he fell to his knees.

The black soldier hadn't cried out only because he'd almost swallowed the penlight. Suddenly a Vietnamese voice rang out crystal clear from around the corner. The high-pitched voice seemed to be talking into the tunnel.

Rose backed up a step and pulled the knife. He pressed himself against the clay wall, staring at the bend. There was a human shadow dancing on the tunnel wall. The Vietnamese voice spoke again with a small chuckle, then something slapped the wall.

Rose bit down on the penlight and inched closer.

Doan Ty, the master teacher, peered into the tunnel and struck the wall again. He knew he had some of the animals trapped. He picked up a net specifically made for rat catching in the tunnel. The net was loosely fitted between two bamboo poles. He would walk into the small confines holding the poles against the walls, and the rats would run to the escape exit, then stop in a frenzied group. Ty recalled how, in the old days, rats were a source of food when times were bad. He barked into the tunnel once again and picked up the two other prepositioned objects needed for the hunt, a small stick to beat them with and an old pith helmet fitted with a flashlight. He turned the light on and placed the helmet on his head, then stuck the club in his waist band.

"Rats, you die for the Fatherland," he said with a laugh

and entered the tunnel. He pushed the poles against the walls and began walking and singing the Provisional Government's national anthem, the first song he would teach the children:

Liberate our South Vietnam!
Heroic Southerners stand firm!
United we will brave the storm!

To save our land we'll fight to the end
March, march, onward, gun in hand.
Our day is . . .

He only saw a blur before falling backward with a shooting pain in his abdomen.

Rose yanked the knife free from the Vietnamese's stomach as he threw the man back and viciously slashed upward at his throat. Doan Ty tried to scream but only gagged on his own blood.

Rose clapped his hand over the man's mouth and drove the knife deeper into his larnyx until the cartilage crunched. The smell of blood was overpowering as Rose raised up and withdrew the knife. His arms and hands were covered in warm blood that smoked in the dim light as he placed the knife in his belt. Without shaking, he took the pistol from his leg pocket and stepped over the body.

Wade whispered into the hole several times, thinking he had heard something. He sent Preacher down the steps, only to have him come back seconds later whispering, "Rats."

Wade handed the small Indian his 9mm. Browning and told him, "Go in just a little ways and wait."

Preacher took the pistol and walked to the first ninety-degree turn and peered into the tunnel. A flashlight was shining toward him from the floor at the end of the corridor.

Rose entered the room swinging his body left, then right, holding the gun with both bloody hands. The room wall was stacked with bags of rice and wooden boxes. The lamp, almost out of kerosene, began flickering. Rose heard music. He stepped quickly across the room to the connecting tunnel just as the light faded out. The music was coming from just ahead, where there was more light. He slid along the wall and stopped as he caught sight of a small Vietnamese sitting at a desk with his back to him. Rose began to step closer when the man spun around as if to speak. Rose fired. The explosion within the tunnel was earsplitting. The shock wave caused his eyes to bulge in terrific pain. He fell to his knees and shook his head to clear the blur before him. Suddenly the lights went out, leaving him in total darkness. From the left came a flash of light spitting flame combined with a thunderous *bloom*!

Rose fell to the floor as the clay wall showered him with dirt. Someone was shooting at him. A loud moan only a few feet away startled him. Rose's ears rang, but the sound caused chills to run up his back. Suddenly the moan turned into a scream and a hand touched his head. Rose fired point blank and spun over just as the room filled with more flashes of light and explosions. *Bloom! Bloom! Bloom!*

Rose screamed out and fired toward the muzzle flashes until the pistol emptied. The radio station concluded its song and a woman spoke softly. Rose heard rustling and grabbed for another magazine. A small flashlight clicked on, its white spotlight shining on the far wall, then swung in his direction.

Rose grasped the magazine just as the light shone in his face, blinding him. Rose shut his eyes, waiting for the bullet, when suddenly a pistol fired behind him. The flashlight clattered to the floor and a body crumpled down on top of it.

Preacher flicked on the old man's helmet light and panned the room.

Rose looked up as the light hit his face. "Sweet Jesus."

"No, it's Black Eagle," said the Indian, kneeling down.

Thumper and Woodpecker sat waiting as the entrance door swung open. A bareheaded Vietnamese popped his head out and then ran up the steps. Woodpecker was about to fire when Thumper pulled the trigger of his .45. The small older soldier was picked up off the ground and flung back into the bamboo. The bullet had blown through his heart, killing him instantly. Woodpecker checked the body as Thumper approached the entrance cautiously.

A voice from within yelled out, *"Thumper?"*

"Yeah!"

"Did you get him?"

"Yeah."

"We're comin' out."

Childs listened as the speaker box crackled and Sergeant Wade's voice filled the bunker.

"We got four weapons, one is a K-54 pistol. There're about twenty sacks of rice and assorted boxes of medical supplies. It looks like a headquarters of some kind. Over."

Child could hardly contain his pleasure as he pushed the transmit bar. "Roger, Three-one, have good copy. We're sending a platoon from the fourth ASAP to police up all captured equipment. Over."

"Negative. Negative. Hotel Three. We think the four we saw this morning will be coming back. All their equipment and packs are here. We will set up ambush and wait. We're Charlie Mikin'. Over."

Childs smiled faintly and pushed the side bar.

"Roger, Three-one, understand. Will keep support ready for your call. Out."

Childs tossed down the handset and pounded his fist on the table. "Ya done good *Wade*! Real good! Hot damn, we killin' them bastards!"

He picked up the other radio handset and took a breath to keep from showing his excitement. "Cloverleaf Three, this is Ranger Hotel Three. Over."

"This is Cloverleaf Three. Over."

"Be advised Team Three-one has found Victor Charles Headquarters bunker and KIA'd four Victor Charlies at same location and . . ."

Rose was still shaking as Wade sat down beside him.

"You feelin' better now?"

Rose raised his head wearily. "Man, it scared me. I don't dig the dark anyway, poppin' caps was a bummer, and my head is still ringin'."

"Here, this will make you feel better," said Wade, handing Rose the Chinese K-54 pistol, one of the most prized war souvenirs a soldier could receive.

Rose flipped the weapon up nonchalantly and caught it in the other hand. He looked over his shoulder and tossed the weapon to the Indian, who was changing the radio battery.

"Preacher, ya got yourself a pistol. I was wrong about you . . . and thank the Good Lord for me that I was, okay?"

Black Eagle nodded in silence and set the gun down as he continued to change the battery.

Wade leaned closer to Rose. "He's takin' it bad, huh?"

Rose stood and chambered a round in his .45.

"The Indian is all right. He'll get used to it. He shot the mutha dead between the eyes. I think we'd better change his name to War Eagle, man."

Thumper walked up and motioned behind him. "We're all set up, Matt. Not many places to put the Claymores, so we're gonna have to fire them up good, if they come."

Wade snapped his fingers at Black Eagle, whispering, "Let's go, Preacher, we're gettin' in position."

Black Eagle put the pistol in his leg pocket and rose. He followed the sergeant to the right of the bamboo thicket and lay down beside him, readying his rifle. Killing another man had not bothered him as he'd thought it would. The sight of the old man's throat cut and the young boy's head partially blown off had bothered him more. They were no longer people; they looked more like dead animals. They had defecated after losing muscle control and the smell of feces, blood, and gunsmoke permeated the air. He would never forget the smell or their look. Death had left its mark on them—and on him, too. He couldn't explain the feeling; neither could he ever tell anyone, but it was a strange, satisfying experience, killing one man who had tried to kill another. He felt no remorse. The dead soldier had had his chance. But he felt sadness for the others.

Black Eagle ran his hand over the M-16. He knew now what his ancestors had felt when they had ridden away from battle. Their songs of victory and of sadness were the same. Only now did he understand why.

Black Eagle lifted his eyes skyward, praying for the dead and for understanding of his tingling pride from the Great One. Today he'd become a warrior.

Wade didn't notice the sweat trickling down his back as he watched the four men approach up the slope. The team had lain in the sweltering tall grass for two hours, almost exhausting their water supply, when Rose lightly snapped his fingers, signaling the enemy's approach.

Wade readied his rifle, aiming at the fourth soldier, who wore the strange, wide-brimmed hat.

Le Can switched his satchel to his other hand. He was looking forward to reaching *The House*. Several hours' rest would be just reward for convincing the An Duc hamlet chief to send the children to An Chon for schooling. The teacher would be pleased.

The three men in front of him carried their rifles over their shoulders like tired hunters. The medical orderly had exhausted his supply of sulphur and bandages on the open sores and infected wounds of the villagers. His only compensation was a lighter medical bag for the journey home. The lead soldier took the weapon off his shoulder as he approached the bamboo thicket, but he halted abruptly. There was dried blood on the ground. He began to scream out when his body was thrown backward violently in an earth-shattering explosion. The medical orderly fell to his stomach, choking in the dust cloud. He coughed up blood and brought his legs up under him to try and stand. Le Can was knocked down, but rolled off the trail just as machine gun fire opened up and stitched the others.

Wade rose, having seen his target crawl into the grass.

He brought his rifle up just as the man sprang to his feet and began to run. Wade aimed carefully and fired.

The .556-mm. copper-jacketed bullet flew for only a millisecond before it ripped through soft flesh, flattened slightly, and penetrated the back of the skull. The mangled hot metal halted its path of destruction only after passing through mushy gray matter and striking the other side of the skull. Le Xuan Can felt nothing. Death came instantly as his body toppled over.

Wade brought the recoiling weapon back to his left and shot again. His team hosed the trail with merciless fire.

In seconds it was over, and the bodies lay in grotesque positions. Russian rose first and nodded to the others. Wade walked to the man who ran from him and bent over, picking up his wide-brimmed hat. It was, as he'd thought, a French legionnaire hat, like ones he'd seen in pictures. He took off his boonie hat and tried the other one on. It fit perfectly.

Thumper turned the last body over and stood. "They're all dead, Matt."

The sergeant spit out a stream of tobacco juice. "Police up all the documents and weapons. Preacher, if ya wanna say some words over 'em, do it now. We gotta radio call to make."

Steer left . . . on course. LZ, one klick out . . . 800 . . .
500 . . . 250 . . . start flare now . . . ya see it?''

"Yeah, I got it, J.D. Good job," responded Lieutenant
Avant over the radio.

J. D. Gibson was flying in the back seat of a small L-
19 spotter plane, directing the other bird dog into a landing
zone as if it was a chopper. And he loved it.

That morning, Major Shane had shown them the tech-
nique on a blackboard. It was simple. The plane flew at
two thousand feet and directed a Slick helicopter, flying
at treetop level, into a landing zone. Choppers flew at max
speed at that level, and their pilots couldn't see an LZ miles
away, so spotter planes acted as their eyes.

Shane had introduced the two L-19 pilots to Gibson and
Avant, then sent them up to practice on one another.

Gibson had found it more difficult than it looked, and
keeping the radio toggles pushed to the right channel was
very complicated. Warrant Officer Gilbert Perry, the pilot,
who had been flying Ranger missions for three months,
had talked Gibson through several missions, and then had
let him try the last on his own. Gibson had done it perfectly.

Perry, sitting in the front seat of the plane, pressed his
talk button on the control stick. "That was super, J.D.!"

Gibson sat in the back seat and pressed a button on the
floor to activate his transmitter. "Thanks, Gil. I had a good
teacher. I don't know why you need me. You seem to know
this stuff."

217

Perry laughed. "You've just gotten started. This was the easy part. When we've got teams out it's a lot different. You're going to have to talk to the teams on their frequency and the choppers on theirs. Then you throw in the gunships, the artillery, the Air Force air controller, *and* report to your TOC all at the same time. I'm here to fly this thing, and you're here to talk and keep everybody informed. You also have to know how to read a map. What's the location of that bare hilltop below us at your one o'clock?"

Gibson oriented his map and found the hill easily. "It's at GD986366."

Perry checked the coordinates on his map and hit his talk button. "Yeah, you got it."

Perry was impressed. The gray-haired officer was a natural. He'd never seen anyone pick up the knack as quickly. It was probably Gibson's six months of experience on the ground that made the radio procedures easy for him. His map skills were excellent, too, and obviously came from plenty of practice.

"J.D., say you have a team in contact on the FM frequency. The guns are on UHF and the Slick's on VHF. Remember, now, the radio is the team's life. You have to talk to the team, but you also have to get the Guns and Slick to the point of contact. What do you need to vector the Guns and Slick to the team for extraction?"

Gibson thought a few seconds, recalling Major Shane's instructions, before depressing his floor button.

"We gotta have a checkpoint, a point of reference that all of us know. From there, I can give them a direction, until I see them and guide them to the team pickup zone."

"Damn, J.D., that's right! For an Aggie, you're not so bad."

"Thanks. You don't do bad yourself for a fly guy. 'Course, if I got paid flight pay, I'd be smart, too."

"Uh-oh."

"What's wrong, fly-boy?"

"You are! You're another one of these smart alec Rangers!"

The small plane plunged suddenly. Gibson held on, dropping his map to the floor.

Perry laughed and depressed the button. "You're gonna appreciate my flight pay, Aggie! I'm gonna see what you had for breakfast before we're through!"

Wade leaned back on his ruck in the shade of the bamboo as a Fourth Division platoon hauled equipment and rice from the underground headquarters. A division military intelligence team had also been choppered out and was sorting through the stacks of documents and maps. Wade looked at his team members sitting around him and felt a tingling sensation run up his spine. It was pride.

Rose was showing Preacher how to operate the K-54 pistol, when Wade cleared his throat for attention. "Guys, you all did good. There's not a thing I could say that any of us screwed up. We worked as a team and everybody did his job. Woodpecker, Preacher, you both acted like old veterans. Looks like Three-one got even better today. I'm proud to call you team members." Wade held his hand out palm up.

Woodpecker slapped his hand into Wade's. "Three-one!"

Preacher felt so much pride he shook as he put his hand on top of the redhead's with a loud "Three-one." He had at last been fully accepted as a team member.

Thumper and Russian both sat up and joined their hands to the group with a "Three-one!"

Rose stood and put his arm around Preacher and his other hand on top of the stack. "Three-one! The baddest news the dinks ever seen, man."

"Fuckin' A," responded all the others except for Preacher, who smiled and said, "Amen."

Just then, an obviously excited captain ran over to the team holding an unfolded map. "You Rangers found the district headquarters . . . and this map shows the exact location of the provisional headquarters!"

Wade exchanged glances with Thumper as if to say "so what."

The captain held the map out, pointing to a red dot. "There it is. A place they call Kim Suu."

Wade sat up and looked at the Vietnamese map, but couldn't tell heads from tails of the strange markings and style of the map. Wade smiled politely and sat back. "Sure enough, sir. Your people will be able to do it a damn damn."

The captain hurriedly folded the map and yelled to his radio operator, "Simmons, get me a chopper in here ASAP!"

Thumper motioned toward the complex. "Sir, how come it took so long to find this place. Surely you've been looking for it?"

"Hell, yes, we've looked for it, but they never transmitted any radio messages so we couldn't triangulate. This district headquarters only received messages over normal AM airwaves from Radio Hanoi or the Liberation Radio station. They had to travel to their province headquarters to transmit and then they used roving radios so we couldn't pinpoint them. By finding the exact location we can destroy their relay station and set them back months, possibly a year. The only problem is we have to do it right now before they find out you've found their district headquarters."

"Sir, the bird is on its way!" yelled the radio operator.

The captain spoke to Wade. "My people will be here until more choppers come out to pick this stuff up. You and your team can go with me and I'll drop you at Mustang."

Wade quickly got to his feet. "You bet, sir!"

Major Shane had picked up Colonel Ellis at noon from the airfield. They were both now in Shane's office, looking at a map the Corps G-2 had spread out on his desk. Colonel Ellis pointed to the map. "You can see it's an extensive area to search. That's why your Ranger teams are needed. Somewhere in that one-hundred square miles is the Second NVA Division. If your team can find the base camp, we'll call a B-52 strike on top of it."

Shane leaned closer to study the terrain when the phone

rang. He reached for the handset and put it to his ear while looking at the map. "Major Shane . . ." His eyes enlarged suddenly and he snapped upright. "Yes sir! . . . Yes, I'm aware one of our teams found a VC headquarters and . . . Yes, sir. In fact, Colonel Ellis, the Corps G-2, is here in my office and . . . Yes, sir."

Shane held the handset out to Ellis, covering the mouthpiece. "It's General Larose from the Fourth Division. He wants both of us to come to his headquarters right now, but he wants to speak to you first."

Ellis took the phone and spoke to the general for several minutes before hanging up and looking at Shane's anxious face. "Looks like your Rangers have stirred up a hornet's nest. It seems the intell people found a map with the exact location of the provincial headquarters and they need your help."

"Sir, they don't need us. Christ, we're trying to train our people," said Shane, knowing Colonel Ellis had to release his company to the Fourth's commanding general.

Ellis shook his head. "This is big, Ed. We don't get many chances like this. I think General Larose is right. An immediate strike is necessary. You'd better call your operation off and get your teams ready to go."

"Sir, we only have four teams in; the rest are in the field. Can't the Fourth handle it?"

The colonel folded his map. "Larose wouldn't ask if his people could do it. At least get your four teams ready, and we'll listen to what he has to say. I'll make the decision whether Corps releases you to his control after we hear him out."

Shane put on his beret and hollered toward the door, "Pete!"

The bespectacled Pete opened the door seconds later. "Sir?"

"Get the jeep. We're going to Fourth Division Headquarters."

Wade washed the last of the camouflage greasepaint

from his face and stepped out of the makeshift shower. The fifty-gallon drums of water overhead only released a trickle of water, but at least he'd gotten the grime off. He'd let the rest of the team go ahead of him, and ensured that Rose went first to wash the dried blood from his arms and hands. Rose was dancing buck naked to the beat of the transitor radio as Thumper and Woodpecker clapped their hands, egging him on. A group of South Vietnamese ARVNs gathered around, giggling and pointing at the well-endowed black soldier as he gyrated back and forth in perfect rhythm.

"Dig it, little people! You checkin' out the Detroit *Dy-na-mo*! Yeah! Jeremiah was a bullfrog . . . he was a good friend of mine . . ."

Rose grabbed Black Eagle and began dancing around him, laughing. The small Indian rolled his eyes at Wade and shrugged his shoulders. Rose tapped the Indian's chest. "Come on, Preacher, loosen up, man."

Black Eagle looked skyward and began a chant while moving his feet. Soon he was in a full victory dance, stealing the show. Rose stopped in shock, then began imitating him. Thumper and Woodpecker joined in.

Childs walked out of the TOC with Lieutenants Gibson and Avant, who had come out to the fire base after they'd finished flying. The three men stood in disbelief just as Wade and Russian joined the other team members chanting and dancing around in a circle.

Childs looked at Gibson, shaking his head. "Ya see what I gotta put up with? A bunch of crazies."

"Hell, Sarge, they gotta be crazy to be in the Rangers."

Avant began shuffling his feet. "Catchy dance. Wonder what you call it?"

Childs snickered. "Dancin' dumb-ass, if you ask me."

Gibson patted the sergeant's shoulder. "Come on, Sarge. Four of your teams are in with kills. You should be happy your training paid off."

The radio operator yelled out from inside the TOC. "Sergeant Childs, Major Shane is on the horn for you!"

Childs walked back inside as the officers watched more

of the teams join in on the dance. Minutes later Childs jogged out of the TOC and hollered out, "Team leaders, get over here!"

"What's up?" asked Gibson.

The sergeant spoke gruffly over his shoulder. "We gotta get ready for another mission."

Major Shane and Colonel Ellis were escorted back into a smoke-filled room where the Fourth Division commander and his operations officer, G-2, and Aviation Battalion commander stood over a map. General Larose quickly introduced his assembled staff, then got right down to business.

"Colonel Ellis, the situation is this: My intell folks have pinpointed the province headquarters in this small valley only twenty kilometers away from the district headquarters the Rangers found this afternoon. The province headquarters is located in thick scrub vegetation with no helicopter landing zones anywhere close. It'd take at least a full day for a company to march over this terrain to get to it. We don't want to bomb it, or we'll lose valuable intelligence. I propose the Rangers go in right on top of it and rappel in. They have the training and men to do it. If needed, I'll follow up with a unit of my own men climbing down from a rope ladder out of a Chinook. We need a sudden strike to catch them with their shorts down so we can capture their radios and codes."

Colonel Ellis studied the map for a moment. "What about enemy strength, sir? The Rangers will be big targets dangling from ropes."

The general nodded to his intelligence officer to answer. "Colonel, the VC usually stay in very small numbers. I would expect only a squad of men, at the largest, plus radiomen and leaders. They definitely won't have any air defense weapons. Mostly small arms. We propose that the Cav lead the attack with gunships shooting only their Gatling guns, followed by small, light observation choppers flying at treetop level to spot the camp. The Slicks will follow behind and drop the Rangers. More gunships will be available to lay supressing fire for the Rangers on the ground.''

Ellis turned to Shane. "What do you think?"

Shane looked at his watch. "Sir, it's 1500 now. By the time we get the ropes and choppers rigged up, it'll be 1700 hours and we've got to brief the teams and pilots. I'd say we'd better wait and plan this out and hit them at first light tomorrow.''

General Larose looked at his G-2, who hesitated for a moment before nodding in agreement.

Larose tapped the map. "Tomorrow morning it is. Let's gather around and work this thing out. Major Shane, we've got birds en route to fire base Mustang right now with the ropes. You'd better call your people and give them a warning order.''

Shane picked up the telephone as he spoke to the general. "Sir, I'll need to keep the birds there so my men can practice rappeling.''

"No problem." The general nodded to the Aviation commander, who immediately picked up a second phone.

Ed Shane rubbed his eyes tiredly and looked at his watch. It was almost midnight. He'd been flown out to Mustang in the late afternoon and briefed the teams on the assault. The team conducted two rehearsals, rappeling into vegetated terrain near the fire base. Based on the rehearsal, he selected Sergeant Zubeck's Team 2-1 and Wade's 3-1 Team to lead the assault, with 2-4 and 1-3 as the second wave back-up, if they were needed. Lieutenant Avant would go in with Zubeck's team to control the operation and Lieutenant Foley would direct the air operation.

Shane sat down on his cot and looked over at Childs, who was writing in a notepad.

"Jerry, get some sleep. The RTO will wake us at four.''

Childs finished making a note to himself and sighed. "You know, sir, I'm not worried about our people. It's them aviators I don't trust. Their assault has got to be timed down to a gnat's ass. Ya see them long-haired Cav pilots? Not one of them took notes during your briefing.''

Shane laid back and shut his eyes. "Get some sleep. They did all right during the rehearsal."

Childs frowned and stood up. "I wish they'd at least cut their damn hair and look military. Them prima donna hippies all try and look like Custer."

Shane turned over without responding. The grizzled sergeant shook his head and sat on his cot. Shane was right; they had looked good during the rehearsal, but their damn hair was . . . aw shit, screw it.

Gibson sat up in his bunk and looked over at Avant, who lay on his bed staring up at the ceiling.

"Can't sleep, huh?"

Avant raised up. "Naw. I was running the operation over in my head. I hope they're there. You know how the intell types can screw up this kind of thing."

"Brad, you just be careful and don't play John Wayne. I might need a good lawyer one day."

Avant smiled. "Don't worry none, cousin. Ol' Brad ain't no he-ro."

Avant laid back and shut his eyes. "You know, J.D., I might not get out and finish law school after all. This Army is okay. On the outside it's hard to find what we've got. It may be just the war environment, but damn, it feels good to be with men who are totally committed to excellence in themselves and the unit. They have such pride and yet are willing to sacrifice for the good of the group. You just don't find that on the outside. It's . . . it's just such a good feeling being a part of them."

Gibson stretched out on his bunk. "The whole Army isn't like this. We're just lucky we have good leaders and good men."

"Yeah, but it's what you make it, my friend. I've been out there in the civilian world, and they care about money, not people. Profit is the bottom line. Their goals are what they can get for themselves. Here it's different. We all have to work together and be the best we can so we all survive. There's a big difference."

Gibson shut his eyes. "Well, hell, I guess I won't have a lawyer friend after all, just another officer to compete against for promotion."

Avant grinned as he shut his eyes. "You'd better believe it. This boy is gonna make a helluva general."

24 SEPTEMBER

The shrill whining of helicopters cranking their engines broke through the early morning quiet.

Matt Wade's stomach knotted into a ball as he reinspected the Swiss seat rappel harness he'd tied round his waist and legs, and checked the metal snap-link's open and closing gate. His men were similarly dressed and were armed to the teeth. Each man wore two eight-magazine bandoliers crisscrossed over his chest and a third tied around his waist. They carried no packs and had their grenades and smoke canisters strapped to their fighting harness. No one wore a hat, but instead wore a red bandana tied around his head for easy identification. In the smoke and confusion, immediate identification was tantamount to survival.

Wade inspected each of his men one more time and looked over at Sergeant Zubeck, who waved and held his thumb up. Wade returned the gesture and led his men to their chopper.

Lieutenant Avant gave Gibson his usual silly smile as J. D. helped him slip the rappeling rope into the snap-link. The assault teams sat on the floor of the choppers with legs extending over the sides. Their ropes were tied to the floor and coiled around dirt-filled sandbags. The sandbags would be placed on their laps and dropped over the target. The weight of the bag would uncoil the rope and ensure that it didn't get snagged in the trees. J. D. placed the heavy bag in Avant's lap and yelled over the engine's roar, "Take care. I'll be monitoring the radio from the other bird dog!"

Avant yelled out, "No sweat, see you later!"

Wade patted his friend's leg and lifted the other bags to the rest of the team members.

After placing the sandbags on the team members' laps, Childs backed up from Wade's bird and raised his hand to Major Shane to signal they were ready. Shane waited until Lieutenant Gibson gave a similar signal, then brought the radio handset to his mouth.

"Eagle flight lead, you're clear for takeoff. Over."

The lead Cav pilot, flying the light observation chopper, gave a quick "Roger" and called the other helicopters behind him.

"Eagle flight, this is lead. I'm lifting in five seconds. Four . . . three . . ."

Childs walked up beside Shane as the four choppers lifted off and shot forward to join the circling gunship above. Shane turned to his sergeant with the look of all commanders who send their men to battle: the look of anguish and pride.

Childs winked confidently. "They're damn good men, sir."

Shane, speaking softly, never took his eyes off the choppers. "Yeah, Jerry, they are."

Signalman Second Class Phu Tan Bic rose from his hammock when he heard the old rooster sing a greeting to the new day. The rooster had much to crow about. The two squads of liberation fighters that had arrived the day before had brought nine hens and a pig for the camp. Bic only hoped the twelve men would hurry and leave after the political classes that afternoon. He was a signalman but also a cook. Cooking for the seven permanent headquarters cadremen was difficult enough, let alone for visitors who would deplete their already meager stocks of rice. Bic put on his sandals and looked toward the stream. Perhaps the traps would be blessed and catch many fish. He yelled toward the first hut, "Tan Phoc, rise lazy brother and check the traps!"

The visitors stirred at his loud words and began sitting up.

Bic walked past their hammocks and entered the radio hut built under the sayo trees. The hut was one of three hidden under the thirty-feet-tall protective trees near the stream's fork. Bic tapped the radioman to get his attention. Phum By took off the headset and smiled. "It is time to eat?"

"No, of course not. Not until the fighters gather wood will there be food."

The radioman grunted. "I am hungry. Hurry the lazy liberators, but before you go . . ." He motioned toward the large radio sitting on the table before him. "The firing device blocks the frequency dial."

Bic stepped closer to the radio to inspect the cylindrical Yankee fuse starter taped to the radio. The orange fuse cord ran only a foot to a block of explosives attached to the side of the radio and a box of code books. Bic pulled off the tape and moved the firing device over an inch.

"You could have done this as well as me."

The radioman frowned. "I do not like touching things that could blow my radio to Buddha's paradise."

Bic shook his head in disgust. "You must pull the ring of the Yankee device if the time comes. You should know such things as well as you know your radio. It is your duty."

The radioman sighed and spoke sarcastically as he put on the headset, "And your job is to feed me. Go do your *duty*."

Bic began to retort when he heard the chickens cluck excitedly. The damn fighters were planning to eat the gifts! He ran to the hut door.

Lieutenant Foley looked out the Plexiglas window of the bird dog to the earth three thousand feet below. The helicopters were circling a small hill at the head of a valley. Foley pushed back his thick glasses and checked his map.

The VC headquarters was supposed to be located eight kilometers up the valley at the fork of the stream. Foley could see the stream glistening with the rays of the rising sun. He pushed the floor button. "Eagle Flight Gun, this is Sierra One, take up heading one-eight-zero."

A voice immediately replied, "Roger."

The two Huey gunships banked right and dropped, rapidly losing altitude, followed by the Cav Loches and two Slicks.

Wade's legs dangled over the lip of the passenger compartment into ninety-knot winds. His fatigue pants fluttered and popped as he opened his eyes after the Slick finally pulled out of its steep descent and leveled just forty feet above the stream. Wade knew it was almost time and yelled as he held up one finger, "One minute!"

Preacher finished his prayer and thought through his actions one final time. They would wait till the bird came over the yellow smoke canister that the Cav pilots had dropped and then he would toss out his sandbag. He'd spin around and place his feet on the skids, holding the rope behind his back in the brake position. Then he'd bound off the skid, throw his brake hand out, and rappel down the rope. He would be on the ground in four seconds and would have to cut the rope free. Oh, Great Father, give this warrior strength to overcome my fears. Guide my friends and me safely, and lead us to victory.

The hungry men gathering around the fire as he poured rice into the simmering water reminded Phu Bic of children. He placed the lid on the large pot and dumped the sliced slivers of fish and pao leaves into a pan of chicken fat. The sizzling sound brought sighs of gratitude from the assembled group of hungry men. Phu Bic couldn't help but smile. His work was appreciated. He poured tea into three cups for his leader and political officers. He picked up the wooden tray and hurried to the third hut.

Foley spotted the fork in the stream and looked at the

position of the speeding gunships. They were only a kilometer away from the target.

"Eagle Gun, one klick out."

"Roger."

The lead Gun copilot flipped down the sight from above him and put his hand on the fire control. He placed his finger to the side of the red button that would fire the two Gatling guns at 1200 rounds a minute and spoke into his transmitter, "Guns up."

Foley hit his transmitter button. "Five degrees right . . . on course. Five hundred meters to target." Foley knew the enemy couldn't hear the choppers traveling at their speed at treetop level until they were only a few hundred meters away, and then it would be too late. He had lined the up gunships to strike the south side of the stream fork where the camp was supposed to be. "Two hundred meters! . . . *Ready . . . . Now!*"

The gunships pulled up to one hundred feet and lowered their noses to fire. The copilot aligned the two red circles on his sight and pressed the trigger. The chopper jolted as the Gatling guns began spinning. Bruuuuuup! Bruuuuuuup!

Phu Bic dropped his tray in terror as the forest behind him erupted in chaos. He turned just as the ground around the cooking fire erupted in smoke and screams. Bullets raked a path beside him and he threw himself behind a tree. The whopping cracks of the helicopters' blades and engines' roar were thunderous and drowned out the wounded's screams. Suddenly there was another sound— a loud, mechanized buzzing as a small, round-nosed helicopter passed overhead and darted to his left. Through the tree branches he could clearly see a Yankee wearing a huge helmet and shooting a machine gun. Another of the round-nosed giant bees came overhead and dropped an object that spewed out a yellow cloud and fell near the first hut. Several fighters ran past him yelling, but he couldn't move. His body was frozen in fear. A big Yankee flying machine hovered close to the first hut and men hanging from its sides began dropping from ropes through the tree branches.

Phu Bic screamed and jumped to his feet. The radio and codes had to be destroyed.

Wade spun around and kicked off the skid, followed by his team. He slid down the rope, throwing on the brake hand only five feet from the ground to slow his descent. He hit the ground and pulled his knife, cutting the rope free.

Preacher slid down and hit hard, falling over in front of Wade. The sergeant reached out quickly and cut Preacher's rope as Thumper helped the Indian to his feet. Bullets cracked over their heads, and they could hear men screaming in Vietnamese. Wade grabbed for his slung weapon just as a wide-eyed VC burst through the smoke cloud running directly toward him and shooting wildly. Wade brought his rifle up, but before he could fire, a loud burst behind him flung the VC sideways. Russian stepped in front of his sergeant and fired again, riddling the soldier with bullets.

Woodpecker fired from the hip at two fleeing figures, knocking one down. Thumper aimed carefully and fired. The second soldier's head snapped back, and his legs buckled. Rose finished off both with a long burst.

When he saw Sergeant Zubeck and his men rushing the first hut, Wade motioned his own men forward. Zubeck fired half a magazine and fell behind a ripped corpse next to a cooking fire. Six other bodies lay in grotesque positions around the small fire. The bodies reeked of blood and torn, exposed intestines. The gunsmoke hung just above the ground like a thick fog as he peered over the body to spot the enemy that had pinned them down. Muzzle flashes popped like light bulbs just to the right of the first hut, where three or four men lay in a shallow depression. One of Zubeck's men rose up to fire but was immediately struck in the side and pitched backward, groaning.

Lieutenant Avant crawled to the soldier and pulled him back behind a tree. Zubeck looked over the body again. There were three thatch huts—two were fifteen meters away and a third sitting twenty meters behind the others.

Wires ran from the trees to the second hut; it had to be the communications hootch.

Wade crawled up to Zubeck just as two Vietnamese ran from the entrance of the third hut. Zubeck's men cut them down in a long volley. Lieutenant Avant looked around the tree he was hiding behind. ''Wade, give me and Zubeck covering fire. I'm going to the second hut. Zubeck, you take the first. On five!''

Wade yelled to his men. ''Cover fire to the right of the hootches . . . on my command! *Ready. . . . Fire!*''

Zubeck and Avant jumped up and ran for the buildings as the teams threw out a protective curtain of lead.

Phu Bic crawled through the back entrance of the radio hut. The radioman had run without priming the fuse starter. Bic ran over and pulled the ring, igniting the fuse that immediately began sizzling and smoking. Bic knew he had only ten seconds. He ran for the back entrance. Suddenly a Yankee burst through the front door, shooting. Bic jumped for the exit but bullets tore into his back, knocking him into the wall. He felt as if he'd been struck by burning coals. As he fell to the floor, he caught a glimpse of the American—an American with no hair. The Yankee stepped closer, smiling strangely, and lowered his rifle.

Avant began to yell out he'd gotten the radio when he saw the smoking fuse. He jumped for the door just as the hut exploded in a vehement blast.

Wade saw the hut disappear in a shattering explosion and ducked down to avoid flying debris. Cursing, he grabbed his weapon tightly and jumped to his feet. ''Mother fuckers!'' He ran directly toward the enemy position, shooting.

Rose screamed out, ''Get some!'' and joined his sergeant, followed by the rest of the team.

The four VC in the depression were still stunned by the blast. Two tried raising up to fire, but bullets plowed the ground in front of them. The other two ran but were shot in the back and legs.

Rose reached the depression first and fired point blank

into the two cowering men. One screamed out, clutching his stomach, and cried pathetically. Rose pointed the barrel of his smoking M-16 at the man's face and pulled the trigger. The weapon was empty. Preacher ran up and fell to his knees beside the wounded soldier as Rose ejected the spent magazine and inserted a new one. Preacher looked up with a pleading expression as Rose lowered the barrel with a cruel grin. "Get back. He's gonna splatter."

Preacher leaned over the soldier in front of the gun barrel and began inspecting the wound.

Rose lowered his weapon slowly. One of the men who had tried to run was moaning. Rose bent over the writhing soldier and pulled a first aid bandage from his harness. He looked at Preacher and winked.

Wade and the rest of the men spread out and began moving toward the hootches. Sergeant Zubeck had been in the first hut and was thrown through the door when the radio shack had exploded. He lay on his back, stunned, as Thumper approached and lifted him to his feet. The sergeant fought to keep his balance and shook his head. "Where's the L-tee?" he asked groggily. Thumper motioned to the smoldering debris. "He didn't make it out."

Zubeck fell to his knees. "God, no."

Lieutenant Foley received a report from the Cav pilot that two of the huts had disintegrated in an explosion and that one of their birds had taken several hits but was flyable. Foley tried calling Zubeck's radio operator, but he wasn't monitoring. It had been three minutes since the teams went in and he should have reported by now. The helmet earphones suddenly popped and an excited voice spoke rapidly. "Camp secured, have one WIA and one KIA. Got fifteen enemy KIA and three WIA. Radio destroyed by dinks, captured bucoo documents, need Demo to blow PZ, need medevac ASAP. Over."

Foley had a list of the men's names with a number beside each. He took a breath before pushing the transmit button. "Eagle Assault, what line number of KIA and WIA? Over."

There was a five-second pause before the answer came back. "Sierra-three, line number zero-one, KIA; line number zero-four, WIA."

Foley didn't need to look at the list to determine the name of the dead soldier. Avant was the leader and was listed first.

J. D. Gibson sat back in the seat of his bird dog circling two miles away monitoring the operation. He dropped his head at the news of his friend's death. His eyes clouded, and he stared at his left hand—it had patted Avant's leg only thirty minutes before.

The image of Avant's silly grin filled his mind as he leaned his head back on the seat and fought back tears. He clenched his fist, wanting to smash something to release his anger and frustration. The death of a friend was always a possibility that lingered in the back of his mind, but the reality of its happening still brought shock. He had prepared for it in his own way, but the incredible empty feeling of loss and the overwhelming feeling of frustration could never be anticipated. Damn, was there a clue or sign of its coming that he should have seen? The answer came back, making him feel small and useless: Dying in war couldn't be avoided. Death could strike anyone at anytime, anyplace. It was always there waiting . . . waiting like a black widow in her web. And everyone in this sad land was caught in a struggle that might make him her victim.

Gibson raised his head, letting his tears fall freely. He cared, damn it! He'd cared and to hell with not showing emotion. His friend at least deserved his tears. God, Brad, he thought, I'm so sorry.

The Huey set down gently in the pick-up zone. General Larose hopped to the ground along with his operations officer and Major Shane. The bird lifted up and a medevac came in behind it.

Larose bent over the wounded Ranger and patted his shoulder. "Thanks, son."

Private First Class Brasseaux smiled through his pain and held up his hand. "We kicked ass, sir."

Larose took his hand, squeezing it tightly. "You sure did. I'll visit you in the hospital and pin on your Purple Heart."

The young soldier's face broke into a grimace of pain as the medic tried to take off his shirt. Brasseaux looked up at the general and clenched his teeth. "I'll be back."

The general released his hand, stood up, and cast a disgusted look at the three wounded Vietnamese lying beside the soldier. Two were hurt badly. He stepped over them and joined Major Shane and Sergeants Zubeck and Wade. Beside them were the remains of Lieutenant Avant, covered with a blood-soaked hammock.

Wade explained what had happened in the assault as he escorted the general through the camp.

The general shook his head after the tour and surveyed the scene one last time.

"Major Shane, your men performed superbly. I'll put all of them in for awards. It's too bad about the radio and codes, but the setback to their operation is more than enough compensation. It'll never replace your lieutenant, but . . . but he died heroically in the service of his country. I'm proud of him, and I'm proud of your men. If there's anything I can do for you or them, call me."

Shane looked at his assembling men, then back at Avant's body. He nodded in silence and knelt down by his dead officer. "Good-bye, Brad."

Gibson ran his hand through his short gray hair and sat down tiredly in the operations briefing room. He'd landed an hour before at the airfield and had driven out to Mustang.

Childs was posting the situation map and looked over his shoulder at the young officer.

"Don't get down, L-tee. Lieutenant Avant is gone. There's nothin' we can do about it but drive on."

Gibson nodded and lifted his head. "I wanna go out on

a team. I need to get back in the field and hold a weapon again."

Childs faced the lieutenant, looking into his pale blue eyes.

"Revenge is a killer. You'll forget the rules and take too many chances. Just forget it and keep flying."

Gibson forced a smile. "I don't wanna go for revenge. I just wanna get back in the bush and feel like I'm doing something useful. Team One-three has a sick man, so I'll take his place."

Childs knew exactly what the L-tee was feeling. He had felt the same way many times. "I'll talk to the major when he gets back this evening. In the meantime, pack your shit. I'll tell Sergeant Selando he's gonna be an assistant team leader and you'll lead the team for training purposes."

J. D. began to offer his thanks when Childs's voice turned cold. "L-tee, don't fuck it up. Selando and his team are good people. Don't be trying to even the score out there or you'll get one of them greased."

J. D.'s eyes narrowed as his jaw tightened. "You know Childs, you really are an asshole."

The sergeant snickered and turned back to the map. "Yeah, L-tee, I am . . . but I'm right and you damn well know it. Lead that team right or I'll personally kick your ass."

Gibson stared at the sergeant's back, knowing he had wanted to even the score. The crotchety sergeant had seen through him and, in his typical direct way, let it be known he was wrong.

The lieutenant stood and walked for the entrance. He stopped at the first step and looked over his shoulder. "Thanks."

Childs kept posting the map and only nodded in acceptance.

24 SEPTEMBER

Gibson raised his hand and halted the team. He looked back at the five camouflaged faces and motioned them down for a break.

Team 1-3 had walked out of Mustang the day before and were en route to a mountain trail. Gibson checked his map. The trail was only a few hundred meters away. The team had not liked the idea of his taking over and only reluctantly accepted his leadership. He knew he was being judged, as his platoon in the 173rd had judged him when he first took command. The looks on the faces were the same. "Does he know what he's doing?" their questioning stares wanted to know. Only with time would their questions be answered.

Gibson took a long drink from his two-quart plastic canteen and motioned his men up. He pointed to Watkins, a baby-faced Kentuckian, and whispered, "Take point. The trail is a couple hundred meters straight ahead. Take it slow."

The soldier glanced at Sergeant Selando, who nodded for him to follow the order.

Gibson noted the gesture and stared at the stocky sergeant, who returned the glare with a surly smirk. Gibson waited for Watkins to pass by him and then stepped close to the olive-skinned sergeant, whispering harshly, "Don't ever do that again! I don't need your approval on anything."

238

Selando still held a condescending smirk. "Yes, *sir*."

Feeling the heat of the sergeant's eyes on his back, Gibson stepped in front of the sergeant and began to follow the point man. Selando was experienced, but so was he. There was no room for two team leaders. Selando hadn't accepted that fact yet and would be watching his every move.

Gibson shook the thought from his mind and concentrated on looking ahead. It don't mean nothing, he said to himself, and stalked forward cautiously.

Woodpecker, lying back on his poncho liner, looked up at the sun and snapped his fingers to the beat of Rose's radio.

"I'm going to tan up this bod and find me a woman tonight."

Rose pushed sand up into a mound and gazed out at the breaking waves. "Man, this R and R shit is what's happenin'. If I'd knowed they was gonna do this for rappelin' outta a chopper and killin' dinks, I'da volunteered."

"You did volunteer," said Preacher blandly.

"Man, you crazy? They told us we gonna do it. I didn't raise my hand."

"Yes, but you volunteered for the Rangers, so it's the same thing."

"Preacherman, you thinkin' like a preacher again. Just cause you say one thing one time don't mean it means it all the time. Why, I told a hundred women I dug 'em. And at the time, I *did*. But that don't mean I really dug 'em, you know what I mean?"

The Indian smiled. "Yes, I understand. And one day I hope *you* do."

As if confused, Rose looked at Preacher and shook his head. "Preacher, you're a heavy trip, man. Hey, Thump, where is Matt?"

The heavily muscled soldier opened his eyes. "He's still trying to call that singer in Saigon."

"Man, he's been gone all morning. The dude is wastin' rays. Look at my tan. I'm ready for *to-night*!"

Russian, the only one of them fully-clothed, shot Rose a warning glare.

"The sergeant say nothing of going to the city tonight."

Rose shoved his sand mound over. "Man, they gave us a three-day I and I. That means intoxication and inter-coursin', and the Rose is in for some intercoursin'!"

"The sergeant say nothing of . . ."

Sergeant Zubeck, holding a football, ran up to the loung-ing men. "Come on Three-one, I got this from the recre-ation guys. How about a little game?"

Thumper sat up and winked at Rose. "I don't know, Zee. Your team is kinda outta our league. Your guys being wimps and all, it wouldn't be fair."

Zubeck threw the ball at Thumper. "Come on stud, you just pissed off the mighty Two-one. We gonna beat you by two TDs or it's a case of Bud."

Thumper tossed the ball to Woodpecker and looked at the others. "Well, we going to play or not?"

Woodpecker stood up, flexing his small arm muscles. "I always did like Budweiser."

Preacher shook his head. "I don't drink beer."

Russian got to his feet and patted the small soldier's back. "I know nothing of your football, but we beat them anyway, yes?"

Preacher smiled and jumped to his feet. "What are we waiting for?"

Virginia put down the phone and wiped away her tears. He called . . . he finally called, and wanted to see her.

At first he'd hemmed and hawed with small talk, but then he'd asked if she could come to China Beach R and R Center in Da Nang to be with him. She couldn't say "yes" fast enough.

Virginia sat down on her bed, trying to remember his every word. His team and another had been given an in-country R and R for doing a good job—three days at Da Nang. They'd just arrived that morning and checked into the recreation camp. He'd been trying to call for three hours . . . three hours, my God . . . Now what was it she had said? She'd have to sing tonight but then she could claim she was sick and needed to rest for a few days. She would catch a flight tomorrow morning and be there by noon. That would give them one-and-a-half days and one entire *night.*

She started to pack.

Wade walked over the sand dune feeling light. Ginny was coming. He wanted to hold her so bad he didn't think he could stand waiting another day.

Someone hollering broke his trance and he looked up the beach.

Sergeant Zubeck tackled Woodpecker just as he received a snap from Russian. Team 2-1's men hooted and jumped up and down, patting their sergeant's back.

Woodpecker threw the ball down and stalked back, mumbling to the huddle.

Thumper knelt down and pointed to Russian. "Once you snap the ball you have to block Sergeant Zee. He's killin' us."

Russian shrugged his shoulders. "He does not stay in one place for me to stand in front of him."

Rose cried out, "You don't *stand* in front of him! You knock his fuckin' head off!"

Russian smiled cruelly. "Now I understand."

Thumper whispered his play and broke the huddle with "Three-one!"

Russian lined up over the ball and eyed Zubeck before bending over. Thumper and Preacher lined up on the right side, with Rose on the left. Woodpecker barked out, "Down! . . . Set! . . . Hut one! Hut two! Hut two! Russian, give me the damn ball!"

The bullish soldier tossed the ball between his legs and charged out. Zubeck easily sidestepped him and began to run for the fading quarterback when suddenly a huge hairy arm stuck out, clothes-lining him in the neck and almost taking off his head.

Woodpecker faked a pump to Rose and threw the ball to Thumper, who was cutting across the middle. Two tack-

lers closed on Thumper for the easy stop when Thumper
lateraled behind him to Preacher, who cut in the afterbur-
ner and streaked toward the goal. A thin soldier chased
hopelessly after him, but the Indian was a blur.

Zubeck staggered to his feet and shook his head in defeat. The score was final: his team, one touchdown, and
Wade's team, two.

Rose put his arm around Preacher's shoulder. "Man,
does the U.S. of A. Olympic team take Indians?"

Zubeck and his men gathered around Thumper. "You
get the beer but we get a can apiece 'cause you cheated."

"Cheated?"

"Yeah, Russian is a foreigner. Foreigners ain't supposed to play like that, plus that Indian has got a jet in his
ass!"

Thumper laughed. "Okay, you get a few hot beers."

Zubeck turned to his men. "You hear that? He said
'hot.' What'd you say we cool off this big ape?"

Thumper began running halfheartedly and was soon
caught and dragged toward the South China Sea.

Rose tapped Preacher and ran for the struggling man.
"They gonna pay for that!"

Wade quickly took off his shirt and boots as the team
members roughhoused each other over in the waves, and
he ran down the sane dune screaming, "*Reinforcements
coming for Three-one!*"

Lieutenant Gibson rose to his knees and snapped his
fingers at the men to his left, then to those on his right,
and signaled them to pick up the Claymores they'd set up
along their ambush trail. They'd been waiting all day. The
sun was beginning to sink and it was time to pull back and
laager for the night. It was dangerous to stay in an ambush
at night. The procedure was to pull back a couple hundred
meters and sleep during the darkness, then return at dawn
to set up again. Gibson stood and walked to the left flank
of the ambush to get in an overwatch position. Watkins
would do the same on the right flank. They would keep an
eye on the trail while the other team members moved for-

ward and picked up their Claymore mines and rewrapped the firing wire.

Gibson leaned up against a tree and glanced down at his CAR-15. He looked back up and saw a hatless Vietnamese soldier casually walking down the trail toward him. His AK-47 assault rifle was slung over his shoulder, and he acted as though he was out for an evening stroll.

Gibson brought the CAR-15 up and fired in a single motion. The bullet tore a gaping hole through his neck and he crumbled to the ground as if he had fallen asleep. The careless soldier never saw his killer.

Sergeant Selando had just picked up his Claymore when the single shot rang out. He spun around, fell to the ground, then noticed the lieutenant, standing ten feet away, looking at his weapon and shaking his head. Selando cursed, got to his feet, and stomped over to the officer.

"Your accidental shot just compromised the whole mission! God damn it, keep your weapon on safe!" the Sergeant whispered angrily.

Gibson kept his eyes on the trail and spoke evenly. "I'll secure the trail. You check the body."

Selando spun around in disbelief. "What body? What bod . . ." He saw the soldier sprawled twenty feet away. "Son of a bitch! You wasted one!"

Ten minutes later, Gibson gathered his team around him in a streambed.

"We're not going in with just one kill. We'll move into a laager tonight and move to another trail tomorrow."

The team exchanged worried glances as Watkins shook his head. "Hell, we got a kill. Let's get out of here."

Sergeant Selando poked the Kentuckian. "The L-tee is right. We haven't blown our Claymores, and he only fired one shot. Nobody will know where it came from. The dink was just a trail runner. We'll get some more tomorrow."

Watkins sighed. "Yeah, I guess it would look silly going in with just one round fired. Childs would hassle us for a month."

Gibson smiled and nodded toward Selando. "Find us a laager."

Childs put down the radio handset just as Major Shane and First Sergeant Demand walked into the bunker. Shane had been at Fourth Division headquarters all day, coordinating another operational area.

"What's up, Jerry?"

Childs pointed to the wall map and stood. "Sir, I got bad news and good news. The bad news is we lost two men wounded from Team Two-three. They tripped a booby trap and the point and slack man were splattered pretty bad in the legs by a grenade. They're both at the An Khe evac hospital. The good news is we've got three teams that got kills. Team Two-two killed four VC, Team Three-four greased two NVA regulars, and Gibson's team killed one VC."

"Gibson?" asked Shane, surprised.

"Yes, sir. Remember I told you the other day he was taking out the team?"

Shane eyed the sergeant. They both knew Childs had never mentioned it, but Childs must have had his reasons for letting the officer go.

"Have all the teams been debriefed yet?" the major asked.

"All but Gibson's team, sir. He's still out. It seems they only fired one shot, and he wants to try again."

"Tell me again why I let Gibson go out on a team," Shane said.

Childs rolled his eyes at Shane. "Shit, sir, the L-tee was hounding me to death. I figured we owed him the chance."

First Sergeant Demand smiled. "I knew that L-tee was a real Ranger the second I shook hands with him."

Shane shook his head worriedly. "Leave 'em out one more day and that's it. We've worked the area enough. The dinks will be on to us pretty soon."

Shane noticed the sergeant's distressed look and threw his arm over the shorter man's shoulder. "I woulda let him go too, Jerry. You made the right decision. Come on, let's go visit the hospital and see our guys.''

Childs began to walk up the steps but Russian's dog jumped up on his legs, looking for a pat. "Git down, Bitch, damn it.''

Shane noted that the sergeant's voice wasn't as gruff as it could have been and winked at Demand. "Jerry, looks like you got a friend.''

"Naw, she just likes the beer I give her. Git down, damn it.''

Childs finally bent over and ruffled Bitch's neck fur and scratched her head. ''I'll be back, ya dumb mutt. Watley, come here and hold her till I'm gone.''

The young Spec-4 radio operator rose from his chair. "She'll just whine. You know how she is, Sarge.''

Shane knew the small dog always stayed close to Childs when Russian was gone even though the sergeant hardly acknowledged her. "Come on, we'll take her with us.''

The three men walked up the steps, with the yellow dog following happily.

The captivated audience of officers stared in fascination at the provocative performer in the clinging black jumpsuit whose husky voice had stolen their hearts. Virginia tossed her mike from hand to hand and danced sensually to the lively beat, then raised the mike to begin singing again.

Seated in the crowd of officers were two Red Cross women and their dates. One of the women was staring at the singer's jumpsuit so intently that she didn't hear the finance captain speak to her. He tapped the woman's arm to get her attention. "Mary Ann, what do you want to drink?''

The raven-haired woman broke her trance only for a moment. "Beer.''

The captain turned to the waitress. "Two rum and Cokes, one vodka Collins, and a beer.''

Sally Ramsey leaned over next to her friend and whispered, "What's wrong?''

Mary Ann shut her eyes for a moment, then turned back in her seat. "Nothing."

Sally knew better. Mary Ann was usually a dynamo of energy and always the life of the party. Sally had noted the change that afternoon after the mail came. Her tall friend seemed to be withdrawn and her constant smile had disappeared. She had hardly spoken a word while they waited in the compound for the captains to pick them up.

The singer finished her song to thunderous applause and nodded to the band to begin her second number. The musicians began playing the introduction to "Bridge Over Troubled Waters" as she spoke softly. "I hope you gentlemen won't mind if I change the words of Simon and Garfunkel's hit tune a little bit. This is a special dedication to a very special person."

She began to pick up the rhythm with her body and raised the mike to her lips.

The finance captain laughed loudly at something or other. Mary Ann didn't know what, but she faked a smile and leaned back.

"Sail on Ranger boy, your time has come . . ."

Mary Ann spun around, hearing the singer's refrain. She now knew why the woman wore the unusual patch over her left breast. Mary Ann had noticed the patch immediately. The red border around the black scroll insignia with the white letters proclaiming "Airborne Ranger" was all too familiar to her. It was the patch of Sierra Company Rangers—Thumper's unit. The singer's words, "Ranger boy," confirmed the woman knew somebody in the company.

"Like a bridge over troubled waters, I will lay me . . ."

Mary Ann had received a letter from Thumper that afternoon. At first she'd been thrilled but then became angry. She'd waited for so long to hear from him and when he didn't write it had hurt her badly. Out of the blue, after so many passing months, his long-awaited letter came too late. She hadn't even opened it.

Mary Ann stood up and held out her hand. "Bill, let me

borrow the keys to your jeep. I've got to go back to the compound for a few minutes."

"I'll take you."

"No, you stay here and enjoy the show. I'll only be a few minutes. I left some medicine that I should have taken."

The captain dug in his pocket. "I thought maybe something was wrong with you. Do you want me to drop you off so you can rest?"

Forcing another smile, Mary Ann took the keys. "I'll feel better after I take the medicine."

She walked hurriedly for the door.

Wade set his beer down and patted Russian's back.

"Why don't you dance with one of those girls?"

Russian frowned. "I cannot dance with those whose brothers I may have killed."

"Well it sure doesn't stop Rose, does it?"

"He is crazy."

Wade laughed and picked up his beer again. They sat in the large recreation hall next to the beach. A ten-piece Philippino band played loudly on stage. Rose and Woodpecker had complained about coming to the hall, but quickly forgot their complaints upon entering. The place held more women than men.

The band took a ten-minute break and Rose walked back to their table with his arm around a beautiful young Vietnamese girl. "Matt, I wanna quit the Rangers and live here forever. This is heaven, man."

The girl broke away from the black soldier's embrace. "I no Evan. My name Vuu Sim!"

Rose laughed and cupped the girl's face. "You bucoo beautiful Vuu. I dig you number one."

Preacher coughed to gain Rose's attention to remind him of their conversation that afternoon.

Rose eyed Preacher and winked.

Woodpecker returned to the table alone and ordered a beer by hollering out to a waitress. Several men behind him turned and surveyed the table surrounded by men

wearing camouflage fatigues. One of the men, a blond
Spec-4, snickered, "Sit down, Air Force REMF!"

Woodpecker knew the Air Force MPs wore camouflage
fatigues and smiled at the Spec-4, pointing to his Ranger
patch.

"We ain't Air Force, man. We're Rangers."

"Same thing, asshole. Sit down!"

Woodpecker began to walk over, intent upon rearrang-
ing the specialist's face, when Wade reached out and spoke
softly. "Sit down, Woodpecker. He's drunk."

The tall redhead gave the blond Spec-4 a last warning
glare and sat down beside Wade. "That son of a bitch is
askin' for it."

"Be cool, forget it," said Wade, looking over his shoulder. The Spec-4 and his four friends wore Fifth Division
patches. One of the soldiers flipped up his middle finger
at him. Wade turned, shaking his head.

Vuu Sim sat on Rose's lap at his insistence and rocked
the table with laughter at her cutting remarks about Rose.
Rose didn't like the woman's chiding.

Vuu leaned over the table toward Wade. "Rose, he say
he numba one Ranger, is true?"

"Yep, if he says so!"

"He say he bucoo lover-boy and love me too much, is
true?"

Wade cleared his throat in embarrassment and began to
answer when Preacher spoke up: "Rose is a very person-
able person who extends his affection to everyone."

The young girl stared at Preacher, then turned to Rose.
"What he say?"

Rose shook his head. "Hell, I don't speak Indian. I
dunno."

The band struck up again and Rose patted the girl's
buttocks. "Let's get down on the sounds!"

She wiggled on his lap and leaned over the table toward
Preacher. "You talk fun-nay. I like you. You dance with
me, okay?"

Preacher's eyes widened in surprise and he shook his
head. "Thank you for asking, but I don't dance."

The girl hopped up and grabbed his hand. "I show you!"

Preacher held on to his chair, resisting her tugging. Rose grinned and waved him up. "Do it, Preacher. She digs you, man!"

The small soldier rolled his eyes as he got up reluctantly and let himself be tugged to the dance floor.

Woodpecker handed Rose a beer. "That was cool, Rose. Thanks."

Rose picked up the can and stood grinning as he looked over other prospects. "She talks too much, anyway. I need one that *believes* the Rose."

The Spec-4 behind their table snapped, "Sit down, nigger!"

Rose spun around, throwing his beer at the soldier. *"Fuck you, leg!"*

The Spec-4 and his friends all stood.

Wade stepped in front of Rose and put his hand up. "Settle down guys. Let's just sit down and be cool."

The blond soldier was the same size as Wade and took a step closer.

"We gonna have to teach you Airborne assholes a lesson."

Suddenly the four men behind the blond soldier were brushed past by Thumper, Sergeant Zubeck, and his four men. Thumper put his large arm over the Spec-4's shoulder.

"What did you just say?"

The soldier stuttered and glanced behind him as Woodpecker joined Wade and Rose. The blond looked up at Thumper.

"I didn't mean nothin'."

Thumper motioned to Rose. "I think you owe my friend an apology."

"Look, man. I'm sorry. We drank a few beers and I'm sorry."

Rose grinned and puffed up his chest. "No sweat, leg."

Thumper removed his arm and took the soldier's chair and slid it up to Wade's table. He sat down and looked over his shoulder at the staring blond. "Good night."

The soldier walked quickly for the exit, followed by his friends.

Mary Ann folded the letter and walked for the door. Damn him, she thought. Damn him for coming back into my life. She drove back to the club trying to sort out her feelings. As she pulled into the parking lot, she could hear the woman singing. His letter had been four pages of apology and ended with, "I still think of you every day." Damn him. The big guzoo had terrible handwriting but his words were emotional and sincere. He said the reason for not writing before was that he couldn't put his feelings into words.

Mary Ann entered the club just as the singer bowed to the clapping audience and walked off stage. Mary Ann paused for a moment only a few feet from her table and then changed direction.

Virginia closed the door to her small room and sat down in front of the mirror. She reached for a glass of water when a knock came at the door.

"Yes?"

"Miss Salin, could I speak to you a minute?"

The voice surprised her; it was a woman's. She stood and opened the door and stared at a woman's bosom. She backed away from the door, looking up at the six-foot woman's smiling face.

"Don't worry, I shock a lotta people. I'm Mary Ann Krueger."

Virginia closed her open mouth and smiled. The tall Red Cross woman was beautiful and had a radiant face that beamed with friendliness.

Virginia put out her hand. "Despite what the club says, I'm Virginia, not Sophia."

Mary Ann took her hand. "I'm sorry to bother you miss . . . I mean, Virginia, but I just have to know about the Ranger patch you're wearing. Do you know someone in the unit?"

Virginia looked down at her patch, "Yes, I met a sergeant a few weeks ago and . . ." She looked up, seeing a strange look in the woman's eyes. "Do you know someone in the same unit, too?"

Mary Ann's lower lip quivered, but she quickly forced a weak smile. "Yes, I had a friend in the Rangers. I'm sorry for bothering you." She turned to go. "Thank you, I just wondered why . . ."

"Mary Ann, please don't go."

Mary Ann stopped at the door and looked over her shoulder. "I'm sorry I barged in, but that Ranger patch just got to me."

Virginia motioned to a nearby chair. "Come on. Sit down and tell me about him. Maybe Matt knows him."

Mary Ann's eyes widened. "Sergeant Matt Wade?" she asked in a rush. "Matt is your friend?"

It was Virginia's turn to show surprise. Her mouth dropped in disbelief that this strange woman would know her sergeant and his unit so well. She stammered, "Ya . . . Yes, Matt and I are friends. In fact, I'm going to China Beach tomorrow to see him. He and the team got a three day R and R."

Mary Ann suddenly felt weak. She sat down and looked up at the small singer. "Did Matt ever mention Kenny Meeks? They call him 'Thumper.'"

Virginia smiled. "I've never heard of Kenny Meeks, but Matt says his closest friend in the company is a big bruiser named 'Thumper.'" Virginia couldn't help but grin at Mary Ann's expression, and she knew at that moment she was going to have a travelling partner to China Beach.

16

<u>25 SEPTEMBER</u>

J. D. Gibson ate another bite of his cold spaghetti lurp ration, then folded the bag and put it in his leg pocket. Cold spaghetti for breakfast wasn't the best meal in the world, he thought.

Sergeant Selando noticed the lieutenant putting away his food and held up a beef jerky stick. "Try one of these," he whispered.

Gibson took the dried meat with a nod of thanks and stood up. "Let's go."

The team moved back in the direction of the trail for 150 meters and came to a halt as Gibson held up his hand. The lieutenant motioned Selando up to him as the others knelt to wait for the two men to move forward and find a location for the ambush. One of them would stay and watch the trail while the other came back and brought the team up.

Gibson and the sergeant approached the trail cautiously and found a good spot by a steep embankment. Selando was about to go back for the others when Gibson suddenly grabbed him and fell to the ground. A Vietnamese soldier wearing a faded pith helmet and gray uniform began making his way down the embankment. Two more soldiers followed him. They were wearing shorts and carried large packs. All had slung AK-47 rifles. The lead soldier spoke over his shoulder and laughed as he lowered his head, watching his footing. Gibson gently pushed off the safety of his CAR-15 and aimed his rifle. Selando raised his weapon and fired at the last man on the hill. The red tracer disappeared into the soldier's stomach and was followed by two more red burning streaks.

Gibson shot the first soldier and raised his weapon up for the second. The small Vietnamese fired his AK on full automatic and slipped. He fell on his pack and slid down the hill, still shooting. Gibson's bullets stitched their way down to the man and struck him in the chest.

Sergeant Selando stood and made his way slowly forward as Gibson covered him. The rest of the team ran up behind the lieutenant, who, without taking his eyes from the steep bank, motioned them to secure the trail.

Two of the Vietnamese were dead. The soldier Gibson had shot was gasping and had rolled over on his stomach and was trying to crawl up the bank. The back of his shirt was oozing bright red blood from the exit wound. Sergeant Selando kicked the AK away from his side and continued walking up the embankment to secure the top. Gibson stared at the pathetic sight of the crawling soldier and walked over to him. He rolled the man over and almost gagged. The bullet had passed through a lung, and pinkish bubbles—like those from a just-opened bottle of champagne—oozed out of the bullet hole. The young soldier's face was turning dark blue and he was gasping for air. Gibson quickly took out the plastic lurp bag, dumped the remaining spaghetti, and placed the bag on the wound. Immediately the soldier took in a breath.

Watkins knelt by the lieutenant. "A sucking chest, huh?" he asked, looking at the wound.

Gibson held the plastic over the hole with one hand and pointed to one of the Vietnamese packs. "Get me something to wrap around him."

Watkins shrugged his shoulders as he stood up. "Aw shit, sir, just finish him. It's a long way to a PZ and we'll have to carry his ass."

Gibson looked into the eyes of Vietnamese soldier. He felt no hate for the suffering man. To kill him now would not be for revenge. It would be murder. Gibson looked at Watkins with a cutting glare. "Do what I said."

Southern Liberation Forces Headquarters

Lieutenant Colonel Sy tossed a booklet of papers on the desk and sat down beside Colonel Chinh. "As I promised, comrade, there will be no surprises during the general's political meeting. Enclosed in my report are the topics to be covered by all the party members. He will have no surprises."

Colonel Chinh picked up the packet but was preoccupied as he looked at the map across from the table. He tossed the report down and sighed. "No surprises from our members but the Americans are surprising us."

Sy could see the colonel was upset about something and spoke softly. "Bad news, comrade?"

Colonel Chinh leaned back in his chair and bowed his head as if he was tired. "We received a report that one of our experienced indoctrination teams was wiped out and that that led to the loss of a local and a district headquarters. It seems the Americans still have some fight left."

Sy's eyes widened at the news. "Our agents did not report signs of any larger operations."

Chinh shook his head. "It was not a large operation. A small unit of commandos was responsible. We are helpless against them. Our agents tell us of the buildup in bases for large operations, but of these small units we know nothing. They don't need massive helicopter support, fuel, ammunition, or weeks of planning. There is nothing for our agents to see or hear."

Sy saw through the colonel's distress. "You are worried about tomorrow's journey to the fortress?"

Chinh rose from his chair and faced the map. "No, the trip should be safe enough. I have sent units ahead to walk the trails, but I am worried about these commando units. They are the American forces' eyes and ears. They could be anywhere, so once you arrive at the mountain base, place a radio security team into operation and monitor the American radio frequencies night and day.''

Sy nodded and made himself a mental note. "I will see to it, comrade.''

The senior colonel sat down and lowered his voice. "Between just you and me, this trip is useless. If it was not for the need of the general to be free from these tunnels I would advise him to hold the Directorate meeting later."

Sy smiled. "But is it not worth the trip for the general to pull Sang's tail and make him squeal?''

Chinh laughed and sat back in his chair. "Yes, I suppose that is another good reason. Sang leads the Second Division fearlessly, but he is too political. The general needs to put him in his place. You must remember every detail of their discussion and tell me of it as soon as you return. It should be worth many nights of laughter." Chinh's twinkling eyes lost their luster as he erased his smile and looked at Sy. "You have much to do, so I will say farewell now. Take care of yourself and watch out for our general. Two weeks without you to pester me is a long time, and I will miss you."

Sy shook the older man's hand, knowing he thought of him as a son. "I will be cautious and take care of our general. I will miss you as well, so take care of yourself and don't find anyone to pester you until I return. Farewell, my friend."

Colonel Sy walked out of the planning room into the tunnel corridor, where Private Nuu was waiting for him. Sy smiled and motioned for the soldier to follow him. "I am happy to see you received my message."

Nuu lifted his pack from the floor and hurried to catch up. "Yes, comrade Colonel."

Sy kept his fast gait and spoke over his shoulder. "After talking to you the other day I thought of something you might like better than patrolling the valley. I talked to Sergeant Thong, General Duc's orderly, and he said he needs an assistant. We are leaving tomorrow on a long march and the sergeant needs help. Do you think you would like such a position?''

Nuu was elated at the chance of leaving the security force. Anything would be better than killing farmers. ''Yes, comrade Colonel. I would be honored to help a man who is the orderly to the general.''

Sy stopped and turned around as if reading the soldier's thoughts. ''You realize eliminating security risks is necessary, don't you?''

Nuu lowered his head. ''They were just farmers.''

Sy couldn't help but smile at the honesty of the boy. He hadn't yet been indoctrinated to give only answers his superiors wanted to hear. Sy pointed to the last room just ahead. ''There is much you don't understand, but you will. Sergeant Thong is in that room waiting for you. The sergeant is gruff, and his ways are a little particular, but he is a good teacher. Learn from him, and your days in the headquarters will be fruitful.''

Nuu looked at the colonel with a questioning gaze. ''Thank you comrade Colonel. . . . But why do you help me?''

Sy put his hand on the small soldier's shoulder. ''Because, my friend, you were happy, and I took that away from you when I brought you here. Perhaps you can find your happiness again by working for the general. He is our hope for the future. Good luck to you.''

Nuu smiled respectfully. ''I will do my best.''

Wade lay on his poncho liner, absorbing the sun's rays and trying not to look at his watch. After all, she'd said there was no telling when she'd catch a flight.

Rose sat beside him and tapped Preacher. ''Look what's comin'!''

Preacher sat up and stared in astonishment as Russian lumbered toward them in a bathing suit. His bull-like body was covered with thick hair. Rose grinned. ''Man, you and me can make us bucoo big bucks. We put a collar on that hairy dude and hit the carnivals. We'll call him *Russian*, the Talking Bear.''

Preacher rolled his eyes and sighed as Russian sat down beside him. "Russian, Rose is talking about you again."

"He always talk."

"Yeah, well, dig it, dudes, the Rose done scored big-time last night, didn't he? That's more than talk. I never done it on the beach before, man. It was a trip."

Woodpecker sat up quickly. "Really, on the beach?"

"There it is. I laid her out and . . ."

Russian growled. "Enough! No talk about such things."

Rose cocked an eyebrow. "Sure, Russian, but I gotta warn you, man, there's one dink broad running around that's got sand all inside her . . ."

Russian grabbed for the black soldier, but Rose anticipated the move and rolled away to his feet, laughing. "She's got sand in it! *Beware, dudes!* The Rose has created a new disease. It's *sandpapered pecker!*"

The team broke up in laughter as Russian tried to catch the elusive soldier. Rose suddenly came to a dead stop as he looked up to the top of the sand dune. Russian caught up to him, but also froze when he saw what Rose was staring at. Wade raised up and smiled.

The small woman ran down the dune and jumped into his waiting arms.

"Well, I'll be damned," said Rose.

Russian smiled. "She is very pretty, no?"

Wade released Virginia and motioned Rose and Russian over.

"Guys, meet Ginny."

Virginia held both hands up and then pointed to the thin redhead.

"You're Woodpecker, and you're Preacher. This is Thumper and you have to be Rose. And of course . . . Russian." She stepped in front of each man and gave him a little kiss on the cheek, but she hugged the startled Czech.

"I feel as if I know you all already. Matt wrote about each of you." She walked up to Thumper with a grin and spoke excitedly. "I have a surprise for you, but you have to turn around and shut your eyes."

Thumper looked confused but did as she requested. She

whispered to Wade and he jogged up the sand dune and waved. The team gathered closer with questioning looks. A tall woman suddenly appeared on the hill and stood beside Wade.

"Okay, Thumper, you can turn around now."

When the big soldier turned around, he followed Ginny's gaze up to the dune. He couldn't believe his eyes. He stood there in astonishment for a moment, and then he began walking up the dune.

Mary Ann felt excitement rising in her chest. She hadn't realized how much she really missed him until that very moment.

Preacher exchanged glances with Woodpecker and turned to Virginia. "Very nice meeting you, Ginny. We're going to have to go; we're going to the PX and then in to see the city."

"Oh, do you have to?"

"Yeah, we gettin' sunburned real bad," added Woodpecker as he motioned Russian to follow them.

Rose didn't catch on and began to sit down when Russian yanked him to his feet. "We go now, crazy one."

"But, man, I wanna rap with Ginn . . ."

"Now."

Wade joined Virginia as his men walked down the beach. "Where they going?" he asked.

"They're leaving us alone. Your team are neat guys. I can see already why you care so much for them. How are Mary Ann and Thumper doing?"

"Just fine. How in the hell did you meet her?"

"It's a long story. Come on, I've got to check in at the officers' quarters so I can get into a bathing suit."

"I can't go. Enlisted men aren't allowed up at that end of the beach."

"Matt, you're in a bathing suit, for heaven's sake. Nobody is going to stop you. Plus, I called and reserved one of the cabins just off the beach."

Wade grinned. "Are you trying to get me alone to take advantage of me?"

She put her arms around his waist and squeezed him tightly. "As you would say—'Yep!'"

J. D. Gibson wiped the sweat from his forehead and gave the radio handset back to the radioman. The team had moved for several hours before finding a suitable pickup zone. The bird dog circled two thousand feet above, and Lieutenant Foley had just called to say the Slick was only one minute out.

Gibson knelt by the wounded Vietnamese, who they'd carried in an NVA hammock tied to a cut bamboo pole.

Gibson knew the soldier was dying. The pallor of death on his young face had told him. He'd seen it too many times before not to know. The sickening, almost gray-white skin and the faraway look in the eyes were telltale signs. He recalled when two men in his old platoon had had that same color and expression. It was just a matter of time.

Gibson patted the soldier's hand as he studied his smooth face. The young man's eyes rolled slowly toward him. They were dull, with that look of acceptance.

Gibson thought of Brad Avant. He had died quickly and without pain. This young soldier, on the other hand, had experienced enough pain for all men, but he never said a word or even grunted. He took the pain inside, and he would die with it there. The pictures in his billfold were of a young, black-haired woman sweetly smiling—probably his wife or girlfriend. Gibson wondered if the worst pain for the man was knowing he would never see her again. But the dying soldier's eyes told Gibson his thoughts were more on the man who had shot him. They were asking why. Gibson could only shake his head. He didn't know.

The whupping of chopper blades could be heard in the distance. Sergeant Selando and Watkins began to lift the pole, but Gibson waved them back.

"Leave him here, let him die in peace."

Watkins began to speak, but the sergeant cut him off with a wave of his hand.

Gibson rose slowly, still staring into the eyes of the soldier, and raised his hand in a final farewell as the landing chopper's wind tore at his fatigues.

Mary Ann stretched out on Thumper's poncho liner and rose to her elbow to look at his heavy, muscular chest. Thumper lay on his back beside her, staring up at the blue sky.

"Thumper, I didn't want to come. I thought you'd forgotten me."

The big soldier sat up and looked into her eyes. "I'm sorry. I tried, I really did, but . . ." He lowered his head.

Mary Ann reached out and took his hand. "It doesn't matter anymore. I'm here now and want to hold you. I don't want to talk about the past—or future."

Thumper cast a lingering look at her, then lowered his eyes again.

"I don't want to hurt you again," he said. "You mean too much to me. I'm not sure why, but it's not the same as it was. Before when we were together I thought of you as a special friend. Time has made you more than that. I'm not sure I can handle it."

Mary Ann sat up. "You're scared of me, aren't you? You think I'll ask something from you that you can't give?"

"Mary Ann, I've never told a woman I loved her. I always thought those words were special. I feel something for you that scares me to death."

"Don't worry, big guy, I haven't got wedding bells in my mind. I don't have anything in my mind but the next couple of days."

Thumper looked deeply into her eyes. "The trouble is, I can't think that way. I want to hold you forever, but I know I can't. I can't touch you, then forget you."

Mary Ann's lower lip quivered. "I guess maybe I'd better go."

Thumper restrained himself from reaching for her. "Can we just be friends again?"

Mary Ann got to her feet and stared at the ocean. "No, I couldn't be around you without wanting you. You've gotten to me, too. I was willing to accept us making love so I could at least hold you a little while. It was foolish to think I could just walk away. Being friends would be torment.''

She threw her head back abruptly, taking in a deep breath, and smiled. ''It was good seeing you. Take care of yourself and don't lose any more weight, huh?''

She picked up her bag and began walking up the sand dune. Thumper didn't watch her. His body went rigid, and he clenched his teeth to fight the emotions that ached in his heart. He raised his head just as she disappeared over the dune.

''Mary Ann!''

He jumped to his feet and ran after her. She kept walking, afraid to turn around and show her tears. He grabbed her shoulder and spun her around.

''I can't let you go again. I . . . I want you to stay. I want us to talk about a future together.''

''We can't.''

''The hell we can't! I'm going home in seven months. You're going back in four. Can't you wait for me for three months?''

''Of course, but . . .''

'' 'But' hell! We can!''

''I don't know, Thumper. My God, why did I come? I wasn't expecting this. I thought . . . I thought we'd . . . oh, hell. Don't stand there, damn you. Hug me!''

Wade lay in Virginia's bed, propped up with a pillow against the headboard. Virginia rested on his bare chest.

''It's not a big farm but the land is good. My granddad wants me to come back and take over the place but I think I'll stay in the Army a couple more years to earn enough for college before I go back.''

Virginia raised her head. ''Somehow I can't imagine you in overalls and wearing a straw hat. Surely you plan on doing something other than just being Farmer Brown the rest of your life.''

Wade smiled at her stereotypical description of farmers

and draped his arm over her back. "I could never let the place go. It's been in the Wade family too long. I think I'll sharecrop it out and teach. I'd really like to help slow learners like I was. It doesn't pay much, but with the farm I can get by."

Ginny lowered her head on his chest, trying to understand. How could anyone love a patch of ground?

"Matt, you could do anything you want. You've got your whole life ahead of you. Surely your grandfather would understand that."

Wade stared at the ceiling. "Ginny, the land is his life. It's all he knows. Roots are important where I come from, and the roots of the Wade family are in the land."

"Roots can strangle you. If it's not really for you, you should walk away and start a new life."

Wade thought of the long days his granddad had sweated on the tractor and of the small cemetery on Black Jack Hill. He answered in a whisper, "No, I can't walk away from that kind of responsibility."

Virginia raised up and looked into his eyes. "Like you can't walk from your team?"

Wade answered without hesitation. "Yeah."

Virginia shook her head. "Your life is run by other people. One day you're going to have to live for yourself."

Wade hugged her to him. "Ginny, I don't do anything I don't wanna do. You've met the guys. If you could see the farm you'd understand. What about you? You love your singing. Could you just walk away from it? You love New York, too. Could you live any place else?"

Virginia sighed. "No, I can't give up my singing. I love it too much. I'm close, Matt, real close to really making the big step up. It's such a good feeling knowing people like my work."

Wade ran his hand over her bare buttocks. "I like your work, too."

She smiled and stroked his lower stomach. "I like yours same-same, G.I. Do you wanna short-time for T-T money?"

Wade reached for nonexistent pockets. "Me cheap Charlie. You souvenir me this time, okay?"

Virginia lay back on the bed, pulling him on top of her. "You'll pay. With your body."

Wade rolled his eyes up, feeling her breasts against his chest, and shuddered. "Damn, and I was gonna save myself for a little Okie farm girl."

"Settle for a New Yorker, buster."

Wade felt a twinge of sadness as he began kissing her neck. He loved this woman, but their conversation had made things clear—their futures were in different worlds. He could never possess her. And he didn't really want to. He couldn't hold her back. He only wanted her to be happy, even if that meant losing her.

Gibson sat in his room at An Khe, nursing a hot beer. Before him was a partially written letter to his dad. The Rangers had moved back to An Khe from Mustang after his team returned that afternoon. The company was throwing a big party in the mess hall to celebrate their success. Gibson didn't feel like celebrating. Something inside him needed to communicate his feelings to a man, thousands of miles away, who would understand.

His dad had been in the Army for twenty-five years and had retired in 1964; his dad knew war. He'd been in Korea with the First Cavalry and had been wounded three times. The horrible white scars told the story. First Sergeant Donald Gibson was a gruff man on the outside, but his eyes often grew misty when he talked about the men he had served with in Korea. His father would know what his son felt.

It was a proud day when his dad put on his old uniform and pinned on the gold bar following college graduation. He'd told his son he was proud and loved him very much, but had also said, "I'm glad you're not gonna be cannon fodder like your ol' man, but damn it, take care of your troops. They fight the war every day. Remember, without them, you ain't a leader."

Gibson leaned back in his chair, took a sip of Budweiser,

and pictured in his mind the small house on the outskirts of San Antonio. His mother's touch was in the flowers and shrubs, and his dad's was in the beat-up Chevy out front. "Can't buy a car when I got kids to take care of," his dad had said. The Chevy was a constant reminder of the sacrifice his parents bore by sending him and his sister to college.

Gibson picked up the pen and began writing again. He'd bought a new car just before shipping to Vietnam and had given it to his mother. He knew his dad would never accept it. The car was his only way of saying thanks . . . until now.

Thumper and Mary Ann strolled hand-in-hand along the beach as the sky darkened. When they arrived at the small cabin, Mary Ann opened the door, but Thumper released her hand and turned away. He sat on the wooden porch steps and looked out at the approaching storm clouds. Mary Ann lowered her head in silence. She'd hoped he would want to take her inside and love her. They'd never made love before, and she desperately wanted to become a part of him. She walked dejectedly inside for her robe.

The sea pounded the beach as a thunderstorm blew in, kicking the waves up into a frenzy.

Thumper watched the lightning flash in the night sky. The wind was cool and intoxicating as it lashed his bare chest with sand.

Mary Ann came back to the door, wearing her robe. "Get in here before it rains."

Thumper held his position, defying the wind's assault, and smiled. "I love it."

Mary Ann stepped out of the doorway, her hair blowing back, and sat down beside him. "You love what?"

The big man took in a deep breath of the cool air, keeping his eyes on the turbulent clouds. "I love it when it storms like this. It's so powerful the earth seems to shudder."

His body was taut as steel as she kissed his shoulder and put her arm around him.

He threw his arms around her. "It's so much better sharing this with you. I want to share everything with you from now on."

She squeezed him again and looked at the rumbling clouds approaching. She'd never thought of them as beautiful before, but there was a strange majesty about them.

The first sprinkles caressed the two lovers as they embraced.

Mary Ann sighed and began to release him, hoping he would now come inside. In private he might finally take her in his strong arms and end her throbbing torment of desire. She'd dreamed too many nights of his heavy muscular body on hers, whispering his need for her. She had finally found a man who finally made her feel small within his grasp. There were few who could ever make her feel that way. This man who loved the fury of a storm was the one she wanted.

She'd come to Da Nang knowing he would become hers or would lose him forever. That afternoon she'd thought it was all over, but now the battle was won . . . almost.

Mary Ann stood and rubbed his thick neck. "Let's go inside, honey."

His gaze was still fixed on the turbulent sea, but he reached up and took her hand, squeezing it tightly. The light sprinkle turned to biting slaps. Thumper turned slowly and pulled her down to him as his eyes reflected another lightning flash.

She lowered herself into his protective arms as the rain began beating down and soaking them. With a dripping hand, he pushed her wet, tangled hair away from her face and kissed her passionately. They both fell back slowly to the glistening wooden planks and he pressed his heated body against hers. The rumbling skies went unnoticed as he nibbled and bit at her neck and lowered his head to her heaving breasts. Suddenly he raised up, putting his arms

under her back and bare legs. He picked her up easily and
stood as the rain whipped their bodies.

She wrapped her arms around his neck and bit his chest
tenderly, tasting his hot perspiration. Thumper kicked
open the door with a powerful shove and walked into the
darkened room.

26 SEPTEMBER

The morning sky showed no trace of the previous night's
fury. A lone man ran up the beach, slapping the wet sand
with his bare feet. Matt Wade dodged and jumped over
washed-up debris and increased his pace. The clean air
and morning coolness felt exhilarating in his lungs as he
pushed his glistening body to the limit. Sweat stung his
eyes but he ran faster. He wanted to feel the pain of the
exertion and going that one step beyond. Nothing was on
his mind but defeating the pain. A washed-up log fifty meters distant was now his goal. He wouldn't quit until he
reached it. He strained harder, pumping his legs and arms
in perfect synchronization, and reached the log but still
didn't stop. It isn't over! It ain't never over! He saw a
clump of seaweed a hundred paces away. A new challenge!
His lungs burned and his legs felt rubbery. His arms
seemed to weigh a hundred pounds and ached at his effort,
but he kept pushing. Reaching the seaweed, he slowed and
sucked air into his pounding chest. Weaving like a drunk,
he put his hands on his hips—they hurt when left hanging—
and as he continued to walk, he tried to take in deep
breaths. God it's great! his mind cried to the heavens. The
feeling of such power, such . . . aw shit, it's great!

Wade stepped out into the cool muddy sea. He needed
the run. It was payment for sleeping with a beautiful
woman who he knew would soon be leaving. He had to

267

clear his mind of her and begin thinking again of his team and what lay ahead. She was wonderful, but only a fleeting dream. The war was reality. The pain of the run had brought that reality back. In a short time he'd have to place her picture back in the scrapbook in his mind.

He felt strong and unbeatable. Alone, he had pushed himself to the point of exhaustion. He was a leader, a man respected by his team, and he was desired by a ravishing beauty who men would die for.

"I love it!" he yelled to the waves that broke weakly around him.

Wade looked up the beach from where he started his run. It was a good two miles away. Nobody could have run it faster, he thought to himself, feeling pride in the accomplishment. He saw a speck moving farther up the beach and froze. It was a running man.

Who the hell is that? Wade thought as he waded from the water. He was furious that another human would spoil his deserted beach. It was like climbing a mountain peak and standing alone, victorious, and then seeing another climber come up beside you and ruin everything.

Wade couldn't make out who it was in the distance, but it was obvious that whoever he was, he wasn't a casual jogger. His arms and legs were moving in a blur. Damn, he thought, the son of a bitch is faster than me.

Wade's joyous feeling of accomplishment sunk to his toes. He knew the approaching runner was another form of reality: no matter how good you were, there was always somebody better. Wade lowered his head and smiled. It had been a good lesson for him. He looked back at the runner and his smile widened. He raised his hand. "Go, Preacher!"

The small, sweat-streaked Indian didn't break his blistering stride as he waved his hand in acknowledgment.

Wade watched him for another minute, then shook his head. "Thanks, Preacher."

The sergeant began a slow walk back to the cabin. It was time to wake from his dream.

Thumper looked at the woman sleeping beside him and listened to her gentle breathing. With Mary Ann he had discovered another world where there was no dirt, grime, or sweat, no M-16s, grenades, or olive drab, no psyching up for a mission or stomach-wrenching fear climbing up his throat. He lay on clean sheets beside a wonderful, loving woman instead of on the ground with five scared men in an unrelenting jungle. For too long he'd been caught up in the other world where death and misery were a breath away. That world had claimed his brother and many close friends. He'd searched too long for answers that didn't matter anymore. It was insane to keep pushing to the edge, believing he'd make it. The odds were against him. It was just a matter of time.

The woman beside him had shown him a world he'd forgotten about. The world where love and affection replaced death and destruction. He reached out and touched Mary Ann's bare skin. Within her embrace was escape and hope for a new life. He felt desperate in his need to take hold of her world before it was too late.

Mary Ann awoke to Thumper's touch.

He looked into her eyes and spoke softly. "I've been looking at you for an hour. Mary Ann, I don't ever want to leave you again. You're the best thing that's ever happened to me. I've been lying here thinking about us and how much I've missed by not being with you."

Mary Ann had never seen that look in his eyes before. He was so sincere and serious. Her smile disappeared as she touched his face lovingly. "I know what you mean. We'll have a whole lifetime together in just a few short months. I hope you'll still love me when I get fat and my hair turns gray."

"I'll always love you. But I don't want to wait for months. Let's get married today. Let's start a new life right now."

Mary Ann sat up. Thumper wasn't talking sense, but he sounded as if he really meant what he was saying.

"Honey, I can't. I'd have to leave if we got married now. You still have seven months left. There's time for us. I'll come and see you every month until I go home and I'll be waiting when you come back."

Thumper put his hand around her neck and pulled her down to him. "That may be sooner than you think."

"Thumper, I can't, I . . ."

Wade and Virginia were sitting in the recreation mess hall eating breakfast when Woodpecker and Preacher set down their trays to join them.

Wade winked at Preacher. "Enjoy your run?"

Black Eagle smiled brightly. "Yes, did you?"

"Yeah." Wade looked over his shoulder at the food line, then back to the two men. "Where's Russian and Rose?"

The redhead exchanged glances with Preacher and lowered his head.

"Rose had a little trouble last night. He's not feeling too good this morning."

Wade rolled his eyes. "What'd he do this time?"

Preacher began giggling and tried to cover it with a quick cough. Woodpecker shook has head, also trying to hide a grin.

Wade set down his fork and, winking at Virginia, leaned back in his chair. "Come on guys, who's gonna tell me?"

Woodpecker raised his head, trying to keep a straight face.

"We went to the recreation hall last night, but there was only about a dozen broads . . . I mean girls, there. . . . Sorry, Ginny. The storm musta kept most of 'em away. Well, the bro . . . girls wouldn't have nothing to do with any of us. They were clinging to these Air Force guys that were throwin' big bucks around. Rose got a case of the butt and starts drinkin' them red sweet drinks called uh . . .

Preacher helped. "Singapore Slings."

"Yeah, Singapore Slings. Well, he drinks bucoo of 'em and gets all dinky dau. Zubeck is with us and is talkin' about this game called 'Rodeo Time.'"

"Oh, shit," said Matt aloud as Woodpecker continued.

"Well, Sergeant Zee is tellin' us how to play and more of the guys at other tables come over to hear."

"What is Rodeo Time?" asked Virginia, never having heard of the game.

Woodpecker looked at Wade worriedly, but the sergeant nodded for him to go ahead and explain.

"Rodeo Time is when you got chicks dancing with only the same guys and think they're too good to mess with anybody else. You pick out one of the gals that is really shaking her ass . . . rear around. A guy runs up to her and bites her on the rear end and holds on for eight seconds."

Virginia almost fell on the floor laughing.

Woodpecker laughed with her and patted her hand. "But the rules are you can only hold on with one hand; the other you've got to wave around like a bull rider to score more points?"

Wade couldn't help but laugh, then suddenly become serious. "Rose wasn't the one who . . . ?"

Woodpecker nodded. "Yeah, Rose stuck up his hand and volunteered. Hell, Matt, you should'a seen it. Everybody kicked in five bucks. We musta had fifty dollars MPC on the table. Rose put on this grunt's bonnie hat and shaped it like a cowboy's, then crept toward the dance floor. He started runnin' and fell to his knees, slidin' into this chick wearing tight pants. Matt, he got hold of that little gal and let her have it right on the left cheek. She jumped a mile high, but Rose held on, even taking off his hat and waving it like a real rodeo star."

Wade and Virginia were in tears from laughing so hard. Woodpecker had to take a few breaths to continue.

"That girl beat, slapped, and clawed that fool like a wild cat. They fell on the floor, her kickin' and yellin' while Zubeck was yellin', 'Six . . . seven . . . eight! *Rodeo Time!*' Man, the place was a zoo. The Air Force guys was all pissed. We were tryin' to keep them away from Rose while that little gal tore into him like a buzz saw. A fight broke out and the MPs came, then everything went even crazier."

Wade stopped his laughter and asked worriedly, "Did they get Rose?"

"Naw, Russian carried him out, but Sergeant Zee got written up."

"How is Rose?" asked Virginia, concerned.

"He ain't feeling none too good."

"He doesn't look any better," added Preacher with a smile.

Woodpekcer stiffened suddenly and whispered, "Shh! Here he comes. Don't say nothin'. We promised we wouldn't tell."

Wade turned in his seat just as the black soldier stepped through the door. The right side of his face was swollen and he had horrible scratch marks running from his neck to his bloodshot eyes. He walked mechanically to their table with his eyes fixed.

Wade pulled back a chair like nothing was amiss and began eating some toast. Rose sat down gingerly and stared at a salt shaker as if in a trance.

Preacher had to turn his back and bite his lip to keep from busting out laughing. Virginia held a napkin to her face as Woodpecker quickly filled his mouth with a sweet roll.

Wade chewed slowly and nonchalantly asked, "Rose, you wanna eat my roll?"

The bleary-eyed soldier kept his dazed look and shook his head meekly.

"How about some cereal?"

Again, he just shook his head.

"Come on, troop, you gotta eat something."

Rose's eyes shifted painfully to his sergeant and raised his hand in slow motion, pointing to his swollen cheek.

"My . . . mouth . . . is . . . sore."

Woodpecker couldn't contain himself any longer and spewed the table with sweet roll as he cracked up with splitting laughter. The rest quickly joined him, with tears running down their cheeks.

Rose shook his head despondently and stood slowly. "Sa' not . . . fun . . . nay, man."

Matt checked his watch and lengthened his stride. It was almost noon. He had to get Virginia to the shuttle bus stop. He carried her bag as she struggled to keep up.

"Slow down, I can't keep up."

Wade grinned. "There you go saying 'I can't' again."

They turned the corner and saw several soldiers waiting along a painted curb. Wade slowed his gait with a sigh. "I told ya I'd get you here on time to catch your flight."

"Are you never wrong, Sergeant?

"Nope."

Virginia hit his arm playfully as they neared the curb.

Wade set down the bag at the curb and wiped the sweat from his brow. "So, you're going back to Saigon, then the Philippines, huh?"

"Yes, we're going on tour of the Navy bases, then heading for home."

"Ya going back to New York?"

"No, Los Angeles. There's an agent there who says he can get me a contract to cut a record."

Wade smiled. "Will you remember this Okie when you make the big time?"

Virginia tried to look happy. "I'll never forget you, Matt. You're . . ." Her smile faded and she quickly turned her head. "You're special to me."

Wade hugged her to him. "I'll miss you, too, Ginny. Please write me and tell me how you're doin'. Hell, I oughta get a cut for saving your skinny butt."

Virginia held him tightly so he wouldn't see her tears. "I'll write, Matt, I promise."

The sergeant backed away from her as the blue Air Force bus pulled up. "Hey, no tears, remember?"

Virginia shook her head. "I don't care about my promise not to cry. I . . . I'm not ready to go yet."

Wade hugged her again. "Go Ginny, go and be the best singer in the U.S.A., like you've dreamed about. You can do it. You're a survivor, remember?"

"Oh, Matt, I'll miss you so much." She looked up at him. "It's been wonderful, hasn't it?"

Wade kissed her forehead. "It's been a dream come true."

The bus began to close its doors. Wade quickly pounded the side and hefted the bag to the doorway.

"Knock 'em dead, Ginny. Take care."

She climbed the bus steps and looked back as the driver shut the door.

Wade tried to wink and raise his hands to say "Click," but his eyes misted and his shaking body wouldn't respond. The bus began pulling away.

Ginny ran to an open window and yelled out, "I love you, Matt!"

Wade tried to yell back but his words only came out in a whisper.

"Bye, Ginny. . . . Good-bye."

Wade sat with Sergeant Zubeck alongside the airfield, waiting for the flight to An Khe. All the men were there except Thumper. Wade stood and walked to the tin shed where his team waited in the shade.

"Preacher, when did you tell him to be here?"

"I told him fifteen hundred hours, just like you said."

Woodpecker grinned. "That's a lot of woman to say good-bye to. Maybe he needs our help."

Wade didn't smile. He only looked up the road. "Damn it, he's late. The plane is gonna land any minute."

A white Lambretta turned the corner and rolled down the road toward them. Russian put his hand to his forehead, blocking the sun's glare.

"It's him!"

Seconds later the Herculean soldier hopped out and ran up to Wade. "You've got to cover for me. I'm staying a couple more days."

Wade walked away from the others, out of earshot. "What the hell you talkin' about?"

Thumper shrugged his shoulders. "I'm staying here a few days, that's all. You can say I'm sick or something."

Wade's brow furrowed as he studied his friend's face. "Does Mary Ann know about this?"

"No, she went to the Red Cross Center, but I'll surprise her."

"With the truth?" asked Wade coldly.

Thumper's eyes narrowed. "Look, Matt, I'm only asking for a few days. Hell, I deserve it."

Wade softened his glare. "Mary Ann wouldn't let you stay. You know that. Come on, Thump, think sensibly. You'll see her again soon enough."

"I thought about it all last night. I'm serious. I don't wanna go back yet. I lost Mary Ann once, and I'm not losing her again."

Wade stepped closer and put his hand on his friend's shoulder. "Look, I know what you're feeling but get hold of yourself. We need you. We've still got a war on. The longer you stay here the harder it will be to come back. Come on, we'll write our ladies as soon as we get back."

Thumper stiffened. "I'm staying. I have to work things out."

Wade dropped his hand abruptly from his friend's shoulder and fixed him with a cold stare. "I'm not going to cover for you. You're going back with us. You can't check out of this war like it's a damn game of some kind."

Thumper's face flushed as his huge body shook with anger. "The hell I can't! I'm the sole surviving son of the family. I can call it quits right now."

Wade shook his head. He couldn't believe what he was hearing. Neither could he let Thumper stay, and then lie to Childs about it. He had no choice but to call his friend's bluff and hope the flight and time would change his mind. "You're going with us. If you want to submit your paperwork . . . well, that's up to you. Get your gear. We're leaving."

Wade turned his back on the big soldier and motioned to the others to pick up their gear as well. Thumper stood fast. He was committed now and had to see it through. He raised a shaking hand and pointed his finger at Wade. "Wade, this goddamn war *is not* that important . . . and I'm through with it."

Wade waved at the taxi driver to take off and looked over his shoulder at the sullen man.

"The team's what's important now . . . and we need you."

Thumper shook his head. "No . . . not anymore."

Major Shane watched the sun's last fleeting glimmer as it disappeared behind the mountains. He turned from the window and sat down at his desk.

"Meeks, are you sure you want to do this?"

Thumper kept his eyes on the wall behind the major. "I'm positive, sir."

Shane lowered his head in disappointment. "Son, you know we have an operation coming up and don't have time to train a replacement. Three-one will have to go one man short. You realize what that means, don't you?"

"Yes, sir, I do. It's over for me. I request relief from the company based on I'm the sole surviving son."

Shane picked up the soldier's personnel folder. "You signed a waiver when you came to Vietnam. It's going to take at least ten days to get your paperwork approved, but I can see your mind is made up so consider yourself relieved from the team. Move into the headquarters barracks immediately. You'll be gone in ten days."

Shane stood and began to motion the soldier out, but instead sighed and ran his hand through his short hair. "Meeks, Sergeant Wade told me about the Red Cross woman. I understand she's a wonderful girl. Do you think it will be the same between you when you see her again? Before you answer let me tell you something. I was here in '67 at Dak To with the 173rd. I was wounded the second day in the battle for Hill 875. It wasn't a real bad wound, but I had an option to leave or stay. I left. The next day twenty-three of the men in my company were killed. I heard about it three days later while in a hospital. I've had to live with asking myself if I'd been there maybe it wouldn't have happened. Son, you have every right to go home. Your family and you have paid enough . . . but please make sure in your mind that it's what you really want."

Thumper's eyes shifted from the wall to the major. "Sir, my brother was killed at Hue. I gave up an education and football career to find the meaning for his death. I found it, and now I've found something else. I've lost my brother and a career. I'm not losing anymore."

Shane turned to the window and spoke softly. "I'll submit your papers. You're dismissed."

The team watched silently as Thumper packed his gear. Wade walked out of his room, but stopped abruptly upon seeing his assistant team leader stuffing his barracks bag. Wade stepped back in his room to avoid him, but suddenly spun around and walked down the barracks aisle. He stopped in front of the soldier and extended his hand.

"Thumper . . . good luck to you."

Thumper stood up and, after a moment's hesitation, took his friend's hand. "I'm sorry, Matt, but it's got to be this way."

Wade forced a smile. "Take care of yourself back in the world. You'll always be a member of Three-one, so write us and tell us how you're doing."

"Sure, Matt."

Wade motioned his men to his room. "Come on guys. We've got a mission to go over."

The team all shook hands with Thumper and filed into their sergeant's room. The big soldier tossed the last items of equipment into his bag and headed for the door. He looked over his shoulder at the empty bay one last time and stepped out.

The column of marching men stopped for the evening. Private Nguyen Nuu walked off the trail, letting his pack fall from his sore shoulders. He sat down wearily and shut his eyes to stop the dizziness.

"Private Nuu, why do rest? You are lazy for such a young man. Your work has just begun! Fetch wood, then fetch water from the stream we passed. Unpack the pots and rice and begin the meal. Our general needs food and tea for his old bones.''

Nuu looked up at his new mentor, Sergeant Thong. The old sergeant was as gnarled as a strangler fig and scolded him like a grandmother. His words always came in a torrent and seemed endless like the monsoons. Nuu rose up, resigning himself to the fact that he was now a slave.

Thong eyed the young soldier and shook his head as if disgusted. "Sit down and rest. You look as if you will fall over and die. I would have to bury you, you know, and then the general's dinner would be late. I will gather the wood myself. Rest for a moment, then fetch the water. Perhaps you carried too much. You did not complain when I gave you all the pots and rice, did you? Foolish! You should have told me the pack was too heavy. Tomorrow we split the load, but only for a day. You are young! Act like it!''

Nuu couldn't help but smile. The old sergeant was loud and liked to hear himself talk but seemed friendly enough. He reminded Nuu of a rooster, the way he strutted and clucked all the time.

Nuu opened his pack and took out the pots for water. It felt good to be in the forest again. It was like an old friend. He walked toward the stream, passing the many escort soldiers that joined them that afternoon. Their drawn faces and thin bodies reminded him of himself only weeks before, but he still wished he were with them. They at least did not make war on farmers.

J. D. Gibson was sitting in the operations center, checking out the team insertion schedule, when Major Shane walked in with Lieutenant Foley and Childs. Shane sat down facing the gray-haired officer. "J. D., you've been practicing your flying a lot, so you've missed out on our recent operations. We need to get you up-to-date so you can start inserting teams.''

"You think I'm ready, sir?''

Shane smiled. "Yeah, you're ready. Foley tells me you're a real hotshot.''

Gibson glanced at the bespectacled lieutenant with an appreciative grin.

Shane nodded to Childs, and the sergeant walked to the wall map.

"We've moved our area of operations to the mountains west of An Khe. We need for the teams to get one more mission under their belts before we move to Phan Thiet to begin the Corps mission. First Platoon was inserted today. Tomorrow, Second Platoon goes in, followed by the Third Platoon the next day. First Platoon teams have seen lots of footprints on the trails, but haven't spotted anyone yet."

Shane leaned forward. "J. D., you're going to insert the teams because I'm sending Lieutenant Foley to Phan Thiet with an advance party to find us a base to work out of. He'll take four commo men and Sergeant Gino to establish a TOC and make liaison visits to the aviation units. Study the map and learn all the team's landing zones. You've had enough practice. Tomorrow you start playing 'quarterback' in the big game."

Shane rose and patted the young officer's back. "You'll do fine, hotshot."

The major motioned Childs to follow him, and the two men strode through the door into the darkness.

Shane waited until he was far enough from the ops center to be out of hearing distance and stopped. "Jerry, I want you to see what you can do to keep Specialist Meeks busy until I get him orders for the States."

The sergeant, in a low voice, said, "Sir, don't be too quick pushing his orders through. I've seen this before. I've got ways to get pussy out of his mind."

"I don't want him pushed to change his mind. He'll be useless to the team if he's forced. Just keep him busy, Jerry, that's all."

Childs gave his major a not-too-convincing, "Of course, sir," and smiled to himself. He knew a proven remedy.

Shane noted the tone. He hoped that whatever the sergeant planned met with his guidance. "I mean it, Jerry. Don't push him."

Childs blustered. "I heard ya the first time . . . sir."

Shane held back his smile. His sergeant couldn't lie worth a shit. "Come on, old-timer, let's drink a beer."

Thumper read over the letter he'd just written to Mary Ann. He'd explained his decision to go home and wait for her. He'd be assigned to a post somewhere in the States for only a few months, then he'd get out and could return to school and they'd get married.

He was about to fold the letter when Childs walked into the barracks and approached his bunk. "Meeks, startin' tomorrow you gonna work in the ops center and be an RTO. We got radiomen leaving tomorrow for Phan Thiet and you'll be replacing them. You'll work a twelve-hour shift and rotate with Dagood."

"Damn, Sarge, I'm not a RTO."

"You are now! Don't complain, lover-boy, I could let Top have you clean his latrines till you leave."

Thumper shook his head dejectedly. He didn't want to know how the teams were doing when they went in—especially Matt's team.

Childs watched the soldier from the corner of his eye. "When Three-one goes out, you'll be responsible for Bitch. She can't stay with Pete 'cause he'll be too busy gettin' ready for the move to Phan Thiet."

Thumper nodded in silence. He didn't mind taking care of Russian's dog.

Hiding a smile, Childs turned and strolled out of the barracks. He knew monitoring a radio all day would give the big soldier plenty of time to think.

Thumper folded the letter and put it in the envelope. Ten days, he thought, ten days, then home. Mom will be so relieved and dad will . . . damn it! Why did the major talk about guilt? I'm right! I don't have to stay. I've paid my dues. Mary Ann and I can . . . damn him!

31 SEPTEMBER

Lieutenant Gibson was tired as he leaned back in the bird dog's back seat and shut his eyes. The past four days had gone by in a blur. He'd flown for seven to eight hours a day, inserting teams and extracting those that had killed dinks in their ambushes. It seemed that every time they turned for home, a team had a contact. The pilot would then turn back, as J. D. directed the gunships and Slick in for pick-up. Only two teams remained out—Wade's 3-1 team and Jenkins's 3-4 bunch. Commo was very bad in the valleys, so he'd had to go up and establish radio contact with both teams and relay to base operations in An Khe. He'd called both teams and they'd reported they'd seen nothing, so he was finally heading for An Khe after a long day.

Wade let the tobacco juice roll down his cheek rather than spitting it out. He'd heard talking. They'd been laying in ambush just off an old trail for two days and had seen nothing. They were perpendicular to a steep-banked dry creek to their right. The noise he'd heard came from the creek bed. He motioned to Russian and Woodpecker, who were ten meters away, to check it out. The two men were hiding behind thick elephant grass only a few meters from the bank and had first alerted Wade to the voices.

Woodpecker crawled slowly to the edge and peered

down the almost vertical fifteen-foot bank to a small pocket
of water, where two khaki-clad soldiers were filling their
tin canteens. The small Vietnamese had left their AK-47s
lying on the bank and were talking in a high, singsong pitch.
Russian saw the soldiers and quickly checked for others
on the far embankment twenty meters away. The land was
higher on the far side, but all he could see was more elephant grass. The two Rangers backed up. Russian turned
to Wade and pointed to the streambed, then raised two
fingers. Matt raised his hand and slid it across his throat,
signaling to kill them. Russian and Woodpecker readied
their weapons. Then Russian tapped the redhead and both
raised up firing. The Vietnamese were flung backward violently, like limp dolls, by the impact of the bullets. Across
the gully on the embankment, four other soldiers suddenly
rose up from the elephant grass where they'd been resting.
Each of their faces showed surprise, but one quickly raised
his weapon and fired at the two shooting Americans.

Woodpecker had seen the movement and tried to bring
his weapon up, but at that instant the bank gave way. The
two men fell, with Woodpecker screaming out.

Wade saw only bullets kicking up around his two men
and then they toppled out of sight. "They're hit," he
screamed, and jumped up. He ran only two feet when a
hail of fire tore through the tall grass stalks around him.
Preacher and Rose raised up shooting but couldn't see a
target. Wade tried to crawl to the bank, but the ground in
front of him erupted in puffs of dust and dull thuds. He
backed up quickly and lay panting. He took a deep breath
and yelled, "Russian! . . . Woodpeck . . ." Bullets cut the
stalks just above his head.

Russian brushed the dirt away from the redhead's face.
Woodpecker immediately opened his eyes and sat up.
They'd fallen to the bottom of a gully where the dirt cas-
cading down after them had partially buried them. They
heard Wade's yell but didn't dare respond. An enemy grenade tossed in the streambed would be devastating. Both
men crawled to the far bank to get out of view of the enemy
shooters.

Wade crawled back to Preacher, who had already called the bird dog for gunship support. The Indian looked at Wade's sweaty face. "What about Russian and Woodpecker?" he asked worriedly.

"They bought it," snapped Wade as he grabbed the handset.

Thumper listened to the speaker box as Lieutenant Gibson reported the information he had received from Team 3-1: "Pinned down by undetermined number of enemy. Two friendly probable KIA."

Childs stood behind him and kicked the chair over angrily. "The dirty motherfuckers!"

Thumper stared at the radio, unbelieving.

Shane ran into the TOC. "What's happening?"

Childs shook his head. "Three-one is in contact. Looks like two of 'em bought it. We got guns en route to help the others."

"Damn!" blurted Shane. "Are they sure?"

"That's all we got so far. The L-tee will be over 'em in a few minutes."

Wade spread his men out and crawled forward in hopes of at least spotting the hidden enemy. He got within a few feet of the bank when a bullet cracked by his ear. Rose saw the muzzle flash and fired. Three more flashes appeared close by the first. Preacher fired a long burst, as did Wade, to try to obtain fire superiority. Both sides were exchanging a steady rate of fire when a grenade exploded just behind the guerrillas. Matt couldn't help but smile. The grenade had come from the gully; at least one of his men was alive. Suddenly, the shooting stopped from the VC side. As Wade quickly changed magazines he heard the droning of an aircraft above. Thank God!

"Three-one, this is Romeo-three. What's your sitrep? Over," radioed Gibson.

Preacher answered quickly. "This is Three-one. Have four or five enemy firing at us from high ground. Will mark our location for guns. Over."

"Roger." Gibson flipped a toggle on his radio panel and called the gunships below him. "Rattler lead, Three-one is popping smoke. Call their frequency for instruction."

"Roger."

"Three-one, this is Rattler lead. I have yellow smoke."

Preacher was engulfed in yellow fog and could barely breathe. "Roger, you have us, Rattler. Enemy located twenty meters due west of yellow smoke. Make run north to south and I'll adjust."

"Roger, Three-one. Keep your heads down. We're coming in hot. *Now!*"

Preacher yelled out to the others, *"Guns inbound . . . stay down!"*

Wade pressed himself into the dirt and clenched his teeth. He could hear the loud popping of the chopper blades as the first bird made an abrupt turn and lowered its nose. The twenty-pound rockets swished out of their firing tubes and screamed to their target. The ground shook under Wade and an earsplitting *whack-boom* deafened him for a moment. The rockets were right on target. The second gunship released its rockets just as Wade looked up. He saw the white smoke trails and again the earth erupted. The thunderous explosion threw up a dark black cloud followed by dirt and pieces of grass that floated like confetti.

Wade rose up firing and ran to the edge of the bank. He paused for only a second, praying that both of his men were alive, and peered over the embankment. Russian and Woodpecker were pressed against the gully's far wall. Wade couldn't speak. The sight of his two men, alive and unhurt, was too much. He was about to yell out when a Vietnamese staggered out of the smoke on the far embankment. His face and the right side of his body were blackened and oozing deep red blood. The soldier, blinded by his wounds, fell down just as Wade raised his weapon. The man got to his knees and tried to stand again when a shot rang out. His head snapped back and a piece of it flew upward.

Rose stood up ten meters away and lowered his rifle with a grin.

Wade yelled to Russian and Woodpecker, then motioned for Preacher to bring the radio up.

Preacher fell to the ground beside Wade, holding out the handset. "I already called the Guns and told them to stand by."

Wade took the handset with a nod and motioned over the bank. Preacher crawled to the lip of the embankment and saw the two men below. "Thank you, Jesus," he whispered and raised a hand skyward.

Wade patted the Indian's leg. "Amen," he said, and pushed the handset side bar. "Romeo-three, this is Three-one, we . . ."

When the updated situation report came in from Lieutenant Gibson, Childs spun around and picked up Bitch. "Well, ya dumb gook mutt, looks like they're all comin' back."

Shane, letting out a sigh of relief, noticed Thumper wiping tears from his eyes. Shane said nothing and walked out of the sweltering bunker. God, it's a beautiful day, he thought. The air seemed cleaner and sweeter than he could remember. The sun's oppressive heat wasn't so bad and . . . they're alive!

Shane threw back his shoulders and breathed in another full breath of air. The problems with the move to Phan Thiet didn't seem important now. Life, the precious stuff they always took for granted, was all that really mattered. His men would soon be back, laughing, bitching, and fighting as always. They'd hung on to life and beat the odds. There would be no solemn ceremony, thank God; only war stories—this time.

"Sir?"

Shane turned around. Thumper walked toward him with his head lowered, speaking almost in a whisper. "Can I speak to you a minute, sir?"

Wade and his team left the ops center after the debrief and walked wearily toward the barracks.

Rose patted Preacher's back. "Man, them dinks really smell when they get cooked, don't they?"

Preacher nodded but tried to block out the images of the torn, blackened corpses of the three men they'd found. The gunship rockets had scored a direct hit on two of the pathetic VC, tearing and burning their bodies into lumps of smoldering, oozing flesh. The smell of cordite and burning human tissue were forever seared into his senses.

Woodpecker saw Preacher's discomfort and put his arm over the Indian's shoulder. "Ya done real good on the radio . . . thanks."

Wade grasped the barracks door handle and looked over his shoulder. "Which one of you guys threw the grenade from the gully?"

Woodpecker pointed quickly to Russian, disgustedly. "He did! I told him not to, but did he listen? Hell no! Said he wanted to kill Communists!"

Russian shrugged his shoulders. "That is our mission, no?"

Wade laughed and pulled open the door. He was immediately attacked by Bitch, who jumped up on his legs excitedly. "Russian, Bitch has missed . . ."

He stopped in mid-sentence: Thumper was unpacking his equipment by his old bunk.

Rose brushed past Wade with a wide smile and tossed his ruck on the floor. "Thump, man, ya shoulda seen me. There I was . . ." The other men walked past their team sergeant, all talking at once to the big soldier as if he'd never left.

Thumper smiled at Rose's enthusiasm.

Wade winked at Thumper. His friend was back. Rose and the others understood, too. It didn't matter how or why he'd returned to them. It didn't matter. He'd returned.

Wade went back to his room, tossed his ruck and weapon to his bed, and walked back into the bay. He wanted to be with his team—the whole team as they came down from the high of the contact. He needed to be with them and to hear the retelling of events.

"Man, it was a real trip. Russian and Woodpecker fired up two dudes big-time and do this swan dive off the cliff. Luke raises up outta nowhere and blasts back, I mean, seriously pissed. Matt shits his pants and sprays . . ." Somehow it was always better when Rose told it.

Mary Ann received a call from Thumper at midnight and wiped tears from her eyes as she replaced the handset. He'd said he sent a letter a few days before and wanted her to tear it up. He'd changed his mind and was staying with the team.

She sat down on her bed. She knew he had to stay or it would never be the same between them. The knowing hurt. He'd been going home to safety but now . . . damn this war! She glanced at the chair across the room where the day before Virginia sat for two hours talking to her before leaving and catching her flight to the Philippines. The little singer knew the same pain. At least Thumper and she admitted they loved each other. Virginia couldn't bring herself to admit the fact, but it was evident the sergeant had gotten to her. As confidently as she'd talked about her singing career, her questions and tears were about love. She insisted that she and Matt were from different, incompatible worlds and that their relationship was just one of two ships passing in the night.

"Looks to me the ships collided a couple of times," Mary Ann had commented.

Virginia hadn't laughed or smiled. Instead, her eyes had grown misty.

The poor girl had never been in love before. Her emotions were tugging her insides out. A career had always been the most important thing in her life . . . until now. The inner conflict Virginia would have to resolve caused Mary Ann to reach out to her and offer the only advice she felt comfortable giving.

"Ginny, go to the Philippines. Work hard and do your best and let time help you sort out your feelings."

Mary Ann broke her trance from the empty chair and lay back on the bed. Her body still tingled inside from talking to Thumper. Just the sound of his voice had made her knees feel weak and her insides flutter. She smiled and shut her eyes to be with him again in her dreams.

19

<u>3 OCTOBER</u>

First Sergeant Demand let his men eat their breakfast in peace. They'd packed their gear the day before and would be moving to Phan Thiet. In a few hours, his Rangers would board Air Force C-130s and fly south, once again leaving him with the administrative duties of running the permanent rear base camp.

As the bantam soldier silently watched the men enter the mess hall, he wondered which ones would never return. The major had told him about the Corps' mission; finding an NVA division would be extremely dangerous. The large numbers of enemy could overwhelm six lightly armed men long before gunships could come to their aid. The senior soldier studied each face and memorized each name. If word came back that one had died, he wanted to feel the loss. They deserved at least that.

There was only one consolation in this kind of situation: his men were Rangers. They were men who knew the danger and yet went willingly. They were a special breed who lived for challenge. They wanted it no other way. Not only did they understand the risk, it was what they sought. Something inside was pushing each man forward to face the ultimate challenge of imminent death.

First Sergeant waited until the last man entered, and looked down at his spot. He wouldn't stand here again until they returned. Raising his head proudly, he strolled out the door without looking back.

Major Shane took a bite of dehydrated scrambled eggs and quickly washed them down with a slug of coffee. "Agh, this crap is terrible!"

"Hell, it's free," said Childs, who had just finished his meal.

Shane took another swig of coffee and shook his head. "Free my ass. This is costing me another year from my wife and sons."

Childs snickered. "If you tasted my ol' lady's cookin' you wouldn't complain."

Shane set down his cup, surprised. Childs had not once made reference to his wife in all the time he'd known him. "Where is your wife, anyway?" he asked.

Childs stared at his tray. "Fort Bragg. She works at the post grade school makin' me beer money."

"She like teaching?"

"Now, she don't teach. She cooks in the cafeteria. We got us a house and her job pays the bills. She don't like cookin' when she comes home, so all I get is shit."

Shane wanted to pursue the conversation, but the sergeant seemed uncomfortable talking about her.

Lieutenant Gibson sat down at their table and motioned to Shane's eggs. "Sir, you gonna eat your . . ."

The major shoved his tray over. "Damn, J. D., you're as bad as Childs. How do you stand the stuff?"

Gibson grinned as he reached for a bottle of Tabasco sauce. "A little of this, sir, and you don't taste a thing."

Shane smiled and picked up his coffee cup. "J. D., we got a call from Foley early this morning and we've had some changes. We're still flying into Phan Thiet but won't be staying there. Corps has given us a base to work out of closer to the area of operation. It's twenty miles northwest of Phan Thiet near a town called An Lom. It's an engineer base and has a fully operational airfield. The birds can all bed down with us. It'll save a lot of time and work out better for the operation."

"We gonna truck to An Lom then, sir?" asked Gibson with his mouth partially full.

"Yeah, we'll be in An Lom by 1500 this afternoon. We'll have three days before we begin operations. Foley says the engineers built super facilities and they're all out on a building site farther north. The only guys left behind are shitbirds, but Foley says they may be a problem. You'll have to be on the lookout while we're there and make sure our guys don't mess with them."

Gibson noticed the hint of concern in his commander's voice. "Sure, sir. I'll brief the platoon before we go."

Shane pulled a folded map from his pocket and spread it out on the table. "This is the area we'll be working. I'll brief the teams in two days, but you need to memorize key terrain features before we go in. Take this map and start sleeping with it. You won't be able to overfly the area until we actually go in."

Gibson let out a deep breath when he saw the size of the marked area. "All of this! My God, it's . . ."

"Almost a hundred square miles," said Shane. "You see, it's almost a perfect rectangle and I've broken it down into four equal recon zones. We'll put our three platoons into the first three zones. It'll take a couple of days to put them in because of distance and establishing radio relay sites."

Gibson shifted his gaze to the fourth area. "How about this one?" he asked, tapping the fourth recon zone.

Shane exchanged glances with Childs. "We hope we find them before we have to work that area. It's rugged and doesn't have very many landing zones."

Gibson lifted his finger and looked closer at the fourth box. The terrain was mostly rain forest-covered mountains, but there was one prominent feature—a river that ran north to south. In the center of the area the river made a large horseshoe bend. Within the bend was a ring of steep hills with a huge open valley in its center.

Gibson looked up. "This looks like a giant football stadium."

Shane smiled and took out a pen. "J. D., you just named the fourth box. We'll call it the 'Stadium Zone.'" He wrote the words on the upper right-hand corner of the map and pushed it toward J. D. "Let's just hope we don't have to play ball there."

Wade and the team sat at the corner table, eating the normal B ration breakfast—with the exception of Russian, who was having his favorite, SOS—shit on a shingle, hamburger and gravy on toast.

Rose leaned over toward the Czech and sniffed the air. "Dig it, dudes. I smell a foreigner who ain't had a shower since he been here."

Russian's eyes narrowed as he picked up his knife and stood slowly.

The men sitting at the next table looked on worriedly, but the team seemed unconcerned.

"Rose, you say bad things again," Russian growled.

Rose took another bite of bacon. "It's true, man. Ain't ya heard Top's speech on being clean? Man, you stink."

Russian tossed the knife expertly to his other hand and leaned over menacingly. "I cut your tongue out."

Rose continued chewing his food nonchalantly. "Then who gonna save your big ass in the toolies?"

Russian's knife flashed, stabbing the sweet roll on Rose's plate and flicking it up. Russian caught the roll in midair and took a vengeful bite.

Rose put his fork down slowly and shook his head. "Aw, Russian, not the roll, man."

Russian sat back and took another bite while glaring at Rose.

The team broke up in laughter and Thumper put a consoling arm around Rose. "You woulda made Top proud."

Rose looked over his shoulder and threw his thumb in the first sergeant's direction. "I'm gonna be just like him one day. I'm gonna be a first sergeant and get rid of foreigners in this Army, like Russian. I'm gonna do it, you just wait and see."

"I didn't know you were lifer type, Rose," Wade said, a little surprised.

"Sure, man. I got it. When I leave the Nam, I'm puttin' in to be an instructor at the Airborne school. They was real professionals, and it's a good place to start my career."

Woodpecker shook his head. "You, an Airborne instructor? Man, us paratrooper's is gonna lose our reputation. Rose, you gonna have to gain some weight. Here, have my roll. You gonna need it, man."

Preacher raised his milk carton. "To the Rose, an Airborne instructor and future first sergeant. There could none be better."

The team lifted their milk containers. "To The Rose!"

The black soldier smiled and pointed his finger at Russian. "And you still stink, man."

Beneath a giant boulder outcrop Sergeant Din Su Thong shaped the last clay hill while looking at his reference map. The terrain model of the fortress had to be perfect to please his general.

A young soldier stood by like an assisting nurse, handing the sergeant the instruments he required for his work. Sergeant Thong held out a muddy hand. "White clay."

Private Nuu reached into a tin bucket and handed over a glob of the special stream clay that dried like iron. Thong placed the goo on the hilltop and flattened it slightly. With a bamboo knife he cut out the ravines and shaped the ridges, knowing his general would want perfection.

Ten minutes later the sergeant stood back from his work and wiped the sticky mud from his hands. The terrain model was complete. Perhaps now the Tall One would smile. The general had been ill-tempered since his arrival two days before. He'd found General Sang's Second Division improperly positioned and was angry that they hadn't dug protective bunkers. Thong stepped closer to the model and motioned his assistant to him. "We are blessed, Nuu, to work for such a leader as the Tall One. You see now why he is a genius of war."

The young private yawned. He saw only mounds of clay on the ground that had taken all morning for the old sergeant to fashion.

Thong angrily kicked at the young soldier's leg. "You are a fool! You appreciate nothing!"

Private Nuu stiffened and stared at his berater. "I know nothing of maps or units. I was a bricklayer in my village before being drafted."

Sergeant Thong realized the boy was right. He patted Nuu's back apologetically. "I'm sorry, my friend. I am taking out my anger on you instead of the others who do not listen to our general. They are fools not to appreciate his wisdom. I will explain the terrain model to you and why the general has been so ill-tempered."

The slight soldier smiled at the old sergeant. "You think a bricklayer will understand?"

Thong winked. "If he does not, the bricklayer may become an infantryman instead of a lazy aide to the general."

Nuu laughed and picked up a stick for his teacher. "Teach me, old one. I like being the aide."

Thong took the stick and pointed at the model. "You see we are in a natural fortress. The river bends around protecting us. We are on the high ground like the lip of an oblong rice bowl, but the bowl has a broken off end. See the large open valley in the center? If you were to stand in its center, you would see the high hills to your north, west, and south. They form a partial ring around the flat valley floor. What would you see to the east?"

Nuu answered quickly, having walked into the valley from that side. "The rain forest. We came in from that direction two days ago."

"Yes, the forest. The forest hides our trails. You see we are in a fortress, but it also is a trap. We can only escape to the east if the Yankees come. The general was furious when he found the Second Division was poorly positioned. General Sang had his three regiments placed all along the hills overlooking the valley. They would all be trapped. Furthermore, he had not ordered his men to dig deeply into the earth for protection from bombs.

Nuu showed confusion on his face. "What was wrong with the unit placement?"

Sergeant Thong squatted down. "Our general was

briefed by General Sang about his regiments' positions when we arrived. The Second's commander said the only danger was the open valley where Yankee helicopters could land. He'd displaced his forces to attack the Americans and destroy them if they dared be so foolish.

"The Tall One's face became almost white. He was so angry I thought he might explode. He sat silently for a full minute before dismissing the others, leaving only the Second's commander. He then told the commander he was a fool. He said, 'We are here to train and prepare for an attack of our choosing. If the Americans come *we* do *not* fight. We escape to fight again.' He then told the commander to place one regiment in the hills to the north and to place his remaining two regiments in the forest at the eastern end of the valley. Should Americans come, one company in the forest would attack and then pull back and delay while the division escaped."

Nuu nodded in understanding and squatted down by his teacher. "The Americans won't come, will they?"

"One never knows. They have planes that see through trees. The general knows this and so directed that bunkers be dug deep. He knows the American ways better than anyone, and he is a fox at outsmarting them. The Americans always bomb just before bringing in their soldiers. If Sang's one company attacks, they will follow like dogs to food."

Nuu looked worriedly at the model. "We are alone here at the western end of the fortress. There is only a platoon here to protect us. How will we escape if they come?"

Sergeant Thong pointed the stick. "We will merely walk down the trail that runs along the top of the hills and follow it to the south, and then go east and escape. The Americans will be too busy fighting the company to try and climb the hills."

Nuu stood and turned around. He gazed down at the open valley floor and looked back at the model. "It truly is a fortress. Your likeness is perfect."

Sergeant Thong rose slowly. "Yes, but it is sad that those who lived here before had to give up their home for the struggle. The Montagnards have lived here for hundreds of years. The fortress was their home. They are the ones who cleared the valley for planting and it's their huts we now use as our headquarters. One day when we are gone and the war is over they will return to be forgotten again. You'd better go and tell our general the model is completed. The party members arrive this afternoon for the council meeting. He will want to see the model before they arrive.''

Nuu walked down an old beaten path to a large, elevated hut and climbed the wooden steps carved out of red teak. A minute later he hurried down the steps and ran to the sergeant. ''Colonel Sy and the general are coming.''

The sergeant looked toward the hut and saw Colonel Sy appear out of the doorway. He was followed several seconds later by his commander, General Binh Ty Duc.

The fifty-eight-year-old general walked down the steps into the diffused light of the forest and approached with his usual precise gait. He was a slender giant, taller than Colonel Sy by a foot, who all recognized immediately. His short, light-gray hair was accented by teak-brown skin, which was wrinkled at the corners of his wise, piercing eyes. His sun-bleached khaki shirt was open at the neck and revealed no rank or insignia on the epaulets or collars. His erect carriage and regal bearing were symbols enough. The taciturn soldier was a genius in the art of war. He had graduated with honors from the Military Academy in Da Lat and later, prior to the colonial war, had attended the French staff college. Fluent in French and a proven leader, he had been one of the staff officers for General Giap in the great victory at Dien Bien Phu.

General Binh Duc studied the model for several minutes before slowly shifting his gaze to Sergeant Thong. ''I am fortunate to have such a soldier as you. My eyes betray me when I only see paper. This, my friend, is a living map made by a true craftsman.''

Thong nodded with a smile. ''Thank you, my General.''

Colonel Sy stepped closer to the general, speaking

softly. "The model will only serve to humiliate General Sang. He is still smarting from your visit."

The general smiled. "It is a reminder to him during the council meeting to keep his thoughts to himself." The general's gaze shifted back to the model and he stepped closer to study the western end of the fortress.

He had assumed the mountains were continuous, but there was a tiny split on the most western end only five hundred meters from his hut.

"Is this an error?" he asked Sergeant Thong, pointing to the small gap in the clay.

Thong pulled out his map and quickly checked before answering. "No, General. The stream that runs through the valley flows to the river through a ravine."

The general snapped his head to Colonel Sy. "Have one of your officers check this. This could be an entrance to the fortress that General Sang has not accounted for."

"Yes, comrade," said the colonel quickly, and motioned Sergeant Thong to fetch one of his lieutenants.

The general strolled past the model to the large table, which was set up under a rock ledge. He sat down on one of the benches and looked around him. Colonel Sy had a map board placed on a bamboo easel showing the disposition of all the Communist forces in the south. Behind the table was the shallow cave where his communications section set up their radios and small generator.

Colonel Sy sat down and handed the general a piece of paper. "Here are the discussion topics the committee wants to discuss with you."

The general squinted, trying to read the small printing, and then tossed the agenda down. "What should I concern myself with?"

The colonel smiled. "The Politburo has several new policies, but as usual they are based on ideology. Our battle will be between the Peiping followers and the Moscow believers. You must ensure you don't embrace either policy with words they can use against you."

The general sighed, tired of such meetings. The rhetoric of the party members was difficult to take. The first several hours would be devoted to briefings from each Directorate, who would espouse their great achievements—all meaningless. Only the last hour would be fruitful. The real statistics and successes would be given for him to assess. The party was a victim of its own propaganda. Failures were never mentioned and exaggerated success only painted false hopes. He was only a soldier, not a politician who had to appease the masses. The only information he needed was the truth.

The general looked at the map and stood. He noted that many of the regular units from the north were not shown. Good. The colonel had followed his instructions to the letter. If the Directorates knew of the real numbers they would scream for more support for their indoctrination program, civilian support, rural cooperatives, state farms, and of course more cadre for the people's liberation armed forces. All made worthy contributions, but victory was not won by spreading his precious trained manpower to the winds. The key to success was the support provided by China and the Soviet Union. Their guns, ammunition, and technical support were the lifeblood of the struggle. Without them the struggle would last another twenty years.

The Sino-Soviet relationship was deteriorating rapidly, but his government had to please both in order to keep their support coming in. Like his government, he had to appease the Directorates by giving them token manpower and promises.

Of course, the war was won. He and General Giap knew this a year ago when the Americans began pulling out and started the Vietnamization program. Victory was close. In perhaps only four or five years they would be strong enough to make a final, all-out assault. Patience was now all that was required, but that meant keeping hotheads like General Sang leashed. The Second Division general would attack today if given a chance. He would win a minor battle only to lose final reunification.

The general picked up the agenda and headed for his hut. Colonel Sy watched his commander go, knowing he would rest and awaken ready to fight the battle of words with the committee. The general was a master and was respected. They would complain and argue but his word was final. When the war ended, the general would return to the North and be a hero, but he would never again lead. He'd made too many enemies, and was a Catholic. He'd never be trusted. He only led now because they needed his military cleverness.

The colonel was about to stand when a familiar voice rang out. "You called for me, comrade Colonel?"

Sy motioned the lieutenant to him and walked toward the model. "I want you to check this gap in the mountains. As you can see, it is five hundred meters. The general wants to know if this can be used as an entry into the fortress. The hills behind us are too steep for a force to infiltrate, but this may be a passage. That would require one of our units to be positioned for security."

The lieutenant pulled out his map and oriented it to the terrain model. "I will return within several hours and report to you, comrade."

General Binh Duc sat on the top step of his hut looking at the valley below. "It is beautiful. The Montagnards knew a wonderful life here."

Sergeant Thong was standing behind the general and squatted in the doorway. "Yes, their village was below us next to the stream. I saw their ruins when Nuu and I collected firewood. These huts we stay in were for the hunters and only used by the men. The small hut behind us was their spirit house."

The general turned to the old sergeant. "You know the Montagnards' ways?"

"Yes, my General, I lived in the highlands as a boy. My father traded with the Jari for fish and wild fruit. This valley would be perfect for a tribe. They had the stream and flat valley to grow food and the hills would provide hunters plenty of birds and animals."

The general looked back to the valley, speaking softly. "It is good to see the sun rise and set. The fresh air renews my strength. The tunnels are no place for soldiers."

Sergeant Thong nodded in silence. He knew his general needed this trip to renew his strength. But meetings such as the one that would take place today also had great propaganda value for the peple. They would see for themselves how vast were the liberated areas. Thong knew the general didn't like meetings, but enjoyed the marches to the different areas.

The general stood up and walked into the old hut. He wrote several messages and handed them to Thong. "Send these to boulder mountain and wake me when the committee members arrive."

Thong took the messages and bowed slightly. To show respect, he waited for the general to turn his back, then retreated quietly.

The sergeant took his time walking toward the boulder outcrop. The great teak and sayo trees smelled of life and provided more than adequate cover from Yankee planes. There was no underbrush and one could see the peaceful valley below. The diffused light cast the small camp in a golden hue. All was calm, quiet, and peaceful.

He entered a shallow cave, where Corporal Din sat at his radio receiver. Five sleeping men lay on the ground behind the corporal.

Sergeant Thong handed over the messages. "It is time for another to make the long journey."

Corporal Din looked at the paper and sighed in relief. "I am blessed not to be young. I would not like having to march the twenty kilometers to the radio transmitter station."

Thong agreed with a nod. The general had only brought twenty men from his staff. When he left the tunnel headquarters, his deputy took command and had full authority to make decisions. The general kept abreast of the situation by monitoring the radio. He could not send out any messages from the fortress location or the signals would be triangulated. The communications platoon had to send runners to radio relays to send messages. The system was slow but guaranteed protection for the fortress.

Sergeant Thong looked at the five sleeping men. "Which one should I wake?"

Lieutenant Huy walked up the ridge trail carrying only a canteen. He had been wounded in the right leg a year before and still had a slight limp. He strolled down the old Montagnard trail until he came to a sudden vertical drop. The mountain seemed to have been sliced by a giant knife.

He looked down the sheer rock face to a stream one hundred meters directly below. Backing up a step from the dangerous edge, he could see the other side of the ravine only twenty meters away. The stream could be used as an entry, he thought, and walked down the steep ridge paralleling the crevice. His leg hurt as he made his way down the incline, and he slowed his pace to stop the throbbing. Three-fourths of the way down the hill he crept back to the crumbling edge and peered over. The stream was only fifty meters down, but any thought that the ravine could be used as an entrance now dissolved. The valley was higher than the river. The stream water gushed out of an opening just below the lip of a solid rock wall in a beautiful waterfall to the stream far below. No one could enter the fortress and no one could go down unless they had ropes.

The lieutenant glanced one more time at the waterfall, then began the long walk back to the camp.

Lieutenant Foley exhaled a deep breath as the first camouflaged C-130 landed with a roar and sped down the runway. In minutes, the aircraft's rear cargo door opened, and the first contingent of Rangers filed out. Major Shane was leading them.

"Welcome to Phan Thiet, sir," said the lieutenant, saluting and joining the major as he walked toward the waiting trucks.

"Thanks, Bob. Is everything set up as planned?"

"Yes, sir, these trucks will transport the men to An Lom. It's about an hour's drive away and all set up, but we have a slight problem."

Shane had been watching the Rangers load the trucks.

When Foley said "problem," he turned toward the be-spectacled officer.

"The engineer camp we're using has some serious racial problems," Foley explained. "I know I warned you before, but it's gotten worse. The engineers are working up at Duc Co, thirty miles from here, and left their trouble-makers and potheads behind. They only have a first lieu-tenant as the rear area commander, and it looks to me as if he's lost control. They've had three fragging incidents in the past two weeks."

Shane waved Childs over. "We got a bigger problem than we thought at the base. The L-tee will bring you up to date. I'm going to Phan Thiet and call Corps and tell them we arrived. I'll see you this evening at An Lom."

Childs and Foley saluted. Childs dropped his hand and looked at the L-tee. "Now, what's the problem?"

General Binh Duc sat at the head of the table, trying to look interested as the Political Directorate droned on about upcoming topics of training by the political commissars. This month's topic was "the armed forces' contribution to the Socialist state." Next month it would be "vigilance against reactionary elements." The general had little use for the rhetoric of the commissars, even if they were powerful in the eyes of the Politburo. They bored his soldiers with political studies and party meetings. Their real purpose was to ensure political loyalty and reliability.

The general leaned back in his chair and looked at the faces of the council members. He couldn't help but be pleased. His plan had worked. The young men who came were only representatives of the key party Directorates and had no decision-making power. The older leaders could not make the long journey. Old Trung Vee, the logistics director, was the only exception. He was a close friend and an ally to the cause. He was a graduate and, later, a teacher at Nguyen Ai Quoc School in Hanoi, and he was greatly respected. The school's ties to the central committee were well known. Between himself and old Vee, the general thought, they would keep the council from making problems. He would be able to push through his policy of patience.

Colonel Sy passed the general a note. General Binh Duc unfolded the paper slowly, thankful for the mental diversion. The note read:

Lieutenant Huy checked the ravine and reports it is impassable. A stream runs to a shear drop-off of fifty meters. The waterfall is beautiful. It is unfortunate the Political Directorate representative likes the sound of his own voice, no?

The general smiled and winked at his adviser as the speaker went on with his monotonous dissertation.

Rose turned the faucet and watched in astonishment as hot water flowed out. He hadn't seen such a phenomenon in some time. Like stateside, he thought happily, as he splashed the warm water on his face to clean off the convoy dust.

The Rangers had arrived at the engineer base of An Lom an hour before and had been assigned their barracks and had stored their gear. The new latrine facility with running hot and cold water was a pleasant surprise.

As Rose looked into the shaving mirror while drying his face, three more black faces appeared in the glass. Surprised, he turned around. The sound of the running water had muffled their steps.

"What's happenin', dudes?"

"What the fuck you doin' here, man?"

The speaker was standing in the center of the three and was of medium height. He wore rose-colored glasses, and his hair was puffed out in a large afro. He spoke menacingly, with his finger pointing viciously at Rose's face. His sleeveless fatigue shirt was unbuttoned, exposing two necklaces made from black bootlaces. Both of his wrists had black leather bands wrapped around them.

The other two men were taller and stood a pace behind their leader. One wore dark aviator sunglasses and had a blue bandana tied around his forehead. The other had a similar headband and wore a thin mustache over a cruel grin.

Rose leaned back on the sink basin, smiling impassively.

"We just got in, man. This is our latrine, ain't it?"

"Your latrine, shit! Motherfucker, us niggers own this whole camp, man!"

Rose casually turned sideways to the leader. He would take him out with a side kick, if there was going to be trouble. He maintained his smile, dropping the corners of his mouth only slightly as he quietly spoke. "It's cool, man. There musta been a mistake. I'll go and get it straightened out."

The leader took a confident step closer, smiling. "You done fucked up, Oreo. We goin' to teach you a lesson."

Rose locked his eyes with those of the approaching soldier. "You fuckin' with Rangers, fool! You best let it be."

The spokesman broke Rose's stare as he chortled through his nose and glanced over his shoulder at his friends.

As if on signal, the others snickered and moved a step closer.

Rose smiled. "You blew it, brother."

The jeering man tensed. He didn't like the confidence the small soldier was displaying. "You gonna . . ."

A toilet flushed to their right. The three men started at the sound. They had assumed the Ranger was alone. Thumper walked from behind a partition and leaned against the wall as he buckled his pants.

He was shirtless, exposing his large, muscular upper torso. He glanced at Rose and winked. "Who're your friends?"

The soldier wearing the aviator glasses spit. "We ain't no Uncle Tom's friends, fucker!"

The leader backed up, joining the others and eyeing the big man who looked like big trouble.

Thumper pushed off the wall and walked slowly up to the soldier who had spoken. Rose's smile broadened when Thump's over-developed chest and shoulder muscles rippled as he held out his hand. "I'll be your friend."

The leader's eyes shifted to Rose, then back to Thumper.

"This honky's shit stinks. Let's get out of here."

The three men backed out slowly as Thumper lowered his hand and shook his head.

When the men had left the big soldier looked at Rose and spoke evenly. "You'd better get the team. They'll be back."

Rose nodded in silence and turned toward the door.

Ten minutes later, Rose stood at the sink shaving. He heard the latrine door open but didn't turn his head. Six blacks entered, led by the same soldier who had acted as the kingpin before. Rose dipped his razor into the sink, swirled it, and casually turned toward the approaching men.

The leader stopped two paces from Rose.

"Motherfuck, you shoulda skyed!" He glanced quickly around the latrine. "Where's your big honky friend? I got somethin' for him." He snickered as he tossed his head in the direction of the other five men.

"I'm right here," snapped Thumper as he walked from behind the partition, followed by Wade, who walked up to the leader.

"There it is, man," said Woodpecker as he strolled out from the shower stall behind the sinks. Preacher walked out from another stall, and both men let the bolts on their M-16s slam forward. The resounding metal echoed through the small building, sending visible chills up the leader's arms as he backed away from Wade and sought protection from his own surprised followers.

Just then, Russian walked in through the door, holding his rifle at port arms. He lowered the muzzle slowly and pointed it at the center of the group.

Wade poked the leader's chest and spoke in a growl. "This is a warning. Don't fuck with Team Three-one or any Rangers. We got problems enough with dinks, let alone the likes of you. Now, move your asses out!"

The leader caught his breath and stood glaring at Wade for several seconds before turning wordlessly and walking for the door. The other sullen men followed.

Russian blocked the exit. He shook his head sadly and

lowered his weapon, holding it in one hand. "You listen to my sergeant or there will be trouble."

The leader raised his hand to brush past the stocky bull. "Get out of the way, fucker!"

Russian's free hand was a blur as he caught the man's arm in mid-flight.

"Do not say such things to me. Is clear?" he grunted, applying pressure. The smaller man bravely took the pain without twisting his body, but his hoarse whisper gave away his suffering. "Cla . . . clear."

Russian released his grip and stepped aside, but not before looking into the eyes of each of the defiant men.

"It ain't over, you know," said Rose, looking at his team leader.

Wade's eyes were still on the door. "I know."

Childs tossed down a pad of paper and stood up.

"Them shitheads will do it tonight! I say blow 'em away and forget it!"

Sergeant Gino shook his head and leaned back in his chair. "You're right, Jerry. They'll probably frag the Third Platoon Hootch. It's a matter of pride and they don't know we know about the previous fraggings, but I don't hold to greasin' friendlies."

Wade was leaning against the wall of the ops center with the other team sergeants. The meeting had been called to discuss how to handle the rabble running loose on the base. Besides his team's incident, one Ranger from 2-1 had been beaten badly in another latrine.

Sergeant Gino looked up at Childs as he paced the room.

"Jerry, we gotta do it legal. If you catch them in the act of fraggin', you gotta let them pull the pin to prove intent. I guess we could secretly evacuate the barracks tonight and stop them after the incident."

Childs glared at Gino. "That's coddling them shits, and you know it."

Gino glared back. "Yes, but it's better than murder!"

Childs stiffened. "Murder? You call ambushin' them

shits murder? They've fragged people already and hurt one of my men. What the fuck is that called?"

Gino lowered his head. "I understand, Jerry, but you can't put a team out there tonight and blow away those GIs."

J. D. Gibson had sat quietly in the corner all during the discussion. Now he stood up slowly and walked to the center of the room. "I think I got a answer to the problem," he said.

Private Nuu squatted down beside Sergeant Thong as he stirred a pot of rice on the small cooking fire. "Where is the Tall One?" asked Nuu.

Silently, Thong motioned behind him toward the ridge.

Nuu glanced up the slope, speaking reflectively. "Does he not grow tired of this war?"

Thong quit his stirring and looked at the young soldier as if seeing him for the first time. "You do not know what tired is, my friend. You are a boy and have not seen enough of this war to be tired."

Nuu looked into the sergeant's eyes with sadness. "I have seen enough. We are killing our own people and are telling ourselves we are saving them."

Thong spoke softly. "Sacrifice is needed for victory. Many who don't understand will die. The general and I understand this, and one day you will."

Nuu sat back on the ground and hugged his knees. The image of the farmer he'd shot filled his mind. As far as Nuu was concerned, both he and that farmer had paid too dear a price for something they could not feel, touch, or see. Words and ideas had caused countless deaths and untold destruction. Ideas could not be planted, used to build a house, or help to love a woman. Nothing was gained in war but death and destruction. Nuu shut his eyes. He didn't want to be like the general and the others who justified dying for the sake of ideas. They were the ones who didn't understand . . . a war such as this one could never really end until everyone cast their ideals aside with their guns.

General Binh Duc stood among teaks, mahoganies, and pines beside the old Montagnard trail above the camp. He needed silence to clear his mind after the marathon committee meeting.

The setting sun painted the western sky in spectacular reds and oranges. The air smelled of sayo and pine. It was a good time to think and renew one's strength. All the posing and handshaking had drained him. He'd won the battle today, but had come away wounded and weary. The government representatives had again attacked religion as antirevolutionary. Internal security forces were being strengthened by the creation of youth organizations and surveillance groups.

The thought of the future made him weary. He and his family would always remain suspect. The endless talking and the seeking out of people not committed to the Fatherland would continue after the war's end. He would never be able to free himself of those who knew of his Catholic background.

There would never be true peace. The government would not allow it. They needed an enemy to keep the people united. Cambodia and Laos would surely be victims. The machinery of the government was built on conflict—conflict he was tired of leading.

The general bid farewell to his silent friends and began walking down the hill. At least the camp would be quiet. He had told General Sang to take the committee members to his division camp on the premise they would feel safer among many soldiers. The real reason was that he didn't want to entertain them while they rested for the return journey back to their homes. He didn't want to talk to those who wouldn't listen.

The forest's solitude and fresh air were all he wanted. In ten days he would have to return to the headquarters tunnel and its demands. Ten days to regain his inner strength knowing the war was won . . . but would never really be over.

"You think this is really going to work?"

Childs sipped his beer and held up the starlight scope again, scanning the barracks only thirty yards away. "I don't know, but it's the first bush I've ever been on where I could drink beer."

Sergeant Gino held back his laughter and tried to make himself comfortable on the corrugated tin roof. Childs checked his watch—0100—and raised the scope again. The pale green light displayed the barracks as a dark green image.

Gino raised his beer and took a sip. At least it isn't raining, he thought. Jesus, if they're gonna come, do it! My butt is getting tired sitting on this damn roof. God, I hope that Claymore the L-tee rigged works.

Childs reached out and tapped Gino, interrupting his thoughts. "We got company."

Gino reached down, grabbed his starlight, and raised it. At first he saw only the familiar image of the barracks, but then he saw light-green shapes moving along the ground. "I'll be damned. I count four."

Childs picked up the Claymore detonator and looked back into his scope. "Yep, it's four of 'em, and they're almost . . . almost . . . come on a little closer . . . just a little . . . *now!*" He depressed the detonator handle.

The explosion was surprisingly small, sounding more like a cherry bomb firecracker than a Claymore blast. Childs cursed as he scrambled for the ladder. Gino raised the scope to see where the men had run, but before he got the night vision device to his eye, he knew he didn't have to worry about finding them. He could hear them. In fact, by now the whole camp could probably hear them.

Childs hit the ground at a full run, but got only ten feet before having to stop. The gas overcame him. He quickly took the small gas mask from his leg pocket, put it on, and turned on his flashlight.

Lieutenant Gibson's gas Claymore had worked beautifully. He had taken the Claymore apart, removed the plastic front cover, the plastic plate of lethal double-ought ball bearings, and three-fourths of the C-4 plastic explosive. Then he'd filled the Claymore with granulate CS persistent gas.

Childs's light beam shone through the white cloud. The four would-be attackers had crawled to within five feet of the modified Claymore when Childs had detonated the mine. The leader had taken the worst of the riot gas. His rose-colored glasses had protected his eyes, but the sand-size fragments had penetrated the skin all over his face, exposed neck, and arms. He lay beating the ground, gasping, vomiting, and contorting in misery. The others were similarly rolling and twisting. Rangers streamed out of the barracks but stayed a safe distance from the choking gas. Childs smiled behind the gas mask as he reached down to pick up the leader.

J. D. Gibson had lain in his bed, unable to sleep, thinking of the secret ambush. When the muffled explosion had come, he'd sat up in a cold sweat, but the ensuing screams had made him sigh in relief. When he had presented his plan to the sergeants, Childs had eyed him coldly and later told him, "This better work, L-tee, or I'm gonna kick your ass just like I did in Ranger school. I want them sneaky shits to remember for a long time they don't fuck with Rangers."

Gibson lay back down. He knew Childs would not be coming to carry out his threat.

21

The briefing room was crowded with Ranger team leaders, helicopter pilots, and liaison officers. Childs entered the door and barked, "Ah-tench-hut!" The men rose from their chairs as Colonel Ellis walked down the aisle followed by Major Shane.

The colonel picked up a pointer and turned to the assembly. "Take your seats. I'm Colonel Ellis, the Corps's intelligence officer. Tomorrow at 0700 we begin Operation Stiletto." Ellis walked to the wall map and pulled down a covering poncho liner.

"Gentlemen, somewhere in this large area is the North Vietnamese Second Division. Your mission is to find them. Before Major Shane comes up here and gives you the concept of the operation, I want to introduce you to key players who are attached to us. Major Cid Orlando is the Air Force liaison who will coordinate F-4 fighter bomber close air support and B-52 targeting."

A slight, dark-haired major stood and nodded to the staring group.

Ellis pointed to another officer on the front row. "And Major Frank Dundee is our Army aviation liaison from the 268th Aviation Battalion."

The major partially stood and raised his hand before quickly sitting back down.

Ellis lowered his pointer. "I'm the Corps's representative only. Major Shane is the operational commander. This operation is vitally important to the V Corps and

312

South Vietnam. Finding and destroying the Second NVA Division will send a message to Hanoi that we are not just sitting on our asses in defense positions. You have been selected because of your outstanding combat records. I feel very proud to be a part of this operation and know you will do your utmost to find the bastards. Good luck to you."

Colonel Ellis sat down as Shane walked to the map and pointed to the recon area. "Tomorrow, the First, Second, and Third Ranger Platoon teams will . . ."

General Binh Duc was in his hut, reading the radio messages he had received that morning, when Colonel Sy entered and set down another stack.

The general glanced at the pile. "Anything of importance?"

Sy shook his head. "No, all is going to plan. The intelligence reports still show no large American changes in disposition. We can safely assume no major operations are planned."

The general closed his eyes for a moment and stood slowly. "When we return to the tunnel, we must begin plans for diversionary attacks along Highways 1 and 14. This will keep the Americans occupied while we consolidate our major units in the west. The Americans cannot afford heavy losses during their pullout. We will use the local people's forces for the diversion."

Colonel Sy raised his brow. "The local units have few experienced troops remaining. Their ranks have given much blood. Perhaps we should consider providing them some cadre from our regular units to bolster morale."

The general walked to the hut's doorway and looked out at the valley. "The People's Liberation Armed Forces are nothing but phantoms with little fight left, and that is exactly what the Americans must think. They must feel they can handle the small threat while still withdrawing. Should we show our strength too soon they would stop their retreat and begin offensive operations again." The general turned slowly and looked at his friend of many years with a sad expression. "The local forces must shed more blood. Supply them with whatever they need in munitions and arms, but no soldiers."

The colonel lowered his eyes. "The reunification will be a hollow victory without shouts of joy from so many who began the struggle. The countless dead will never know of their success."

The general sat down and picked up a message from the stack. His eyes glanced tiredly at the paper, then up to the colonel. "The dead will be with us when victory comes. Their shouts of joy will be heard by you and me."

Wade walked out of the stifling briefing room, drenched in sweat. The hot afternoon sun attacked him unmercifully as he strode toward the barracks holding his map and notes of the upcoming mission. He paused in the doorway and turned around. He wasn't ready yet. Changing direction, he strolled to the plateau edge.

Below him was the airfield. Simmering heat waves off the runway distorted the shapes of the parked helicopters. The surrounding area was flat except for the mountains looming far to the west. The base was on a plateau that rose up twenty meters. It was the only high ground for miles. Wade wiped sweat from his eyes and glanced at the map he held in his hand. Tomorrow they would again be in the jungle, but this time not to kill. His men wouldn't object to searching for an NVA division. They'd listen to his briefing and accept the mission as routine, but tonight when they lay down to sleep each would ask themselves the question: Is this the mission where I buy it? Maybe this time, this mission, their luck and skill would run out. The odds were against them; if seen they would die. They didn't have the firepower to hold off a large force before the gunships arrived. This mission would be unlike any other. He knew it . . . and soon his men would know it, too.

Wade took a deep breath and shook the doubts from his head. He was ready now.
_____

Major Shane took off his sweat-soaked shirt and sat behind his desk. He picked up a one-page report and waved it in one hand. "Do you expect me to believe that four engineers *accidently* gassed themselves beside one of our barracks last night?"

Childs stood beside the major's desk, looking up at the ceiling. "Sir, don't ask no questions and I won't tell no lies. It's a dead issue. The problem we had is solved. We gonna keep this real quiet and it'll all pass."

Shane stared at his sergeant's weathered face and tossed down the paper. "Okay, it's dead. I won't ask, but damn it, let me know next time. When that Claymore went off last night, it scared the hell outta me. I ran to a bunker and stayed there half the night!"

Childs rolled his eyes and sat down. "Sir, your briefing went well. The aviators seem to have their shit together and didn't piss and moan like they usually do. The Air Force major worries me a little with those dumb-ass questions he asked, but we can keep an eye on him."

Shane agreed with a nod and looked over his briefing notes. "Colonel Ellis got us plenty of air assets, so things ought to go pretty smoothly, but I'm still worried about the fourth recon area, the Stadium Zone. I'll bet a dime to a doughnut they're in that area exactly for the reason we don't like it—no landing zones for infiltration."

Childs leaned back in his chair. "Sir, it'll take us four days to check out the three other areas. Don't get excited and start losing sleep over somethin' that ain't a problem yet. Let's see what the teams come up with first."

Shane looked up with a frown. "Okay, but I'm going to order some photo missions just in case. The Mohawks fly high enough not to be seen or heard. You better talk to the team leaders tonight and make sure they know how important moving quietly is in their areas. If they even think they hear or see something, I want them reporting in."

Childs noted his major's worried tone and nervous fidgeting. "Goddamn, sir, you're makin' me antsy just listenin' and watchin' you. Relax, for Christ's sake!"

Shane had picked up a pencil and was jabbing the point

into his desk. He tossed the pencil down, exasperated. "What the hell am I supposed to do?"

Childs stood and walked to the door. He paused and looked over his shoulder. "Ya start by leading by example."

Shane picked up the pencil and grinned before throwing it at his sergeant. "Get out of here so I can relax!"

Wade sat on his bed with his map spread on the floor in front of him and his team surrounding him as he explained the mission. "The Third Platoon is going to recon the third area. It's broken down with four team recon zones. Our RZ is here. L-tee Gibson will be infilling us tomorrow at 0700. We're going in a couple of klicks outside our area, so we'll have to walk in, but it'll be safer that way. Once we get in we'll establish a patrol base and break up into two-man recon teams. We'll clover-leaf out and return to the patrol base. If you see or hear something, get your ass back to the patrol base and wait until we all get back. This is gonna be slow and tiring. Be alert and rest when ya have to. No shooting. Just run if ya get compromised. Me and Preacher are Team One. Thumper and Woodpecker, Two, and Russian, you and Rose, Team Three. What're your questions?"

Rose hopped to his feet and pointed at Russian. "No, man, not me and the foreigner."

Wade ignored the irate soldier and spoke to the others. "We're travelin' light and quiet, so pack accordingly. The dinks won't know we're there, so they'll be half steppin'. Check the wind constantly for their cooking fires and voices. Move slow and keep an eye out."

Rose stamped his foot for attention. "Man, I can't be snoopin' and poopin' with that hairy dude. The foreigner is an ox. He makes more noise than a herd of elephants.

Russian, patting Bitch, eyed the black soldier coldly. "You speak untrue things, crazy one."

Wade smiled. "Rose, you know Russian is as good as you. You're just worried he'll show ya up."

Rose's frown turned into a calculating grin. "I'll go with the foreigner if you split the care package."

Wade's eyes showed confoundment. Thumper smiled and pulled a big, brown-paper-wrapped box from under his bed. "The mail came when you were in the briefing."

Wade looked at the box and grinned. It had come from Ginny. "If it's food we'll all split it," he said, and pulled his knife. He slit the sides and, raising the lid, peeked in.

"Well?" said Thumper.

Matt slammed the lid back. "Nope, it's not chow. She sent me underwear. Sorry, guys." He stood up and lifted the box to his shoulder. "See y'all."

The sergeant started for the barracks' door, trying to contain a smile.

"Matt!" yelled Thumper, jumping to his feet.

"Hold it, man! Let me check it out!" added Rose.

Wade spun around and dumped the contents on the floor. Small cans of smoked ham, shrimp, oysters, and colored packages of cheese and breads scattered over the map and concrete floor.

"Thank you, Lord!" sighed Preacher, grabbing up a can of ham.

Russian raised a red-foiled package to his nose. "German Gouda. It is very best."

Rose smirked as he rifled through the stack, picking up cans, reading the labels, and discarding them. "This is all foreign shit, man. Ain't there any canned hamburgers or fries?"

Thumper picked an envelope out of the pile and handed it to Wade. "I think this is all you really wanted anyway."

Wade took the letter with a smile. "How 'bout you. Did Mary Ann write?"

The big soldier patted his breast pocket and winked. "You bet."

Childs walked out of the tactical operations center into the midday heat. In his hand, he held an unopened letter that Pete had just handed to him.

Childs stuffed the letter into his leg pocket. He already

knew what his wife had written. She always wrote the same things. She'd tell him how much she missed him and what other improvements she'd made to their small house. The last few paragraphs would be the bad news—news of his friends who'd been killed or wounded and how their wives were doing. The words she didn't write were the ones that affected him most, the words that said she understood why he'd extended his tour instead of coming home. They were words she'd never write because they both already knew why. She was a professional soldier's wife and understood he loved his men as much as her. And for that reason more than for any other he cared for her so much.

The sergeant walked to the barracks and sat down on his bunk. As he opened the letter he felt empty inside. Her letters always did that to him. Her words were no substitute for her touch and smile.

Linda was a small woman whose hair had turned gray on the ends when he was gone on his first tour. Her face had finally wrinkled around her green eyes during his second. She was growing older without him, but loved him more each time he returned. They were friends as only a man and wife could be, special friends who needed and understood each other. Unable to leave his job at the office, he was cold and gruff to her at times, but she always ignored his roughness and touched his heart with her understanding. He loved her, but rarely told her so. He needed her and never spoke of his desire. He missed her and put the hurt somewhere else. Linda Childs understood all that and loved him anyway.

Jerry Childs read the letter, then crumpled it into a ball. He'd fight the empty feeling like he always did and promise himself he'd make it up to her. There was no time to think about that now.

Sergeant Thong held the bamboo pole steady and pushed upward. The green mango broke loose from the cluster and fell fifteen feet to the waiting brown hands of the old grinning sergeant. Thong had walked down the hill to the valley floor to gather wild fruit from the old Montagnard fields. The elephant grass had almost taken over, but near the stream there were still mango trees and wild pineapple plants interspersed with huge clusters of yellow and green bamboo. Thong sniffed the mango and placed the ripe fruit in a canvas bag. Tonight he would prepare a feast for the general to lift his spirits. The sergeant hefted the bag to his shoulder and walked along the streambed to collect bamboo shoots. The cooling shade and the crystal clear water beckoned to him.

Thong found young shoots and picked the most tender. He could already taste the meal he would prepare. He followed the stream until he was blocked by huge, rounded boulders that allowed only a deep narrow path for the water. Beyond, he could hear a faint roar. That meant there was a waterfall just past the boulders. Curious, he dropped his bag to the bank, rolled up his pant legs, and waded into the stream to follow its narrow path. The water came to his waist and forcibly pushed him forward. Only by bracing his hands against the gray boulders was he able to stay on his feet. Ten meters into the passageway the corridor widened, to reveal a magnificent pool. The quiet pool formed a wide oblong behind a rock dam. The land to his left and right first ascended gradually and then became steeper. Higher up it was covered by hundreds of large, green, moss-covered boulders. Thong paused; he could still hear the roar of falling water, but there was no spillway. He took a step forward. His foot didn't touch bottom but was pulled downward. He lost his balance and fell forward. His body was being sucked under. Gasping, he frantically fought the powerful undertow, kicking back toward the boulder. Regaining his footing in the shallower water, he climbed up the boulder and sat shaking. From the height of the boulder he could see at the end of the pool a large swirling hole in the water. A whirlpool the size of four men's heads churned in deadly silence. Thong stood and hopped from boulder to boulder around the pool. Jumping to a large, flat-topped rock, he caught his breath and sank to his knees. Two feet away was a vertical drop of forty meters. The height and precarious position made him feel faint and weak. The pool had an underground passageway that led a few meters below the lip of the dam. There it spewed out to a rock-strewn stream far below. The spray misted upward in a cloud that danced with hundreds of rainbow prisms. Had he not been able to break the undertow's grasp he would have surely fallen to his death.

Thong crawled back from the boulder's edge and slowly made his way back to the narrow boulder passageway. Afraid he would not be able to fight the current, he decided to climb over the boulder.

Twenty minutes later he sat down tiredly beside the canvas bag of fruit. His hands and legs were bruised and scraped from the climb. He lay back on the bank, looking up at the countless leaves of bamboo. He was too old to be curious. The stream had almost lured him to his death. A younger man would have had no problem, but his old body was too weak for exploring. Still, the thought of the adventure brought a smile to his lips. It would be a tale he could tell his grandchildren for many years.

The old sergeant rose and picked up his bag. He would collect two more of the mangos and place them in the spirit house. The Montagnards believed in making an offering to the spirits after a good hunt or a significant event. He didn't believe in spirits but it seemed fitting to thank someone for his life.

Thong walked up the bank with a spring in his step, feeling young again.

Ku Toan laughed loudly and raised his fish trap. The fish spirit had slept and let his family stray. Six small fish flopped madly at the bottom of the rattan basket.

Reaching into the small opening, Ku Toan grasped one of the smaller fish and tossed it back into the river. "Go and tell the spirit I release you."

Toan ran a reed through the fishes mouths and gills and tied a twig to its end. Holding up his catch to sparkle in the fading sun's light, he could see the mountains looming across the shallow river. The mountain had been his home for sixty years. He and two other free men had stayed when the tribe was moved to a resettlement village five years before. He was the only one left to appease the spirits until his people returned. The other men had died—one by snakebite and the other by sickness that had eaten his body from within. He alone, the tribe shaman, was left to watch over the mountains. The Sedang were strong people and would one day return and claim their rightful home. The lowlanders that had come would leave soon. They knew nothing of the spirits and did not appease those who provided.

Ku Toan walked back to his hut and stirred the embers of the small hearth. The fish would be wrapped in mud balls and baked on the coals. His dark skin turned golden brown in the fire's glow as he squatted down and poured water from the rusted can to make his mud. Soon the rain would come and he wouldn't be able to climb the trail to his old village. He had to go quickly or he wouldn't be able to make the journey until the red-streaked fish mated.

The blackbird squalked beside him at the sight of the fish. Toan cut one of the fish into tiny pieces and held a portion in his fingers. The bird poked its head through the bamboo-strip cage, striking ferociously at the pink meat. Toan laughed and tossed the pieces into the cage. "Eat well tonight, my black friend. Soon you fly again over the mountain."

Toan placed a pot on the embers and put in a handful of maize with a little water. Tonight would be a feast. The spirits would provide strength to climb the mountain and see his home again.

The lowlanders may have gone and left his land alone. Only a full moon ago, the first had come. He had to leave before they saw him and made him their slave. If they were still there, he would have to return, but the spirits would understand. They knew of the lowlanders' ways.

The bird threw his head back, swallowed the fish, and pecked frantically for another piece.

Toan gently laid the mud balls into the embers. When the mud split, the meal would be ready. He was happy. In only five days he would return to his home and enter the spirit house once again.

The Huey plunged down into a valley at ninety-five knots, then pulled up abruptly to avoid a stand of tall trees. The Slick dipped and raised with every terrain contour and obstacle, always keeping as low as possible to avoid detection and becoming a target. The six passengers with camouflage-painted faces appreciated neither the pilot's skill nor the magnificent view. They sat on the floor of the aircraft, feeling sick and holding on for dear life.

The copilot turned in his seat and held up two fingers. Sergeant Matt Wade mumbled a "Thank God" and yelled to the others, *"Two minutes!"*

Wade wanted out of the chopper. The low-level flying had lasted for over twenty minutes, longer than any mission he'd ever been on. The extended time at low level was for his team's safety, but their stomachs hadn't understood. Each man felt like a landlubber in a dinghy in high seas. The abrupt sinking and rising had taken its toll. Rose had vomited first, and that had caused a chain reaction. The smell alone was enough to gag a maggot. Wade had emptied his stomach's protesting contents, but he kept on dry heaving until he thought his intestines would heave out. The vibrating floor was covered with half-digested breakfast food, as was the back of the chopper, which pissed off the door gunners and encouraged them to likewise add their stomachs' goodies to the countryside.

Wade scooted out to the edge of the open compartment and readied himself, as did the others. The copilot raised one finger. Wade didn't need to yell out the one-minute warning. His men were positioned. They wanted out as bad as he did.

The Slick began its flare and Wade scooted farther out, stepping down on the skid in preparation to jump. The bird dropped into a small open area surrounded by thick scrub trees. Four feet from the ground, Wade jumped and hit the ground at a run. Preacher jumped to the earth beside him, but the weight of his pack with the added weight of the radio threw him off balance and he pitched forward face first. Russian pulled him to his feet with one hand and pushed him toward the tree line as the chopper pulled up and streaked away. Wade lay panting as his men fell to the ground in the standard wheel formation. Thumper tried to breathe through his mouth. He didn't want to smell his vomit-soaked fatigues. Woodpecker gagged and started another dry heave session among the team.

Wade disgustedly pulled the map from his leg pocket and confirmed his position. He wanted to find the closest river or stream so everyone could clean up. They couldn't begin the mission until they'd gotten rid of the horrid smell; the dinks would detect them a klick away. Wade sighed in relief. There was a stream only five hundred meters to the west.

Jerry Childs sat in the ops bunker, staring at the situation map, with an unlit cigarette hanging from his lips. Gibson had called in a few minutes before to report that he'd inserted the last team.

Childs's experienced eyes translated each team's location into a visual picture of mountains, draws, streams, and vegetation. He calculated their movement and how long before they'd laager for the night. His biggest concern had not come to pass—none of the teams had been hit upon landing. The silent radio told him the operation was going smoothly. If his men had landed close to a large enemy concentration, the dinks would have sent patrols out to investigate and would have been seen or heard by now.

Bitch lay sprawled on the cool cement floor at his feet.

She raised her head and placed it on his boot. The sergeant broke his concentration and looked down at the yellow mongrel. "Just you and me again, huh?"

Bitch rolled her eyes up, but didn't move.

Childs looked into Bitch's eyes, wondering if she felt as empty as he did. Both of them had waited through countless days, unable to feel whole until the teams were in. Bitch waited for Russian and he waited for them all. Maybe that's why she always waited with him. She needed someone to share waiting's torment.

Childs looked back at the map. The next few days would drag by, but somehow he felt better knowing the little animal resting on his foot would be there with him.

Rose, Woodpecker, and Thumper sat in the shallow stream, rubbing mud into their fatigues, while Wade and the others stood guard on the banks. The gritty mud would take out the foul smell as well as lye soap. Each of the men cleaned himself and his equipment, then exchanged places with the guards.

Minutes later, Wade walked downwind of the assembled team and sniffed the air. The mud bath had worked; there was no trace of their breakfast. Wade frowned as he motioned Rose to move out. Remembering Childs's rule of six P's—prior planning prevents piss-poor performance— he'd planned everything, in perfect detail, everything but the extended low-level flight. Damn, he should have known!

He reached in his leg pocket for his chewing tobacco pouch, but his stomach rumbled a warning—it wasn't ready yet. Wade brought his hand back up to his weapon in disgust. The mission hadn't started off any too hot and now he couldn't even chew. Goddamn fly-boys!

Four hours later, Wade toyed with the gold medallion on his chest as he sat back on his rucksack waiting for the rest of his men to return to the patrol base. They'd broken up into two-men recon teams to do the search. He and Preacher were the first ones back. They'd only found a few trails and no signs of recent activity. Wade let the medallion fall. Someone was approaching. Preacher patted him with a grin, pointing to Rose and Russian as they appeared through a tangle of vines.

Rose sat back tiredly on his ruck and shook his head at Wade's questioning stare. Russian spoke in a whisper. "We see nothing. What you find?"

Wade whispered back, "Nothing," and lay back, shutting his eyes. The local terrain was thickly vegetated because the small trees allowed in so much sunlight. Each man's sweat-soaked uniform was torn in several places where the damnable vines known as Wait-a-Minutes had taken hold.

Thirty minutes later Thumper and Woodpecker walked into the patrol base and fell to the ground, exhausted. Their recon area was more rugged than the others', and their gaunt faces looked drained of strength.

Wade reported in by radio that his team had found nothing and would be staying in the patrol base for the night. Tomorrow they would continue the mission. He then ordered his men to drink a full canteen of water and to eat, even though they didn't feel like it. Heat could be just as deadly a killer as the enemy, especially jungle heat, which was like no other. Long ago, on his first patrol, he'd fallen flat on his face from heat prostration, though he'd never received the normal warning signals from his body. The pumping adrenalin covered the danger signs. If you felt thirsty it was too late; you were already dehydrated. There was nothing like it. The teeming green plants seemed to radiate heat and suck all life from the air. Sweat-soaked fatigues became sweltering, chafing torture and movement had to be consciously forced. The air was oppressively sultry and reeking with rot.

Wade pulled out his map to find some water, but there was no stream close by. Tomorrow they'd move their base and recon another area that promised more of the thick vegetation. Shit!

He opened his ruck and pulled out a C ration can of peaches. The sweet juice and fruit was the most prized of all rations. Using a P-38 can opener, he quickly punctured the metal and rocked the small device back and forth, cutting the top off. The delicious fluid helped him to forget the heat.

Childs saw the NVA soldier rise up from the corner of his eye, but it was too late. The AK-47 spit out a tongue of flame and bullets tore into his chest.

The sergeant snapped upright in his cot, drenched in sweat, and felt for the gaping holes. There was none. Hot perspiration—not blood—clung to his fingers. Childs stared into the blackness, shivering.

He'd seen the bullets coming toward him in slow motion. They'd pierced his skin and burrowed into his heart like red-hot drill bits, twisting, plunging deeper. The crushing, searing pain had been too real to be a dream. Had he screamed? Was it a heart attack?

Childs raised his head, breathing in deeply to try and stop his shaking.

Bitch rose from the floor and laid her head on his trembling hand. Childs blinked his eyes and tried focusing on the dog. The heat and lack of sleep had gotten to him. He'd had nightmares before but none so real as this one. He patted the dog's head and lay back on a wet poncho liner. The past three days of waiting had been the worst that he could remember. The Second and Third Platoon teams had found nothing, but the First Platoon teams had reported seeing numerous large groups of NVA pushing bikes packed with equipment and munitions. They'd all been heading east.

Major Shane and Colonel Ellis sat with him every day, listening to the reports. They knew the supplies had to be heading for the Second NVA Division. The First Platoon teams had cautiously moved east to find the base camp, but had come to the end of their recon area. The dinks were moving into the Stadium Zone.

He, Shane, and Ellis had stayed up until two a.m. that night, planning how they would search the area. The teams would be extracted in the morning, given two days' rest, then reinserted. The search was almost over, and the noose was tightening. One of the teams would soon be calling in excitedly and reporting it had found the base camp.

Childs shut his eyes, even though he knew he wouldn't really sleep until after that call came in and the mission was over.

Peteroski stood outside the door of the orderly room watching Childs cross the compound toward the barracks. Just then Sergeant Gino walked by. "Hey, Pete, was Childs givin' you a hard time again?" he said with a grin.

Peteroski frowned. "Does Childs seem alright to you?"

Gino shrugged his shoulders. "He's still cussin' and kickin' ass as far as I know." Gino waited for a smile from the clerk, but when none came, Gino let his own smile drop. "Look, Pete, he ain't been sleepin' none too good. Hell, none of us have. The teams just got back in and a couple of them gotta go back out real soon. The operation is a hairy one, and he's worried about it, that's all. Nothing to be concerned about. Childs's been through this before."

Peteroski nodded, but he wasn't convinced. Only minutes before, Childs had come into the office acting so strangely. The sergeant had given him an envelope for safe keeping and told him not to tell anyone about it. It wasn't like Childs to be so secretive.

Gino opened the screen door and motioned Peteroski inside. "Worry about Childs when he stops drinkin' beer. If that ever happens, *then* we'll know somethin' ain't right."

Preacher shut his eyes and sank to his knees in the shower bay floor. The cool water washed away three days of sweat, grime, and frustration. It was the most glorious feeling he could remember. The team had been picked up by chopper an hour before. The tired men had landed at An Lom, dumped their gear, and walked straight for the showers.

Rose plugged the shower drains with his fatigues and the water rose to a three-inch-deep pool before spilling over the shower bay doorway. The team sat and lay in the pool under the refreshing spray of water.

Woodpecker, sitting on the floor, looked up at the kneeling Indian. "I've never been so pooped," he whispered.

Preacher laughed. "What are you whispering for?"

The redhead looked around him at the naked men sprawled in the pool and yelled crazily, *"I'm tired, naked, and sittin' on the damn floor! I can't get up and I don't care! I'm stayin' here till I wrinkle up and . . ."*

Woodpecker's voice caught in his throat when he noticed Childs standing in the shower doorway, scowling with his hands on his hips. "You people all gone queer?" he barked. "Ya look like you're all auditioning for a damn California porno flick!"

Rose got to his feet. "Aw, Sarge, we was just . . ."

"Plain crazy!" snapped Childs, then pointed at Wade, who rose up to a sitting position. "Wade, you and your collection of perverts are going out again in two days. Clean this mess up and get your ass to the TOC in thirty minutes for the mission brief."

Wade nodded in silence. He'd already realized they'd have to go out again. It'd been obvious none of the teams had found the enemy base or the Ranger camp would have been buzzing with the good news.

Childs shook his head as if in disgust, shoved the latrine door open, and whistled loudly.

Bitch bounded up the steps of the TOC and ran straight for him. Childs held the door open for her and walked back to the miniature pool. The dog saw Russian lying in the water and immediately jumped into the water and pounced on him.

Childs growled, "Russian, keep that mangy mutt away from me! She's chewed up two pair of my boots and ruined my poncho liner."

The hairy soldier looked up innocently. "Yes, Sergeant, I will teach her no do such things."

Childs grunted and strode for the door, mumbling, "Goddamn gook mutt ain't worth a shit. She ain't nothing but . . ."

He stepped out and lowered his head. He already missed her.

Colonel Ellis lowered his magnifying glass and looked up at Major Shane. "You're right. It looks big enough to land a bird." He tossed the aerial photo to the tabletop, walked to the wall map, and pointed to a spot ten kilometers due west of the horseshoe bend in the river. "I make it about here."

Shane tapped the map. "The only other spot suitable for landing choppers is this huge open area inside the horseshoe bend, but we sure as hell can't use it. It's ringed by hills, and if dinks are in there it'd be suicide. Of course, there's the river itself. There's plenty of open space and right now it's shallow enough, but that sound will carry down the river and anybody along the banks will hear the bird land."

Ellis shook his head dejectedly. "What are we going to do?"

Shane picked up a pointer. "Sir, Sergeant Childs and I discussed the problem this morning. We think there's just one way to handle this operation safely. The first thing we have to do is check out the Stadium. We need it as an LZ and to establish a radio relay. From there we can put in the rest of the teams and then they can recon the whole fourth zone. What we plan is to put one team in the small LZ west of the Stadium. Their mission will be to head directly for the valley itself. We put in two more teams on the river just above the horseshoe bend. They'll climb up the ring of mountains at the most eastern end of the Stadium and split up. One team'll check out the ring of hills around the valley to the north and the other'll move south. They'll link up with the team that comes in from the west and then we'll know it's safe and begin the big search."

Ellis pulled at his chin as he looked at the map. "The backside of those mountains looks steep as hell. You sure your men can climb the eastern end?"

Shane picked up the aerial photo. "Sir, I'm sending Lieutenant Gibson out as patrol leader of Sergeant Wade's and Sergeant Zubeck's teams. The teams are the best we have and Gibson has plenty of field experience and is a graduate of the Mountain Climbing School at Fort Carson. If there's a way up, they'll find it.''

Ellis stared at the map. If dinks were sitting on the top of the eastern end of the Stadium, the men Shane spoke of would be like ducks in a shooting gallery. ''There sure are a helluva lot of *ifs*. *If* the teams fly in undetected, *if* they can climb the mountain, *if* the valley is clear.'' His eyes shifted to the map for a moment, then back to Shane. ''But we don't have much of a choice, do we?''

Shane's eyes met the colonel's with determination. ''No, sir, we don't. In ten minutes I brief the teams that'll be going in.''

Ellis lowered his head. ''At Corps, we move divisions and brigades around to find the enemy. Here, the biggest opportunity to find the enemy the Corps has had since Cambodia lies with a handful of men. I should be excited. I'm not. I feel shitty.''

Shane looked at the map as if hating it, and then spoke softly. ''I know, sir . . . I know.''

Matt Wade shut his eyes tightly and jumped. He fell ten feet before splashing into the river and sinking to his waist. The rest of the team splashed into the water beside him as the Huey lifted up and nosed over, gaining speed for the getaway.

Wade walked as fast as he could toward the near bank, cringing, half-expecting bullets to tear into his body. They were completely in the open. Anybody on either bank could easily hose them.

Another Slick streaked in low and came to an abrupt hover. Its rotor wash kicked up miniature waves and whipped spray onto Wade and his men.

Lieutenant Gibson jumped into the shallow river. Sergeant Zubeck and his team followed. Within seconds the bird was gone, leaving the struggling men in deathly quiet.

Wade reached the sandy riverbank and ran toward a green wall of vegetation. The seemingly impenetrable obstacle was only a leaf and vine facade. Wade busted through into a dark, dank world of brown decay and rot.

Wade fell to the ground beside the base of a huge teak and raised his Colt automatic rifle to a ready position. His men fell beside him, facing the forest.

Gibson, Zubeck, and the others broke through the leafy curtain and hit the ground behind Wade's team, then turned to face the river. If the dinks had heard the choppers hovering, they'd come to investigate.

Preacher whispered almost inaudibly into the radio

handset, "Hotel-three Alfa, this is Papa One. Papa is on first base. Over."

Lieutenant Foley, sitting in the back seat of a bird dog a mile away and three-thousand feet up, answered immediately. "Roger, Papa One, I'm standing by with guns. Out."

Preacher tapped Gibson's leg and gave the L-tee a thumbs-up.

Gibson nodded and rolled back over to his stomach. The next ten minutes would be critical. If dinks were close by, they'd be here within that time. Lieutenant Foley had a pair of gunships standing by to help, but everyone knew they'd probably be useless. The only way the patrol could get out was to use the river as a pickup zone. It was too open. The men and Slicks would be easy targets.

Gibson raised his head and looked over his men. They all lay on their stomachs with their weapons readied. Russian carried an L34A1 British Sterling submachine gun with a sound suppressor. If the dinks sent only a few men to investigate, they'd die silently. If they sent a lot of men, there'd be a battle.

Gibson lowered himself and looked at his watch—0731.

Colonel Ellis and Sergeant Childs sat in the Ops Center, watching Shane pace back and forth in front of the wall map. The small radio speaker box suddenly crackled with static and Lieutenant Foley's voice filled the bunker.

"Base, this is Three Alfa. One-three and Papa One are on first base. No hits, no errors, they are moving to second base in one mike. Out."

Shane had frozen in his tracks listening to the voice and let out a sigh of relief. He exchanged smiles with Ellis and nodded toward Childs. "Phase one down."

Childs showed no expression as he continued patting Bitch's head. It wasn't time to smile; there were three phases left and a helluva lot more waiting before the mission would be over.

Sergeant Selando's One-three team had been inserted into the small LZ that was ten miles west of the Stadium.

Lieutenant Gibson's team, a combination of Wade's and Zubeck's, was called Patrol One and had been put in several klicks north of the horseshoe bend. Foley's radio message meant both teams had gone in safely and had waited the required ten minutes. Both teams were now moving toward the Stadium. The second phase would be complete when Gibson's patrol reached the Stadium and reported in.

Rose took a deep breath and cautiously stepped out onto a small trail. They'd been moving for only fifteen minutes, paralleling the river, when he'd spotted the path.

Rose knelt down to touch the ridges of a footprint. The impression left by the heel was still damp. The person was small and had an unusually wide foot. It had to have been a Montagnard. Vietnamese regulars wore sandals or Chicom boots. Rose stood and motioned Wade and Lieutenant Gibson up.

"A Yard walked down this trail less than an hour ago," whispered Rose.

Gibson looked to Wade for advice. Wade shrugged his shoulders. "We gotta take it. It's heading in the right direction. The Yards this far in the boonies are hiding out. They shouldn't be a problem."

Gibson turned around and whispered to Thumper. "Pass it back. We're taking a trail. Last man pull rear security."

Thumper nodded and whispered to the next man.

Gibson looked back at Wade and Rose. "Well . . . shit, let's do it."

Rose brought his weapon up and began walking.

Ky Toan sat on the riverbank, searching the sky. He had released the blackbird from the cage a few minutes before. The black one's wing had mended well, for the bird had made several circles over him, then had soared toward the mountains across the river.

Toan's heart was heavy. He had hoped the raven would

return to him, but he knew it would not. All black living things were messengers of the spirits.

Toan lowered his gaze from the white, billowing clouds to the mountains across the river. It was almost time to visit his old home and the spirit house. His snares and traps had caught many rabbits and fish to strengthen his body for the journey. Perhaps tomorrow he would go. Perhaps the blackbird would welcome him there. Perhaps the lowlanders were gone. Perhaps . . .

Toan began to rise but heard a strange noise and spun around. The forest plants were thick, but he knew an animal of prey was looking at him. The noise he heard was a large branch snapping. Only an animal of size could make such a noise. His eyes searched the vegetation for several seconds and froze abruptly.

He saw two large white eyes staring at him from behind the broad leaves of the chaoc. Toan shut his own eyes and fell over in the sand. It was a black spirit, not an animal. His life was over. The spirit never appeared until it was time to begin the long sleep. Many whom he had tried to heal spoke of seeing such a spirit just before they died.

Wade positioned his men in overwatch positions and nodded toward Rose. The black soldier walked out of the jungle, pointing his rifle at the old man.

Toan trembled at the sound of approaching steps and began mumbling chants of contrition.

Rose stood over the pathetic, shaking man and lowered his rifle. The old Montagnard was wearing a dirty scarlet loincloth. His gray hair was matted with dark grease and was full of clinging sand. His small body was thin but his legs looked like those of a man thirty years younger. His calves were big as baseballs.

Rose reached down and grabbed the mumbling man's arm and yanked him to his feet.

Toan cried out upon feeling the spirit's touch and opened his eyes. He sank to his knees again. It was not a spirit, but a black-skinned soldier who would surely kill him.

Rose lifted the Montagnard again and dragged him toward the trees.

Toan sat on the ground outside the front of his hut, watching the huge, light-skinned soldiers search his house and camp. He felt better now, and had finally stopped shaking. They wouldn't kill him, he could tell by their eyes, but they might take him with them. Three of the light-skins knelt in front of him, talking in a strange language and motioning with their hands.

They were the light-skins the lowlanders battled. He had seen their kind a few years before when they had come in iron birds that dropped from the sky and took his people away. Another of the light-skins who had come many years before had learned the Sedang language and told of a great spirit called Jesus. The light-skin had come from a place called France. His language was different from that of these men. He'd taught the language to the Sedang and had shown them new ways to grow their crops.

Wade lowered his hands in exasperation and shook his head at Gibson. "It's useless, sir. He doesn't understand a word of English or any of our sign language."

Gibson leaned closer to the old man and spoke in slow Vietnamese. "Dung sa Vietnamese?"

The Montagnard cocked his head to one side, obviously not understanding.

Damn! thought Gibson. The old man could tell them if there was a way up the Stadium.

"Parlez-vous Francais?" asked Gibson as an afterthought.

The old man's eyes widened and he broke into a grin. "Oui, Monsieur. Parlez-vous Francais?"

Gibson's mouth dropped open in shock. Wade clapped Gibson's back. "Damn, sir, ya did it. I sure didn't know you spoke French."

Gibson looked at Wade with a frown. "I don't. You just heard all the French I know."

Wade smiled. "Russian does—he learned it in the mercenaries."

Gibson broke into a wide grin. "Get the bull over here and let's find out how we get up that." He pointed in the direction of the looming Stadium hilltops.

Childs listened to the radio report and made some notes. He spun around and barked to the runner, "Get the major!"

Minutes later Shane walked into the bunker with Colonel Ellis and the Air Force liaison officer. Childs was about to speak when the radio crackled again. "Base, One-three has found a high-speed trail. They've spotted ten NVA pushing bikes to the east toward the Stadium. Over."

Childs picked up the handset. "What is One-three's position? Over."

"Base, they're six klicks from the western end of the Stadium. Over."

"Three Alfa, have One-three remain in their location. Do not, I say again, do not move until we give orders to do so. Over."

"Roger, base. Out."

Childs turned and looked into Shane's eyes. "Sir, the dinks are in the Stadium." Shane's knees felt weak. He sat down as Childs continued. "Gibson reported in a few minutes ago and said they found an old Yard who says dinks moved into the Stadium a month ago. The Yard knows a way up the eastern end and will lead them up tomorrow morning. You just heard what One-three reported. The reason I stopped them was that we need to keep this coordinated. We'll have One-three move at first light tomorrow, too."

Colonel Ellis slapped Shane's back. "My God, this is it. They've found them!"

Shane let out a breath, stood up, and turned to the Air Force liaison. "Orlando, we have a lot of work to do. You'll need to target the whole Stadium area and contact your people that we'll need every F-4 available on call. When my men go in tomorrow, I want to guarantee they'll have air support in minutes."

Shane stepped up to the map and looked at Childs. "Get

the Army liaison in here and have two more maps hung
up. We all can't work around one map.''

"Sir," said Shane, nodding to Colonel Ellis. "I need
several maps of the Stadium area blown up as big as we
can get them. Can someone in Corps do it for us?''

Ellis walked to the telephone. "Yeah, I can have the
photo people do it right now and have them flown down
in a couple of hours.''

Shane nodded and looked at his watch. "It's 0945 now.
We've got about twenty hours to plan this out. In one hour
I want everyone here, and we'll go every contingency.''

Each of the men nodded except Childs. He was staring
at the map, lost in thought. The NVA Division they sought
was in the Stadium. Three of his teams were close. Real
close. They had to sneak in, find the main base, and get
out undetected. Selando, Gibson, Wade, and Zubeck were
good. He couldn't have picked better men for the job.
They'd do it. They'd find the bastards.

Shane stepped up beside the sergeant and spoke softly.
"Jerry, can you think of anything else we should be
doing?''

Childs broke his stare from the map. "No, Ed, you're
doin' good. When we get everybody here, let the Air Force
brief us on the B-52s and what lead time they need for
planning a target. We need to know how far away the teams
have to be before they start droppin' their bombs.''

Shane smiled. Childs had never called him by his first
name before. It wasn't a slip of military discipline. He was
telling him in his own way he was a friend, a close, respected friend who would support him during the upcoming
trial of leadership.

Shane put his hand on the sergeant's arm. "Thanks,
Jerry.''

J. D. Gibson sat alone at the edge of the Montagnard's
camp, looking across the silty river at the mountains. They
couldn't really be called mountains—they weren't high
enough—but they sure as hell couldn't be called hills,

either. They were like the pictures he'd seen of Hawaii where the mountain chain was steep on the windward side and gradual and rolling on the other. His men would not have been able to climb this side. It was almost straight up. The old man had said there was a streambed they would follow and that there was a small passageway hidden in darkness that would lead them to the valley. The path was used by his tribe, the Sedang, to travel to the river for fishing.

Gibson looked at his watch. It was almost noon. He'd wanted to take the path today, but old Toan insisted on waiting until tomorrow. He'd said he needed rest before making the journey.

J. D. felt a tingling sensation run up his back. The NVA Division was in the Stadium. The only question was where. The tingling feeling came from knowing that tomorrow the question would be answered.

Matt, the team, and Toan sat in the Montagnard's hut, eating the rice and fish the old man had prepared. Toan jabbered to Russian for several minutes before taking a mouthful. Russian laughed and quickly translated. "He talk of crazy one. He think Rose was maybe a black spirit who had come to take him to his heaven. He say he know Rose not spirit when he come closer, because he smell like wild pig."

Rose frowned. "That's not funny, man. The dude is a redneck, Yard, racist. I don't stink. He do!"

Russian smiled. "We all smell to him. We eat different foods, and our bodies give off strange odors."

"Well, the dude smells like a gook to me!" blurted Rose.

Wade got to his feet and motioned Russian to follow him outside. The two men stepped out of the small hut and walked to a nearby tree and sat down.

"Carl, what do ya think?"

The Czech's head swung to the Stadium. "We can trust Montagnard only to top of mountain. I walk point with him and watch him close. . . . We must be very careful, my Sergeant. The Communists could be anywhere. Keep radio close and move very slow. We will stop and listen to the forest many times tomorrow.''

Wade stared at the Slavic face of his mentor. He wanted to tell him he felt confident because of his presence. Russian was a man he would give his life for. Russian broke his stare from the Stadium and looked into the eyes of his sergeant.

Wade knew he didn't need to say a word. Carl Rostov's eyes told him he already knew.

Woodpecker sat back against the hut wall, cleaning his machine gun. Preacher sat beside him trying to disassemble his M-16, but his mind was on the mission. He fumbled with the weapon and finally set it down.

Woodpecker tapped the Indian's leg with his cleaning rod. "Relax, warrior, we're going up there tomorrow and play Indian. We gonna snoop and poop just like your ancestors did. Looks to me you got an advantage on us.''

Preacher smiled and held out his hand. "You are a good friend, fellow warrior, I am truly blessed to have you by my side.''

Woodpecker took his hand. "Three-one, buddy.''

Sergeant Din Thong pointed to the stream ahead. "Is it not beautiful like I say?''

General Binh Duc smiled as he stared at the inviting, crystal-clear water and bamboo-shaded banks. "Yes, my friend, you were correct. It is truly a place of beauty.''

Thong awkwardly pulled the AK-47 from his shoulder and sat on the stream bank. "I will protect you while you bathe and rest. Remember, do not get close to the boulders. As I told you, the stream becomes a demon beyond the big rocks.''

General Duc took off his uniform and waded out into the cool, refreshing water. The old sergeant had been right. The stream was just what he needed.

He lay down in the water perfectly still for a few moments and could feel the gentle tugging toward the boulders. He could also hear the faint roar of the waterfall

Thong had spoken of and closed his eyes to imagine its beauty.

Thong felt happiness inside at seeing his general relax. The Tall One had been very busy and could not sleep at nights. Because of this, his health was fading and he could not keep his mind on all that he had to do. Some of the staff spoke badly of his short temper and sullenness.

Thong smiled. The general needed only to be near a stream's tranquility and away from the radio.

The general rose up and waded to a flat rock under the coolness of the protective bamboo. He lay down and shut his eyes to absorb the quiet.

Thong shifted his gaze from his sleeping leader to the boulders on the far bank. They were covered with thick, strangling, ropelike vines. A tree grew from the top of one of the boulders, its tendril roots snaking down the body of the rock and into the earth for nourishment.

Thong looked back at his general, who was resting comfortably. His chest was rising and falling in much needed sleep. Thong lay back on the bank. The war would not care if his general rested. The war didn't care about anything.

Colonel Ellis glanced at the enlarged maps that had just arrived by chopper from Corps. He made a mental note to send a memo of thanks to the photolab. They had done a good job in the short time they had been given.

Ellis handed the maps to Childs and motioned to the captain sitting in the corner of the TOC to follow him. The captain had also come in on the chopper and held a briefcase that was handcuffed to his wrist.

Ellis had requested information on General Binh Ty Duc, but had not expected this level of response. The captain was from the 525th Military Intelligence Group out of Tan Son Nhut, the Army's intelligence clearing house, and he was a member of the "Community."

Ellis shook his head at the thought of the involvement by the Community and wondered what "great" secret about the general could be important enough to justify sending an armed courier.

The Community consisted of the CIA, the Defense Intelligence Agency, the Army Security Agency, and every other gathering group or agency that dealt in intelligence. All worked sitting on their asses and all had failed. None had predicted the disastrous Tet offensive of 1968 or had pinpointed any major Communist political or military headquarters since then. With all their agents, analysts, spy planes, and tons of electronic equipment they couldn't provide the commanders in the field what they needed most: hard, updated intelligence.

They were all victims of their own secrecy. The compartmentilization of information, and its dissemination on a "need to know" basis, made for a complicated system that assured sluggish response, kept coordination to a minimum, and made outside interpretation unthinkable. The result was always too little, too late. The Community had lost its credibility with the field commanders long ago.

Ellis walked into his room with the captain and locked the door. He sat down to listen to the ritual he'd heard too many times before only to be disappointed and frustrated. The captain began his monotone of instructions, explaining the contents of the message the colonel was about to become privilege to. He was not to discuss, write, or in any way communicate to a second party, the secret contents of the message without an explicit okay from the issuing authority.

Ellis rolled his eyes as the captain quoted regulations and codes that would be used to ensure his incarceration if secrecy was violated, then described the procedure for destroying the document, once read.

Finally, the captain unlocked the briefcase and had Ellis sign three forms acknowledging that he understood the rules, then pulled out a plastic-covered envelope marked *"Top Secret Eyes Only."*

Ellis opened the envelope and began reading. The first page was a synopsis of the general's life; place of birth, civilian schooling; military schooling and assignments, family, party status, close friends, and enemies. The second page was different. Ellis sat down. He now understood

why the captain had been sent. He reread the page with a
pounding heart:

Hanoi's latitude for political and military initiative
in support of the war is limited by Peiping and Moscow differences over the general question of strategy
and tactics. North Vietnam has to rely largely on aid
from Peiping and Moscow, not only for material support for the war effort but also for its own economic
survival. As a result of the worsening relationship
between the two Communist powers, practical ne-
cessity requires Hanoi to remain neutral to the dis-
pute. The divergent viewpoints of Peiping and Moscow, the former advocating uncompromising, total
victory versus the latter's demand for a more moderate and conciliatory approach, is a major concern
to the premier, Pham Van Dong. (*Secret*)

Despite appearances in the recent announcement
of a new Communist government formed in the South
(Provisional Revolutionary Government of the Re-
public of South Vietnam', the real military and political leader of the South is *General Binh Ty Duc*.
(*Top Secret*)

Bottom Line

General Binh Ty Duc is the only true moderate
leader in the South not associated with either Chinese
or Soviet factions, and is the *de facto* leader appointed by Premier Pham Van Dong. (*Top Secret*)

Termination of *General Duc* would cause tempo-
rary paralysis of military and political decision-making processes within the South. All future major Communist military actions would be delayed for
unspecified time based on realignment of leadership
and/or appointments. (*Top Secret*)

*General Binh Ty Duc's termination is authorized
category 1-Alpha-1.* (*Top Secret Eyes Only*)

Copy furnished Corps commander

End Report

Ellis took a deep breath and set the paper down. Category 1-Alpha-1 was the code that meant heavy friendly casualties were acceptable in accomplishing the mission.

"Sir, are you finished?" asked the captain, obviously wanting to be done with his duty and to be gone.

The colonel nodded in silence. The captain pulled a lighter and flat metal tray from the briefcase. Ellis held the report over the tray as the captain lit the corner of the document.

Ellis watched the report burn, grateful that B-52s would do the killing and that good men didn't have to be sent to die for a purpose they and their leaders would never know about or understand.

24

It was quiet as only the early morning could be. The jungle still slept as the sky changed from black to dark gray and a white mist oozed from the river into a lingering cloud. Lieutenant Gibson stood on the riverbank and shut his eyes. The mission was about to begin. He absorbed the tranquil silence for a moment, then turned and motioned for Russian and Toan to cross.

The two men immediately stepped into the river. Gibson watched them disappear into the white vapor and then he went to his knees in the sand. He would wait five minutes, time enough for the two men to secure the crossing site. Behind Gibson, the rest of the patrol waited.

Russian stepped onto the far bank and halted. The silence was total except for the slight gurgling of the river and the water dripping from his fatigue trousers. Toan stood behind him, burdened with a rattan basket-pack filled with fruit for the spirit house. The old man listened a few seconds, then continued up the bank. His experienced ears told him they were in no danger.

Minutes later, dark shapes began to emerge from the mist. The patrol was coming: first Lieutenant Gibson, then Wade and the others. Gibson motioned for Russian and Toan to lead on. Walking single file, the patrol snaked down the riverbank. They had traveled only several hundred meters before they came to the junction of the Stadium valley stream and the river. Without pausing, Toan turned toward the mountains and began following the gradually ascending stream. Within fifty paces they reached the base of the mountains and entered the narrow ravine whose rock walls rose straight up to a height of over three hundred meters.

Russian, feeling as if he'd entered another world, cautiously followed the old Montagnard. The dark canyon became progressively steeper and led to a succession of beautiful, stepped, stream-pools and miniature waterfalls. The looming rock walls were rough with ridges and outcrops that supported a profusion of tropical plants. Splashes of thick, brightly colored mosses clung to the walls in irregular patterns like patchwork. The sky was turning light gray streaked with pale blue, but inside the ravine the eerie mist still lingered.

The farther into the ravine the patrol went, the more difficult the climbing became. It was like walking up a never-ending flight of stairs as they hopped and scrambled up boulder after boulder, and soon their legs and backs cried out in tormented agony. Even their necks and shoulders grew sore and stiff from constantly looking up at the cliffs for the glint of a rifle barrel or a sign that the enemy was watching.

The sound of their steps and heavy, labored breathing was gradually drowned out by the sound of crashing water. Toan climbed up a large boulder and stopped. Before him was the rainbow-colored cloud that always made his heart sing.

Russian crawled up beside him and stared in awe. A waterfall fell in a white, turbulent froth from some forty meters above to crash onto flat, worn boulders. The thick, showery mist made a rainbow with colors so vibrant that they seemed painted.

The rest of the patrol climbed up the boulder and stood in the drenching spray. It was a once-in-a-lifetime sight.

Lieutenant Gibson broke the spell. "Russian, ask Toan where we go from here." He had to half yell to be heard over the crashing water.

Russian leaned over the old man and spoke into his ear. Toan turned wordlessly and pointed toward the falls only thirty feet away. Russian looked at the rock wall looming ahead and shook his head as if confused. He spoke again into the Montagnard's ear. Toan again pointed toward the falls and spoke a few words before walking toward the splashing water.

Shrugging his shoulders, Russian looked at Lieutenant Gibson. "He say we go into the darkness."

Gibson began to ask what darkness, but Russian had already begun to follow the old man.

Minutes later, Gibson understood. Past the curtain of drenching water was a small cavern. The patrol stood just inside the entrance, staring into a dark void.

Rose shook his head. "I ain't goin'."

Preacher patted the small soldier's back. "We have flashlights. You'll be okay."

Rose stood frozen. "Men, I ain't goin'. I had enough of dark places."

Preacher pulled a flashlight from his pack and handed it to Rose. "You'll do fine. Thumper will be in front of you, and I'll be behind you."

Rose sighed and turned on the light. "You stay on my ass and tell me where to go. I'm shutting my eyes, and I ain't openin' them till we out."

Toan talked to Russian for several moments and Russian translated to Gibson. "He say have men lay down close to entrance and cover their heads. He go into cave and scare out flying demons."

Gibson rolled his eyes up at the absurdity and began to step deeper into the cave. Russian blocked his path. "He speak of bats."

Gibson's mouth fell open, and he quickly turned around. "Everybody move close to the entrance and lay down. Stay as low as possible and cover your heads. The old man is going to scare out some bats."

"Bats?" whined Rose. "I hate bats. I hate caves, too, man."

Thumper and Preacher moved back, pulling Rose with them, and lay down beside Woodpecker and Wade. Sergeant Zubeck and his men moved to the side of the cave and sprawled out.

Russian turned on his flashlight as Toan picked up a rock and stepped into the darkness. Russian, walking behind the old man, was trying to light the way when they came to a narrow, deep crevice in the rock floor. Toan hopped over the obstacle and as about to turn to give a warning when Russian jumped and cleared the crevice easily but slipped on the icelike surface on the other side. The big Czech lost his balance and slid into Toan with a jolting crash. Both men struggled to keep their balance and stayed on their feet by holding on to one another. Russian finally got his feet firmly beneath him and panned the light on the slimy floor.

The cave angled sharply on the other side of the crevice, and a stream of water flowed down the incline into the deep crack in the floor. The water was slimy gray and stank of ammonia.

Toan walked several paces up the incline and pointed up. Russian slowly trained his light to the ceiling fifteen feet above and immediately froze. The light shone on a teeming sea of life. There was no visible rock, only hundreds and hundreds of brown-black bodies pressed so closely together that they breathed as one. Their wings were folded over their sleeping forms like cocoons. The sight above him explained the smell and the slick floor. Bat excrement was being washed down the floor by the water in a natural cleaning process.

Russian pressed himself against the rock wall and motioned Toan to his side. The old man heaved the rock upward and the two men covered their heads.

The stone struck with a dull thud, then fell back and splashed into the stinking stream. At first there was a faint fluttering. Then the sound grew into a roar as the bats, in a frenzy, flew to escape.

Rose's screams went unheard as hundreds of two-pound flying rodents rushed past in a black, turbulent cloud of furry flesh, slapping with their wings the exposed portions of the men's backs. Woodpecker held the flaps of his boonie hat tight against his face, but still almost lost his hat to the beating. Preacher, praying aloud, held on to Rose with a death grip.

Wade curled his body into a ball and gasped for air. The multitude of panicking animals was taking all the oxygen. In twenty seconds it was over. Wade lifted his ringing head and opened his eyes. The diffuse light in the cave entrance was thick with dust, as if a rug had been beaten there. The other men began to rise up slowly.

Lieutenant Gibson shook his head to clear it and spoke in a rasp: "Report."

Wade checked his men with a quick glance. "Three-one okay."

Zubeck chimed in, "Two-one ready."

Toan stood up, walked deeper into the cave, and disappeared.

Lieutenant Gibson held Russian back and pointed his light into the darkness. The old man stepped into the light and pointed to his right. Gibson took a deep breath and motioned the others to follow.

Rose shook his head again at Preacher. "I ain't goin', man."

Preacher took his arm. "Come on, you can't stay here."

Rose frowned and began walking. "I hate this shit, man. I mean totally, big-time, *hate it!* You know, man?"

Preacher patted the small soldier's back. "I know."

Gibson followed the old man into a corridor that angled sharply right and abruptly slanted upward at a forty-five-degree angle. The rock floor was rippled and a small stream of clear water ran down its center, glistening with iridescent specks. The cave narrowed to a three foot width and a four-foot height. The darkness was total except for the beam of yellow light from the flashlights. Toan scampered up the corridor like a monkey while Gibson hunched over awkwardly, panning his light nervously.

The tunnel angled again and became even steeper. The men had to crawl on their hands and knees, dragging their packs behind them.

Rose bumped his head for the umpteenth time and spun

around, shining his light in Preacher's face. "I shoulda killed that stinking Yard the first time I see him! When I get outta here I'm gonna wring his puny neck. Then I'm. . ." He turned back around, mumbling, and began climbing again.

Matt Wade wasn't sure what claustrophobia was, but he knew that whatever it was, he had it. Twenty minutes in the darkness, seeing nothing but occasional flashes from a flashlight, had done him in. His heart pounded so loud and hard that he couldn't breath anymore. The walls were closing in and suffocating him. He froze, unable to move another inch. He tried moving and clamped his eyes tightly shut to will his body to move, but he was caught in unyielding fear.

Thumper nudged him. "What's wrong?"

Wade whispered, trying to form his words without screaming. "I . . . I'm sick."

Thumper crawled past and, taking Wade's arm, tugged him forward. "Don't worry. It'll pass. Put your mind on something else and shut your eyes."

Wade shivered all the way inside. The dampness and darkness combined to make him so cold he thought he might freeze to death. Thumper pulled him along roughly, but talked confidently and calmly. "Just move your legs and push forward. You doin' fine. Think about Ginny and keep pushin'."

Toan had disappeared out of Gibson's light for several minutes, but the lieutenant didn't give a damn. He was too tired to worry. He was struggling just to move one bruised knee in front of the other. Suddenly his light shone on the old man's grinning face. The cave widened and Toan was standing. Gibson crawled a few more yards and joined him. Toan pointed up the steep corridor to a glorious sight. An opening. At least Gibson thought it was an opening. A strange, green-tinted light was twenty meters distant.

Gibson had to brace his hands on the cave walls to pull himself up the steep incline so as not to fall backward. He approached the opening cautiously, not sure what might be outside. As he neared he saw it was covered by an intricately woven spider web. Beyond the web was a tangle of leafy vines so thick that not a single speck of sunlight shone through.

Gibson slashed through the sticky web with the CAR-15 barrel as the others came up behind him. He then reached out carefully and made a small opening through the tangle of vine to see if they were in danger. All he could make out was a steep, tree-covered embankment a few meters distant. Pushing more of the vine back and bringing up his CAR-15, he slid out into the glorious sunlight.

He found himself at the base of a huge, ten-meter-high boulder that had a strange dwarf tree protruding from its top. The tree was beautiful, but it had hideous, snaky roots that crawled down the rock face. Gibson readied his weapon and peered cautiously around the boulder. A tranquil stream shaded by bamboo was only a few meters away. The muffled roar of a waterfall behind the boulder told Gibson his exact location. They were in the saddle between the ring of the mountains. Gibson motioned the others out.

Childs shut his eyes, listening to the radio-relayed message from Lietuenant Foley, who was flying five miles away from the Stadium.

"Base, Patrol One reports reaching the top and will soon begin search, over."

Childs snatched up the handset. "Three Alfa, have you got a sit rep from Team One-three, over?

"Base, that's a negative. Haven't heard from them in an hour since they began moving toward the Stadium. Over."

Childs cursed under his breath. Selando wasn't following the standard procedure of calling in every hour with a situation report. It could be negligence or . . . "Three Alfa, keep trying to contact Team One-three and report contact immediately. Over."

"Roger. Out."

Sergeant Bill Selando held the handset to his ear, listening to Lieutenant Foley call him, but didn't dare whisper a response.

His team had moved toward the Stadium at first light, following a densely vegetated streambed. They'd moved only three kilometers when the point man froze in his tracks and slowly sank to the ground. The morning ground fog had dissipated, and when the point man parted a stand of large ferns he found himself staring at rows of strung-up blue hammocks full of lounging NVA. The team had walked part of the way into a huge NVA camp. Selando had tried to back the team out, but several NVA had awakened close to the stream and had started a small fire. Now they were eating. The camp was only fifteen feet from the six men hiding in the bamboo thicket. Selando was afraid to breathe, let alone try and whisper a message.

Lieutenant Foley tried calling again. Selando carefully pushed the side bar twice to break squelch.

Foley immediately sat up in his seat. The squelch breaks meant Selando had a radio problem or couldn't talk.

"One-three, this is Three Alfa. If you are having radio problems break squelch twice."

There was nothing but static in the headphones. Foley held his breath for an instant then hit the floor switch again. "One-three, if you're in trouble break squelch twice." The static in his earphones stopped two distinctive times.

"Shit!" blurted Foley to himself. "One-three, are there dinks close by?"

Again there were two breaks.

"One-three, understand you're close to dinks. Are you close to their camp?"

Selando squeezed twice, wishing he could yell. "Hell, yes, we're close—you wanna talk to some of 'em?"

"One-three, this is important. Break squelch once for each kilometer you're away from the Stadium."

Selando pressed the bar three times. Foley's palms were slippery from sweat. He shut his eyes, forcing his brain to think of other questions he should ask. He pressed the switch. "One-three, I'll remain on station and alert Guns.

Get out of there as soon as possible. I'm going off push to report your situation, then I'll be back.''

J. D. Gibson watched Sergeant Zubeck and his team disappear up the slope, then motioned for Wade to move the team out. The two teams had split according to plan. Zubeck would recon the ring of hills to the north and he and Wade's team would check out those to the south. Russian led, with Toan walking close behind. The old man had told Russian of a trail that ran along the ring of mountains and of the spirit house only a short distance away.

The Czech crossed the stream and began climbing the steep slope. The team had seen footprints on the creek's bank and held their weapons ready. Rose had whispered that the prints were only a day old.

The TOC was a beehive of activity. Childs had received the excited message from Lieutenant Foley about Selando's predicament only minutes before. All the officers were gathered around maps, talking to their respective units by telephone, reporting the NVA camp location. The Army liaison had already alerted two sets of Guns. The Air Force liaison had called for a pair of F-4s to stand by and was waiting to get a time for a B-52 mission. Colonel Ellis was talking to Corps Headquarters.

Major Shane sat silently in his chair. He looked at Childs worriedly and glanced back at the map.

Childs walked over and sat down beside him. "Don't worry, Ed, they're in a good hide position. They'll be able to wait it out and get away."

Shane nodded without taking his eyes from the map.

The Air Force liaison set down his phone and stood up. "We've got a B-52 cell diverted to us! The 307th out of Thailand is diverting three B-52s. They'll be over target in three hours."

Shane glared at Colonel Ellis, then at the Air Force major. "They're not dropping if the team is still in there!"

Ellis raised his hand as if quieting a child. "Of course,

Ed. There will be no drop if your men are in danger, but we should think positively and let the mission stand as is.''

Shane stood up without taking his eyes from the colonel. ''Okay, but they don't drop unless I say.''

Ellis forced a smile and spoke softly. ''It's your ball game.''

Russian moved slowly, stopping every few minutes to listen and ''feel'' out what lay ahead. The rocky trail they followed was a killer. It ran along the top rim of the mountains. To the left was an almost sheer vertical drop to the river far below. To the right the land sloped moderately to the Stadium valley. Towering pines and mahoganies interspersed with magnificent teaks destroyed all undergrowth under the thick canopy. There was no place to take cover to let an enemy patrol pass. Russian would have to see them first and pray it was only one or two men. He could kill them quietly with the silenced British Sterling. If there were more, there would be a fight—a fight they couldn't win. And, of course, if he or the team was seen first, they'd die.

Russian wiped his sweaty hands on his trousers and grasped the weapon again. On the trail up ahead was a group of large boulders. They would make good cover for an NVA trail watcher or sentry.

Russian whispered to Toan to stay down and motioned Wade and Rose to cover him. The two men took up firing positions as Russian crept forward cautiously to check out the danger.

Russian hunched over his submachine gun and swung it along his arc of vision. The closer he came to the boulders the more apprehensive he became. The rocks were waist-high and constituted a natural defensive position because of the way they formed a partial circle with plenty of firing positions. Russian sneaked around the rocks, anticipating a sleeping soldier on the other side, but there was none. He took a deep breath and began to raise his arm to wave the others up. A noise froze his arm in mid-flight. His feeling of relief from a second before was blocked out by a sudden cold jab of fear. The noise was distant, but it was unmistakably man-made, and it told him they were in trouble.

Russian looked back at the team. They had heard the noise, too, and were facing down the slope with weapons readied.

Toan sat on the trail crying silently. The sound below him, that of a man chopping wood, meant the lowlanders were still in his valley. A man didn't chop wood unless he felt safe, and he wouldn't feel safe unless there were many others of his kind nearby. The old man got up slowly and moved closer to Russian. He pointed down the slope and whispered, "The hunter's hut and spirit house rest below a stone ledge three hundred paces down."

Gibson directed the team into the protection of the rocks as Russian told him what Toan had said. The lieutenant knelt down. "Wade, you and Russian will go with me. We'll sneak down and check out the huts. Thumper, you organize a defensive position here. We'll be back in thirty minutes. If we're not back in that time wait five more minutes and head back to the cave. Questions?"

No one spoke.

Gibson smiled. "Okay, that's it, let's see what we got."

The three men took off their packs and began crawling down the slope.

Sergeant Selando sighed inwardly with relief and thanked God and every saint he could remember as the NVA soldiers left their positions and joined a large gathering a hundred meters away for what looked like a class of some sort.

Selando led the team as they cautiously crawled out of the thicket into the streambed and crept down the bank to escape. In ten minutes they had only traveled one hundred meters, but had reached the end of the camp. Every painstaking foot was another foot closer to survival. Safety was only a few more hundred meters away.

Selando breathed easier but couldn't chance getting to his feet to make better time. Their low profile in the shallow water was barely noticeable. He crawled on, praying for strength, praying that no sentries were posted by the creek.

Fifteen minutes later he raised his exhausted body from the water and fell on a carpet of moss. He had no more strength. His muscles seemed like spongy rubber. The others joined him on the bank, trying not to wheeze or throw up. The radio operator held out the handset to his team leader with the last of his energy. Selando dragged the handset over his heaving chest and pushed the side bar.

Lieutenant Foley sat in the backseat of the small plane, eating C ration pound cake. The earphones crackled and the whispering voice of Selando ran through his earphones. Foley nearly choked on the half-eaten cake.

"Three Alfa, this is One-three. We're out. Over."

Foley slammed his foot on the transmit button.

"Thank God, One-three. Report everything you saw. How big was the camp? Which direction did it spread? What was your exact location? How many did you see? What was their activity? Give it all to me *now!* Over."

Selando gasped in several breaths and began whispering back the information.

Russian crawled toward the distinct smell of smoke. Wade and Gibson inched along the ground behind the Czech. They knew they'd found something big. They had crawled down the slope for a hundred meters before smelling the faint trace of smoke. In another fifty meters they heard voices along with the chopping sound. Russian halted. They'd come to an expanse of smooth rock covered with moss. Russian could see the valley, but not what was directly ahead. He motioned for the others to wait, and he crawled forward. He moved for twenty feet and stopped. There was no rock ahead, only sky. From the sounds and the faint cloud of smoke, he knew he was on a ledge. Somewhere below was what they were looking for. He inched up to the rock's edge and peered over. One glance was enough. He quickly lay flat and pushed back.

Russian crawled back to the others and got so close to

Wade's face to whisper that they touched noses. "It is a camp."

Gibson began to crawl forward but Russian put out his hand. "Is too dangerous here."

Gibson understood immediately. A man's head peering over the ledge would be easily seen. He raised up and saw a tree next to the ledge fifty feet away. A strangler fig had attached its twisting tentacles to its base and to a nearby boulder, providing cover and an observation point.

Gibson crawled toward the tree. The others followed.

The message that came through the radio speaker caused Major Shane to smile. Team One-three was out of danger and heading for the pickup zone.

The Air Force liaison tapped Colonel Ellis's shoulder. "Sir, can we go with the B-52 mission now?"

Ellis listened to the last words of Foley's transmission and stood up.

"Ed, what's the status from the other teams? Are they far enough away to go with the strike?"

Shane studied the map for a minute, calculating the distance. The minimum safe distance from a B-52 bomb run was 1500 meters. The team's teeth would rattle and they'd be shaken a bit, but if they took cover, they could ride it out safely. It was five kilometers from the western end of the Stadium, where the NVA camp was located, to the eastern end. Shane motioned the Air Force officer over and handed him a red grease pencil. "Mark on the map how the strike will go in."

The officer drew a long rectangle box as he explained: "The three BUFs will come in at 30,000 feet at four hundred knots in a vee formation. They're carrying 108 five-hundred-pound MARK 82s apiece. They'll make their strike perpendicular to the western end of the Stadium, guided by ground-based radar. There's a five-hundred-meter plus or minus error factor . . ."

Shane computed the error factor and looked up at Ellis. "Sir, they'll be safe enough. Go with it."

The Air Force liaison shrugged his shoulders. "Why

don't you just pull the two other teams? We found the camp.''

Shane was about to answer when Ellis clapped the young Air Force major on the back and pointed to the map.

''The two teams still have to check out the mountains to ensure there aren't more of them. I'm sure the western end holds the main base camp, but it's unlikely the whole division would be there. If the other teams find more, we'll finish them off with your fast movers and our gunships. Somebody needs to be on the ground to direct them, right?''

The major smiled sheepishly, realizing his question had been dumb, and raised his wrist to look at his watch. ''Well, gentlemen, I've gotten a lot smarter in the last couple of minutes and, just so you know I'm good for something, it's exactly two hours and ten minutes before bombs away.''

Shane nodded toward Childs. ''You'd better call Gibson and tell him to warn his teams.''

Gibson lay beside the tree, observing from between strangler roots the small NVA camp below. He'd been watching the scene for several minutes and counting the personnel. He knew within seconds it was not the main base camp. There were less than fifty people. But he also knew this camp was special. There had to be big brass here. He'd never seen so many NVA officers and senior enlisted before. They were easy to identify by the K-54 pistols they carried. It had to be a headquarters of some kind. On several occasions he saw soldiers carrying papers to the large hut thirty-five meters from the ledge. Each time the soldiers came back empty-handed. Another interesting thing was a terrain model of the valley fashioned on the ground in the center of the camp. A platoon of regular infantry was camped just below the hut and seemed to have positions dug in facing the valley.

Russian and Wade, lying away from the tree, protected the lieutenant's back. Wade poked Gibson's leg and whispered, ''We'd better get back and report this.''

Gibson was about to back out when a soldier emerged from the hut. He was extremely tall for a Vietnamese and had silver-gray hair. He had no rank on his khaki shirt, but by the actions of the soldiers who all stopped work to look at him as he walked down the steps, Gibson knew he had to be the big cheese.

Gibson backed out slowly and looked into Wade's anxious face. "It's a headquarters of some kind."

Wade whispered over his shoulder as he started crawling. "Let's get the hell outta here."

25

Thumper looked nervously at his watch, then stared down the slope again. "Where are they?" he asked himself for the tenth time. Preacher had received a message twenty minutes before that One-three had found an NVA camp and that a B-52 strike was on the way.

Thumper's eyes caught a movement. He immediately tapped Woodpecker to get ready to fire just in case. Thumper eased the safety off his weapon, but didn't put his finger on the trigger. Lieutenant Gibson's head became distinct, then his shoulders. Thumper marveled at how effectively camouflage fatigues and painted faces made the approaching men difficult to see.

He raised up and walked toward the lieutenant, repeating the radio message in an excited whisper.

Gibson's eyes widened and he looked quickly at his watch. It was 1220. The strike would hit at 1400 hours. He walked past Thumper and held his hand out toward Preacher. The small Indian immediately gave him the handset and whispered, "Zubeck's team already knows about the strike and has laagered up to wait it out."

"Have they seen anything?" asked Gibson.

"No, sir, they're on a trail on the top of the ridge, but they haven't seen any signs."

Gibson brought the handset to his mouth and smiled. "Wait till the major hears this." He pressed the side bar and began whispering.

The operation center's inhabitants were quiet and still as Foley's voice filled the room, relaying Gibson's report: NVA Headquarters had been found.

Colonel Ellis showed the only reaction by clapping his hands together when Foley reported the sighting of a tall Vietnamese officer with silver hair.

Shane looked at Ellis with a questioning stare. Obviously the Colonel knew something he and the others didn't.

Ellis stood up and spoke in a rasp, as if his throat was parched. "The team has got to kill him."

"Kill who?" asked Shane, perplexed.

Ellis stared at the wall map as if in a trance.

"General Binh Ty Duc, the commander of all Communist forces in the south. I thought he'd be in the main camp, but Gibson's description is unmistakable. It's him."

"Sir, you never mentioned him before. We didn't plan. . ."

Ellis interrupted, talking as if to himself. "I didn't think it mattered. He was supposed to be in the main camp. But now . . . now, we've got him!" Ellis's far-off look dissolved and he looked directly into Shane's eyes. "Your men have got to kill him!"

Shane shot up out of his chair. "What the hell are you talking about? You heard the report. There are forty men in that camp! It'd be impossible to kill one man and escape."

Ellis's eyes didn't leave Shane's as he spoke coldly. "It's got to be done. The general is more important than the NVA Division—or ten divisions, for that matter. He's the mastermind, the tactical genius of the whole southern war effort. He has to be killed!"

Shane's jaw muscles rippled as his eyes burned holes through the colonel's forehead. "Sir, there is no way that. . ."

Childs stood up abruptly between the two men, facing his major. "Sir, may I speak to you outside, *now!*"

Shane ignored the sergeant and began to finish his reply

to Ellis when Childs stepped closer and spoke roughly. *"It's important, Sir!"*

Shane spun around and marched up the TOC steps, followed closely by the sergeant.

Ellis looked around the room at the other faces staring at him. He knew they felt as Shane did—he was ordering the team to commit suicide.

Once outside, Shane angrily turned around. "I'm not doing it! The son of a bitch can go fuck himself!"

Childs lowered his head and spoke quietly. "He's right."

"No! No, Jerry, God damn it! You can't mean it."

Childs looked up at his major with eyes set. "He'll relieve you. He'll relieve you on the spot and order the mission himself. Believe me, I know. Ed, he's looking at a bigger picture than you and me. He don't see faces, he sees only statistics. He's got a job to do, a shitty job in a shitty war, and he knows he's right. He'll do it and he'll be able to live with himself after it's over." Childs stepped closer, almost as if pleading, "God damn, Ed, you gotta do it! We know those men. They're ours. With our experience we can plan out the mission, and they'll have a chance. If Ellis takes over . . . then it's finished for them."

Shane stared at his sergeant for a long time, then lowered his head. "Ellis may be able to live with himself, but how about me? How am I if I order that mission?"

Childs turned slowly and began walking toward the TOC steps. He paused in the entrance and looked over his shoulder. "How ya gonna live if you walk away from it?"

Childs stepped into the lighted room, walked to the radio, and sat down. He avoided the stares from the others by looking up at the hanging aerial photo map.

Colonel Ellis, still waiting, was about to speak to Childs when Shane walked down the steps and strode up to the seated Air Force liaison. "How much time we got?"

The Air Force officer quickly lifted his wrist. "Uh . . . one hour and twenty-one minutes."

Shane nodded toward the radio. "Jerry, call Foley and have him relay to Gibson he's going to hit the general. . . . Tell him to plan the hit to coincide with the B-52 strike. Other info will follow in fifteen minutes."

Shane looked into the surprised face of the Air Force major. "Get me a pair of Phantom-4s over the Stadium once the bomb run is over. Gibson will direct them if they're needed. And make sure others are standing by."

Shane turned to the Army Air liaison. "I want two sets of Guns orbiting a couple of miles from the Stadium. Once the bombing is complete, have them report immediately to Gibson for instructions. Have two more sets ready, and get two Slicks rigged with ropes so we can McGuire-rig the teams out if needed."

Both liaisons reached for telephones as Shane looked up at Colonel Ellis without showing any expression. "Sir, you better call Corps and make sure no paper-pusher denies or fails to understand the importance of these requests. I need first priority on every air asset this Corps has till this is over."

Ellis stared at Shane for an instant, then smiled. "You've got it!"

Childs finished his radio transmission to Foley as Shane yanked the aerial photo from the wall and spread it on the table.

"Jerry, give me the exact location of the team and the NVA camp . . ."

Sergeant Thong stood in front of the tired private and smiled. "You have cut enough wood for today, Nuu. Stack what you have cut by the hut. You will find a cup of cool tea on the first step for you."

The young soldier wiped his sweat-beaded brow with his shirt sleeve and began to offer his thanks when a signal corporal yelled out to Thong.

"Comrade Thong, you are needed!"

Thong walked to the terrain model where the signalman was standing holding two pieces of string.

"Old one, Colonel Sy wants you to place the string on

your model to represent the phone communications wire we laid this morning.''

Thong beamed with pride. Colonel Sy respected his skills and knew he would place the strings expertly.

The old sergeant had seen the signal team walk into camp earlier that morning holding the bamboo pole, unreeling the spool of commo wire. Thong took the first string. ''Tell me now exactly the route of the wire team.''

The signalman knelt at the western end of the model. ''The Second Division Headquarters is located directly across the valley and five hundred meters into the forest. We ran the wire out to the edge of the open fields, then, to hide it, we skirted along the mountains to the north. It is along the path hidden by the trees.''

Thong knew the trail. It was the trail they had taken to reach their present camp.

''And the second string?''

The signalman pointed to the ring of mountains to the north. ''We ran wire from the Thirty-third Regiment down the mountain to the trail and followed the same path to here.''

''Is the Thirty-third still camped along the top of the mountain?'' asked Thong.

''Yes, they are twenty-five hundred meters from the Second Division Headquarters and three kilometers from this camp.''

Thong placed the string and stepped back to look at his work. ''The phones are working now?''

''Of course. I do not walk all this way for nothing. Your general can talk to anyone in the Second Division. Do you want to see for yourself?''

Thong smiled. ''No, I am too tired. I just laid your phone wire across the valley.''

The signalman laughed and walked toward the boulder outcrop to his new field phones.

The headquarters radioman tossed off his headset and hollered to his communications sergeant. He had just received a message from the radio relay team that they had picked up American traffic on their radio.

The sergeant read the message and quickly walked over to Colonel Sy, who was updating his maps for a briefing to the general.

"Comrade, the radio team has heard several messages over the radio on the FM frequency. They say messages are being relayed by a plane."

Colonel Sy immediately dropped his pencil and grabbed the report. Radio traffic on FM frequency meant ground units! Planes used higher frequencies to communicate. FM transmission was limited by distance, which meant American units were somewhere close by . . . but where? The colonel spun around to the easel map. The Americans could be anywhere in a twenty-mile radius.

Lieutenant Huy, bringing out another easel for the briefing, noticed his colonel's distress. "What is wrong, comrade?"

The colonel pointed at the map. "Call the Second Division Headquarters and tell them American units may be in the area. Have them send out patrols to search outside their camp. Then call the Thirty-third Regiment on the mountain. Tell them to send two platoons to this location. Have one take the valley trail and the other patrol along the rim of the mountains. Have them also check the stream you visited the other day and the trail behind us."

The lieutenant began to pick up the phone handset, but paused. "Do you want me to wake the general and tell him?"

The colonel shook his head. "No, the Americans may be miles from here. This is only a precaution. He needs his rest. I will tell him later."

The lieutenant rang the field phone handle and began talking.

Sergeant Zubeck and his team lay in a depression made by a large, uprooted tree only fifty feet from the mountain trail. Zubeck waited with the radio handset held to his ear. Five minutes before, he had overheard Gibson receive orders to make a hit on a general. Zubeck knew the recon mission was over. Gibson would be ordering him to come to their location or to move back to the cave entrance and wait.

The static in the radio suddenly turned into silence, then a voice whispered, "Zulu One, move back to First Base and secure it. We will be running after hit so don't fire on us. We will arrive at approximately 1415. Over."

Zubeck whispered a quick, "Roger. Out," and tossed the handset to his radio operator. "Okay guys, we're going back to the cave to set up a defensive position. The other team has found an NVA headquarters and they're going to grease a big general. They'll be running back to the cave, so no shooting unless you're sure it's not our guys. Let's move it."

Lieutenant Gibson motioned to the small terrain model he'd made and whispered, "It's simple. Russian and I will be hidden on the ledge. When the first B-52 bombs hit across the valley, the dinks will be confused and run for cover. The general will run out of his hut, and Russian will pop him with the silencer. Nobody will know what happened. Matt and Rose will be on the left flank of the ledge. Woodpecker and Thumper on the right. If we're seen and they try to flank us, you guys blow 'em away and throw gas to slow 'em down. If the general isn't in the hut, he'll probably be in a briefing area just below the ledge, so he'll be an even easier target. Either way, if you see us jump up and start running, *everybody* run. We all come back to here, where Preacher will be securing the patrol base. We'll grab our rucks and run to the cave entrance, where Zubeck's team will be waiting. Any questions?"

Russian pointed to the old Montagnard. "What about Toan?"

Gibson shook his head. "We don't need him involved in this, but I can't let him go. He'll stay here with Preacher."

Gibson looked at his watch. It was forty minutes before the bombs hit. "Okay, that's it, then. Remember, I'll be carrying the radio. If something happens to me, make sure one of you gets the radio . . . it's our lifeline outta here."

Gibson looked into the painted faces and smiled. "Well, let's go kill us a general."

Major Shane, sipping coffee from a brown-stained cup, watched Childs scratch Bitch's stomach. The yellow mongrel was sprawled on her back on the floor, whimpering in ecstasy. Childs looked up, self-conscious of Shane's stare, and abruptly sat up. Bitch lay perfectly still for a moment, then turned over and began whining for more.

"Go on, Jerry, I won't tell anybody," said Shane, smiling.

Childs looked at his watch. It was ten before two. "Jesus H. Christ, I wish this was over!"

Shane stood and stretched his back. "In ten minutes hundreds of men will be dead. Most will never know what happened. God, it's a horrible thought."

The Air Force major leaned up in his chair. "But it's only gooks. What do you care?"

Shane looked over his raised coffee cup at the major. "You ever see what your bombs do?"

"Sure, I've seen the pictures. So what?"

Shane sat down tiredly and leaned back. "Never mind."

The Army air liaison walked down the steps into the TOC. "Ed, the Slicks are rigged with the McGuire rigs you ordered. I hope we don't have to use them. Men are awfully vulnerable hanging from those ropes."

The Air Force major put his feet up on the desk. "How's that work, anyway?"

The Army pilot sat down. "We lower ropes down from the bird. The team hooks in with snap-links and we lift them out. We only use it when there's no LZs 'cause the Slick is a sitting target, too."

"They won't have to use them if they get to the cave, right?"

The Army pilot lowered his head. "Yeah, *if* they make it to the cave."

Senior Sergeant Tran Quy held up his hand to stop his platoon. He looked at his map to confirm his location to call back to the Thirty-third Regiment Headquarters and report his progress. His thirty-man platoon had been ordered to move out immediately and patrol the mountain trail that led to General Duc's headquarters. According to the map he was only a kilometer from the stream and waterfall. He took the radio handset and called the headquarters to give his exact location. He did this to coordinate his movement with the other platoon from his company, which was taking the valley trail. If they reached the stream at the same time, they could mistake each other for the enemy. The headquarters radioman reported the other platoon was two kilometers away from the stream.

Quy smiled to himself. His men were moving more quickly than Sergeant Chuong's third platoon. Chuong was young and overly cautious.

Quy put his map inside his shirt and waved his men forward. He would reach the stream first and wait for the third platoon before continuing. His men would gain strength from laughing at their slower third platoon comrades and he would be able to chide his fellow platoon leader for being so cautious.

Russian crawled into position behind the gnarled roots of the strangler fig and peered down into the camp. The general was not in the briefing area, but several other high-ranking officers were. They seemed to be preparing for a briefing. The general's hut was thirty-five meters away with no obstructions to hamper his shot.

Gibson slid in beside him and tapped his leg twice, signaling that the others were in position. Russian raised his Sterling and rested it on the roots to steady his aim.

Gibson looked at his watch and felt his stomach tighten. It was almost time. He backed away from Russian to give him room and crawled to the other side of the tree. When the bombs hit he would peer over the ledge and back up Russian if he missed.

Sergeant Zubeck dipped his hands into the refreshing stream and splashed his face with cool water. His team had refilled their canteens and had taken a defensive position in front of the cave entrance. Zubeck walked to the large boulder with the small tree growing from its top and looked over his men's position. It wasn't the best place to be. There was high ground on both sides of the stream, but it was all he could do. His men were hidden behind small boulders and clumps of bamboo, facing the stream toward the valley. They'd placed their Claymores out and were ready.

Zubeck sat down next to his radio operator and looked at his watch. "Charlie," he whispered, "it's almost show time."

General Sang, the Second Division commander, folded the letter he wrote to his wife and put it into his shirt pocket. He stood up and walked out of the open tent. The huge camp was quiet except for the loud voices of the political officers giving classes to assembled groups of men. Sang strolled to the closest group and sat down. He didn't listen to the officer, but instead looked around at the magnificent beauty of the forest. The sun's rays penetrated the thick canopy in only a few places, allowing narrow shafts of golden light to spot the forest floor.

General Sang reached out a hand for one of the spots when the ground suddenly shook. He jumped to his feet just as a horrible *"Crunch-Barooom"* traveled the five hundred meters from the first bomb's detonation. The men around him screamed in terror and ran in all directions for protection as he stood frozen in disbelief. The rumbling of the first explosion was quickly blotted out by a continuous succession of other earthshaking explosions that grew louder in intensity as they approached. The ground pitched and rolled, knocking him down as the hurricane-force wind and shock waves rushed through the trees carrying smoke, dirt, debris, and death. *Crack, Crack, Boom, Crack, Boom, Boom.*

Sang grabbed the exposed roots of a tree to stop himself from rolling on the lurching ground. He screamed in agony; he felt as if his brain was being sucked out through his bulging eyeballs by the concussion. He could no longer breathe or hear, but he held tight to the roots. Suddenly, he was yanked upward viciously. He last saw his hands and severed arms still holding the roots as he was flung skyward.

Russian held the Sterling tighter, trying to ignore the thunderous explosions across the valley. Blocking out the yelling and screaming from the camp below, he sighted down the barrel toward the hut and waited for his target.

Private Nuu stood under the general's elevated hut, afraid to move. He was scared and confused by the horrible rumbling and screaming from the camp. He looked at the hut floor above him and yelled for his sergeant.

Sergeant Thong dropped the mango he was cutting as the hut vibrated from the violent eruptions. General Duc sprang wide-eyed from his bed and rushed for the door. He took one step out the door and turned, yelling for Thong. The old sergeant had followed but stopped just inside the doorway upon seeing the dark clouds billowing across the valley.

Russian aimed at the general's chest and began to pull the trigger. The general grabbed Thong with one hand and shoved him toward the steps. Russian saw his target blocked just as he squeezed the trigger. Thong jerked sideways with the bullet's impact and clutched the general. He slid down the general's chest, smearing blood on his khaki shirt. He tried to speak and raised his hand as if for forgiveness as a second bullet ripped through his outreached hand into the general's shoulder and knocked him off the porch.

The general hit heavily on his back and lay gasping. Above him his old friend lay on the porch jerking spasmodically, his head and arm dangling over the ledge.

Russian looked over the smoking barrel for his target, but the general had fallen from view. J. D. Gibson cursed under his breath, seeing what had happened, and crawled to a higher vantage point. He could just see the general lying on the ground and that he was moving. Shit! Gibson brought his rifle up, knowing he had to finish the job.

Nuu had heard the footsteps on the porch and couldn't believe his eyes when the general fell to the ground only a few meters away. Nuu forgot his fear and ran to help his leader.

Gibson raised his rifle and took aim, but his target was partially blocked by a soldier who'd just run from under the hut. Gibson fired anyway.

Nuu's right leg jerked out in front of him uncontrollably and he fell forward. He tried to catch his balance but was suddenly knocked violently to the side. He struck the ground beside the general, screaming in excruciating pain. He felt as if his lower body was burning from within. He gagged and jerked as he bounced and rolled on the ground trying to find release from the burning, tormenting agony.

Soldiers of the general's security platoon turned around as they heard the American rifle's report and began raking the ledge.

"It don't mean nothin'," said Gibson as he stood up to get a better shot. He ignored the bullets cracking by his ears as he braced the weapon against the tree. His target was clearly visible as he held half a breath and squeezed the trigger. The small projectile slammed into the general's side and knocked him over.

Gibson was beginning to drop back down when he was knocked backward as if he'd been hit in the face with a baseball. He fell to the ground, feeling nothing, then sat up quickly. Russian was crawling back to him, yelling. "Lie down! Lie down!" When Gibson put his hand up to check his face, blood spurted over his arm. He tried to speak but somehow the words wouldn't form. His mouth wasn't working.

Wade and Rose waited for the four NVA running up the side of the slope to come within ten meters of them, then rose up shooting. The shocked men were knocked down instantly. Rose tossed a gas grenade down the slope and he and Wade began running.

Russian quickly wrapped his parachute scarf around Gibson's lower face and yanked him to his feet. The AK-47 round had passed through the lieutenant's lower jaw and exited out his upper right cheek. His tongue wasn't hit so he wasn't choking, but his lower jaw and back teeth were destroyed, and the upper teeth were grotesquely exposed by the open wound.

Gibson was stunned, but stayed on his feet as Russian pulled him along up the slope.

Woodpecker sprayed the NVA rushing across the open campground as Thumper pumped round after round of 79-fire into huddled groups of them.

The NVA seemed confused and were firing wildly. Woodpecker changed his rate of fire to short bursts, making every shot count. When he saw Russian helping the lieutenant up the hill, he realized he had to buy them more time.

Three men ran up the slope, firing at the place where Russian had been. Woodpecker calmly swung the barrel of his M-60 and stitched them all.

Thumper tapped his leg, motioned to his grenade, and handed one to Woodpecker. They both pulled the pins and tossed them down into the camp. After the explosions, the two men pulled the pins of gas grenades and threw them. The grenades were still in the air as they ran.

Colonal Sy pressed himself against the outcrop, afraid to move. The gas was choking him and his eyes were burning as if touched by hot coals. Lieutenant Huy lay a few feet away in a large pool of blood, his face ashen white. The camp was in chaos. Men coughed, gagged, and screamed. Some lay wounded; others fired wildly at the ledge above him. Fragments of rock fell like rain all around. The deadly machine gun fire from above had ended, but two explosions had killed and maimed still more of his men. When the crescendo of firing finally decreased, three men ran to where he stood.

Sy felt his own fear dissolve as he looked into their terrified faces. He knew he had to be strong and give them

direction. "You," he pointed at the first soldier, "find the **general and see** if he is hurt. You others gather the able-**bodied and have** them help the wounded. Post sentries, but **do not follow** the attackers. I will call for help to find **them."**

The three men left to follow their orders as Sy ran to **the field phones** and rang the handle to the Thirty-third **Regiment. He** looked across the valley at the billowing **black clouds of** destruction, knowing no one would answer.

Senior Sergeant Tran Quy and his platoon stood on the **mountain trail** staring in morbid fascination at the destruc-**tion of the Forty-second** and Thirty-ninth Regiments. The **bombs were carpeting** the rain forest and made occasional **hits in the open** valley. The white-orange flashes and the **violent upheaval** of dirt and debris were strangely hyp-**notic.** With each explosion, the ground seemed to lurch **upward, as if in** pain. The spreading circles of deadly shock **waves were clearly** visible. The sound would reach them **a few seconds later.** A voice over the radio handset broke **the radio operator's** trance. He handed Quy the handset. **The excited voice** told him that the general's headquarters **was under ground** attack. He was to proceed directly to **the camp and find** the enemy. Quy quickly briefed his men **and began jogging** down the slope. They were only a few **hundred meters from** the stream and the headquarters was **only five hundred** meters beyond.

After one look at Lieutenant Gibson's wound, Wade **knew he was now** in charge. He pointed at Rose and Wood-**pecker.** "Get in position down the slope aways and shoot **anything that moves!** Preacher, get the radio from the lieu-**tenant and get us** some Guns support in here!"

Wade changed magazines while Thumper rewrapped **Gibson's face with** a sterile bandage. The sergeant nodded **at Russian.** "Tell Toan to help the L-tee while we're **moving."**

Preacher held up the handset. "Guns inbound. They **need a smoke to** mark our location."

Thumper finished tying off the bandage and pulled a star cluster round from his leg pocket. "I'll mark with this." The big soldier opened the breech of the M-79 and slipped in the shell. Wade nodded and Thumper raised the weapon and fired.

The shell exploded two hundred feet above them, releasing three miniature glowing red stars.

Preacher gave the location of the NVA camp from the cluster and picked up his weapon. "They're inbound!"

Wade yelled at Rose and Woodpecker. "Come on, we're moving!" The first gunship lowered its nose and released four rockets that spiraled toward the earth.

Colonel Sy felt weak and helpless as he watched Private Nuu and the general carried into the communications cave. They both had been wounded badly. Sy was stepping over other wounded to see what he could do for the general when he heard the approaching helicopter. He threw himself toward the cave entrance and rolled just as the ground behind him erupted in a series of vehement explosions.

The ensuing screams of the wounded and dying outside the cave tore through his heart like saber slashes. He shook uncontrollably and couldn't stop from crying. Someone touched his head. He jerked up, looking into Private Nuu's anguished face. The young soldier had sat up and reached out his hand in desperation. "Am . . . am I dying?"

Forgetting his own fear, Sy took the boy's hand and looked at his ugly leg and side wounds. Both would be painful, but were clean exit wounds. Sy patted the boy's hand and forced a smile. "You will live to tell your children of this day. Rest, my friend. Soon you will be going home."

Sy released the boy's hand and stood to find the general, when he heard the approach of another helicopter making its rocket pass.

Sergeant Zubeck smiled at Charlie, his radio operator. "Man, the Air Force really did a J-O-B on them suckers, didn't they?"

Charlie was about to answer when they both heard

someone splashing through the stream. Zubeck raised up just as one of his team members detonated the Claymores.

Sergeant Quy had waded into the stream, followed by his radioman, and was about to turn around to tell his men to spread out when he was knocked back into the water by a violent blast.

He gagged under the water and fought to his feet, but his right leg buckled under him in pain. He fell back as the water kicked up in miniature fountains of bullet spray. Three of Quy's men lay dead on the bank, and a fourth was wounded. The rest of the platoon was still strung out along the slope. They immediately hit the ground and returned a devastating barrage of fire toward the ambushers. Quy surfaced again, supported by his left leg. Beside him, his radioman floated face down. Dark red blood clouds expanded in the water under the man's body.

Quy pushed off his good leg toward the far shore to reach the protective cover of the bamboo as his radioman drifted slowly toward the gap in the boulders.

Zubeck lay behind the boulder, yelling into the radio handset, "I need Guns! We're pinned down at the stream!"

Foley could barely hear Zubeck's words over the sound of rifle fire in the background, but he'd heard enough to know the situation was on the verge of turning into a disaster. He flipped a toggle and blurted into the handset. "Ghost Rider, lead, we have another team in contact. They're located by the waterfall in the gap of the mountains. Do you have a visual. Over?"

The Gun pilot replied immediately. "Roger, we'll be there in two mikes. Have them pop smoke and we'll come in hot, over."

"Roger, break. Zulu-One, pop smoke and direct strike."

The radio operator's body tumbled with the current between the boulders and was pulled to the center of the quiet pool. There he bobbed up and down and began spinning around the periphery of the whirlpool's vortex, faster and faster, until suddenly he was sucked down as if consumed.

Zubeck pulled a smoke grenade from his harness and heaved it. "Christ, Charlie, they're almost on top of us!" Zubeck had his back to the radio operator and turned around to give him the handset. The young blond soldier sat against the boulder with blood oozing from a hole in his forehead.

"Charlie!"

A bullet careened off the boulder just above Zubeck's head, stinging him with fragments. The NVA were moving higher on the slope so they could fire down at them. Zubeck knew it was only a matter of time before grenades would come in. He jumped up and ran for the cave entrance. Bullets slammed into the rock all around him as he dived in head first. He spun around and yelled over the incoming fire, *"Move back to the cave!"*

Only two of his men heard him. The rest were dead.

Jenkins and Burris were in a shallow depression they had dug out behind a trunk-size boulder. They'd been the ones who blew the first Claymores. Jenkins peered around the protective rock and ducked back. "Throw a smoke to the right and they won't see us," he said.

Burris pulled a smoke grenade from his webbed belt and threw it. It seemed to take forever for the red cloud to mushroom and spread.

"Go!" yelled Jenkins, hopping up and firing his M-16.

Burris broke for the cave, jumping over rocks like a hurdler. Jenkins followed. The NVA on the slope, unable to see their targets, threw grenades in the general direction of the boulders. Explosions threw up gravel and rock chips like deadly shrapnel.

Jenkins buckled over, screaming in agony. He'd been hit in the legs and stomach. Burris turned around to help, only to be blown backward, mortally wounded in the legs and chest.

Zubeck cried "Nooo!" as he saw Burris fall.

Quy's men attacked. Zubeck heard their shouts and readied his CAR-15. His first target appeared out of the red smoke only ten feet away. He fired and swung his rifle toward another screaming attacker.

The gunship pilot called again. "Zulu-One, Zulu-One, this is Ghost Rider, Two Zero. Over."

The helicopter passed over the stream at eighty knots, but didn't fire. He couldn't shoot unless he knew where the enemy was in relation to the team's position.

The door gunner yelled into the intercom, "Jesus, dinks are all over down there!"

"You see any friendlies?" asked the exasperated pilot.

"Negative, just dinks! Jesus, they're all over the rocks."

The pilot pulled up as he called the gunships behind him. "No friendlies. Dinks in the open along the stream. Get em!"

The second chopper streaked in, firing its mini-guns. *Burrrrrrrp! Burrrrrrrp!*

Quy lay balled up on the bank. The machine gun bullets churned the stream into a muddy froth. Water dripped from the bamboo. Screams of pain came from the direction of the boulders, but were quickly masked by the other helicopter's beating blades as it bore down on its target.

Zubeck lay in the floor of the cave, wounded in the back by a ricocheting bullet. He couldn't move his arms or legs. His head was cocked and frozen at an odd angle, looking out of the entrance. The second machine gun pass went unheard by him. He couldn't hear anymore. An image appeared in front of him, a figure of a small man raising a rifle.

Quy heard a single muffled shot from the boulders and stopped crawling. He hadn't thought any of his men could have survived the air attack. He called out to his platoon to report. Across the stream and in the forest along the slope, he heard many voices respond. He gritted his teeth in a cruel smile. His platoon was still intact.

26

They don't answer the radio and Ghost Rider gunships report enemy in the cave area. We must assume Zubeck's team is KIA'd or captured. Wade's team has been notified and has moved back to patrol base in rocks above NVA camp. They report they are in a good defensive position, but have one WIA. They have seen no activity since initial attack. Over."

Childs bent over the radio mike. "Roger, Three Alfa, what is air support status? Over."

"I have a set of F-4s with a forward air controller and one set of Star Blazer gunships. Ghost Rider Guns are returning to rearm. Star Blazers have ten minutes more of station time before they have to refuel. Will need additional gun support ASAP. Over."

Childs looked up at Shane. "We gotta get 'em out now before it's too late."

Shane grabbed the mike. "Three Alfa, this is Six. Have Three-one mark their location and bring in the F-4s to blow an LZ on top of the ridge. A Slick will follow for extraction. Over."

"Wilco, Six, out."

Shane set the mike down and shut his eyes. Come on guys, get outta there . . . you gotta make it.

Wade held the radio handset to his ear, listening to Lieutenant Foley, as the team frantically piled up large rocks and dug in around the boulders for more protection.

377

Foley told Wade the gunships reported seeing the dinks leave the stream and head in his direction, but they had disappeared under the thick canopy. Wade knew the F-4s' bombs would kill some of the approaching enemy but not all. It would be too risky to blow the LZ to the north. He keyed the handset. "Three Alfa, I'm gonna have the F-4s make their drop three hundred meters south of my location on top of ridge. Have Slick ready to come in."

Rose crawled back into the boulders after setting up the Claymores and, as he started digging, mumbled, "Them gooks fucked up big-time, man. They messin' with the Rose."

Thumper tried to make Lieutenant Gibson sit back against the boulder and rest, but he insisted on keeping his position and watching the trail. Thumper knew the pain must have been terrible for him, but didn't dare give him morphine. When they ran for the chopper, they couldn't afford to carry anyone.

Tears streamed down the lieutenant's face as he rocked back and forth, trying to keep his eyes on the trail. His jaw ached so badly that he felt as if it might explode. He dug his hands into the plastic stock of his CAR-15 and stifled a scream inside himself.

Wade pulled out a smoke grenade and called the forward air controller's call sign that Foley had given him. The Air Force FAC responded immediately. "This is Pretty Bird, Five-zero. Go."

"Pretty Bird, am popping smoke, now. From smoke make drop three hundred meters due south on top of ridge. Over."

Wade tossed the smoke canister as the pilot answered, "Roger."

Colonel Sy and a corporal carrying a radio stepped over the wounded as they approached the general, who sat propped up against the outcrop wall.

Sy knelt down and patted the old man's hand. "We will carry you out soon."

The general's eyes were sunken, and his face drawn.

He looked as if he'd aged twenty years in the past twenty minutes. His wounds had been tended, but he needed serious medical attention—medical attention he knew he would never receive in time. His eyes told Sy this as he whispered, "What is the situation?"

Sy lowered his head. "The Thirty-ninth and Forty-second are finished. There are some survivors, but the numbers won't reach a hundred. The Thirty-third has sent two companies to help the wounded. Here, at the Headquarters, we have twelve dead and sixteen wounded."

Sy looked up at the general. "A platoon from the Thirty-third engaged a small American force by the stream and killed them all. Another platoon has joined them, and they are now beginning to search the mountain behind us for others."

General Duc took Sy's hand, whispering in a rasp. "Leave now. Take the wounded and fight another day."

The radioman raised the handset to his ear, hearing a call, and grabbed the colonel's shoulder. "The Third Platoon reports seeing a colored cloud on the trail behind us!"

Sy sprang up to leave but felt a tug on his trouser leg. The general was holding him and whispering again. Sy bent over to hear his words. "Let them go. The men are more important . . . you must leave now."

Sy gently pulled the old man's hand away from his leg and called for the able-bodied to pick up their weapons. The radio operator looked into the colonel's determined face with a questioning stare. "What did the general say?"

Sy glanced at his general, then at the slope behind him. "He said, 'Destroy them.'"

Senior Sergeant Chuong crawled behind the base of a huge mahogany and peered around. A yellow smoke cloud a hundred meters down the trail was billowing up toward the canopy. Chuong slid back. The American position would be located in the rocks just off the trail. He motioned his first squad leader closer and whispered, "You and the men from the Second Platoon stay here and pin the Yankees down with your gunfire. Colonel Sy has called on the radio. His men will attack up the slope in a few minutes. It will be a good diversion for us. I and the rest of the platoon will crawl along the slope and get closer. After the colonel's assault, we will follow with our own. Begin shooting when you hear the colonel's attack commence.''

The squad leader nodded and crawled back toward his men. Chuong smiled to himself as he motioned the other squads to follow him. Second Platoon leader Quy had chastised him for being too slow in binding the sergeant's leg wound at the stream, but now, *he*, the cautious one, was leading half of the Second Platoon. Yes, he was cautious and maybe even slow, but *he* was not the one lying wounded back at the stream.

The first Phantom-4 jet streaked in and released one of its 250-pounders. The bomb overshot the ridge by two hundred meters and exploded so far down into the river valley that Wade could barely hear it.

Woodpecker looked at Thumper and whispered, ''Them boys need some practice, don't they?''

The Air Force spotter plan called the second inbound fighter. ''First strike, two hundred long.''

Preacher was watching down the slope to the west when he saw two light-green-uniformed men pop up and run in a crouch over to a tree. They were only forty yards away. He was about to warn the others when he saw two more do the same thing. ''Here they come,'' he whispered loudly.

Every man looked down the slope, except Wade, who spoke angrily. ''Watch your own area, damn it! Don't shoot till you've got a target. Preacher, get me some Guns in here. Thump, the dinks will lay a base of fire to pin us down . . . probably from down the trail. When they do, pump a couple of gas rounds into 'em. Remember, everybody, wait till you have a target, and make your shots count.''

Lieutenant Gibson laid his grenades in front of him and straightened the pins as Preacher lowered the handset.

"Matt, the Guns went back to refuel. L-tee Foley says another set will be here in ten minutes."

Wade slapped the stock of his weapon angrily. "Shit!"

The second jet pulled up after releasing its bomb and began banking. The projectile crashed through the forest canopy and hit the slope one hundred meters short of the ridge. The ground shook violently, rolling over the grenades the team had laid out. Then the shock wave struck like a sudden, blistering, sixty-knot windstorm, sucking up all the air. The earshattering *barooom* left the men deaf and cringing in their shallow holes.

Colonel Sy was about to begin his assault when the bomb hit. The quaking ground knocked him over onto his radio operator. Sy quickly got to his feet and yelled for his men to attack, but even he couldn't hear his words over the racket. He shouted again and began running up the slope, waving frantically for his men to follow him. One by one, the stunned soldiers rose and came up behind him, shooting toward the rocks.

"They're attacking," Preacher yelled and sighted down the barrel of his M-16. There were six easy targets struggling up the slope directly to his front only twenty meters away. He panicked, not knowing which to shoot first. Finally, he fired at the closest attacker, knocking him down. Preacher immediately fired at the next closest. That soldier, too, fell backward, holding his chest.

When Quy's first squad leader heard the colonel's men yelling, he gave the order to fire. A barrage of bullets slammed into the boulders from the north, sending up rock chips and dirt in a gritty cloud, but Rose and Preacher were oblivious to their shooting. Facing down the slope, they were well protected by the heavy rock, and had a perfect field of fire. The attacking NVA were running and shooting wildly. They made easy targets for Rose and Preacher, who fired in short bursts, systematically mowing them down.

Thumper fired his M-79 gas canister toward the shooters to the north. The round exploded in a choking white cloud

close to the first squad leader. In seconds, the firing ceased
as the men gagged and fought to breathe.

Colonel Sy fell behind a tree and stared at his pistol.
He hadn't fired a single shot. He spun around for the radio
handset but his radioman lay five meters behind, clutching
his thigh. Deep red blood spurted up in a thick stream
between his fingers like a ruptured hose. Five more soldiers lay sprawled further back. The rest of his men were
running down the hill away from the battle. Suddenly a
cry went up that froze his blood. To his left, only twenty
paces away, a wave of men screamed and ran toward the
boulders. The Third Platoon!

Wade, Thumper, and Woodpecker were positioned facing north, so they saw the screaming men jump up only
twenty meters away to their left front. Woodpecker immediately began raking them with M-60 fire as Wade
opened up with his sub-machine gun. Thumper had just
fired another gas run down the trail and quickly inserted
a buckshot round.

Rose smiled as he picked up the Claymore detonator.
He'd placed the mines in the perfect position. He even
chuckled as he pushed down the electrical firing device.
    The lead attackers were ripped and thrown backward
by a black-brown cloud of lethal ball bearings. For an instant, there was complete silence. Then, suddenly, four
men came charging through the smoke and over the mu-
tilated dead and wounded.
    Wade raised up firing. The first soldier lifted off the
ground with the top of his head partially blown off. Thumper fired the buckshot round as Woodpecker stitched the
others. All went down jerking and twisting in a strange
death dance, but one managed to toss a grenade.
    Gibson was in the middle of the ring of boulders, chang-
ing magazines, when the bamboo-handled grenade fell beside him. He grabbed for it frantically and tossed it toward
the slope, but it exploded one foot from his hand. The air

burst sent the hot deadly fragments downward and tore into the exposed team.

Colonel Sy peered around the tree toward the rocks. A thick vapor floated in suspension over the boulder, and the smell of gunsmoke and plastic filled his nostrils. Grotesquely crumpled bodies lay in front of the American position. The attack had failed. The Third Platoon soldiers ran down the slope. Only for fifty meters were they out of view of the Americans. A sergeant stood barking for them to regroup and for the leaders to report to him.

Sy holstered his pistol and began crawling toward the sergeant. The battle was far from over.

Sergeant Quy stood shaking. He knew the attack was doomed as soon as the Yankee machine gun began firing. The first squad had failed to keep the Yankees pinned down behind the boulders. He grabbed the closest soldier and yanked him to his feet. "Go to the trail and have the first squad leader and his men report me, *now!*"

A horrible rumbling, followed suddenly by a high-pitched screeching sound, forced both men to fall to the ground. The Phantom-4 pilot was not going to miss again. He came in at five hundred feet and pulled the stick back to escape the blast of his own bomb. The top of the ridge exploded in a crunching blast.

"Bingo!" yelled the FAC pilot into the helmet transmitter, then calmed himself and spoke to the second jet as it began its attack. "Okay, Cisco Two, your buddy got a direct. Let's see you do same. Over."

The Phantom pilot snickered a "No sweat" and aligned his target.

Quy poked the shaking private lying beside him. "Go now! Get the first squad!"

Wade turned over in pain and tried to sit up. The backs of his legs, back, and buttocks were peppered in fragments. Woodpecker lay over his M-60, stunned and unable to move as Thumper rolled him over to see of he was alive.

The back of the redhead's shirt and trousers were soaked with expanding spots of red.

Preacher wasn't hit, and Rose only had a few fragments in the back of his right leg. They both crawled to the open area between the boulders to help the rest of the men. Gibson lay unconscious over Toan. The lieutenant's hand was partially amputated from the index finger to down past his little finger, and his arm was ripped open and spurting blood. Russian was on his hands and knees, patting the ground, as if searching for something.

Rose grabbed Gibson's arm and began tying a tourniquet with his parachute scarf as Preacher lifted Russian's head. The Czech had looked up just as the grenade exploded. The fragments had hit his face and chest. He was blinded by blood oozing from deep gashes in his forehead and scalp. Preacher wiped the blood away with his hand to see the damage and gagged. Russian's right eyelid was laid back, exposing a jagged fragment embedded in the eyeball. Blood and a clear jellolike substance oozed and bubbled around the fragment.

Thumper had felt no pain until he tried to change positions to help Woodpecker. Suddenly his back and legs felt as if there were burning hot marbles lodged inside the muscle. It wasn't marbles, but searing metal fragments that had ripped into him. He bent over, vomiting.

The jet's 250-pound Mark-82 hit twenty meters to the right of the other smoking crater on the ridge and exploded, shattering the silence.

Wade gritted his teeth and rolled to his side, lifting himself up after the ground quit shaking. Like Thumper, the initial shock had worn off and the gut-wrenching pain began to race through his body. He felt dizzy and nauseated, as if he had been stabbed by hot knives—all at the same time. He looked up at the others and forced himself to speak: "Report!"

The single command rang out crystal clear, like a slap. Each man fought to evaluate his wounds as if he was outside his own body. The pain, blood, smoke, and chaos were all set aside for another priority—responding to a command.

Preacher spoke first as he tore open a sterile bandage and placed it on Russian's eye. "Russian is hit in the face, blinded. I'm not hit."

Rose finished tying the tourniquet on Gibson's arm and glanced at the pool of blood under the old Montagnard's head. His neck was ripped open. "The L-tee is alive, but fucked up bad. The Yard bought it."

Thumper gritted his teeth in pain as he pulled up Woodpecker's shirt. The readhead was moaning and trying to get up. His back and legs were spotted with dark bluepurple spots where the shrapnel had embedded itself. "Me and Woody are hit in the back and legs, but. . ." He was going to say "okay," but he knew they weren't.

Wade shook his head violently to clear his thoughts and tried testing his movements. The pain was horrible but bearable. He picked up his CAR-15 and depressed the magazine release. "Back to your positions. Rose, put out the rest of the Claymores and drag some bodies up for more protection. Preacher, get me the radio."

Preacher sat Russian back against a boulder and crawled for his radio. He could hear a voice over the handset.

"Three-one, Three-one, this is Three Alfa. Over."

Preacher put the handset to his mouth. "This is Threeone. Go."

"Three-one, the Slick is inbound for your extraction. Move to LZ, *now!*"

Preacher picked up the radio and crawled over to Wade. "The Slick is inbound!"

Wade tried to stand but the effort was too painful. He knew he couldn't walk, even if he got to his feet. He fell back, looking at his men and knowing they couldn't make it. He held out his hand for the handset. "Three Alfa, this is Three-one. Over."

Foley was watching the Slick make its approach to the ridge and depressed the floor button. "This is Three Alfa, are you en route? Bird is almost there."

Wade spoke between clenched teeth. "We're . . . we're not going to make it."

Foley slammed his foot on the floor switch. He couldn't believe what he'd just heard. "What? God damn it, Wade, you gotta make it! What happened? What's the problem?"

Wade tossed the handset to Preacher. "Explain the situation. And tell him to get the Guns in here until they figure out how they're gonna get us out."

Wade crawled to Thumper and Woodpecker. "We gonna have to suck it up and hang tough."

Thumper picked up Gibson's CAR-15 and chambered a round. He looked at Woodpecker, who held up his thumb and rolled over behind his M-60.

Foley lowered his head. Preacher's report on the NVA assault and Ranger casualities made Foley feel sick, but he dutifully relayed the information to Childs.

Sergeant Quy faced his squad leaders. "We will crawl up the slope in a line. Once we are close to the boulders, all squads will fire on my command, except the first squad, which will rush the position. Third squad will follow, then fourth."

The first squad leader looked up worriedly at the canopy. "We all heard the helicopters! What do we do if the helicopters attack us?"

Quy glanced up, then stared at the corporal. "The branches are thick and will protect us. Just do your duty when the time comes. If the helicopters attack, they will not be able to see us. Their rockets will explode in the branches high above. Your only worry is the American fire." The sergeant's eyes shifted to the other leaders. "We attack in thirty minutes. This will give you time to brief your men and get into position. We move forward on my command."

Shane's jaw muscles rippled as he listened to Foley's report. Childs sat stone-faced, staring at the radio. Colonel Ellis paced back and forth and halted abruptly at the end of transmission. "Surely some of them could get out? He said some were only lightly wounded."

Shane shook his head. "They won't leave their friends."

Ellis shook his head. "I'm sorry, Ed, truly sorry."

Childs stood abruptly and walked to the corner of the room. He picked up his M-16 and looked up at the Army air liaison. "How many Slicks ya got on the airfield?"

"Three, but . . ."

"Crank 'em up!"

Ellis raised his hand, "Hold it, we can't afford any more losses. We . . ."

Childs had turned around and picked up Shane's rifle and tossed it toward his major.

Shane caught the weapon in front of the colonel's face. He spun around, facing Ellis with a scowl. "You have another suggestion, sir? You know a way to get them out?"

Ellis stammered, "Well . . . no . . . but . . . hell, let's face it. It's over. We can't send more men into a hopeless situation."

Childs strode for the door and stopped in the doorway, pointing at Ellis. "It ain't over, God damn it! It ain't never over!" He spun around and jogged up the steps, followed by Bitch.

Shane nodded at the Army pilot. "Get the birds ready. We'll be on the airfield in ten minutes."

Ellis grabbed Shane's shoulder as he began to walk for the steps. Shane turned with a look of defiance. The colonel began to speak but lowered his head and put out his hand. He raised his eyes to Shane. "Good luck."

Rose pulled the last body up and placed it on the platform he had created by laying two AK-47s across four other bodies. He'd stacked the NVA like sandbags, forming a firing port for Woodpecker. Thumper gagged. The smell of the ripped corpses was too much for him. Preacher called the gunships in for another rocket run. Preacher had put the choppers to work immediately when they had arrived a few minutes before. He was directing their fire northwest, in the direction of the retreating NVA.

Wade crawled back to Lieutenant Gibson, who was unconscious. Gibson was lucky, he thought as he inspected the dressings, lucky to be in a dreamless sleep and away from all this. Russian sat back against the boulder, with his bandaged head raised, as if listening to the forest. Wade crawled up beside him and took his hand. "Sorry about this, Carl."

Russian turned and squeezed Wade's hand. "Are you hurt, my Sergeant?"

"Only a few fragments in my ass," said Wade, trying to sound convincing.

Russian swung his head toward the valley. "They will attack in waves. They will have men shooting trying to knock out the machine gun. Do not shoot the gun until you must. Let the first wave come close and blow Claymores at the second. Throw gas then . . . it will disorient the others."

Wade listened well. His friend had more experience than the whole team combined. Russian brought his other hand up and patted Wade's arm. "The enemy cannot attack on all sides or they would shoot each other. They must attack from one direction. Stop the second wave, my Sergeant. You must."

Wade smiled through his pain. "We will, old-timer. I'm gonna get you home . . . I'm gonna get us all home. And that's a promise, you hear? A promise." He released his friend's hand and crawled to the others to pass on the defensive plan.

Childs climbed into the lead Huey and spun around to take the rucksack Pete had insisted on carrying for him. Pete grabbed Child's hand with a worried expression. "Be careful, Sarge."

Childs looked at the typist with an atypical smile and winked. "It's a piece of cake. Take care of that dumb-ass dog for me . . . and take care of yourself, kid."

Childs turned and gave the pilot a thumbs-up. The chopper lifted immediately and dipped forward to gain air speed.

The two Slicks lifted off behind the lead bird and followed. Childs leaned over to Shane and yelled over the engine noise, "We'll be there in twenty minutes. Guns are going to join us and lead us in."

Shane nodded and chambered a round into his M-16.

Childs had selected twelve men—two medics, four M-60 gunners, and six of the biggest men in the company. He needed the medics for the wounded team members, the machine gun gunners for firepower, and the big men to carry the wounded.

Foley had reported that the blown LZ on the ridge was only big enough for one bird. The first two Slicks carried the rescue force, and they would have to go in one at a time. They'd be extracted in reverse. The third empty Slick would pick up the team; the other two would retrieve the rescue force.

Childs pulled out a magazine and inserted it into his

weapon. He leaned back on the padded firewall and
thought of his wife. She'd be in the school cafeteria cleaning up after the noon meal. Her face would be flushed from
the heat of the kitchen and her hair would be tied back and
covered by a hairnet. The thought of her working made
him angry at himself. She deserved better, damn it! Her
hair was so pretty when it hung down and . . . Damn!

Colonel Sy and Sergeant Chuong walked past the line
of waiting men, talking calmly, urging them to relax, but
the effort was difficult, for three men had already been
killed and four had been wounded by rocket fragments
from the gunships. The helicopters had made passes up
and down the slope searching for their position. The gun
and rocket runs had come close, but were haphazard and
mostly ineffective.

Chuong looked at his watch and centered himself along
the ragged line of men. He lifted his arm and brought it
forward. The platoon rose and began the trek up the slope.

Preacher set down the handset with a smile. He whispered to Wade loudly enough for all the team to hear. "A
rescue force is coming in to get us out! They'll be here in
fifteen minutes!"

Wade shut his eyes to put the throbbing pain somewhere
else and raised up. "You heard it, Three-one. We gotta
hold!" He'd promised Russian—and himself—that they'd
all make it home . . . and by God, they would!

Rose pushed off the safety of his rifle and blurted,
"Fuckin' A!"

Thumper looked behind him at Gibson and Russian. His
face contorted in anger upon seeing their wounds, and he
whispered in determination, "Fuckin' A!"

Woodpecker lay beside his M-60, holding a rifle. He let
the bolt slam forward and nodded to himself as he spoke,
"Fuckin' A!"

Russian lifted his head with a quick "Fuckin' A!" as
Preacher finished his prayer asking for forgiveness for what

he was about to say. He looked down the slope and raised
his rifle. "Fuckin' A, brothers!"

Chuong could just barely see the boulders on the ridge
and lowered himself to his knees. He turned to face his
men and raised the hinged bayonet on his AK-47 to its
extended position.

The line of men all sunk to their knees and followed
their leader's example, locking their bayonets for close
combat.

Chuong motioned them forward and began to crawl.

Rose's eyes darted back and forth. He knew the NVA
were close. He *felt* them. He turned over and whispered,
"They're comin'!"

Preacher picked up the handset and directed the Guns
to make a pass in front of their position. He knew Rose
too well to doubt his instincts.

The lead gunship banked hard right and lowered its
nose.

Chuong crawled a few feet toward the boulders just
ahead, then raised his rifle. The men behind him crawled
up and got in position. The sound of the attacking helicopter unnerved a few of them, who flattened themselves
as minigun bullets ripped through the canopy above.

Chuong raised up, ignoring the helicopter, and yelled,
"Fire!"

Wade and the team stayed hidden as the bullets tore
into the battle-scarred boulders and NVA bodies. Wade
was waiting for a change in the tempo of firing and yelling
that would signal an assault. He and the others had all
pulled pins on grenades and held the spoons down, waiting.

Suddenly the fire decreased, and the soldiers of the first
squad jumped to their feet, cried out at the top of their
voices, and began their assault.

Wade judged their voices to be twenty yards away and
closing fast. He counted aloud, *"One . . . Two . . . Three
. . . Now!"*

Each man tossed his grenade over the boulder and readied his weapon.

The first squad leader was only a few feet away when a succession of explosions threw him forward into the rocks. He hit his shoulder and fell back. His shirt was ripped open and his intestines were bubbling out up from a gash in his stomach. Screaming, he grabbed at the slimy pink flesh as Woodpecker rolled into position. Woodpecker fired point blank at the soldier's face, ending his agony. Two men lying wounded among the dead tried to get up when Wade and Thumper rolled over and fired. The two NVA fell back into silence.

A second wave of men fired from the hip and ran toward the boulders. Woodpecker dropped the M-16 and got behind his M-60. He aimed low and pulled the trigger. The first three men fell, shot first in the legs and then hit again, this time in the face and shoulders. Now Wade's weapon was empty. He grabbed for another magazine as Thumper fired a burst into the chest of a charging soldier. Thumper saw the red glow from the last bullets as they disappeared into the falling man and knew his own gun was empty— he always loaded tracers last to signal the end of the magazine.

Two remaining NVA ran up to the boulders, firing steadily. One of them jumped to the top of a rock and fired into the first target he saw. Russian jerked back, struck in the chest, and toppled over.

"No!" screamed Wade in anguish as the NVA soldier swung his weapon and fired the last of his ammunition into Gibson and the body of Toan.

Wade forgot his wounds and yanked the pistol from his shoulder holster. He screamed as he raised it up, viciously jabbed the barrel into the startled NVA's side, and fired. The small Vietnamese was blown off the rock by the deadly blast. The second NVA lunged forward with his bayonetted rifle. The long, narrow blade struck Wade in the left side, deflected off his rib, and sunk in three inches below his breast, just missing his lung. Wade fell back with the

momentum of the thrust but raised his pistol and fired
point-blank into the NVA's screaming face.

The third wave was avoiding the M-60 fire by running
up the slope toward Preacher and Rose. Rose waited for
them to get a little closer and blew the last of the Claymores. Preacher fired at two men who had run past the
mines and were about to toss grenades. The first man had
pulled the firing wire and was about to throw when his
right eye disappeared and the back of his head blew out.
He fell beside his primed grenade, never knowing it blew
his comrade's legs out from under him. Preacher raised up
and put a bullet into the squirming man's head.

Woodpecker and Thumper threw gas, as they'd
planned, and waited for the fourth wave, but it didn't come.

The gas and failed attacks had demoralized the remaining men—except for Sergeant Chuong, who stood in the
white cloud, with tears running down his face, coughing
and yelling for his men to continue the attack.

Colonel Sy, following the soldiers as they ran down the
slope in search of protection, slowed to a walk and looked
over his shoulder at the pathetic sergeant. His general had
been right; they must survive to fight another day.

Rose raised up cautiously and looked behind him.
Preacher was kneeling in a pool of blood beside Russian.
Wade lay on his stomach with his arm outstretched, hold-
ing the dead Czech's hand. "Carl? Carl, you'll be okay.
I'm gonna get you home. We're gonna make it."

Thumper checked Gibson's neck for a pulse and closed
his eyes. Despite the bullets that had struck him in the
stomach and side, the young officer was somehow still
alive.

Rose was taking a step to help Thumper when a shot
rang out. Rose stumbled forward, grabbing at his back,
and fell in front of Preacher. Woodpecker screamed,
"Motherfucker!" and swung the M-60, firing at the running
NVA who had jumped up from behind a tree. The soldier

zigzagged down the slope followed by the red tracers of the 60 and dived for cover out of sight.

Rose lay on his stomach, looking up with a strange grin at Preacher and spoke in a tired voice: "They got the Rose, man."

Preacher grabbed his friend and rolled him over. He tore open his shirt, "No. God. No!" Frantically he put his hand over the one-inch exit hole to stop the blood flow.

Rose rolled his head back and forth along the ground, shaking violently. "Preacher . . . Preacher, pray for me. Pray for . . ." He stopped shaking.

The tears that streamed down Preacher's face left trails in the grime on his cheeks. He tore at the plastic of a sterile bandage. His hands shook as he looked at Rose's still face. It was no use. His friend was dead. The bandage fell from his hands as he fulfilled Rose's last request and began to pray for him.

Thumper eased Wade over on his back to check his bayonet wound, but the sergeant brushed the big man's hand away. He rolled his head to the side and looked at Russian and Rose. "They're gonna make it, aren't they?"

Thumper shut his eyes and shook his head. "They're gone, Matt."

Wade frantically broke from the big soldier's grasp and hugged Russian's lifeless body. "*No*, they can't die! I promised! I . . . I *promised*."

Thumper lowered his eyes. There was nothing he could do or say. His sergeant was delirious with pain and couldn't be reasoned with.

Wade rocked Russian's body back and forth. "You'll be okay, Carl. You and Rose are gonna make it."

Chuong ran down the slope to the group of remaining men who stood in groups beside the wounded. "There are only a few Yankees left. I shot one as he stood up! We can take them now!"

Colonel Sy stepped forward. "No, it is over! We must help the wounded and leave!"

Chuong spun around, facing his men. "The Yankees

killed your comrades. Can you let their deaths go una-
venged? The Yankees are finished, they . . .'' Chuong
stopped in mid-sentence; a large group of soldiers was approaching. He recognized the first man immediately. It was
his company commander, Captain Trung.

The sweat-soaked officer saluted Colonel Sy and motioned behind him. "The regiment commander has sent us
to help destroy the Yankees."

Colonel Sy shook his head. "No, captain, enough have
died. You must help the wounded and leave the fortress."

Captain Trung glared at the colonel. "My regiment commander has ordered me. You do not have the authority to
change his orders." Trung's eyes shifted from the colonel
to Sergeant Chuong. "Where are the Yankees?"

Preacher raised his hand to his face and ran two blood-
covered fingers down his cheek. The blood was Rose's.
He dipped his hand into the sticky pool beside Russian and
made two more streaks down his other cheek. Reaching
out, he touched both of his friends and began the Fallen
Warrior's Chant of his ancestors. The spirits of the two
men would join as they made their long journey. They
would be together as warriors should be. Together forever,
they would be honored by countless other fighters who
would understand that their deaths had meaning.

At hearing the sorrowful chant, Woodpecker turned
painfully and lowered his gaze to the small Indian. He
turned to face the trail again, sniffing back his tears, and
began humming along.

Colonel Sy walked to the outcrop and stood over the
general. The Tall One was dead, but his face showed no
sign that he had suffered pain in those last moments. Sy
felt strangely relieved for the old man. The awesome responsibility that the general had endured for so many years
was finally over.

Sy pulled a ground cloth over the body and walked over
to Private Nuu, who was lying beside the rock wall. The
colonel knelt down and took the boy's hand.

"You must be strong and endure a little longer. I have ordered the evacuation. Soon we will be leaving and will find you medical help. I'm sorry we have nothing to give you for the pain."

Nuu's face was flushed and his jaw taut from clenching his teeth. He looked up at the colonel and spoke with tears in his eyes. "Is there a victory for us . . . an end?"

Sy looked at the bodies and wounded lying about him and thought of the soldiers lying still on the ridge. He could hardly bear to look at the young man as he shook his head. "For the soldier, there is no victory, there is only survival."

The wind from the helicopter's rotor kicked up a dust cloud as the big machine lowered onto the ridge. Childs jumped out first. Shane and the others followed. They ran a few yards and got down to wait for the next bird.

Childs brought the handset up. "Three-one, this is Rescue-one. Over."

Thumper picked up the radio. "This is Three-one. Go."

Childs turned his head to avoid the biting dirt kicked up by the approaching second Slick and spoke quickly. "We're on the ground and on the way. Hang tough, Ranger!"

Captain Trang had brought the first platoon with him. Combining his troops with those remaining of the Second and Third Platoons, he had forty-three men for the attack. He heard from Sergeant Chuong how the past attacks had failed and decided to place his two machine guns on the trail to the north. He would have them fire as his soldiers crawled forward. There would be no charge. He wouldn't expose any of his men until they were almost on top of the Yankees' position. He motioned for the machine gunners to move into position and waved his troops forward.

Wade lay on his side, still holding Russian's hand. Preacher had cut off Wade's shirt to bandage the bayonet wound, but instead decided to place the compress over a fragmentation wound that was still bleeding. Wade's pants were soaked with blood from the frag wounds in his buttocks and legs. None of the wounds by itself could kill him, but Preacher worried his sergeant might die of blood loss from the combination of all of them.

Thumper wasn't better off. His body was so stiff he could barely move his arms without shuddering in pain. And Woodpecker bit down on a rolled-up portion of his parachute scarf, his eyes watering in silent agony. Preacher had just finished checking Woodpecker's wounds when he heard a shout that made him shut his eyes in relief and thank his savior.

"Rangers comin' in!"

Two 60 gunners ran up to the boulders and took up positions beside the rocks. Then Childs stepped into the opening between the boulders, and the sight and smell before him seared into his brain forever. The small open area in the center of rock formation was carpeted in shell casings, strewn equipment, blood, vomit, and his dead and wounded Rangers, covered in gritty rock dust and splattered with blood. The staring eyes of the survivors were distant and emotionless.

Childs took two steps forward, as if entering hallowed ground, and knelt by Rose and Russian. The smell of blood was overpowering. Wade looked up. "Get Carl to a doctor," he said. "He'll be okay if he gets to a doctor."

Shane ran up with the others and put his hand on Childs's shoulder. "Come on, Jerry, let's get 'em home."

Childs stood abruptly and barked, "Litter teams pick 'em up and move out! Security teams move into their old positions and keep an eye out!"

Shane looked away from his wounded men, feeling sick. In front of their position NVA bodies were stacked and sprawled. He'd never envisioned anything like this. The sight before him was beyond imagination.

Shane shivered and began to turn around when a bullet cracked by his head. A second tore through his ear and grazed the back of his head. He fell backward behind the protection of the chipped and scarred boulders just as the other enemy machine gun opened up. All four of the security team's machine guns returned fire, spewing out a curtain of red tracers down the trail.

Childs and the men carrying the wounded were lying on the trail on the other side of the boulders. Childs, realizing the big rocks were blocking the fire, rose up and yelled out, "Move it! Keep going!"

He grabbed the handset in his leg pocket. "Rescue Flight lead, this is Rescue Ground. Bring in the Slicks. We've picked up wounded, and we're proceeding to LZ. Break, Gun lead, we're under fire and need support to disengage. I'm marking our position with pen gun flare. Enemy located north of our position, fifty meters."

Childs took out the small black cylinder from his shirt pocket and screwed in a red cartridge. He pointed the device toward a gap in the tree limbs high overhead and pushed the spring-loaded firing-pin knob with his thumb. *Psssssst!* The flare burst a hundred meters directly above him.

Preacher had remained in position at the boulders as the Rangers picked up his team. He would stay until his friends were safe on board the chopper. When he saw Shane fall, he crawled over to him to check his wounds. The major sat shaking his head, trying to stop the spinning sensation. Preacher lifted his head and inspected the damage. Shane had lost a piece of his lobe and had a narrow gash on the back of his head where the bullet had grazed him. Bright red blood from the ear wound cascaded down his neck. He was stunned but alright.

Shane shook his head again and brushed Preacher's hands away. He spun around just as Childs crawled back into the boulders. "The wounded?" he asked the sergeant.

Childs threw his head toward the trail. "They're moving them to the bird. What the hell happened to you?"

Shane frowned as if embarrassed. "Never mind. Ya got Guns coming in?"

Childs nodded and crawled up behind the gunners. They had ceased fire, as had the NVA guns.

"When the gunships make their run, you men back out

and haul your ass outta here back to the LZ! You," he pointed to the closest gunner, "leave your gun and ammo. I'll fire a belt to cover your butts, then catch up."

Shane sat up about to protest when the lead gunship streaked overhead and unleashed four rockets.

Childs yelled, "Move it!"

The four Rangers jumped up and began running as the rockets exploded in the canopy.

Shane began to crawl toward Childs, but the sergeant pointed viciously at Preacher. "Get the major out of here, Indian! *Now!*"

The miniguns of the second gunship rattled overhead, sending a barrage of bullets into the forest.

Preacher grabbed Shane's arm and yanked him up. Shane felt dizzy and fell back to his knees. Preacher pulled him up again. "Come on, sir, move your feet!"

Captain Trung had halted his men when he heard the four machine guns open up from the American position. Sergeant Chuong had told them there was only one. He was not about to move forward into a bee's nest. The close rocket and machine gun passes by the gunships had solidified his decision not to proceed with the attack, but then he heard a yell and saw Chuong rise up, shooting. The remaining men of Second Platoon hadn't seen him wave to get them down and were continuing the attack.

Trung yelled to his men to stand fast and turned to watch the slaughter.

Childs sighted over the 60 and pulled the trigger. Three of the nine attacking men went down in a single long burst. Childs swung the barrel slightly and fired another burst when the gun jammed. He yanked a grenade from his harness and pulled the pin, then crawled backward and tossed the grenade toward the rushing NVA. He saw Woodpecker's 60 to his right and jumped for it as the grenade exploded.

Chuong was knocked down by the man in front of him, who took most of the shrapnel, but three more of his men

were still on their feet and almost to the boulder. Chuong
jumped up and ran screaming to join them.

Childs raised up from behind the boulders firing the 60
from the hip. The surprised attackers were riddled only a
few feet from the smoking barrel. Childs saw the last man
coming from a few yards farther back and pulled the trigger. Nothing happened; it was empty.

Chuong lowered his rifle, about to fire, when his head
snapped back from the impact of an M-16 bullet hitting just
below his nose and crashing through his brain.

Childs spun around. Preacher, twenty feet behind him,
was lowering his rifle. He'd taken the major up the trail,
where he ran into three Rangers. Everyone had been lifted
out, and the last bird was sitting on the LZ waiting. The
three ran back to see if they could help. Shane took one
of them, and the other two followed Preacher, who went
for Childs. Preacher outran the men and had arrived just
as Childs fired the last of his ammo.

Childs broke into a run toward Preacher, but he had
barely made two steps when he was almost cut in two by
a fusillade of bullets. The old veteran felt no pain as his
riddled body crumpled to the ground.

Captain Trung had ordered his men to attack as soon
as it became apparent that only one man held the position.
The lead attackers swarmed over the rocks after Preacher
as he bolted down the trail yelling for the other two Rangers, still forty yards off, to turn and run.

Preacher dropped his rifle and sprinted as fast as he
could. He'd run a lot of races under pressure, but never
for his life. Bullets cracked by his ear, but he never broke
stride as he churned his arms and legs for all they were
worth.

Shane jumped out of the vibrating helicopter when he
caught sight of two Rangers running toward him. He
couldn't hear over the chopper's screaming engine, but he
knew by their expressions and pace that they were taking
fire. He then saw Preacher. The Indian's mouth was open
and dirt was kicking up around him from bullet strikes.

Preacher could see the helicopter a hundred meters

ahead. The sight of the bird was all the incentive he needed. He strained with all his might, tapping his last reserve of energy. The trees and trail became a blur as he pushed his body to the limit. Suddenly he felt shoved forward, as if by a giant blow to his lower back. A tingling sensation spread through him and he began falling forward. The ground seemed to leap toward his face so quickly that there was no time to raise his hands to protect himself. He slammed into the dirt headfirst and everything turned black and cold.

Shane saw the Indian fall and ran toward him just as the gunship passed overhead, firing. The trail behind Preacher disappeared in a succession of explosions that sent up clouds of smoke and debris.

Shane grabbed the unconscious soldier, threw him over his shoulder, and began running. He slowed twice to look back for Childs. A Ranger met him halfway and took Preacher.

"Where is Childs?" yelled Shane as the Ranger began running.

"Dead." The young Ranger didn't look back.

Shane suddenly felt tired and weak. He began to jog slowly. He didn't care anymore if he made it or not. The second Ranger screamed for him to hurry, then cursed and ran after him. Shane slowed to a walk and looked back once, hoping his friend would appear miraculously. The Ranger grabbed his arm and pulled him toward the bird. Suddenly, Shane screamed, "Jer-reeee!"

Shane stood against the wall of the emergency room as an orderly cut Preacher's shirt away and started on his trousers. Nearby, Wade, Woodpecker, and Thumper, all nude, lay face down on gurneys with their arms attached to IV tubes. Their blood-stained clothes were scattered on the floor. Lieutenant Gibson was on a table in the back of the room. A doctor and an assisting nurse feverishly worked on him, while another doctor with blood stains on the front of his green smock leaned over Wade, tying off a bleeder in a deep wound just below his buttocks.

Wade's doctor looked up at his assistant. "That's all we can do for him. Get me another set of gloves for the last one."

The doctor pulled off his bloody rubber gloves and turned to Preacher. He stared at the back wound as he raised his hands to receive fresh gloves from the orderly. The doctor leaned closer and placed a finger next to the bullet wound. "Looks like a fragment of a ricocheting bullet; too close to the spinal cord for me to screw with. Start IV with ringers and send him with the others."

An orderly took Shane's arm and led him to a nearby stool to begin cleaning his head wound.

"You're the lucky one of the bunch, aren't ya?"

Shane looked up at the freckle-face Spec-4 with a questioning stare. "What are they going to do with my men?"

The orderly realized the major wasn't feeling so lucky and erased his grin. "Sir, they'll be med-evaced to Sixty-first Med at Cam Ranh. The surgeons there will take out the shrapnel, then they'll be sent on to Japan."

"What about Gibson?"

"Who?"

"The lieutenant, over there. What about him?"

"He's pretty bad off, sir. The stomach wound messed him up and he lost a lotta blood. Doc Little is doing the best he can."

The doctor with the blood-stained smock walked over and inspected Shane's head wounds.

"Uh huh . . . Well, major, you'd better sit back. Looks like I've got some sewing to do. Why don't you give the orderly here your unit phone number, and he'll call and have someone pick you up."

Shane looked up at the doctor. "Are they going to make it?"

The doctor took a needle from the orderly. "The three with the shrapnel wounds will be all right. The small man with the bullet in the back may be in trouble. The bullet is lodged close to the spine. It depends on the surgery whether he walks again. The lieutenant has a fifty-fifty chance. Sit back now; this is gonna sting a bit."

Colonel Ellis had called for a chopper and flown to Nha Trang as soon as he'd heard the last situation report from Lieutenant Foley. Ellis had arrived at Corps Headquarters and briefed General Wayland on the operation for several minutes.

"And the B-52's bombs hit the main camp at 1400 hours. The Rangers located at the eastern end of the valley then attacked the NVA Headquarters and shot General Duc. They had difficulty in disengaging and . . . "

General Wayland stood up abruptly. "Excellent! This ought to make Region sit up and take notice of this Corps! Put this report in briefing format and have it on my desk in an hour. I'll fly to Saigon and personally give it to General Abrams."

Colonel Ellis coughed and stepped closer to gain the general's attention again, but Wayland turned to his G-1.

"Charles, have a photographer ready to go up with me and . . . "

"Sir!" said Ellis loudly.

The general eyed his G-2 coldly. He did not like being interrupted. "Yes, what is it?"

"Sir, I think you should fly to An Lom and personally thank the Rangers."

Wayland shook his head and began to walk for the door. "I don't have time for that. Draft me a letter of appreciation and give them some awards."

Ellis shook with anger. He restrained himself from yelling, but his voice still rang out forcefully.

"Sir, don't you want to know the Ranger casualties?"

The general paused in the doorway. "Put it in a follow-up report. And Colonel . . . after you finish writing the briefing, get some rest. You look terrible." Wayland walked out the door, followed by his aide.

Colonel Ellis lowered his head, feeling defeated.

Colonel Wright, the portly G-1, smiled smugly and stood up. "It doesn't matter about the Ranger losses. We won't replace them anyway. While you were playing hero in An Lom, we received a new list of units to be deactivated for the draw-down. It seems your Rangers aren't needed anymore."

Ellis jerked his head up. "What?"

"Yes, colonel, your prima donnas are being deactivated effective within a few months. You can call the Ranger commander and tell him it's all over."

Ellis stared past the pudgy colonel, thinking of the last words sergeant Childs had spoken to him. Ellis's eyes shifted to the colonel in a cutting stare. "You're wrong, asshole. It ain't never over."

Pete sat on the jeep hood outside the Phan Thiet Emergency Room, waiting for his major. He was watching the sun sink behind the distant mountains. Somewhere in those mountains was the body of a man he respected and cared for very much. The grizzled sergeant had been gruff at times, but he knew Childs had liked him just by the little things the sergeant had done—a look, a pat, a small conversation now and then all told Pete that Childs had respected him.

The door of the emergency room swung open and Shane walked out. The right side of his head was bandaged. Pete hopped off the hood with a look of concern. "You okay, sir?"

Shane headed straight for the jeep and climbed into the front seat. "Get me outta here."

Pete jumped in quickly and started the engine. He glanced at Shane, wanting to say how sorry he was, but the major was obviously upset. Pete pulled away from the curb and shifted to second gear.

Shane closed his eyes. He wanted to be away from everything and everybody. He wanted to be in a place where he could sort his feelings and find some reason behind life's absurdity.

Forty minutes later the jeep's lights shone on the camp. A large group of Rangers was waiting to see how their leader was. Shane didn't seem to notice. He pointed ahead to the operations center and spoke for the first time since leaving the hospital. "Drop me off at the TOC."

Pete pulled up beside the deserted operations center. Shane hopped out, walked down the darkened steps, and slammed the door behind him.

The waiting Rangers gathered around Pete as he stepped out of the jeep. "How is he?"

"Is he hurt bad?"

"How's he takin' it?"

"What'd he say?"

"How're the wounded doin'?"

Pete shook his head in silence at their questions and walked toward the orderly room to pick up the letter Childs had given him a few days before. The sergeant had come into the office and looked around to see if anybody else was there. He had spoken as if embarrassed, and then had thrown the letter on the desk. "Pete, put that away in a safe place and give it to the ol' man if somethin' happens to me."

Pete had looked up as if he hadn't understood. Childs had leaned over the desk and scooted the letter closer to him. "Look, Pete, this whole operation is fucked up. Just put the damn thing away just in case. Don't ask me no questions and don't say nothing to nobody, okay?"

"Okay, Sarge."

The vision of the incident faded as Pete opened the orderly room door and walked toward the desk.

Shane sat staring at the silent radio. He was finally alone. His head throbbed, but the pain was just reward for ordering the damn mission—a mission that had killed nine of his men, one of them a special friend.

The TOC door opened and Pete walked in. "I'm sorry to bother you, sir, but I was supposed to give you this."

Shane wanted to scream, "Get out!" but clenched his teeth, restraining himself as Pete held a letter out to him. Shane grabbed the letter without looking at it and tossed it on the desk. The clerk stood in front of him without moving. Shane looked up and saw tears running down the young man's face as he fought to speak.

"Sa . . . Sir, Sergeant Childs gave the letter to me to give to you in case something . . . something . . . " Pete couldn't bring himself to say anymore.

Shane stood up and put his hand on the clerk's shoulder. "I understand, son. Thank you."

Pete turned to leave, but spun back around. "Sir, we're getting him out of there aren't we? We're bringing them all back?"

Shane's eyes widened. He hadn't thought of a recovery mission. He hadn't thought of anything but his self-pity at Childs's loss. He straightened his back and patted Pete's arm. "Yeah, we're going to bring them back. Get me the liaisons, Sergeant Gino, and the radio operator. Have them report to me here in ten minutes."

Pete looked up into his major's face with determination. "I volunteer to go, sir. The whole company has volunteered."

Shane cracked a small smile, envisioning the slight, bespectacled clerk carrying a rucksack and weapon, but nodded. "Sure, son, you can go. Now get the men."

Pete ran for the steps as Shane picked up the letter and sat down. The envelope had a stained water ring on its front. Probably a beer can ring, knowing Childs, he thought. Shane closed his eyes for a moment to gain strength for what had to be done, then ripped the end of the envelope open and pulled out the folded single page of yellow tablet paper. Taking a deep breath, he began reading.

Ed,
   I never wrote a letter like this one and it ain't easy for me. I have drank three beers and started this damn thing four times, but fuck it, here goes. Ed, if you read this I got wasted. I'm writing this 'cause we are friends and I know you'll do something that is very very important to me. Ed, write my old lady and tell her we used to talk a lot about home. Tell her I talked about her a lot. I know we didn't but I should have and it bothers me that I didn't. My old lady is the best. I have thought about her more in the last few weeks than I ever have when I been away. Ed, she needs to know I really cared. I didn't write much and that bothers me bad. Write her, Ed. Please.
   One more thing. 'Cause we was friends, I know you are feeling bad readin' this. Don't. Hell, I'm going out as a Ranger, like you know deep inside the way you wanna go. You got a company to run. Get your head up and Charlie Mike. Charlie Mike and take care of my Rangers.

Respectively
Jerry Childs

P.S. Make sure Russian takes care of that dumb-ass dog.

Tears fell on the paper as Shane reread the letter. He

THE LAST RUN

knew that he had been wrong. His friend wouldn't be gone forever. Jerry Childs would always be with him and in the memories of every Ranger he had ever taught.

Shane felt a nudge on his leg and looked down. Bitch had walked into the TOC and sat under the desk. She lowered her head and brushed up against his leg, again wanting a pat. Shane kneeled on the floor and hugged the surprised dog. He hugged her tightly, like he wished he had done to his friend just once.

Thumper felt the dull throbbing coming back. He'd been in the Camp Zama, Japan, hospital for eight days and knew the feeling all too well, but this time they wouldn't give him a shot of pain killer. His last shot had been given four hours before, and Miss Pisser had proclaimed there would be no more.

Thumper raised his head to see Woodpecker in the next bed. The redhead was lying on his stomach, with scattered bandages over his back and legs. Most of the fragments had been close to the surface and had been easily pulled out and closed by stitches. A few, however, had gone deep and required cutting out along with damaged tissue. The deep wounds, left open to form their own scar tissue, were the most painful.

"Hey, Woody, looks like Miss Pisser meant what she said about no more shots."

"Man, I was diggin' on the high, too. You think Pisser would bitch if we asked for aspirin?"

"Naw, I'll scream in a minute and get her attention."

Woodpecker raised up to his elbows and looked over his shoulder at Wade's bed across the aisle and five beds down. The sergeant lay on his side, facing away from them.

Woodpecker sighed and lay back down. "Matt has got to snap out of it, man. The shrink has seen him more than Miss Pisser or Doc."

"You calling me names again, Specialist Stecker?" A petite, blond first lieutenant nurse wearing white uniform, stockings, shoes, starched cap, and a scowl stood with her hands on her hips at the foot of Woodpecker's bed.

Woodpecker rolled his eyes. "Aw, hell, ma'am, I didn't hear you draggin' your chains like you usually do. Ya gonna beat me and big guy again?"

"The name is Lieutenant Pisa, Specialist Stecker. I would appreciate it if you and Specialist Meeks would refrain from the colorful nicknames and any innuendos that my medical care is less than superb."

"Sure, ma'am. How 'bout a steak, French fries, and a shot of su-perb painkiller?"

Thumper quickly added, "Or lobster tail, salad, and a couple of painkilling beers?"

The nurse's scowl dissolved into a genuine smile. "Well, well, food is on your mind for a change! That's a good sign. There *is* progress in the pits. What shall we have today? Liver or chicken cacciatore?"

Thumper made a face at the selection. "Just give me C rats."

Woodpecker nodded. "Yeah, I'll take a beef and rice lurp."

Lieutenant Pisa stepped in between their beds and nodded her head toward Wade. "You guys are a pain, but I'd give a month's pay for your sergeant to bitch or complain at me just once."

Thumper and Woodpecker exchanged worried glances.

"How's he doin'?" asked Thumper.

The nurse let out a sigh. "He's a little worse off than you two complainers, but it's his mental state that is slowing down his healing. He's been off the shots for two days and hasn't once asked for anything. It's like he's taking the pain inside and feeding on it."

"Move him over here next to us so we can talk to him," said Woodpecker.

"We can't. Depression is just as contagious as infection. Besides, he doesn't talk to you now, does he?"

"No, but . . . "

"We're moving him to the south wing in a few minutes. Oh, I have some good news for you two. Your friend Private First Class Black Eagle's surgery was a success. They got the bullet out without much nerve damage and it looks like in time he may walk again.''

Thumper and Woodpecker both smiled half-heartedly. The news was good, but it still implied Preacher had a long way to go.

"How about Lieutenant Gibson, ma'am. You heard how's he doin'?" asked Thumper.

"Nothing more than I told you yesterday. He lost about three feet of small intestine and will be shipped to Walter Reed today or tomorrow. . . . Well, I hate to leave such terrible company, but it's time for me to talk with your sergeant. Wish me luck, huh?"

The nurse marched straight for Wade's bed as if into battle. "How are we feeling today, Sergeant Wade?"

Wade's eyes shifted slowly up toward her, but he didn't speak.

"Sergeant, I spoke to you and would appreciate a response."

Wade's eyes showed no expression. "I'm fine, ma'am."

"Good. Well, I brought you something. Will you lift your head, please?"

Wade lifted his head as instructed. The nurse reached in her pocket and pulled out the gold chain Ginny had given him. "I got this from your personal belongings . . . thought you'd like to have it." She slipped the chain over his head.

Wade lay back again without changing his expression. The nurse had hoped for a glimmer or sign of recognition, but there was nothing. He had held that same look ever since coming into the ward.

The nurse pressed the button on the wall above his head. An orderly stuck his head out of the office at the end of the hall, and she waved him toward her.

"Wade, we're moving you to the south wing." She bent over and unlocked the bed rollers and began to pull his bed away from the wall, but stopped and stared into his eyes. "You know, your friends care about you very much. They're worried about you. I know you don't care, but for their sake, please say something to them. They need to know you're okay. They'll be leaving in a few days for the

States and you'll probably never see them again after you
leave this ward. I'll push you down to them for just a minute so you can say good-bye if you want.''

Wade closed his eyes for a moment and nodded.

The nurse smiled and motioned for the orderly to help
push.

Thumper and Woodpecker raised up to their elbows as
Matt's bed rolled in between theirs.

"Matt, damn, it's good to see you, man.''

The sergeant raised his head, looking at Woodpecker,
then Thumper. His eyes still showed no emotion. "I want
to tell you both I'm sorry for what happened. I will never
forget you, and I'll miss you. You were like brothers to
me and . . . '' Wade's eyes suddenly clouded and his monotone voice began quivering. He closed his eyes for a moment, then opened them, releasing tears down his cheeks.
He tried to speak but his words came out in a whisper.
"Good-bye . . . Good-bye, my brothers.''

Thumper and Woodpecker were crying and reached out
for their sergeant. Wade took their hands and squeezed
them tightly. "Good-bye . . . and take care of yourselves.''

Lieutenant Pisa pulled Wade's bed back and motioned
for the orderly to help her push. They pushed the bed down
the aisle to the hallway. Another nurse passed by and
looked at Pisa strangely. "Why are your crying?''

The lieutenant wiped her tears away with her hands and
shook her head. "Just one of those days.''

Mary Ann hadn't known about Thumper's injuries until
she'd called An Lom to talk to him. Then Pete had told
her everything, and she'd immediately sent a telegram to
the Philippines for Virginia. The next morning, Virginia
called her, and they'd both cried and speculated, knowing
nothing more than that Thumper and Matt were wounded
badly enough to be sent to Japan. Both of them decided
to meet in Tokyo and drive to Camp Zama to see the men.

Two days later Mary Ann and Virginia were taken to

the patient affairs office at the hospital where a doctor
pulled the men's files.

"You'll find Specialist Meeks on Ward B in the north
wing, Miss Krueger. You're awfully lucky to have gotten
here when you did—he leaves tomorrow for the States.
Uh . . . I need to speak to Miss Wolinski for a few moments, so why don't you go on down and see him. I have
an orderly waiting outside to show you the way."

Mary Ann got to her feet and put her hand on Virginia's
shoulder. "I'll see you back at the hotel tonight. Don't
worry, everything will be fine."

Virginia smiled nervously and patted her friend's hand.
"Tell Thumper hello for me."

Mary Ann walked out of the office, leaving Virginia fidgeting in her chair.

"Would you like some coffee, Miss Wolinski?"

"No, thank you," said Virginia anxiously.

The doctor leaned back in his chair. "Miss Wolinski,
your friend, Sergeant Wade, will recover completely from
his physical wounds, and he'll be able to carry on normally.
However, psychologically, we're concerned about him."

"What does that mean, doctor?"

"It means, simply, that don't expect to see the same
man you knew before. He is severely depressed and we
haven't been successful in helping him yet. Perhaps seeing
you may trigger something, but I doubt it. It was my mis-
fortune to have to tell Sergeant Wade a week ago that his
grandfather had passed away. He took the news without
a trace of emotion. I found this surprising and discussed
the matter at some length with the psychiatrist who is han-
dling his case. He told me Sergeant Wade was involved in
some very heavy action and that several of his team members were killed. The sergeant somehow feels directly responsible for what happened to those men. All this has
produced a depression that is proving very difficult to treat."

The doctor could see by the young woman's expression
that she wasn't taking the news very well. He got up,
moved around his desk, and sat down beside her. "Miss
Wolinski, I'm afraid the sergeant is dealing with his emo-

tional pain in the worst possible way. He's completely withdrawn into himself."

Virginia shook her head in disbelief. "I don't understand. What are you telling me?"

The doctor lowered his eyes, searching for an explanation that wouldn't sound like medical mumbo jumbo. He looked back up at her. "Sergeant Wade has created a barrier in his mind to stop everything but the hurt and suffering caused by his feelings of guilt. The problem is, this barrier shuts us out, too. It's shut out everything, even his grandfather's death. In fact, he may in some way feel he's responsible for that, too."

"He couldn't possibly!" Virginia blurted, choking back her tears.

The doctor took her hand and spoke softly to reassure her. "The problem is, he probably *does*. It's the reason he won't take any painkillers for his wounds. He believes that pain is what he deserves for his failure as a leader. He's punishing himself for crimes he didn't commit. In his mind, he wasn't good enough to do the job, even if no one could possibly have done it, and he's made a little hell for himself to hide in. Unfortunately, right now, there is nothing and no one that can help him but time."

Virginia stood up with determination and wiped her cheeks. "No, you're wrong, doctor. There is something and someone. He has his land in Oklahoma and he has me. Take me to him, please."

The doctor stood and walked to her to the door. "I'll escort you myself, but please don't get your expectations up. These things *do* take time."

Wade opened his eyes and saw a dream. It was a woman whose pictures had kept him going once—a long time ago, it seemed. But she was just that, a dream, a passing person in his life. And he didn't want to hurt her like he had the others. She spoke to him and pleaded, but she just didn't understand. Her tears were real, but they'd soon dry and be forgotten. As she'd soon forget him. She had her own life to live. She was saying things and making promises and probably believed all of it. But that was because she didn't know that love wasn't enough. In the face of pain and death, love couldn't do a damn thing. It didn't mean nothin'.

Virginia cried and reached out, touching his face, speaking through her tears. "Matt, talk to me, please talk to me. I can't stand for you to do this to yourself—to us! Tell me you love me. Tell me you understand what I'm saying to you."

Wade looked deeply into her eyes and spoke the only words that seemed to make sense in a world that took all the people you love away: "Good-bye Ginny."

1971

It had been a year since Matt Wade was discharged from
the hospital, and shortly after that, the Army. He'd returned to the farm when he'd gotten out, only to find his
hometown friends had become strangers to him. They'd
tried to talk to him and help in his adjustment to the 'world',
but their efforts only pushed him farther away. Finally,
he'd left the farm empty and begun an aimless search. He
drifted from state to state, East coast to West, trying to
find something—he couldn't explain what. Whenever he
found himself pulled back to the farm, letters from Virginia
would always be waiting there, as they had while he was
in the hospital, but he threw them away unopened. He
didn't want to reopen old wounds, he told himself. Usually
he'd stay a few days, sometimes a couple of weeks, but
inevitably he would leave again.

The drifting finally ended on a late summer day in Or-
egon, when he suddenly and quietly came to a realization:
Whatever he'd been looking for couldn't be found anywhere except in himself. The faces of the men he'd loved
and failed could not be left behind. There was no place,
person, or thing that could give him a miraculous release
from the guilt he felt. He'd failed his beloved team. He
had not gotten them home as he'd vowed. Two were gone,
and the others would carry the scars of his failure of responsibility for the rest of their lives. Those were the facts,
and he grimly determined to live with them.

Matt went back to the farm and began college again. He found he could forget the faces of his men for awhile by burying himself in the pages of his schoolwork. He became a model student, but one without purpose. He changed majors three times, searching for something, anything that had meaning.

Then, one day in early summer, a Special Education student teacher asked him to fill in for her while she was on jury duty. The young woman explained that the college helped local grade school children who were having learning problems by sending out Special Education majors during the summer session to teach them.

Matt reluctantly agreed to help the teacher only after she offered to pay him. He walked into the small classroom the following day. There were five students—four ten-year-old girls and one nine-year-old boy.

Matt handed out questions for the students to fill out after they had read a story from their textbooks. He then sat down to complete an American history report. The girls began reading, but the blond boy sat staring out the window.

Matt ignored the boy and started on his report. An hour later he asked for the papers and excused the children for a ten-minute recess, then shuffled through the questions until coming to the boy's. He'd only partially completed two questions out of twelve. His printing was barely legible and half the letters were written backward. Matt stared at the paper for a few moments, remembering back to a time when he, too, stared out a window hoping to become magically smarter, to understand the words he had read.

Matt pulled the boy's progress file from the desk and read not about Robert C. Canning, but Matthew Wade, fourteen years before.

The boy sat on a swing, watching the girls play on the merry-go-round. He saw the new teacher approaching and lowered his head guiltily.

"What's your name?" Matt asked him.

The small face looked up with large, clouded, brown eyes. "Robby."

"Hi, Rob, I'm Matt."

The boy's eyes never left the face of the big man towering over him as he nodded and waited for the teacher to ask why he didn't complete his work.

"Rob, you play baseball?"

The boy's eyes misted and he lowered his eyes.

Matt knelt down to the boy's level and saw tears trickling down his face. Rob lowered his head farther to hide his tears.

"What's the matter, Rob? You don't have a reason to cry."

The boy shook his head and hopped from the swing to get away.

Matt grabbed the boy and hugged him to his chest. "I know, son, I know why . . . you know you aren't getting any better in school and will have to be put back a grade. All your friends will go on to the fifth grade and you won't know anybody."

The boy sniffed back his tears. "How . . . how did you know?"

Matt shut his eyes, fighting back his tears. "Because once I felt the same way."

Matt Wade left the classroom that afternoon and walked straight for his curriculum counselor's office to change his major to Special Education. There was something new in his step that any student who knew him would have noticed. Matt Wade was walking with a purpose—he was walking toward a future. A young boy needed him and, Matt knew deep inside, he needed the boy and other children like him.

1976

The driver smiled as he stopped his cab along the curb in front of the Hilton Hotel. He'd seen his passenger half a block away and knew it was his lucky day.

A small woman wearing a black-sequined dress and waist-length coat fur stood in front of the door waiting for him.

The driver broke his own rule. He never got out to open the door for a fare, but this fare was special. It was Ginny. He'd seen her on television three years before when she sang her hit song "Waitin' in Line" on the prime time special. She was a knockout then and still was. Her auburn hair was fixed the same way as it was when she was on TV, and her breasts looked as if they'd pop out of her low-cut dress.

The driver smiled brightly as he opened the door and she began to step in. He backed up a step to look through the window to see if maybe . . . just maybe . . . damn, she'd put her hand up, holding the top of her dress as she got in.

The driver ran around the front of the cab, hoping none of the other cabbies had seen him open the door. The assholes will give me a ration of shit for weeks! he thought. He hopped in the front seat and looked in the rearview mirror. "Where to, Ginny?"

Virginia Wolinski was immediately disappointed. He hadn't read the papers and seen where she was playing.

Probably nobody in Nashville had read it either, she thought.

Virginia sighed to herself and spoke evenly. "Printer's Alley, please."

"Sure thing. Be there in five minutes. Which club you singing in?"

"The Captain's Table."

"Sure, I been there. Maybe I'll get off early and catch the second show."

Again, Virginia felt a pang of disappointment—she'd been booked into a tourist restaurant where even cabbies hung out. It was a reminder of her present popularity. Three years ago, when she'd been in Nashville, she'd sang at the Center to a standing-room-only crowd. Her great comeback had turned out to be a pipedream. Her booking agent had told her she was lucky even to get this gig, let alone the Center. After all, she hadn't had a hit since "Waitin' in Line." The new single had done well but the album sales barely reached the top fifty.

The driver talked the whole way, and she was thankful that most of his questions required merely a nod for an answer.

"Captain's Table on your right, Ginny. Good luck, and I hope I can catch the second show."

Virginia opened the door herself and stepped out. She didn't want to disappoint the cabbie by telling him there was only going to be the one performance and leaned forward, giving him ten dollars. "Keep the change . . . and thank you."

"Thank *you*," the driver exclaimed with a smile.

Virginia glanced at the marquee as she walked down the steps of the club.

GINNY SINGING HER OLD TUNES
MAKE RESERVATIONS NOW! DINNER AND SHOW $22.50

The marquee had angered her. She tossed her fur to the maitre d' and walked straight toward the bar, where Bob, the manager, was inspecting the silver water goblets.

"What's this about 'old tunes?' When I spoke to you this morning, I told you I'd be singing my new release."

Bob smiled as if he was a politician. "Now, Ginny, the crowd here tonight will be the older set. They're not into the disco scene. I'm doing you a favor."

"What do you mean 'older set'?"

"We got a call and a bus tour from Florida is coming in. They're from an old-age home or somethin'. Hell, Ginny, they reserved twenty tables!"

Virginia backed away from the bar in disbelief. The manager didn't know it, but he'd just thrown her the third and last disappointment of the evening. It was like three strikes and she was out. Her pipedream was over.

She forced a smile and walked through the deserted restaurant to the dressing room, where she would wait for her nine o'clock performance . . . her last.

Matt looked at his watch and quickened his steps. The plane had arrived late and he'd just tossed his bag into his room and headed for the club. He knew he wouldn't make it in time for a table and hoped there would at least be a place to stand. He saw the marquee and ran across the street. Her picture was on the door as a coming attraction. For years he'd been following her career, until he'd read she'd married a real estate agent in California. That was two years ago. By chance, he'd later read that she'd been divorced after some kind of scandal, and that her husband taken most of her money and run off with a Spanish actress. He'd never tried to get in touch with her. Only after reading about the divorce did he write, but the letter came back marked "Address Unknown."

Then he'd read about her new single in the *Daily Oklahoman* and how she was trying to make a comeback, but according to the article the record wasn't doing well. He'd called the record company and then her agent to get her show schedule, then picked the one place where he could go on a weekend. School was in session, and between his duties as teacher and school principal, it was the only time available.

Matt felt his body tingle as he walked down the steps. He couldn't believe that after six years he could still feel the way he did about her.

The darkened club's tables were full, as he expected, but the bar in the back had three empty stools. He sat down and looked over the lounge to see if he could spot her at one of the tables, but they were filled with gray-haired women and a few aged men.

Matt ordered a beer as a side door opened next to the small, lighted stage and the band came out. Matt spun around but she didn't appear. The band played one melody, then the lead guitarist took the microphone. "Ladies and gentlemen, here is the moment you've all been waiting for.

Here she *is!* All the way from sunny San Diego, California, the little lady with the big voice . . . GINNY! Come on, folks, let's make her welcome in Nashville!''

The door opened and Matt held his breath as the applause grew louder.

The woman who walked out the door was not the Ginny he knew. She'd been a small bundle of energy then, and hardly wore any makeup. She'd had a quick smile and a bounce in her step. The woman who appeared in front of the lights was a ravishing, refined beauty who never could have followed him out of a jungle. No, the woman in the tight jumpsuit who spoke in the microphone wasn't the girl whose mental picture he looked at every night. His Ginny wasn't a girl anymore.

Matt turned toward the bar and picked up his beer. It had been a mistake to come, he knew that now. One look at her told him he was crazy to think that after all the years he had any more to offer her. He lifted his beer and saw his reflection in the mirror behind the bar. His hair had receded and . . . he realized he was older, too.

Her voice filled the room, making the old familiar tingle crawl up his spine. Her words tore through his heart and embedded in his soul. He realized he could remember every word she'd ever spoken to him and every time they'd made love. He could especially remember when she touched his face that last time at the hospital. And remembering all that, he could not force himself to leave. He was stuck in his seat. Her songs, her voice, glued him there.

Her last song got her a standing ovation, and she stood there like a queen, accepting the adoration of her audience, then bowed her head as if saying good-bye forever. When she left the stage, she raised her chin proudly and walked off without looking back.

Matt shook his head with a smile, and thought, "You've become quite a lady, my little Ginny." He got up to leave, but then stopped to look at the closed door at the side of the stage.

A hostess tapped his shoulder. "Can I get you another drink?"

"No ma'am . . . well, do you think you could do me a favor. Could you give a note to Miss Salin for me."

"Who?"

"I'm sorry, to Ginny, we're old friends."

The waitress eyed him with a sly grin. "Sure you are."

Matt returned the smile. He wouldn't have believed himself, either. He took out his billfold and gave the hostess a ten dollar bill. "Could you give her a note from an admirer?"

The hostess looked into the eyes of the good-looking customer and smiled again. "Sure, I've got to take a drink to her anyway. Keep your money, but if she doesn't read it, I will. I like admirers! I'll get her drink and be back for the note."

The pretty hostess walked toward the bar as Matt pulled out his pen and leaned over a table, picking up a napkin.

The hostess returned a minute later. Matt handed her the folded napkin and she gave him one in return.

"My number is on the back," she said with a wink.

Virginia sat in a chair, staring at herself in the large mirror. She had put on a good show, she thought, and been a trooper for not going ahead and singing her new song. She smiled wryly at herself. It wasn't that good a song anyway.

A knock at the door dissolved her smile and she grabbed for a Kleenex to start wiping off her makeup. "Come in."

"Ma'am, here is your drink . . . and a gentleman at the bar asked me to give you this note."

Virginia picked up the drink from the tray and flipped open the napkin. She thought for a moment her heart had stopped beating, as a rush of memories raced through her mind. The glass slipped from her shaking hand onto the carpeted floor with a thud.

Virginia jumped to her feet. Only one man in the whole world could have written the note. Only one man knew the one word that she'd dreamed of so many times for so many nights. He was here, after all the lonely years, after so long a time she'd almost forgotten . . . . She dropped the napkin and ran for the door.

The hostess bent over to pick up the glass, but instead picked up the note. She turned the napkin over and shook her head. Why a single word could make a celebrity act like that was beyond her, especially such a dumb word as "Click."

WASHINGTON, D.C., NOVEMBER 13, 1982

Two women and two young boys sat beside a barren oak to break the wind's cold chill. Scattered on the grass mall around them were thousands of veterans and their families. All were waiting for the Vietnam Memorial parade to begin.

Mary Ann began to raise her coat collar, but suddenly reached out, slapping her son's hand. "No more cookies!"

"Mom."

"You heard me. Sit next to your brother and put the blanket up over you both before you catch your death."

"But, Mom."

"Do it!" Mary Ann raised her collar, shivering, and looked at Virginia. "When is Matt going to make an honest woman of you?"

Virginia looked at the two boys and smiled at Mary Ann's directness. Her friend hadn't changed.

"It's going to take time. We're different people than we were in Vietnam."

Mary Ann frowned. "Virginia, you've been going together for six years. You can't tell me you don't love each other. My God, I've seen how you look at one another. What is it, Gin?"

Virginia lowered her eyes, knowing she couldn't hide her feelings from Mary Ann. "Matt doesn't want the responsibility." Virginia raised her head and looked into her friend's eyes. "He still feels he failed the team and he doesn't want to fail with me. That's the way he explains it. Living together he can handle, but not marriage. He didn't want to come here, you know. I forced him. It almost broke us up but I insisted and told him I'd leave him if he didn't. This . . . this getting together with his friends I thought might help.''

Mary Ann reached out and took Virginia's hand. "You were right in making him come. It has helped. It's helped us all." She patted Virginia's hand, knowing she'd better change the subject, and broke into a smile. "You should see yourself. You sure don't look like your album cover now.''

Virginia laughed and wrapped her hands around the warm thermos. "That was years ago." Virginia was wearing Matt's old Army field jacket, jeans, and a stocking cap pulled down over her ears.

Mary Ann patted her coat. "Well, at least you haven't gained weight like I have. I must look awfully fat to you.''

Virginia smiled again at her old friend. Mary Ann had gained a few pounds through her hips, but she was still a beautiful woman. "No, you look great. Everybody looks great, don't they?''

"Yeah, everybody but Woodpecker. My God, he looks like a Hell's Angel with that red beard and long hair. I didn't remember him being such a character.''

"I didn't remember him that well, but boy did he put the booze away last night. I'd forgotten how bad they all talked. Matt hasn't cursed like that since . . . since I don't know when.''

"Yeah, it was like they were back in Vietnam again. You'd think it was yesterday the way they carried on. Oh, who was that good-looking prematurely gray-haired man with the scarred face you were talking to in the room?''

Virginia lowered the thermos. "That was Lieutenant Gibson. He was with the team when they were wounded. He's an investment broker here in Washington and helped pay for the hospitality suite we were in last night. The booze was donated by one of his investors.''

Mary Ann laughed. "Well, there wasn't any left after the Rangers got through. My God, it was so crowded in there I couldn't move.

A small woman wearing a quilted coat and calf-length boots approached the women. "I finally made it!"

Mary Ann patted the ground beside her. "Sit down, Mira. This old tree kinda blocks the wind off us."

The round-faced woman tossed her long black hair with a flip of her head and sat down. "How are your men doing? When we left last night they weren't feeling any pain."

Mary Ann shook her head as if disgusted. "Kenny puked his guts up half the night. It's a good thing your husband doesn't drink or he'd feel like mine did this morning."

Mira nodded reflectively. "Black Eagle laughed more than I've seen him in years. I have you and Thumper to thank for that. If you all hadn't insisted on us meeting here, he wouldn't have come."

Mary Ann smiled. "It was Kenny's idea. He wanted so bad to see his old team. He worked for months trying to find everybody and this parade and dedication seemed the perfect time."

Mira scooted over next to Virginia and took her hand. "I'm so glad to be here and meet everyone. Black Eagle talks about the team all the time and . . . and, well, I just wanted to touch a part of his life that I never knew. Seeing him with his friends makes it easier to understand."

Virginia patted Mira's hand. "I know."

Mira's eyes lowered. "Black Eagle has done so well. He has accepted his handicap and is a respected elder of the tribe, but . . . but he needed this. Really needed this. At times he becomes so depressed it breaks my heart."

Mary Ann moved over and put her arm around Mira. "What is it that gets him down?"

Mira looked up and stared across the park. "He does fine except when he sees people running. He so loved to run. Oh, he tries to hide it, but I see the change."

Mary Ann glanced at Virginia. Neither woman knew what to say to comfort her.

Mira broke her trance and smiled. "I pray every night for a miracle. The Lord one day will allow his last run, I know it."

"Where's the food?"

Mary Ann rolled her eyes upward and turned around as Thumper and Matt walked up. "The cookies are in the bag and . . ."

Matt laughed out loud and put his arms around Thumper's huge shoulders. "She's still passing out cookies?"

Thumper bent over and kissed Mary Ann's forehead. "That's why I married her . . . but don't tell her."

Virginia looked at Matt's bloodshot eyes. "How you feelin', honey?"

Matt winked. "Great!"

Thumper chortled, "Hell, Matt, tell her the truth. You puked in that trash can back there."

Matt punched Thumper jokingly and frowned. "The rum and Cokes got to me last night. I shoulda stuck to beer."

Mira got to her feet. "Where's Black Eagle?"

Thumper tossed his thumb behind him and picked up the bag of cookies. "Woodpecker and him are comin'. They were talking to J. D. Gibson." Thumper tossed a cookie to each of his sons and offered one to Matt.

Matt shook his head and stood beside Mira. "He looks good, Mira. You've taken good care of him."

Mira saw her husband coming and smiled. "No, the Lord has."

Matt felt the same pain now as he'd felt when he'd first seen Preacher yesterday.

Woodpecker walked slowly beside Preacher, being careful not to make him hurry. Preacher stepped normally with his right leg but had to toss his left leg in a jerking motion. He supported his movements with a cane.

Matt smiled through his pain. "About time. We gotta get lined up."

Mary Ann stood quickly. "I'll say it's about time. The kids are freezin' to death. Where do we go to see the parade?"

Thumper pointed toward the Washington Monument. "To the right of the monument is Constitution Avenue. They've got bleachers set up and a reviewing stand. You all can sit in the bleachers. Sierra Rangers will be marching behind the 173rd Airborne Brigade, so when you see them pass, get ready to see the best damn company in the world.''

"Amen," said Preacher.

"There it is!" said Woodpecker, holding up his thumb.

"Damn straight!" added Matt, feeling light inside. Seeing his men smile and laugh the past days had taken away his fears about coming. The first time he saw them he'd stood and cried, unable to move. They'd come to him, crying, too, and hugged him like a lost brother. There was no anger in their faces, only love. Love that he'd forgotten for too long. Ginny had been right. They'd needed each other.

Matt put his hand out to the woman who stood by him over the years waiting for him to understand what she'd known all along. Memories can change—not the facts, but the feelings behind them.

Virginia came to him and he hugged her for strength. There were two more memories that had to be faced.

The women sat the boys between them and pulled the blankets over their shoulders as the Army band marched by the reviewing stand. The crowds in the bleachers and lining the streets all clapped and stood. The band peeled off next to the bleachers and continued playing as the first contingent of veterans approached. They were led by General Westmoreland. The veterans behind him walked with heads held high and waved to the crowd. They wore every conceivable type of uniform and civilian attire. Some were in jungle fatigues, while others walked in T-shirts. Mary Ann squeezed Virginia's hand tightly. The men she cared so much for weren't young men anymore. Most were in their thirties; their faces had lost their innocence long ago, but their smiles and waves warmed her all the way to her toes. Group after group passed, some following state banners, others, unit banners—the 101st Airborne Division, the First Cavalry, Delaware, Texas, First Infantry Division. Some walked arm and arm while others marched

along with the beat of the music. As they passed the reviewing stand, many would salute while others just waved.
Finally, after thousands had passed, Mary Ann saw the
173rd banner a block up the street.

"There they are! They're behind the 173rd!"

The women all stood, holding each other and waiting
excitedly.

The Rangers were led by J. D. Gibson, who marched
to the side of the formation of forty-five men calling out
cadence. Hut . . . two . . . three . . . four. Hut . . . two
. . . three . . . four. The Rangers marched in perfect step.
Their heads were set to the front. They marched proudly,
wanting everyone to know they were still a unit, a unit
deactivated with no fanfare, no banner-waving, but still a
unit, a unit of proud men who had not forgotten.

Gibson halted the formation one hundred yards from the
reviewing stand to get more distance between his group
and the 173rd. He began to say "forward march," but
stopped himself and faced the formation.

"Rangers, we can march or we can by God show who
we are! Whatddya say we double-time!"

The men yelled back, "Double-time!"

Preacher stood beside Thumper and Woodpecker in the
last rank. The march had been difficult for him. Many times
he'd had to grab Woodpecker's arm to keep his balance.
The decision to run meant he'd have to fall out to the side
so as not to embarrass his fellow Rangers. He backed up
just as Gibson commanded "Double-time . . . March!"

Matt saw Preacher walking slowly to the curb and yelled
at Thumper, "Get him!"

Both Thumper and Woodpecker broke from ranks and
picked their friend up by his arms and jogged back into
position. They held him tightly between them, allowing him
to hop on his right leg and hold the left one up.

Gibson sang out, "Here we go! All the Way! One Way!
Ranger! *Ranger!*"

The women saw their men approach and stood with

tears running down their faces. The crowd came to their feet, clapping and hollering as the proud Rangers ran by in perfect unison.

Then Mira saw Black Eagle and suddenly felt weak. His head was held high and his cheeks glistened with tears of pride. He was together with his beloved friends and running. Running not like the others, but still, with them, as he had in his mind for so many years.

Mira looked skyward and thanked God for the miracle.

The march ended a few blocks past the reviewing stand at the new Vietnam Veterans Memorial. Matt, Thumper, Woodpecker, and Preacher walked toward the monument arm in arm, as they'd promised they would the night before.

They held each other tightly as they walked down the slight grade past the polished black granite panels covered with too many names. They stopped at the seventeenth panel and began their search. It was Preacher who pointed, finding what they sought, but Matt turned away, overcome by the emotions that seemed to engulf him. Woodpecker tearfully put his hand on the last two names on the thirty-sixth row—Carl Rostov and Jeremiah Flowers—and looked at the other team members. "Three-one!"

Preacher hugged Woodpecker and put his hand on top of the redhead's. "Three-one!"

Thumper put his arm around Matt's shoulder and spoke softly. "It's time, Matt."

The ex-team leader raised his head and took in a deep breath to stop his crying and looked at his friend, forcing a smile. "Yeah. It really is."

He walked to the wall, following Thumper, who threw his arm around Woodpecker and Preacher and slapped his hand on top of the others. "Three-one!"

Matt looked into the faces of his crying team members and joined their embrace. He slowly raised his hand, laid it on his men's, and shut his tear-filled eyes. Then he could see Rose's grin and Russian's little smile as they joined him in saying, "Three-one!"

OCTOBER 1983

Men of the newly activated First and Second Battalions of the Seventy-Fifth Infantry Airborne Rangers parachuted under fire onto the Communist-controlled airfield at Port Salinas, Grenada. The Rangers took the airfield, spearheading the successful invasion. It ain't never over!

GLOSSARY

Airborne Personnel or equipment dropped by parachute.

Airmobile Personnel or equipment delivered or inserted by helicopter.

AK-47 A Soviet-Bloc produced semi-automatic or automatic 7.62mm assault Rifle, known as the Kalashnikov AK-47, easily identified by its distinctive popping sound.

AO Area of Operation.

Arty Artillery.

Assets Aircraft Support.

ARVN (AR-VIN) the South Vietnamese Army. Sometimes referred to as "Little People."

AWOL Absent Without Leave.

Azimuth A direction in degrees from North, a bearing.

Ballgame An operation.

Base Camp An administrative and logistical camp for a unit, usually semi-permanent and contains unit's support elements, i.e., mess hall, supply.

Baseball Baseball-shaped grenade, $2\frac{1}{2}$ inches in diameter.

BDA Bomb Damage Assessment.

Beaucoup French for big or many. We pronounced it Boo-Coo.

Berm Parapet around fortification or buildings.

Bird Helicopter or plane.

Bird dog L-19, Light fixed-wing observation airplane. O-1A or O-1E.

BN   Battalion. 400 to 600 men in U.S. Unit. 200 to 500 NVA battalion.

Boonie hat   Soft jungle flop hat.

Boonie rat   Infantrymen, grunt, dogfaces, line doggies.

Boonies   The bush, jungle, field.

C's   C-rations, canned meals.

C-4   Plastic explosive.

C-130   Air Force medium cargo plane.

CAR-15   Colt Automatic Rifle . . . Colt Commando submachine gun, same as M-16 but shorter.

C&C   Command and Control.

CH-47   Chinook, a large twin-rotor cargo helicopter.

Charlie Mike   Continue the Mission.

Cheap Charlie   Stingy or Cheap.

Cherry   New Troop.

CHICOM   Chinese communist, weapon or equipment made in China.

Clacker   Electricell detonating device for Claymore mines.

Claymore   Fan-shaped lightweight anti-personnel mine, detonated electrically. Plastic cased with a C-4 charge behind a plastic wall of steel balls.

Co   Company.

Cobra   AH-1G Huey Cobra Helicopter Gunship—Snake.

Commo   Communications.

Conex   Large corrugated metal container.

C Rats   C rations.

CS   Riot control gas.

Daisy chain   To attach one Claymore to another by det cord, firing one also fires the other. No limit to number of Claymores that could be attached in this manner.

Det Cord   Detonating cord for explosives, used in daisy chaining in ambushes.

Didi   (*Dee Dee*) Vietnamese to run, move out quickly.

Dinks   Derogatory expression for Vietnamese, enemy and friendly.

Doughnut Dollies   Red Cross girls.

Escort   Armed helicopter flying escort.

Extraction   Withdrawal of troops by air.

FAC Forward Air Controller, Air Force spotter, to co-ordinate artillery or Air Strikes.

Fast Movers An Air Force F-4 Phantom Jet.

Frag Grenade. Also a term to mean "kill a lifer."

Freq Frequency.

Green Used to mean safe.

Gook Derogatory term for enemy or any oriental person or thing.

Gunship Armed helicopter.

HE High explosive.

Heat Tabs An inflammable stick tablet used to heat C's or boil water for Lurps.

Hootch Your bunk, whether a room or poncho.

Horn Radio handset.

Hump To walk carrying a rucksack or to perform tough duty.

Insertion Placement of soldiers in AO by helicopter.

Jody Bastard who takes your girl when you're gone.

KIA Killed in action.

Klick Kilometer.

Lifer Career soldier.

LOH (loach) Light Observation Helicopter.

LRRP (*Lurp*) Long Range Reconnaissance Patrol.

Lurps Long Range Recon Soldier or lightweight freeze dried food packet.

LZ Landing Zone.

M-16 Rifle used by U.S. soldiers, weighs 7.6 pounds.

M-60 U.S. light machine gun, fires 7.62 bullets.

M-79 Single shot 40mm grenade launcher.

Medevac Medical evacuation by helicopter.

MP Military Police.

Nap-of-the-Earth Flying as close to the ground as possible.

NCO Noncommissioned Officer: Sergeant.

No sweat Easy.

Number one (*Numba one*) The best, first place, the highest.

Number ten (*Numba ten*) The worst, loser, the lowest.

Nuoc mam Tangy Vietnamese sauce.

NVA   North Vietnamese Army or solider.

OD   Olive Drab.

OJT   On Job Training.

On Station   Gunships, Slicks or fast movers in position for mission or operation.

OPS   Operations—Tactical Operations Center.

P-38   C-ration can opener, small and folds, comes in C-ration case.

PZ   Pick up zone.

R&R   Rest-and-Recreation vacation.

Recon   Reconnaissance.

REMF (Rim-ph!)   Rear Echelon Mother Fucker.

Rock-n-roll   Firing full automatic.

RPD   Soviet bi-pod mounted, belt fed light machine gun similar to American M-60.

RPG   Russian made anti-tank grenade launcher.

RTO   Radio Telephone Operator.

Ruck, Rucksack   Backpack issued to infantrymen.

Same-Same   The same as, or to do likewise.

Sapper   Enemy soldiers trained in demolition and infiltration.

Sit Rep   Situation Report.

Short-short timer   A soldier who has little time left in country.

Sky   To leave or move out quickly.

Slackman   The second man behind the point man.

Slicks   Lift helicopter, Hueys.

Snakes   Cobra gunships.

Tee Tee   Vietnamese, small or little.

TOC   Tactical Operations Center, Operations.

TOP   First sergeant of a company.

USMA   United States Military Academy.

Ville   Village.

VHF   Variable High Frequency.

Wake-up   Short timer expression "four days and a wake-up" (going home).

Waste   Kill.

WIA   Wounded in Action.
WIMP   Weak Incompetent Malingering Pussy.
World   U.S. of A.
X ray   Commo site.
XO   Executive Officer.

About the Author

Leonard B. Scott is a career Army officer who served in Vietnam with the 173rd Airborne and 75th Rangers as a Rifle Platoon Leader, Patrol Platoon Leader, and Operations Officer. His combat decorations include the Silver Star, Purple Heart, and Combat Infantryman Badge. His hometown is Minco, Oklahoma. He now lives with his wife and children wherever the Army assigns him. He is also the author of *Charlie Mike*.